The Archers

THE AMBRIDGE CHRONICLES

The Archers

THE AMBRIDGE CHRONICLES
PART ONE

Family Ties

1951–1967

JOANNA TOYE

BBC

In memory of Godfrey Baseley – and all that followed.

This book is published to accompany
the BBC Radio 4 serial entitled *The Archers*.
The Editor of *The Archers* is Vanessa Whitburn.

Published by BBC Worldwide Ltd,
Woodlands, 80 Wood Lane, London W12 0TT

First published 1998
Reprinted 1998, 2000
Copyright © Joanna Toye 1998
The moral right of the author has been asserted

ISBN 0 563 38397 6

Designed by Tim Higgins
Text set in Adobe Plantin and New Caledonia Semi Bold Italic

Printed and bound in Great Britain by
Butler & Tanner Ltd, Frome and London
Jacket printed by
Lawrence Allen Ltd, Weston-super-Mare

Contents

The Archers

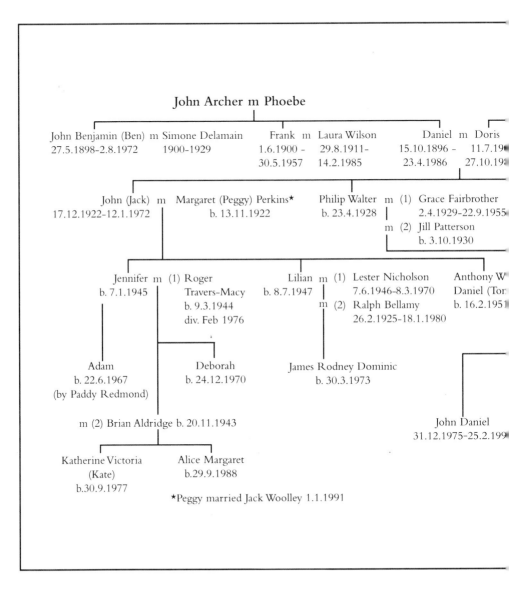

John Archer m Phoebe

John Benjamin (Ben) m Simone Delamain   Frank m Laura Wilson   Daniel m Doris
27.5.1898-2.8.1972   1900-1929   1.6.1900 - 29.8.1911-   15.10.1896 - 11.7.19
    30.5.1957 14.2.1985   23.4.1986 27.10.19

John (Jack) m Margaret (Peggy) Perkins★   Philip Walter m (1) Grace Fairbrother
17.12.1922-12.1.1972   b. 13.11.1922   b. 23.4.1928   2.4.1929-22.9.1955
    m (2) Jill Patterson
    b. 3.10.1930

Jennifer m (1) Roger   Lilian m (1) Lester Nicholson   Anthony W
b. 7.1.1945   Travers-Macy b. 8.7.1947 7.6.1946-8.3.1970 Daniel (Tor
    b. 9.3.1944   m (2) Ralph Bellamy b. 16.2.195
    div. Feb 1976   26.2.1925-18.1.1980

Adam   Deborah   James Rodney Dominic
b. 22.6.1967   b. 24.12.1970   b. 30.3.1973
(by Paddy Redmond)

    John Daniel
m (2) Brian Aldridge b. 20.11.1943   31.12.1975-25.2.199

Katherine Victoria   Alice Margaret
(Kate)   b.29.9.1988
b.30.9.1977

★Peggy married Jack Woolley 1.1.1991

Family Tree

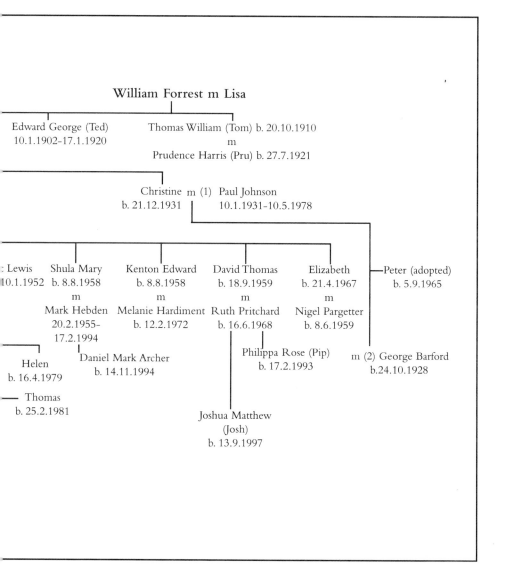

William Forrest m Lisa

Edward George (Ted)
10.1.1902–17.1.1920

Thomas William (Tom) b. 20.10.1910
m
Prudence Harris (Pru) b. 27.7.1921

Christine m (1) Paul Johnson
b. 21.12.1931   10.1.1931–10.5.1978

Lewis
10.1.1952

Shula Mary
b. 8.8.1958
m
Mark Hebden
20.2.1955–
17.2.1994

Kenton Edward
b. 8.8.1958
m
Melanie Hardiment
b. 12.2.1972

David Thomas
b. 18.9.1959
m
Ruth Pritchard
b. 16.6.1968

Elizabeth
b. 21.4.1967
m
Nigel Pargetter
b. 8.6.1959

Peter (adopted)
b. 5.9.1965

Helen
b. 16.4.1979

Thomas
b. 25.2.1981

Daniel Mark Archer
b. 14.11.1994

Philippa Rose (Pip)
b. 17.2.1993

m (2) George Barford
b.24.10.1928

Joshua Matthew
(Josh)
b. 13.9.1997

Acknowledgements

No book about *The Archers* can ever truly be the work of one person. Over the years so many dedicated writers, performers and production staff have moulded the programme's character and characters.

It would have been impossible to write this book without the support of the Editor of *The Archers*, Vanessa Whitburn and her team, especially *Archers'* Archivist Camilla Fisher. At BBC Worldwide, Nicky Copeland and Lara Speicher have been nothing but encouraging, but I owe the biggest debt of gratitude to Heather Holden-Brown who originally commissioned the three-book saga. I became a regular visitor to the BBC Written Archives at Caversham, where Neil Somerville and James Codd helped me in researching past script material by Edward J. Mason, Geoffrey Webb, Bruno Milna, John Keir Cross and David Turner.

Although I had access to the scripts and did in some cases draw on them, I also had licence to invent, and my hope is that the reader will not be able to see the joins – or want to look for them. For those who listened in the 1950s, I hope that the book recreates *The Archers* of memory. For newer listeners, I hope that reading about those dark, post-war days will illuminate what they are hearing today.

Joanna Toye
September 1998

·1·

New Beginnings

'Will this be enough, do you think, Chris?'

Christine laid down the last of the already spotless cake forks, which her mother had nonetheless insisted that she polish. The chintz curtains were drawn tight against the sharp December afternoon and the cutlery glimmered gently in the glow of the logs in the grate and the gas jets on the wall. She looked up. Doris Archer was holding out an enormous willow-patterned platter. On it were arranged overlapping slices of roast beef, home-cured ham (one of her husband Dan's prized Large Whites, killed at Martinmas) and cold, pressed tongue. There were rumours that the meat ration was to be reduced at the end of January, but in the countryside, and especially the countryside at Christmas, you would have been forgiven for thinking there was no rationing at all.

'Just remind me how many we'll be tonight, Mum? Twenty, was it?'

'No, just our Jack and Peggy, you and Philip ...' Her mother broke off. 'You're teasing me, aren't you?'

Chris jumped up, took the platter and squeezed it on to the dining-room table between a dish of piccalilli and the pork pie with its glistening crust. No-one could make hot-water-crust pastry or pickles like Doris Archer, as her several certificates from the Women's Institute and Ambridge Flower and Produce Show proved. Then Chris turned and wrapped her mother in a fierce and impulsive hug.

'Can you blame me?' she smiled. 'Of course there'll be enough. Have you ever known anyone leave Brookfield hungry?'

'Walter Gabriel's always saying he could manage another helping.'

'That's because he only comes up here for a good feed!' Chris shook her head, amused. 'This fretting wouldn't have anything to do with the fact that Grace Fairbrother's coming this evening, would it?'

Doris busied herself with the butter dish, moving it a fraction of an inch to the right and laying the pearl-handled butter knife next to it. Chris watched her covertly.

'Come on, Mum, you'd love her and my dear brother to make a match of it.'

'It's not up to me, is it?' replied Doris stoutly.

'But you have to admit Grace is rather more suitable than Rita Flynn. Philip Archer and the barmaid at The Bull! I bet that little escapade had you and Dad lying awake at night.'

'You needn't be so smart, young lady,' retorted Doris. 'I wouldn't mind seeing you walking out with someone.'

'And who did you have in mind? Nelson Gabriel, I suppose,' said Chris indignantly.

'I don't know what you've got against the boy –' Doris began.

'*Boy*, mother dear, exactly. He's two years younger than I am. His ears stick out – though admittedly, not as much as his Adam's apple. And he's got sweaty palms.'

'And how did you find that out, I'd like to know?'

'I don't need to find it out.' Christine wet the end of her finger. She dabbed up some crumbly flakes of cheese straw and popped them in her mouth. 'His sort always do.'

'Oh, Chris, what are we going to do with you?'

Christine was twenty. When Doris was her age, she had been courting Dan for two summers. It had all started at the Midsummer's Eve bonfire on Lakey Hill, when, along with all the other giggling village lasses, she had put a sprig of St John's wort down her blouse, the local saying being that the man who came and took it would be the girl's future husband. Doris had been working as a lady's maid up at the Manor House at the time and she'd always thought Dan Archer was a fine figure of a man – not that she was about to let him know it!

When she met him again at a dance in the village hall at Christmas, he asked if she'd still got the St John's wort safe. She told him not to be so cheeky, but by the end of the evening he'd somehow got her to agree not to let anyone else take it off her and that, pretty much, was how they came to be engaged to be married. Everything had seemed much simpler, much more innocent in those days. Doris could just imagine Chris's reaction if she'd told her the story – shrieks of laughter and a knowing shake of the head.

'You don't need to *do* anything with me, Mum, that's the point,' Chris was saying. 'I've got a job I'll like all my life. Lab work, research and all that.' Christine had only been at Borchester Dairies as an outside milk tester for six months, but her boss, Mr Grove – or Basil as he'd told Christine to call him over a festive sherry in his office the day before they all packed up for Christmas – was well pleased with her progress.

Doris smiled at her youngest child – at last, a daughter!

'I know, it's lovely, Christine. I'm so glad you're happy. And if you get married, well, I know you'll choose sensibly.'

'Married! Not me! I'm going to get somewhere in life on my own before I get married.'

Doris smiled to herself. The world had certainly changed – and fast – since she was a young woman. Dan said the same. Look at the changes in farming. When Dan was a lad, most of the Brookfield land had been grass. Two world wars and a hungry population had seen fields that had only ever been pasture go under the plough. When Doris was young it had taken a day to plough an acre with a team of horses: now there were ten-horsepower tractors that could make a day's work of a four-acre field. After hand-milking all his life, Dan had invested in a milking machine for Brookfield in 1947. 'Cows'll slip their calves,' prophesied his farmhand, Simon Cooper. 'They'll all get bad quarters. It'll make their milk as poor as water.' In the end, none of these things had happened. The milk yield was high, the butterfat content good, the calves as sturdy as ever. And as if that weren't enough, Philip, Dan and Doris's younger son, had come back from his training at the Farm Institute talking about silage and combined harvesters and Lord only knew what. And Doris had no doubt that, in due course, they would come to Brookfield.

The grandfather clock in the hall struck six. Doris gasped, a pantomime of panic.

'Is that the time? The scullery's full of crocks and I want to put some pins in my hair!'

'I'll do the crocks – you go and get ready,' soothed Christine, hustling her mother out of the room. 'And put on some of that 'Devon Violets' Dad gave you for Christmas. This could be an important evening. You might be about to become a mother-in-law again.'

Doris shook her head at her daughter, affectionately exasperated.

'If Grace is impressed with the cake forks, of course,' added Chris as an afterthought.

• • •

'How about some more of that rich and ripe old cooking port, Dad?'

Jack Archer, his high colour attributable to rather more than the heat of the fire, held out his glass. Doris noticed Peggy's darted look, but Dan refilled his elder son's glass to the brim before either mother or wife could get a word in.

'Cooking port!' Dan protested. 'You've got no palate on you, lad! Your mother bought that at old Mrs Benson's sale two years ago and goodness only knows how long it had been laying down in her cellar.'

'Doesn't seem to have been lying down in very good company,' grinned Jack, raising his glass. 'Cheers!'

It was well after midnight. After the chimes of Big Ben on the wireless, and the inevitable arrival of Walter Gabriel, first-footing his way round all the neighbours on the correct assumption of a free drink, Doris had rather hoped for the blissful comfort of her bed, but the men were still raring to go.

Dan got to his feet – steadily, she was pleased to see. It would be lack of sleep that would affect her and Dan in the morning, not an excess of alcohol. Like Peggy, who was eight months pregnant, Doris hadn't touched a drop all night. She preferred the taste of her elder-flower cordial – her grandmother's recipe – anyway.

Dan cleared his throat and the chatter subsided. Chris, seated on the footstool by the fire, looked up at her father. Philip and Grace broke off their intense conversation.

'Now we've all got our glasses filled,' began Dan importantly, 'here's a toast.'

'Pray silence for the Lord and Master of Brookfield Farm and Sire of the illustrious Family of Archer,' ragged Phil.

Christine told him to shut up.

'Well, all of you – and that includes your two youngsters, Peggy m'dear, and one on the way – I haven't got much to say, but – somehow –'

'You're going to take a long time saying it,' piped up Phil again.

Dan continued, undeterred, bathed in the glow of his family's affection.

'All I want to say is: here's to the coming year and may we all get what we're after, may we go on being as happy and united a family as we've been up to now – and –' he paused for effect, 'may the weather be a bit kinder to all farmers.'

'Hear hear,' roared Jack.

Doris wondered silently if all the mishaps at Jack and Peggy's smallholding could really be blamed on the weather. Jack had forgotten to spray against mildew last spring, and when he should have been lifting his leeks he'd found himself a driving job for a fortnight. ('But it'll pay a few bob, Mum!')

'May I say something, Mrs Archer?' It was Grace.

Doris nodded.

'Why not, dear?'

'I just wanted to say – I hope you'll always be here – and that I'll be able to . . .' She stopped and put the back of her hand to her lips. 'Oh, I'm sorry, I can't go on. I always get like this on New Year's Eve.'

Phil reached over and squeezed her other hand and Christine arched her eyebrows. She didn't believe this tentative, faltering 'little me' act for one minute. Grace's father, George Fairbrother, had made a fortune in plastics before buying his farm in Ambridge, and still divided his time between the village and his factory. He was dynamic, forceful – some would say ruthless – and Chris had detected before something of the father's steeliness in Grace. Still, if Phil was taken in . . . But her father was patting Grace on the shoulder and she was looking up at him, her eyes brimming.

'There is something sad about the old year going out,' agreed Dan. 'But it's gone now. It's the first of January and another working day. Time we packed it all up and went to bed.' He turned to his daughter. 'You've got an early start, Christine, remember.'

'I know, Dad. Half past five.'

Chris got up and smoothed down the skirt of her emerald wool dress. As her hands brushed lightly over her thighs she wondered how Basil had spent Christmas. He'd said something about having his wife's parents to stay. And how he wasn't looking forward to it.

'Blessed if I'd do your job, Chris,' joked Phil, who was helping Grace up from her chair as if she were an invalid. Poor distended Peggy struggled up by herself. Jack, Chris noticed, had poured himself another glass of port and was helping himself to a handful of cobnuts. 'You ought to have a word with your bosses, get them to nationalize cows into being milked at a human hour.'

'You've got to be at your best, too,' Doris warned him. My goodness, would she be glad to get her feet out of these shoes! And her corset was digging into her unmercifully. 'If you go before the Board looking worn out, you won't give a very good impression.'

'After another job, Phil?' enquired Jack.

'Junior livestock officer,' said Doris proudly.

'What d'you mean, another job?' teased Phil. 'The offers I've had so far weren't jobs. They were just slavery and a waste of talent!'

Jack punched his brother playfully in the chest, but Doris laid a hand on his arm.

'Jack, I think Peggy's tired,' she said softly.

'Thank you so much, Mrs Archer, for a lovely evening,' Grace was saying. Phil had fetched her coat – a beauty, with an astrakhan collar – and she was putting on her gloves.

'Philip'll get your car out of the yard,' insisted Dan. 'There's a sharp frost and the road may be slippy.'

Chris watched, amused, as Grace put on her uncertain, kittenish face again and Phil sped off obediently to get a scarf.

'Goodnight, Chris, dear.' Grace approached and offered her cheek. 'I hope I'll be seeing a lot more of you in the coming year.'

She was tiny beside Chris, who felt like a carthorse next to her.

'I'm sure you will, Grace,' Chris replied, as Phil came bounding back into the room. If Phil has anything to do with it, she thought to herself.

. . .

Grace even let him drive the car, her Christmas present from her father. Would it be too shameless to compliment him on his driving? Tell him he was a better driver than she was, even though he'd crashed the gears changing down as they approached the village and the car had wandered alarmingly on a patch of black ice near the forge? Oh, why not? Philip Archer might not be everyone's idea of a romantic hero – he was no Montgomery Clift, that was for sure – but there was something about that dimple in his chin, the curl of his blond hair and the look in his eyes when they met hers that melted her insides.

So, she complimented him on his driving. He grinned at her endearingly and pulled up in a shower of pebbles on the drive. Her father was travelling back from London that night and the house was dark. But the sky was clear, scattered with stars and illuminated by a huge disc of moon. They sat in silence for a moment. The car's engine ticked companionably.

'It's – it's a lovely night,' ventured Phil. 'Almost too good to waste.'

'Yes, isn't it?'

'Grace . . . ?'

'Yes?'

'Grace, I . . .'

She had wanted this all evening, but now it was so close, she was so nervous she could hardly think straight.

'Good luck tomorrow, Phil,' she heard herself blurt out. 'I hope you get your job all right.'

'I'll take it if it's what I'm looking for,' said Phil brusquely. He sounded rather puzzled at the sudden shift in the conversation. Grace knew she had to recapture the mood.

'What are you looking for, Phil?' she asked gently.

The question hung in the air between them. She knew Phil was looking at her mouth, moistly parted. She wanted so much to feel his lips against hers.

'I . . . oh, that's tomorrow.' And suddenly, he reached for her. His mouth closed over hers. His arms cradled her and, with one hand against his chest, lest he think her too forward, her other hand crept round to caress the springy softness of the hair at the nape of his neck. The party spirit? The moon? Sheer desire? Grace didn't care. Philip Archer was kissing her in the car on the first day of a new year. Anything could happen.

• • •

Nothing quite seemed to connect for Phil the next day. Astonished by his own boldness, amazed and flattered by Grace's enthusiastic response, he found himself gazing into his shaving mirror for an absurdly long time, quite unaware that Doris had called him three times for breakfast. Then there was a not untypical run-in with Jack, who had borrowed his father's car to drive Peggy home the previous evening, on pain of death to return it by nine o'clock so Phil could set off in good time for his appointment with the Agricultural Advisory Board.

Ten past nine came and there was no sign of the car, so Phil had to leg it over to the smallholding where Jack not only claimed he'd 'forgotten all about it, old chap', but had also mislaid the ignition key. Finally tracing it to the trouser pocket of Jack's best suit, Phil was left with twenty-five minutes in which to get into Borchester, park, and present himself as the most suitable applicant for the job of junior livestock officer, Ambridge and District.

Not that it had been worth breaking his neck for, he thought, as he emerged from the offices of the Agricultural Advisory Board shortly before eleven o'clock. In fact, it had been a complete waste of time. Only the prospect of a cup of coffee and a teacake in The Copper Kettle did anything to restore his spirits. Yes, a quiet sit down with the paper would console him. On second thoughts, he might just sit there and remember last night.

• • •

'Canoodlin', they was.' Walter Gabriel hitched up his collapsing corduroy trousers and sniffed. 'No other word for it.'

Dan continued ladling out mash for the pigs. Walter chuckled.

'Winders were proper steamed up. You want to watch that lad o' yourn, me old pal.'

'And what were you doing sneaking around George Fairbrother's shrubbery in the early hours?' Dan clanked the handle of the bucket violently as he put it down. 'Or don't we ask?'

'You know what I was doin'! I came a-doin' it 'ere! If there's a tot o' rum or a drop o' port bein' given out to first-footers, then it might as well be coming in my direction.'

Walter Gabriel was Dan's neighbour, another tenant of the Estate. There the similarity ended. Walter's farm was at best ramshackle, at worst a dilapidated ruin. His fences were the shabbiest in the district, his hedges the patchiest, his crops the puniest. He took good care of his stock, such as it was: a few Jerseys and a straggling flock of sheep. Walter loved all animals whether or not they were supposed to be making him a profit: on no other farm nearby did the cats have the run of the dairy or the birds eat as well as the person who fed them.

Dan's relations with Walter were based on give and take. On the face of it, Dan gave and Walter took, whether it was a roll of barbed wire, a bolt cutter or one of Doris's famed ginger cakes. But Dan knew that the relationship was more reciprocal than it seemed. What Walter could not give materially he gave in his company, his anecdotes, his peculiarly individual slant on life. Dan, never the most imaginative or daring of men, recognized in Walter a real original, and he somewhat reluctantly admired him for it.

'Well, that was last night, you old rogue,' chided Dan. 'And what are you after this time?'

Walter rubbed a dewdrop from his nose with a knotted wrist.

'Water. Pipes is fruzz up.'

Dan picked up the bucket and walked out into the yard, away from the squalling pigs. Walter followed him.

'I might've known. Didn't you put that lagging on them like I told you to?'

Sometimes Dan felt more like Walter's father or older brother than his neighbour.

'No. I don't hold with it.' Walter stuck out his bottom lip, just as young Jack had been inclined to do – still did, Dan suddenly realized – when he was crossed. 'Makes the water too hot in summer.'

'Gorblessme, that's a ripe 'un!' exclaimed Dan. 'Too darn lazy and that's the truth. You'll be writing to the Ministry next to send someone along to run your farm for you while you sit with your feet on the mantelpiece!'

'You'd never catch me writing to that bunch of . . . ' Walter broke off. 'Here, what's wrong with this calf, Dan?'

Walter was peering into the calf shed where Daffodil, one of Dan's best Shorthorns, was boxed up with the calf she was suckling.

'Darned if I know,' replied Dan, unnerved that it was so obvious. 'She's getting plenty of milk, there's no sign of scour . . . '

Walter chewed his lip.

'Well, she'll probably get over it – or die,' he pronounced cheerfully. 'Now, about this water . . . '

'I suppose I've got no alternative,' grumbled Dan. 'Are you bringing some churns over?'

Walter opened his filmed, baby-blue eyes wide.

'Bringing 'em over? Don't be daft, me old beauty. I'm going to borrow yourn.'

If the sum total of Dan's worries had remained at helping a neigh-bour and dealing with a sick calf, he might have felt that 1951 had indeed started on a benign note. But when he came in for his dinner – Doris had promised him rabbit – he found the three of them – Doris, Philip and Christine – seated round the table as if the King had died.

'Phil was in with a chance for that livestock officer job – and what does he do?' he fulminated to Doris later as he chopped logs for the house. 'Tells them he won't work for chickenfeed? Where does he expect to start if not on the bottom of the grade? Anybody who's going to do a proper job o' farming has got to start at the bottom.'

'Philip has been through the Farm Institute, you know.'

'Fat lot of good it's done him, too.' Dan swung the axe down with far more force than was necessary and the huge elm log skittered in two halves on the concrete of the yard. Dan picked one half up and placed it on the block again.

Doris knew what the problem was. Dan had set his heart on Philip working with him at Brookfield. But Philip took that to mean work-ing *for* him, and since each was equally stubborn, there did not seem to be any area for compromise. In the end, as always, it would fall to Doris to bring them together, to create the atmosphere in which they could at least talk – she had given up hope of their ever agreeing – and to affect surprise and pleasure when Dan told her, as he usually did, that 'young Philip's seen sense at last'.

'Nice bit of haddock for your supper tonight, love,' she said mildly. 'Boiled potatoes, carrots and I might run to a drop of parsley sauce.'

Dan grunted. Doris delivered her *coup de grâce*.

'Bakewell tart for afters?'

It was both Phil and Dan's favourite.

• • •

'So Philip's said he'll give working at Brookfield a try.' Christine was round at the smallholding, helping Peggy to hem flannelette cot sheets.

'He's a better man than I am, Gunga Din.' Jack Archer knocked his pipe out against the grate. 'I don't know that I'd want to work alongside Dad.' He gestured at his wife's stomach with the stem of his pipe. 'How's young Anthony William Daniel today?'

After two girls, Jack was convinced that the next baby had to be a boy.

'Fancies himself as a bareback rider, I think,' smiled Peggy. Then, suspiciously, 'Have you sterilized the ground for the early tomatoes already, Jack?'

Jack sat down with the *Daily Sketch*.

'Finished? Don't be daft. I haven't started yet.'

'But you went out an hour ago!' Peggy bit off a length of cotton.

'I know,' said Jack reasonably. 'But I got sidetracked. I was looking at the pram.'

'Looking? For an hour?'

'And thinking.'

'What's the matter with the pram?' put in Christine quickly.

'Nothing. Just a bit shabby.'

'Jack, it's falling to bits!' Peggy shook out the sheet she'd been hemming and her thimble dropped to the floor. Christine bent to pick it up. She hated being caught in the middle of these spats between her brother and sister-in-law.

Jack and Peggy, who was originally from London, had met in Norfolk during the war, when she had been a stores orderly in the ATS and Jack had been a corporal with slicked-back hair, his beret through his epaulette and a clever way of procuring nylons from a 'contact'. Peggy, whose life had been bounded by the back-streets where she had been brought up and the millinery shop in Tottenham Court Road where she'd worked, had been, she'd once told Christine, completely bowled over. They'd had a wartime wedding – which Christine remembered chiefly because she'd been sick on the train coming home – a honeymoon in Clacton and, in the space of two years, two little girls, Jennifer, who was now six, and her younger sister Lilian.

Chris supposed it had seemed romantic to Peggy, marrying a

soldier – not that there was anything unusual about that during the war – but the romance seemed to have worn off very quickly. Chris could remember them visiting Brookfield when Lilian was a baby. Peggy had been going on about wanting a New Look frock, which she could get made up on the quiet, but there wasn't enough money because Jack had frittered it away on some get-rich-quick scheme with a 'pal' of his (there was always a 'pal' with Jack). In the end, Doris had given her some clothing coupons and told her to buy a new blouse, and Peggy had had to be satisfied with that.

She had seemed so doll-like and pretty at the wedding, Chris remembered, clinging to Jack's rough khaki arm in her dress of slipper satin. Now, hemming old sheets in a crossover pinafore, her swollen ankles propped on a stool, her hands roughened by washing soda and field work, she looked like just another frowsty housewife. Oh, they were probably happy enough. Peggy always said she couldn't be cross with Jack for long: he always managed to joke her out of a frown. But it was not the life Christine wanted for herself. And Doris wondered why Chris wanted to live a bit before she got married . . .

• • •

'Fancy a bar of chocolate cream, Grace? I think I've got enough coupons on me.'

In the crowded foyer of the Plaza Cinema, Borchester, Grace smiled up at Phil.

'If you're going to spend your time eating chocolate,' she remarked, 'why have you bought tickets for the back row?'

'Well, I . . .' Phil realized she was teasing him. He handed his coupons to the girl behind the counter. 'You needn't think I'm sharing it with you after that,' he retorted.

Grace pouted.

'All right. But I hope I get some reward for listening to you banging on about how dreadful it is working with your father all the way into town.'

Phil looked dejected.

'I'm sorry, Grace. It's just that he's so . . .'

'Like you?' she suggested.

'No! Well, I hope not!' Phil took her arm and guided her towards the sweeping staircase that led to the balcony. Errol Flynn, in naval uniform, glared menacingly at them from a poster advertising a coming attraction. 'I was going to say blinkered. Take this idea of the electric fence. Even old Walter can see the value of it – at least, he's going to let me rig one up for him on a trial basis. But not Dad. You'd think I'd suggested laying landmines in the kale instead of a bit of wire and a six-volt battery.'

Grace, enjoying the pressure of his hand on her arm, looked at him affectionately.

'It takes time for two people with ideas of their own to sit down and work together.'

'There's no working together where Dad's concerned. He gives the orders and you darn well take them, like it or not. And where's that going to get me?'

'Your father has got a lot of experience,' offered Grace tentatively.

'You're on his side, are you?' Phil edged them round a pillar.

'No more than on yours.' Grace stopped and turned to look at him. She was wearing a pale camel coat with a marcasite brooch on the collar, and a small fur hat with a spotted veil. It half hid her deep-blue eyes – with her dark hair, the sign of real beauty – and she looked up at him from beneath it. 'I only know what Daddy finds. You can't run a farm like a factory – what happens one week or one year may be quite different the next. In fact, something fresh crops up every day and it's never quite the same.'

'Maybe he needs a manager,' said Phil shortly.

'Maybe he does,' mused Grace. 'Well, shall we go in?'

• • •

Maybe he did, maybe he didn't. Maybe the idea was George Fairbrother's own, maybe Grace put it there. However it came about, whatever the reason, barely a week later, Phil received a summons to go and see Grace's father. Fairbrother, it transpired, had decided to appoint a manager. The older man walked him round the farm, explained his ideas and asked Phil what he thought.

Phil's enthusiasm was boundless. In Fairbrother he recognized a modern man – an urban man, maybe – but someone who was willing to embrace change, who couldn't cling to the old ways for the simple reason that he had never known them. Someone who was not afraid of the idea of mechanization, who thought tractors 'vital' and the combined harvester 'the coming thing'. Someone who had never heard the old adage, which Dan was so fond of quoting and which, he said (only inflaming Phil more), *his* old Dad had quoted at him: 'Be not the first by whom the new is tried, nor yet the last to cast the old aside.'

'But we *will* be the last!' Phil had fumed. 'The first tractor in Ambridge was five years ago! At the rate we're going, Walter Gabriel will have one before we do!'

'I doubt it, lad,' Dan had said annoyingly, patiently curry-combing Blossom, the old shire horse. 'Walter's always said he'd give Blossom and Boxer a home when we've done with them. Isn't that right, girl?' Blossom seized another mouthful of hay from the rack in acquiescence.

In any event, Phil felt his meeting with Fairbrother had gone well. Fairbrother asked for time to think about it, saying he was seeing a couple of other candidates the following week. Phil could do nothing but wait. But as he laid hedges for his father, his hands stinging from the billhook, even through his leather gloves, as he patted the warm rumps of the cows at milking, as he mucked out the horses or fed the pigs, he could see himself up at Fairbrother's, driving around in the Jeep, dealing with the seed merchant, making decisions – farming.

• • •

It was after a particularly frustrating day, during which he'd tried unsuccessfully to persuade his father to take out an overdraft to buy machinery, that Phil told his mother he'd get a bite of bread and cheese at The Bull and took himself off there for a quiet glass of beer instead of having supper at Brookfield. Anything rather than sit round the table with his mother passing the potatoes and making small talk about the village choir, Chris smirking and his father grimly silent.

He'd hardly had time to sit down and wipe the froth of his first sip from his lips when Rita Flynn appeared. On the pretence of wiping the table where he was sitting, she perched on a stool and leant forward.

'Can I ask you something?' Rita's soft Irish accent would never leave her, and it was probably her most attractive feature, for all her other more obvious charms.

'Ask away.' The previous autumn, Phil and Rita had spent several nights in the back row of the cinema. Phil had kissed her diffidently and, though he didn't know it at the time, inexpertly, and she had smiled to herself at his inexperience. They had walked arm-in-arm to the bus station and there, while they waited for the service to Ambridge, Rita had kissed him full on the mouth and had slid her hands up his back under his jacket.

Phil had been pleasantly surprised but slightly alarmed, and after another couple of dates when the same thing had happened, he began to feel that Rita was, perhaps, rather 'fast'. But being the well-brought up boy that he was, he didn't just drop her. He told her that he didn't think they were suited, but that he'd like to remain friends. And Rita, who by then, in addition to Phil, was seeing a commercial traveller in haberdashery who covered the Borchester area, had accepted his verdict graciously. To their credit, they had managed to remain friends. Phil bought her a gin and lime when he saw her in the pub; she told him the latest gossip. But he went home alone and Doris Archer had been able to relax for the first time in weeks.

'I need some money, Phil,' Rita said now.

'Money? How much?'

'Fifteen pounds.'

Phil let out a breath. 'That's a lot.'

'I know.'

'I just haven't got that much. Can I ask . . . can I ask why you need it?'

Rita looked down at the floor. She moved a discarded cigarette end about with the toe of her shoe.

'You're not . . .'

'No! How could you even think . . .' She stood up, offended. 'It's all right. Sorry I troubled you.'

'I only get what Dad pays me,' blustered Phil. 'And that's darn little. Don't take on, Rita.'

'I'm not. I understand,' she said, in a tone that showed that she didn't. 'Don't bother yourself. I'll manage.'

She flounced off back to the bar, flicking the tables with her towel as she went, and picking up dirty glasses. Phil sighed. It seemed there was no way of escaping some sort of confrontation this evening. He opened his copy of the *Pig Breeder* with relief.

• • •

Phil owed Rita nothing, and she wouldn't have held him to it if he had. But all that churchgoing, all that singing in the choir, all the Sunday evenings at home with his Grandmother reading from the family Bible had left their mark on him. He couldn't see a person in need, especially someone like Rita, who was a nice girl at heart, and not do something about it. The next night he sought her out in the little back yard at The Bull and offered her his last two weeks' wages if she could find the rest from elsewhere.

'You're an angel, Phil!' she exclaimed, giving him a smacking kiss. 'I've a bit put by myself, and I can get an advance against my wages. Ten pounds might do it, anyway!'

'Can you really not tell me what it's for, Rita?' asked Phil. 'You're not in any sort of trouble, are you?'

'No, bless you.' Rita's eyes, with their sooty coating of make-up, held his. 'This money's going to keep me *out* of trouble, you'll see.'

·2·

Secrets and
Surprises

But Rita Flynn was always going to be trouble as far as Phil was concerned. Two days later, he was digging out a blocked culvert in Long Meadow – was it his imagination, or was his father giving him the dirtiest jobs on these dank January days? – when Rita, of all people, in her inappropriate shoes and her best coat, came running up the lane.

'Phil! Oh, Phil!'

Phil threw down the spade.

'Rita?'

'I have to ask you, there's no-one else. Oh, Phil, can you take me to Hollerton to catch the train?'

'What, now?'

'I've got to get the four o'clock to Birmingham. There's only a ten-minute wait and then I can change to –'

'Look, you don't have to go through the whole timetable.'

It was already ten to three and the sky was being inked in beyond the trees.

'You could borrow your father's car, couldn't you?'

Phil thought quickly.

'I'm sorry, Rita, but no. He's gone in to see Mr Helston, the bank manager.' Not about the overdraft that Phil was so keen on, sadly, but about a cheque from a cattle trader at Waterley Cross that had bounced.

'Oh, no.' Rita was close to tears. 'I've got to get that train.'

Phil rubbed his forehead, a nervous habit of his when under pressure.

'Look, there's only one thing I can think of,' he said. 'Grace has always said that if I needed it, in an emergency I could borrow her car.'

'This is an emergency!' cried Rita. Her feet must have been freezing in her thin-soled shoes, Phil thought, and her hands were blue.

'Look, I'll dash across and see Grace at home, borrow the car and meet you at The Bull in – say – fifteen minutes.'

'Oh, Phil!' Rita grabbed his hands and kissed them. 'I'll never forget this!'

• • •

Nor will I, thought Phil, as he stood in a muddy lane not two hours later and watched Grace's car being winched up on to the breakdown truck that had come out from a nearby garage. What he could forget, he felt sure, were his hopes of the manager's job with Mr Fairbrother.

He should have realized, he thought bitterly, that the mission was doomed when, arriving at the Fairbrothers' to beg the loan of the car from Grace, he had found her not at home. Betty, the maid, launched into an explanation – a new hat and a train journey to Felpersham came into it somewhere – but Phil had no time for any of that. He gave Betty a garbled explanation of his own, promising to return the car within the hour ('Grace won't even need to know!'), seized the car keys from their usual Benares brass pot on the hall table and disappeared before the poor woman could protest.

Taking every corner on two wheels and hoping against hope that the Ambridge policeman, Constable Randall, was, as usual, still recovering from the after-effects of a heavy lunch, he'd collected Rita from outside The Bull, loaded her mean cardboard suitcase into the boot and hurled the car into gear. And as they sped through the darkening afternoon, along the bare lanes, she had told him, finally, because he insisted, what was so important.

'You won't go blabbing this all over the place, will you?' she pleaded. 'If I tell you, you'll keep it to yourself?'

Phil slowed down as they came to a T-junction.

'Let's hear it first.'

'All right.' Rita took a breath. 'I've got to catch that train and I need the money because . . . I'm going to see my husband.'

Husband! Phil felt his hands tense on the wheel. Try as he might, he couldn't recall any mention of a husband when he'd been buying her chocolate caramels or feeling her hand on his knee in the back row at the flicks. He pointed this out to Rita.

'I've never told a soul,' she said in a low voice. 'I've made a point of not telling.'

'But why? Where is he?'

'Scotland.'

A momentary quiver of relief ran through Phil. Far enough away not to come looking for him, anyway.

'So what's the worry?'

'He's coming out tomorrow.' Phil looked blank, so she added, as if stating the obvious, 'Out of prison.'

Numbed, Phil nodded. Rita carried on matter-of-factly, 'He's been doing five years – robbery with violence. Nasty job. Post office outside Aberdeen.'

Bit by bit, as Phil drove, the rest of the story emerged. The husband – Terry – had written to Rita about a week ago saying he was due for release – hence the need for the money. And in this morning's post she'd had confirmation that the release date was today.

'I don't want him back, Phil – not ever. When I came to Ambridge three years ago it was like starting a new life.' Her hands wound round each other as she talked. 'Oh, I know what the village thinks of me. I'm not respectable enough for them – but I've been as happy here as I'm ever likely to be. Much happier than when I was with him. I was scared of him, to tell you the truth.'

'So why rush off to meet him now?'

Rita shook her head wonderingly.

'You don't get it, do you? I'm afraid he'll come back to me. He'll start all his old tricks – getting on the drink, hitting me around –'

Shocked, Phil took one hand from the steering wheel and laid it over hers. Rita shook it away.

'Look, I'm not asking for sympathy and I don't need any. I can take care of myself – at least I can with him out of the way. That's why I've got to see him.'

'To talk him into leaving you alone?'

Rita looked at him witheringly. He really had no idea.

'You can't talk to Terry. But you can give him money. He said something about going back to Ireland. If I meet him and give him enough for his fare – and a bit extra for beer and cigarettes – and if I actually go with him and make sure he buys the ticket . . . Well, maybe he'll go and leave me alone.' She shrugged. 'That's what I'm hoping, anyway. And then I can come back to Ambridge and carry on as before. But . . .', she turned to Phil, 'I couldn't if the truth came out. So don't you say anything about me to anybody – promise?'

Maybe it was the enormity of taking all this in that caused Phil's concentration to lapse, or maybe, at the crucial moment, his mother's face floated in front of him as she learnt that her son, her precious son, had been involved not just with a barmaid but a married woman with a jailbird husband . . . the tractor, anyway, turning out of a gateway, took him by surprise. Phil wrenched at the wheel but he couldn't prevent the car from bouncing into the ditch and up into the hedge, scattering an indignant flock of fieldfares and dislodging a patter of desiccated leaves, which dropped on the bonnet. Neither of them was hurt: it was the car that had borne the brunt of the damage.

Phil would willingly have coped with a broken arm or a mild concussion if only the car could have been spared, but it was clear that it was in a bad way. Apart from the mud and a fretwork of scratches, the offside wing was buckled and the wheel arch was digging viciously into the tyre. Phil rubbed his forehead as if to clarify his thoughts, but Rita grabbed his wrist to look at his watch and, seeing the time, began jabbering about her train. The tractor driver, a whiskery fellow in a moleskin waistcoat, approached.

'Want me to drag you out?'

Phil shook his head. The priority was Rita. He had to get her on that train, not just for her own sake, but so that he could start to think straight.

'This young lady's got a train to catch,' he explained. 'If you could just take her to the main road, she'll be able to pick up the Lavershore bus. That gets to Hollerton in time for the four o'clock.'

Having dispatched Rita with her knight on shining Fordson, who in addition promised to stop off and phone the garage on the Hollerton road, Phil slumped down on the verge. It was damp and muddy, but he was past caring. It was not the damage to the car that bothered him – he could pay for that – but the damage it represented: damage to his relationship with the Fairbrothers – father and daughter.

• • •

Grace certainly didn't make it easy for him to apologize – but then why should she, especially when Walter Gabriel, who just happened to have been sitting in his favourite window seat at The Bull supping his ale and who just happened to have seen Phil collect Rita, just happened to mention to Mr Fairbrother that it was 'real generous' of Grace to loan young Philip her car to run another young lady about in. Walter hadn't deliberately been making mischief – he was simply taking his role as a sort of village oracle rather too seriously – but word got to George Fairbrother and to Grace before Phil could tell them his side of the story.

Phil knew before he set out to see Grace that same evening that there was a high chance that his turning up at the Fairbrothers' might only make things worse. When he got to the house, she wouldn't even let him inside. Her coolness could have caused frostbite in the height of summer, and on a raw January night, with the wind smarting in his eyes and the tip of his nose freezing above his scarf, it was almost more than Phil could bear.

'I'm – I'm very sorry, Grace,' he said, when she had had her say. 'I did a darn silly thing taking the car but – well, circumstances were such that I –'

'Yes?'

Phil knew he couldn't renege on the promise he had made to Rita.

'I can't tell you what it was all about,' he agonized. 'But there were very good reasons.'

'Well, I'm afraid that sort of explanation isn't enough to convince Daddy,' replied Grace icily. 'He's very annoyed about it.'

Grace had already explained that her father was in Birmingham seeing clients.

'I see. Yes, I expect he is pretty mad.'

'He's disappointed, Philip. Disappointed in you and his first impression of you. And you might as well know,' she added, as if Phil could have formed any other opinion, 'that I'm disappointed in you, too.'

'But, Grace –' Phil made one last attempt to put his case, which sounded pathetic even to him. 'I can't tell you the reasons in detail, but they're genuine – honestly – Rita needed help and –'

But Grace was already shutting the door.

'Good night, Philip.'

Phil was left staring at an expanse of black paint and a highly polished door knocker in the shape of a fox's head. He had to fight the desire to seize it, hammer the door down and tell her everything, but he knew he had made an intractable promise to Rita and anyway, with Grace in this frame of mind, he doubted if anything would get through to her. Shoulders hunched to face the frozen walk home, he turned and stepped out of the shelter of the porch. He was not at all surprised to find that it had started sleeting.

• • •

'Go easy, young Philip, you'll have her teats off!'

Phil's pace didn't slacken. He was having to handmilk Clover, who had mastitis in one quarter and whose milk couldn't go in the tank with the rest.

'She's not complaining.'

'Poor old Clover, what's he doing to you, hey, girl?' Simon Cooper, the farmhand, patted the cow's neck, then spoke to Phil. 'Your Mum wants to know when you'll be in for your breakfast.'

'I'm not hungry. You can have it, if you like.'

'Not hungry? You've got that hedge by the Five Acre to finish laying this morning, lad, you'll want something inside you.'

'I'll finish here and then I'll get off and make a start,' said Phil stubbornly.

'What's up wi' you? Is sommat the matter?'

No, not really, thought Phil. I've just thrown away my chance of the best job there is in this neighbourhood, working for a modern, go-ahead chap like Fairbrother. I'll be stuck here working for Dad for the foreseeable future, on a miserable 100-acre tenant farm, with no modern machinery and attitudes to farming rather less enlightened than Turnip Townsend's. I've smashed up the car belonging to a girl I'm really beginning to get quite keen on, and she thinks I'm two-timing her with a bottle blonde who, for good measure, happens to be married to a violent thug who might just come looking for me. In fact, the way things are going, it might be a mercy if he did. But apart from that, Simon, no, nothing's wrong. God's in his Heaven and all's right with the world.

Phil got up abruptly, kicking over the stool.

'Oh, you finish her off, will you?' he said. 'I've had enough.'

'I should think Clover's had enough of you an' all,' muttered Simon as Phil departed. 'Face like that's enough to turn the milk.'

• • •

Of course, it would be that night that Grace had been invited round to Brookfield for supper. After a long day in the fields, breaking the ice on the water troughs, taking fodder to the sheep, and the seemingly never-ending task of hedge-laying, it was already dark when Phil got back to the house. All afternoon, he'd had visions of a nice cup of tea or three, perhaps a scone or bit of bread and jam, and his mother's comforting presence as she started preparations for the meal. Surely, over supper with his parents, Grace would have to open up a bit, and then if he could get her on her own he might be able to talk her round? But though the gasjets flickered in the kitchen, the fire was raked low and he suddenly remembered that Doris had said she was going to tea with Peggy, whose formidable mother, Mrs Perkins, had arrived from her home in London to stay until after the baby was born. She had, though, left a note on the kitchen table. Phil snatched it up eagerly. 'Cake in tin,' perhaps? 'Grace rang,' he read. 'Unable to come for supper. Didn't say why. Love, Mum.'

Grace's unexplained absence at supper meant that Phil had no alternative but to tell his parents the full story – at least, the part about giving Rita a lift to Hollerton. Their reaction to that – which had been, he thought, a harmless enough act of Christian kindness – in itself convinced him, had he thought of wavering, that Rita was absolutely right not to want the reason for her hasty departure spread around. Ambridge folk like his parents judged her by her appearance, decided that she was 'no better than she should be' and automatically assumed the worst.

Incensed on her behalf, and helpless to save himself, Phil kept his pact with her: he said nothing about Terry. For the next week, he hid himself away. He didn't attempt to see Grace, and his dealings with his parents were restricted to the barest essentials as his mother asked him to pass his plate for more cabbage or his father instructed him to inject a new litter of pigs. Tense and miserable, he went about his work with a pinched face and tight lips, always waiting for the phone call or message – from George Fairbrother or his daughter – which never came.

By the time a week had passed he was (perhaps a little theatrically) resigned to his role as the spurned lover and martyred work-horse. His hands were blistered from wielding the billhook. His back ached from mucking out the cow pens and sweeping the yard. His head throbbed with the injustice of it all. And then, one night, he came in with a tiny posy of winter aconites he had found in a sheltered spot on Lakey Hill and which he intended giving Chris, to find his father and mother seated at the table looking solemn.

'Why didn't you tell us?' his father demanded, before Phil had even had time to take his boots off.

'Tell you what?'

In his thick, marled socks, Phil carefully crossed the quarry-tiled kitchen, picked an egg cup off the dresser and went into the scullery to fill it with water for the flowers.

'Rita Flynn's been here,' his mother called.

'She's told us what you should have told us a week ago,' his father added tersely, in case Phil might have thought everything was going to be smoothed over without an argument.

But for once Phil didn't care about arguing with his father. At the scullery sink, he looked out into the yard. An improbably rosy sun was balanced on the dark horizon. Lady, Dan's sheepdog, was worrying a bone by her kennel. From the parlour, he could faintly hear the swish of milk into jars as Simon coaxed and chatted his way through the herd. Water splashed over Phil's hands and he turned off the tap. He arranged the aconites in the egg cup, which itself was in the shape of a chicken. He noticed again how fragile the flowers were, their green-veined petals almost transparent. Rita had told his parents the truth. It didn't mean he could tell Grace, but it was, perhaps, a start.

• • •

As far as Dan was concerned it was more than a start. He had stood back for the best part of a week, silenced by Doris into not pressing Phil about the accident to Grace's car and why he was running round the countryside with Rita Flynn when he was supposed to be courting Grace Fairbrother and, more to the point, when he was supposed to be digging out a culvert in Long Meadow. Lord knew, he could have shaken the boy, but he'd seen the dull eyes and the defeated slope to the shoulders, that told him Phil was suffering enough.

If Rita Flynn had been in the village, he'd have gone and got the truth out of her himself, but when he'd enquired casually at The Bull, Sam Saunders, the landlord, had said she'd taken some holiday owing to her and gone to see a relative in Scotland. Dan privately thought it was a funny time of year for a holiday, especially in Scotland, but he just took a sip of his pint, retamped his pipe and said nothing. And then, out of the blue, in the half light of a January afternoon, Rita Flynn had come and found him in the yard and said she needed to speak to him and to Doris, and the whole sorry story had come out.

'Philip only did it out of the goodness of his heart, to help me get to see Terry because I begged him, and because there was no-one else!' she said as Doris poured the tea, but not into the best cups, because it was only Rita Flynn and she was hardly the President of the WI. 'And it was only when I got back to The Bull and they were saying in the public that him and Grace Fairbrother were all washed up because of it that I knew I had to tell you!'

Touched, Doris passed her the teabread and patted her hand. Maybe Rita Flynn wasn't all bad.

Dan kept his own counsel. The girl looked like a trollop – the outline of her mouth was printed in lipstick on her cup – and his son's involvement with her could have cost Phil his future. But at least that involvement was limited to giving her lifts to the station. Worse, far worse, had crossed Dan's mind, including the ultimate possibility of forgetting about Phil and letting Jack take on the tenancy of Brookfield, something that he knew deep down would be a disaster. But now that Dan knew the full story, what was he to do about it?

• • •

When he was suddenly summoned to see George Fairbrother, Phil had every reason to expect the worst. Over and over again he had weighed up in his own mind the desirability of seeking out Grace's father to apologize about the car, but as Grace had so convincingly conveyed her father's displeasure, there didn't seem to be much point. Now, perhaps, Fairbrother felt he'd waited long enough. He wanted to carpet Philip. George Fairbrother, Phil imagined, had spent a week brooding on what he would say, flexing his muscles, honing his barbs. He's going to flay me alive, thought Phil glumly as he waited in Fairbrother's study, and there's nothing I can do about it.

But when Grace's father came in, apologizing profusely for

keeping Phil waiting, his eyes were flashing good humour, not fury, and his handshake was friendly. It didn't stop Phil from beginning to burble an apology.

'Never mind about that. It's over and done with. Sherry?' asked Fairbrother.

'Um, yes, thanks,' replied Phil cautiously. Was he being softened up for the real body blow?

'The whole episode has been satisfactorily explained to me.' Fairbrother replaced the crystal stopper in the sherry decanter and crossed the room to Phil.

'Explained? Who by? Not Grace?'

Fairbrother handed him his glass.

'No. By the same person who usually keeps a fellow on the rails.'

'Dad?'

Dan, Mr Fairbrother explained, had been to see him. Dan had told him all about Rita and the urgent need for her to get to Hollerton, and the complex reasons for secrecy. Overnight, Phil had been transformed in Fairbrother's eyes from an uncaring opportunist to an unassuming hero, too gallant to break a promise, too modest to protest his innocence. This, allied to the fact that Fairbrother had met old Renshawe, the principal of the Farm Institute, at dinner and had clearly enjoyed passing the port and taking a cigar with him whilst talking about old pupils, made Phil, as Fairbrother put it, by far the most suitable person for the job of farm manager, which was still open.

'Can you start on Monday?'

'You bet, sir!' Phil leapt up from his chair to shake Fairbrother's outstretched hand. 'This is going to be a test for me – a real test – but you can be sure I'll give it my best shot. And thanks for being so decent about the car and –'

'That's all forgotten. I'm sure we'll work together well. And Philip?'

'Sir?'

'Can I give you a piece of advice?'

'Of course.'

'At a time like this, just when you're beginning to get started on a career, sometimes it pays you to concentrate on your job and not bother your head so much about the girls. Don't misunderstand me,' he added, raising his hand in that slightly schoolmasterish way he had. 'You and Grace are good friends, I believe, and I've nothing whatever against that. But I do know that if you get too involved in your personal life, your work suffers.' Phil nodded in what he hoped was an appreciative manner.

'I do see what you mean, sir.'

'Just bear it in mind, Philip, bear it in mind.'

Phil nodded again. There was no problem bearing it in mind when, as Fairbrother had told him, Grace was in London visiting an old schoolfriend. Whether he would be able to do so on Monday, and every successive day when he might see her, was another matter entirely.

• • •

The first few days of Phil's employment with Fairbrother were all he could have hoped for. Fairbrother listened to Phil's comments and tempered some of his wilder ideas with caution, but in the main he seemed willing to give Phil free rein, and, while there was no blank cheque, he was certainly more receptive to ideas that might cost money than Dan would ever have been.

Phil knew that, in a sense, the comparison was unfair, because Fairbrother had money to throw at the farm and, if it all went horribly wrong (which it wouldn't, Phil swore, as long as he was in charge), he still had his plastics business to bring him in a sizeable income. Brookfield, on the other hand, was Dan's all. He had no assets and precious little spare cash, and in his heart of hearts Phil knew that he was guilty of trying to push his safe, reliable father too far, too fast.

He knew he was lucky to have found a rare opportunity with Fairbrother and he was determined to make the most of it. He arrived early in the morning and left late at night, poring over figures in the farm office when daylight had long gone. Fairbrother was delighted with him and told him so. Phil was relieved and pleased, but felt slightly guilty. The real reason he stayed late was in the – now receding – hope that Grace might come and seek him out.

He had seen her coming and going across the yard, her slim figure dangerously exciting in jodhpurs and a hacking jacket. He had seen her getting into her car, now mended, dressed for town in a new tweed costume with a fox fur at her neck. He had once, tantalizingly, seen her at her bedroom window with her hair in a towel and, as far as he could make out, nothing else on. But she had not once acknowledged him, not even to cut him dead.

His parents had forgiven him the Rita Flynn episode, Grace's father had forgiven him: only Grace remained resolute. What was it they said about a woman scorned? Except Grace hadn't been scorned. Phil would have had to be crazy to prefer Rita over Grace, especially when he and Grace had been on the verge of something different from anything he had felt for anyone else before. He wanted passionately to tell Grace all this. He needed to tell her. But how could he if she wouldn't even look him in the face?

• • •

'Grace!'

Grace pulled her horse, Flash, up short and turned in the saddle.

'Hello, Chris!'

Phil's sister, Christine, cantered up behind her on a roan mare.

'Isn't it a fabulous day?'

'About time!'

It was true that January had been a foul month: wet, cold and sleety, damp and grey, and the first two weeks of February had been the rainiest on record. But now, mid-month, the skies had lifted and you could almost believe that there would eventually be a spring. The winter aconites had been joined by the first spears of crocus, those impossibly pointless flowers that only seemed to grow to give the birds the pleasure of destroying them. The proud spikes of would-be daffodils were also starting to strike through the earth and down here by the Am the first furry catkins were fluttering in the breeze.

'Haven't seen much of you lately.' Chris loosed her grip on the rein to let her horse crop the struggling grass.

'No, well . . . I didn't know how welcome I'd be up at Brookfield.'

'How welcome *you'd* be? Hang on, I may have got this wrong but I thought it was my brother who smashed up your car, not the other way round.'

Grace looked down. She pushed her fingers rhythmically through her horse's mane. For once, Chris felt, her little-girl-lost act wasn't put on.

'Oh, Chris,' Grace began. 'I've been so stupid. Daddy's explained to me all about what happened with Rita and why Philip had to help her out. And he and Philip are getting on like a house on fire – Daddy's never been more positive about the farm and what he can do with it. So there's no reason at all why Philip and I shouldn't be . . . friends again, is there?'

Chris shrugged. 'None at all.'

'But it's me!' Grace burst out. 'Or my silly pride, or something. I just can't seem to forgive him – not for taking the car, or even for helping Rita, but for not telling me!'

'But Grace,' said Christine gently, 'he couldn't, could he? He was sworn to secrecy.'

'It's torture having him up there every day and not speaking to him, and yet I just won't let myself!' Grace went on. 'I suppose I'm waiting for him to make the first move.'

'I think there's something you'd better know about my brother,' said Christine. 'When it comes to stubbornness he takes some beating. But I think in you he might have met his match. The two of you need your heads banging together!'

Grace smiled wryly. 'Perhaps we do,' she said. 'Any volunteers?'

'Come back to Brookfield for tea,' suggested Chris. 'Phil usually finishes a bit early on a Friday, doesn't he? When he comes in, I'll steer Mum out of the way and maybe you and he can finally make up your differences.'

'Well, I don't know . . .'

'Grace! I'm not asking you, I'm telling you! You ought to have tried living with Phil over the past couple of weeks. He may be a little ray of sunshine for your father but at home he's been a downright misery. Just make it up with him and do us all a favour!'

Grace smiled. She tugged on the reins to raise her horse's head.

'All right, then,' she said. 'But I'm going home first. I don't want him to see me looking like this!'

Chris took in Grace's slender legs in their jodhpurs, her soft lovat-green tweed jacket and her cream twill shirt with a silk scarf at the throat. Chris was also wearing jodhpurs, but topped with an old shirt of Dan's and a sweater of Philip's. Where Grace had glossy riding boots, Chris had wellingtons. Grace's hat was of matt black velvet: Chris's was worn and shiny with age. Apart from the absurd idea that Grace could look any better than she did already, Chris also had to struggle with the ridiculous notion that anyone should be bothered to dress up to impress her brother, but she suppressed her smile. She wheeled her horse round.

'See you later, then,' she called, suddenly remembering that if Grace and Phil made it up and his mood improved, Phil might just lend her the few bob she needed to get a new blouse made out of the material she'd bought with her carefully hoarded coupons. Basil, her boss, had said something about taking her out to lunch next week – supposedly to discuss 'her future with Borchester Dairies'. Chris wondered. She was still puzzling over the identity of the person who had sent her a Valentine's card and a spray of orchids to the office. It couldn't have been Nelson Gabriel. She had seen him biking furiously away from Brookfield, having left her a card and a box of chocolates (either black market or a year's sweet ration) on the back doorstep.

Basil was everything that Nelson wasn't. He was older, sophisticated – and married, of course – and therefore fatally attractive to a girl like Chris. So she decided she'd let him take her out to lunch next week and over mulligatawny soup in the lounge bar of The Station Hotel they could discuss her future, by all means – and maybe more. And she certainly felt that a new blouse – rayon, pink peony print – would be appropriate.

But when Chris got back to Brookfield, it was clear that her careful plan to bring Phil and Grace together was destined for failure. Peggy's baby had started and Doris, her father informed her, had gone down to the smallholding, presumably to boil kettles and to hold Jack's hand while Mrs Perkins did the same for Peggy. Jack and Peggy's girls, Jennifer and Lilian, were cutting out paper dolls at the kitchen table, having been left in Dan's charge, and he was itching to get out and start the milking. So Chris, and Grace, when she arrived, had to act as babyminders – and while Grace boiled eggs for the girls' tea, Chris took a call from Phil saying that work digging drainage ditches at Fairbrother's had been held up and he'd have to stay on until the job was completed, and then he'd got paperwork to do . . . There goes the reconciliation, and there goes my new blouse, Chris thought.

'I'm sorry, Grace,' she said, when she'd explained. 'It doesn't look as if matchmaking is my forte.'

'Oh, that's all right.' Grace helped Lilian to peel the shell off her egg. 'I'm enjoying myself here, anyway. I shall give the girls a bath in a while and then tuck them up for the night. If they're very good, I've promised I'll tell them a story, haven't I, girls?'

'Oh yes?' Chris got down some mugs for the children's cocoa. 'And what will that be about?'

'Oh, the usual,' smiled Grace. 'It's about a beautiful princess who lives in tall tower. And there's a handsome farmhand who's in love with her, but he's captured by a wicked fairy who drives him away in her carriage, puts a spell on him and makes him her slave. And the princess pines away, but the farmhand doesn't realize it until it's almost too late, and then . . .'

'Go on!' cried Jennifer, waving an egg-coated spoon.

'Well?' Chris put the milk on to boil.

'I don't know the end yet,' said Grace thoughtfully. 'I'll have to work it out as I go along.'

• • •

'Jack, for pity's sake, sit still.' Doris laid down her knitting. 'That's the third time you've got up and sat down again for no reason at all.'

Jack paced the length of the numdah rug in front of the fire, then turned and paced back again.

'Can't take all this long,' he grumbled. 'Midwife said it was nearly all over when the doctor went up. Been up there half an hour already. What is he doing?'

Doris calmly counted her stitches.

'Why don't you go up and ask him, tell him how to do his job?' she queried. 'I tell you, Jack, I heard that baby cry ten minutes ago when you went for the coal.' A faint mewing sound floated down the stairs. 'Hear that! There it is again!'

'I heard it . . .' Jack's face was alight. 'Why don't they hurry up?'

The stairs creaked as the doctor, who was only there because he'd jokingly promised Doris he'd be the one to deliver her first grandson, came down. Doris caught his eye as he came into the room and he nodded imperceptibly.

'All right, Jack, lad,' he said. 'You go and see your missus and tell her how proud you are.' As if he needed to, he added, 'It's a fine baby boy – eight pounds!'

Jack bounded up the stairs, but on the landing a terrible shyness overcame him and he had to resist the urge to knock at his own bedroom door. He took a deep breath, smoothed his hair down, wiped his hands on his trousers and, opening the door very quietly, went in.

Peggy was propped up in bed, holding a little bundle in a lacy shawl. Her face was lowered to the baby's and her fuzzy blonde hair made a halo round both their heads. Jack stood in the doorway watching them and at that moment he resolved that everything would be different. He'd concentrate on the smallholding instead of his 'schemes', as Peggy called them. This summer they'd have the best crop of tomatoes in the district, their cucumbers would be second to none, their lettuces would be crisp and juicy. He'd never again (as he had just had to do) have to cadge the money for the coke bill from his Dad who, as he'd said more than once, was sick and tired of having to bail him out. If he said he was going to turn over the ground for the marrows, that's what he'd do, instead of sitting in a wash of early sunshine with the racing pages. If Peggy wanted the coal carrying or the copper lighting, he'd do it without complaint. He'd play snakes and ladders with the girls, and push them on the swing, and be proud to walk out with the new carriage pram that Dan and Doris had bought them when he'd finally had to admit that the old one was beyond repair . . .

'What are you looking at?' Peggy was smiling.

Jack moved towards the bed. He put out a hand and stroked her cheek with his fingertips.

'You. Seems such a – well, such a long time since I saw you.'

Peggy caught his fingers and brought them to her lips. He bent to kiss her.

'You haven't looked at Anthony William Daniel yet,' she chided. 'Look . . . isn't he beautiful?'

Jack looked at the little screwed-up monkey face, the shock of black hair, the tiny, tight-curled fists.

'Beautiful,' he repeated. 'The first Archer grandson, eh? Gosh, Peg . . . aren't we clever . . . you and me?'

·3·

Difficult Decisions

'Look healthy enough, don't they?'

It was the first week of September and a sluggish summer had roused itself into a day of brilliant sunshine. Phil shielded his eyes and looked with satisfaction round George Fairbrother's poultry flock and the fold units he had set up on the rich pastureland by the Am. A quivering breeze from the river lifted a strand of Jane Maxwell's blonde hair and laid it across her cheek. She tucked it behind her ear.

'As healthy a bunch as I've seen anywhere,' she agreed.

Contented hens clucked around their feet.

'And you're quite clear regarding the feeding?'

'It'll be easy. It's just what I was taught at college.'

Phil nodded his approval. Jane had only been at the farm a day and a half, but he could already sense that he'd chosen the right candidate to look after the poultry. She was confident, capable and, most compelling of all, she could only be doing the job because she loved the work, since she came from a wealthy family near Bath who, she had told Phil at her interview, couldn't understand her interest in getting her hands dirty.

'Well, you're obviously not going to have any trouble in coping with the job,' he grinned. 'And how do you think you're going to like Ambridge?'

Jane laughed. When she laughed she had a way of tilting her head back and exposing her throat. A blue vein beat in the hollow at its base.

'Oh, I'm used to country folk,' she said. 'I've been a country girl all my life. No, I'm not worried about that . . .'

Her voice trailed away and Phil sensed a wariness.

'You're not worried about anything, I hope.'

She was practically the same height as he was, and he could look directly into her eyes. They were a pale tawny brown, the colour of dried barley straw, and the sunlight danced in them.

'Well, not worried, exactly . . .'

Phil opened his hands, gesturing helplessness and the wish to understand.

'What? Tell me. Please.'

'Phil? Phil!'

Grace was standing at the field gate. Phil sighed.

'Want me?' he called.

'If you can spare a minute.'

Phil pushed his hand through his hair.

'Won't be long,' he said to Jane. 'Perhaps you could start . . .'

'Checking the feed hoppers? Of course.'

The light in her eyes was gone. She moved away, inscrutable. Phil tramped over the long grass to Grace.

'Hope I didn't break up anything,' she said sweetly.

'Break up what?'

Grace's eyebrows made two perfect arcs.

'You must admit you're giving Miss Maxwell rather a lot of attention. In fact, you're fussing round her like an old hen.'

Phil felt suddenly tired. He'd been up at six to help his father with the milking: Simon was on holiday in Rhyl. He'd started work in Fairbrother's farm office at eight-thirty, talking to the grain merchant on the phone, chasing a delivery of cattle feed, checking with Angus, Fairbrother's herdsman, about the Ayrshires, supervising Jim Benson, who was ploughing in the stubbles. He had hoped that Jane's appointment would at least relieve him of responsibility for the poultry, but he could see that any time saved would have to be spent pacifying Grace.

His relationship with her never seemed to run smoothly. They had made up eventually after the incident with Rita Flynn and the car, but just when Phil had started to feel that they were a couple again, Grace had begun to seem restless. Squire Lawson-Hope, the Estate owner, had had an old friend, Helen Carey, staying with him. She was an attractive woman in her early forties and Grace seemed to think that she might be a suitable match for her father. She began asking Helen over for tea and to dinner, and when Helen's son, Alan, had come to stay as well, it seemed only natural to include him. The threesome turned into a foursome for games of croquet or canasta and for trips out in the car. Phil, tearing into the yard to get a spare belt for the tractor at the height of harvest, had seen them all piling into Fairbrother's Daimler. Grace, in one of her summer print frocks sprigged with lily of the valley, was supervising the loading of the picnic hamper into the boot.

'It's such a shame you can't join us, Phil,' she'd called, and Phil had made some curt reply about someone having to do some work. That night, when he'd taken Grace over to The Fox at Edgeley for a drink, she'd snuggled up to him on the rustic bench and told him she'd rather be with him than anyone. But Phil couldn't help but wonder about the day she'd spent with Alan Carey, who'd been with a tank regiment in Korea, and whose dark hair flopped moodily over his eyes.

'For goodness' sake, Daddy and Mrs Carey were there, it's not as if we weren't chaperoned!' Grace had teased when he asked. 'All we did was drive to Worcester and have a walk by the river! All four of us!'

Phil had rubbed his finger round the ring of wetness left on the table by his beer glass. It was hard for him to object to what, on the face of it, was a perfectly innocent summer outing. Grace was at home all day with nothing to occupy her. Once she had taken out her horse in the early morning, instructed the cook and done any errands, the rest of the day hung empty ahead of her. Phil, on the other hand, was working flat out. Even nights like this were rare. To catch the weather during harvest they would often work on after dark with lights, and on the nights he wasn't working he was ready for bed at ten.

He had looked at Grace as she sipped her drink, at her fine-boned hands and her pert, elfin profile. He wondered if she would feel less restless if she had something to occupy her, like a home of her own and – well, dash it – a husband. Or was there something in her – and this was what really worried him, tempering his natural caution even more – that would always be yearning for something or someone else?

Now, as he stood at the gate with her, he asked her, more brusquely than he had intended, 'What do you expect me to do with Jane? Say, "There are the hens, there's the hen food – I'll leave it to you?" I don't know about you lately, Grace,' he went on. 'First you run around in circles over Alan Carey, then you behave like Cupid off a wedding cake trying to throw your Dad and Mrs Carey into each other's arms – now you're getting the needle because we've got a girl working on the farm.'

Grace gave him a narrow-eyed look.

'Finished?' she demanded.

'Yes. Yes, and I'm sorry.' Phil reached for her hand, which was resting on top of the gate. He couldn't bear quarrelling with her. 'I'm tired, that's all. Did you want to see me about something?'

'I *did* want you to play tennis this evening.'

'Tennis?' Phil was taken aback. 'But we were going for a swim. We arranged it.' There was a natural bathing pool in the Squire's woods which he allowed several of the villagers to use.

'I'd rather play tennis,' said Grace coolly. 'If you don't mind.'

Phil took his hand away.

'You know what a duffer I am at the game. All the people who can play just stand around and take the mickey out of me.'

'I particularly feel like a game of tennis tonight,' said Grace stubbornly. Her mouth clenched tight and Phil suddenly saw Jane's brown throat and heard her laugh.

'And I particularly feel like a swim,' he replied, unusually defiant. 'That's life, isn't it?'

When he went back to Jane, she was quietly collecting the eggs. A couple of bantams murmured at her heels.

'What were you going to say, earlier?' he asked her. 'Something was worrying you?'

'It's nothing.' She placed a smooth brown egg in the basket that rested on her smooth brown forearm, fuzzed lightly with golden hair.

He touched her elbow. 'Jane. What?'

She stooped and put the basket down.

'I don't think Miss Fairbrother likes me very much.' She spoke to the middle distance as she straightened.

'What? Oh, nonsense. Why in the world should she like or dislike you?'

A cloud capped the sun.

'That's what I'm beginning to wonder myself,' said Jane slowly. 'Why should she?'

'Look,' said Phil abruptly. 'I honestly think you're imagining things.'

Jane's mouth twitched.

'Maybe,' she said. 'Anyway, not much I can do about it, I suppose. Oh, by the way,' she added, 'someone's told me there's a place to swim round here. A natural pool. A swim tonight would be wonderful.'

'Tonight?' Phil thought quickly. 'Well, why not? I'll take you.'

• • •

He might have known it would happen. He and Jane had had their swim. They were sitting in the last shaft of sunlight of the evening, talking about Jane's family, when they heard the crack of twigs. Someone was coming. Phil turned his head, utterly relaxed. He didn't know who he was expecting, if, indeed, he had formed the thought. Chris maybe? With Dick Raymond, a reporter from the *Borchester Echo* she had been seeing lately? But the person who stood in the gloom of the elms in a shimmering short white tennis dress was not his sister.

'Grace!'

'I see now why you were so keen on having a swim, Phil.' Her voice was high and hard. 'I'll leave you to it.'

He sprang to his feet. Droplets of water fell from his hair.

'Grace, don't be silly. Come and join us.'

'Us? I wouldn't want to intrude.'

Jane spoke for the first time. 'You wouldn't be.'

'Oh, I think I would.' Grace swung her tennis racket lightly. 'I'm so glad to see you're settling in so well in Ambridge, Jane. It must be nice to have someone to show you around.'

She turned in a whisper of pleats and was gone before Phil could say any more. He sat down again on the bank. Jane pulled a face.

'And you still say she doesn't dislike me?'

• • •

'Bill Slater? What was he doing on my land?' Fairbrother's voice came crisply down the phone. It was the next day and it looked as if it would be another difficult one for Phil.

'Well, sir, it was like this,' he began. 'Bill, as you know, is pretty good with machines, and because the tractor was playing up, I thought he'd be a good chap to have a look at it . . .'

It had seemed a perfectly sensible idea at the time. Bill Slater was a cousin of Peggy's. He'd come to Ambridge because he had a weak chest and he'd been told to get away from the smog of London. Jack had put in a good word for him with Dan, and since Bill's arrival had coincided neatly with Phil's full-time job for Fairbrother, Dan had agreed to take him on. He hadn't instantly regretted it, but as the summer had worn on, Dan had been less and less pleased with Bill. In short, he was a waster. He had no real interest in country life, no feeling for the stock. He did the minimum possible in the maximum time, leaving Simon to complain that he'd be better off working on his own.

All Bill was interested in was the tractor that Dan had finally bought (whilst still managing never to acknowledge that it had been Phil's idea). In fact, Bill was interested in anything mechanical – which is why he had been Phil's first choice to come round and have a look at what he suspected was a kink in the fuel pipe on Fairbrother's new tractor. Bill had sorted out the problem in no time but, being Bill, he could not leave it at that. Fairbrother's tractor was a big, new, shiny, tempting machine, and, while Phil was in the yard sending off a lorryload of late lambs, Bill had taken the tractor into a field – and had promptly driven it over a hummock that turned out to be solid rock, causing rather more damage than a kinked fuel pipe.

Over the course of the next few months, Phil asked himself many times what would have happened if, instead of calling in Bill, he'd tried to sort out the fuel pipe himself, or if he'd asked the bloke from the garage to come over and have a look. When Fairbrother had first arrived back from London and had looked at the damage to the tractor, he had done exactly what Phil had expected and called Bill up to the farm to give him a talking to. But then afterwards, when Fairbrother had walked with Phil to look at the rock in question, he had gone very quiet. He had started to rub and pull at his moustache in a way that Phil knew, after six months of working for him, meant that he was dealing with a big idea. Fairbrother did it because in the action of smoothing his moustache, his hand hid his mouth. When he had a big idea, Phil had learnt, he was often concealing a smile, because Fairbrother's big ideas usually translated into a lot of money.

'Going to make a phone call,' he'd said cryptically, adding, 'I'm beginning to regret giving young Bill such a roasting. I've a feeling I may have reason to thank him.'

• • •

It was ironstone. Fairbrother called in a mineralogist, Keith Latimer, and his survey revealed that it stretched for hundreds and hundreds of acres – not just beneath Fairbrother's land but under most of the Squire's Estate – under most of the tenanted farms on both sides of the river. And Fairbrother wanted to mine it.

'He'll never get away with it – will he?'

Keith and Christine, who had struck up quite a friendship, were sitting in the garden at The Bull, drinking shandy. Keith shrugged. He was a bookish-looking twenty-nine-year-old with a slightly dilapidated look to him.

'Fairbrother strikes me as the sort of chap who likes getting his own way,' he said thoughtfully. 'He's not going to take no for an answer. You know he's already bunged in an application for development covering both his land and the Squire's?'

'Can he do that?'

'He says the Squire gave him permission. But according to Jim Benson, who was bedding down the calves at the time, the Squire was in a tearing hurry – he was off to catch a train or something – and I don't think he really took in the implications.'

Christine let out a sigh. The Squire was a sweet old thing, he really was, but he was not exactly of the modern world. He belonged to an age when history and tradition had counted for something. There were Lawson-Hope graves in the churchyard dating back to the seventeenth century. The Gabriels had fought alongside the Squire's ancestors in the English Civil War. When the present Squire had commanded the 2nd battalion of the West Borsetshire Regiment in the First World War, thirty-five men from the village had enlisted under him.

The Squire's interests were in maintaining and preserving the legacy that his family inheritance had left to him. He planned meticulously the replanting of woodlands, the coppicing of trees. Chris's Uncle Tom, her mother's brother, worked as his gamekeeper, rearing pheasant and partridge, woodcock and snipe for the huge, almost Edwardian shooting parties that the Squire held and for which the woodland on the Estate was preserved in its ancient form. But if the Squire was the past, Fairbrother was the future. Chris knew from Phil the power of his arguments for mining the ironstone.

'Fine, the country needs food – but it also needs iron and steel,' Fairbrother had insisted when Phil had first challenged him about his plans. 'You people down here, you don't see the big industrial conurbations as I do. Of course you depend on the land, and people depend on what you produce from the land, but millions more depend for their livelihood on the shipyards of the Tyne or the smoking chimneys of the Black Country. That's who I'm interested in serving.'

Phil had told Chris that he'd got very angry at that, but he couldn't tell Fairbrother what he thought of him because he was his boss. And, worse still, Phil had had to agree to drawing up two sets of forward plans for Fairbrother's farm: one set that took account of the ironstone mining, and another that didn't. But Phil knew which one Fairbrother thought they would be following.

'So what do you think'll happen, Keith?' Chris put down her glass and turned on the bench to face him. 'You must have been involved with this sort of thing before.'

'Well, wherever there's public opposition – and there usually is – there'll have to be a public inquiry,' he replied. 'Fairbrother will have to engage a lot of expensive experts – lawyers and the like – to explain why it would benefit the village –'

'Benefit?' Christine looked incredulous.

'I've heard it all before. Increased trade for the pub and the shop, Department of Transport have to provide better roads, maybe even street lighting –'

'Better roads so that heavy lorries can thunder through, you mean? Street lighting showing up those ugly pitheads and cranes and grabs? It's ridiculous. This is a village. Surely no-one could be taken in by those arguments?'

Keith shrugged.

'I hate to tell you this, Christine, but they are. If you asked me to put money on it, I'd say Fairbrother has an even chance.'

'But surely when the Squire comes back he'll put a stop to it?' demanded Christine. 'Fairbrother caught him off his guard when he asked him about the permission. And maybe it wouldn't be worth Fairbrother's while developing only what lies under his land.'

Keith drained the last drop of his drink.

'Come on, drink up, or we'll miss the start of the picture,' he said. 'Have you heard about these open-air cinemas in America?' he went on as Christine pulled on her cardigan and retrieved her handbag. 'Drive-in movies, they're called. Who knows, if ironstone comes to Ambridge, maybe they'll come to Borchester.'

'Well, you can keep them,' said Christine firmly, taking his arm. 'I like Ambridge – and Borchester – just as they are.'

· · ·

'Come on Grace, eat up. Duck with green peas – I thought this was one of your favourites?'

George Fairbrother poured himself another glass of claret. Grace's glass was still untouched. Slowly she pushed a sliver of duck on to her fork, placed it in her mouth and chewed obediently.

She had been out for a ride that afternoon. The leaves were truly on the turn now and crimson hips and haws bloodied the hedgerows. Flash had plunged through the crackling leaves in the woods, then she had cantered him up Heydon Berrow to look down on Ambridge. But instead of the familiar cluster of cottage roofs or flocks of swallows on barn tiles that might have attracted her eye, the only thing visible to her had been the crude outline of the experimental drilling equipment against a pearly sky.

From the moment her father had come back in from examining the damage Bill Slater had done and had headed for his study calling, 'Tea, please, Grace!' she had known he was hatching a plan. He was like this. He got enthusiasms. Last year it had been aluminium ('The metal of the future, Grace!'), the year before that new-style caps for milk bottles. Grace knew that so much of it was a frantic attempt to fill the gap left by the death of her mother. George Fairbrother seemed to think that if he kept busy he would not notice she was gone, or perhaps he would notice, but could somehow anaesthetize himself against the pain. Grace knew, because she missed her mother every day, busy or not, that this was not the answer, but it was the only one a man like George Fairbrother could think of.

Grace knew no details of her father's business interests and normally she did not care. When they had moved to the country she had not expected to enjoy it, having always scorned the slow pace of life and the limited entertainments available. But despite herself, she had come to love Ambridge. She found the rhythms of the country-side soothing. She enjoyed listening for the first cuckoo, hearing the call of the dog fox on a moonless night, smelling the hay as it lay in the fields waiting to be carted. She still enjoyed her trips to town, but increasingly found she was happy to come home, to take gasping lungfuls of air as she drove back through the lanes and to rush to the rose garden in front of the house to see which bushes had bloomed in her absence.

There was no-one in Ambridge whom she would have described as her type, but she liked Christine Archer's company, and their shared love of horses gave them a bond that went deeper than a simple friendship. And then, unexpectedly, there had been Phil. Grace had never even considered that she might meet a man she would care for in Ambridge. She had assumed that she would commute between the country and parties up in town, staying with schoolfriends in Chelsea, going to dances, drinking cocktails, being driven back to the flat on the Embankment and kissed under a streetlight while Thames tugs hooted on the water. But then she'd met Phil with his honest grey eyes and strong embrace, and she'd begun to wonder if, perhaps, settling in the country might just have been the best enthusiasm her father had ever had. Until, of course, Jane Maxwell's arrival, and now the ironstone.

'Daddy –' she began.

'Yes, darling?'

George Fairbrother laid down his knife and fork. Grace took a deep breath. She had always been rather in awe of her father.

'You know when Philip Archer first started work for you? And his father telephoned to let us know that there was a dog that everyone thought was responsible for sheep-worrying heading in the direction of the farm?'

Fairbrother nodded.

'And you said to me that it marked a turning point. That we were accepted at last in the farming community here – we weren't out-siders any more?'

'What are you getting at, Grace?'

Grace wondered how he could be so shrewd in business and such a bad judge of people.

'Everyone's turned against us,' she said urgently. 'Everybody. Even people I thought couldn't be shaken by a thing like this. All of Ambridge is cool.'

'Nonsense!' He looked at her indulgently. 'You're overreacting.'

'But I'm not! You ought to try it – go down to the shop or the pub – you'll see how people almost shy away. They hate what you're thinking of doing to this village!'

Her father shook his head in disbelief.

'They don't understand, that's all. When I've had the surveys printed up I can distribute them round the village and people will see what a lot of good it will do them. Jobs for their sons in the mine and their daughters in the offices. Better transport links with the cities, which will benefit ordinary folk just as much as the mining business –'

Grace pushed her plate away. Either he didn't understand or he didn't want to. She felt irritated with herself for even raising the subject. His refusal to consider her point of view made her feel worse than if she had never tried to make him understand in the first place.

And deep down she knew that though her plea had been on behalf of the village, there was one person in particular whose animosity she could not bear. Grace had thought that she and Phil had had an understanding. They were very different, of course, but she liked to think that those differences complemented each other, whilst in the important things they were alike. She appreciated his seriousness and his steadiness, which calmed her excesses. She liked to think that she could tease him out of his earnestness and bring out the sense of fun which was never far below the surface but which often had to be sacrificed to his determination to prove himself in his work. Now he felt like a stranger. She didn't want to forget the times they had shared together, but remembering them just made her feel more desolate.

In the last month she had felt Phil move further and further away from her, not helped by the fact that he was thrown together with Jane Maxwell every day. It wrenched her heart to see them working together, heads bent over columns of figures or hauling a trolley-load of eggs to be sent off to the packing station. In their ease with each other, she could see everything she had tried to articulate to her father: two people, bound together by their work on and love for the land, who would instinctively close ranks against anything that threatened their existence from the outside.

She made one last try.

'I know you don't want to listen to me,' she pleaded. 'You're determined not to. But I'm . . . afraid . . . of what might happen if you carry on with this ironstone scheme. Can't you drop it, Daddy? Please?'

'My dear Grace.' Though she had often benefited from his indulgence, the thing she hated most about her father was the way he spoke to her as if she were a child. 'Let's be practical for a moment. The country's in need of steel and there are ten million tons of ironstone under our land and on the Estate. The only practical thing to do is to mine it.'

Practical for whom? thought Grace. It could only drive Phil further and further away from her. And push him closer and closer to Jane Maxwell.

'Now,' said her father, in a way that clearly meant 'case closed', 'dessert. Did I hear hothouse peaches mentioned?'

• • •

Supper at Brookfield was long over and with both Christine and Philip out for the evening, Dan and Doris had decided to take a stroll. It wasn't often that they had the time to walk the farm together. By the time Doris had seen to the hens and the butter-making, stoked the range, lit the copper, cooked three meals a day and kept up with all her village activities, there was little time left for leisure. So it was pleasant, on a mild autumn evening, as the weak sun slanted long over Lakey Hill, to stroll the fields arm in arm.

'Thank goodness this ironstone business doesn't affect our land, Dan,' said Doris. 'Look, the mushrooms are coming through.'

The hedgerow at the lower end of Pikey Piece was a favourite hunting ground for them.

'Aye,' agreed Dan. 'But if the scheme comes off, it'll be a different Ambridge. An ironstone mine would change the place beyond all recognition. Even when they've finished, who knows how long it would take to get the land in good heart again – or even if we could.'

'When's the Squire due back?' asked Doris. Dan had stopped to tie up a gatepost more securely.

'End of the month, I think,' he replied, wrapping binder twine round the post. 'I just hope he says "no" and means it when he comes back. All this uncertainty's bad for everyone.'

'Especially Phil,' fretted Doris.

'You'd be the same if you got a job as farm manager and when you'd just got the place running how you wanted it your gaffer comes along and says it's all going to change.'

Dan had got over his disappointment that Phil did not seem to want to work at Brookfield – for the present, at least. On balance, he thought it was probably better that he should make a start somewhere else. His own father had died young and Dan had had no option but to take over his tenancy. But there'd been a time during the war when his father had been ill and Dan had been recalled from his posting – with the intervention of the Squire, as it happened – to run the farm.

He could still see his father, weakened by the quinsy, lying in the big old iron bed, demanding to know if the corn was heating up and if the ricks had been sheeted properly. 'Who's in charge here?' Dan had said impatiently and his father had croaked, 'Till the good Lord takes me, I am.' So though he could never have let on to Phil, Dan did understand the frustrations the lad felt.

It was far better that Phil worked out his youthful enthusiasms on Fairbrother who, after all, had the money to indulge them – always assuming that Fairbrother carried on farming and didn't go wholesale for the mine. Dan knew that Phil's main worry was that the

siting of the mine would bisect the farm, making it fiendishly difficult to bring the cows in for milking or get arable machinery where
it was needed.

'I think I'll tell him he'll have to construct a new parlour,'
Phil had threatened when he and Dan had last discussed it. 'But
knowing Fairbrother, he'd just manage to find some way to set it
against tax. When he's got his business head on, Dad, nothing can
touch him.'

Dan knew that this was the fundamental difference between a
man like Fairbrother and the rest of the farming community in
Ambridge. Even an old rogue like Walter Gabriel, whose farm was,
frankly, a disgrace, had more claim to the name of 'farmer' than a
man like Fairbrother. What mattered was where your heart and your
instincts lay and Dan feared very much that Fairbrother's still lay
in town.

Dan and Doris strolled on up the dirt track.

'It's weeks since Grace was here,' mused Doris. 'It's a shame for
her. She's a sensitive girl.'

'She'll have picked up the feeling in the village even if her father
hasn't,' agreed Dan. 'And I suppose she thinks we feel the same.'

Doris paused for a moment to catch her breath. Her handspan
waist had long since disappeared into comfortable rolls of flesh and
her ankles had a tendency to swell if she was on her feet for too long.
Dan could have carried on walking for hours but he paused with her,
watching the Shorthorn cattle curling their long tongues round the
tussocky grass. Doris wondered what the outcome of the ironstone
would mean for Phil and Grace. Though she had her worries –
heaven knew, what worries! – about Christine and her love life, at
least Chris would talk to her about things. Phil just withdrew, leaving the house earlier and earlier each day, getting back later and
later. He had asked the new poultry girl, Jane Maxwell, round for tea
the other Sunday, and though she seemed very pleasant, Doris
hadn't taken to her.

On the face of it, she was far more suitable for Phil than Grace.
She was a country girl, they shared an interest in all things

outdoor and she seemed down-to-earth and practical. But what had Doris's mother used to say? Jane was 'hanging her hat up' to Phil rather too obviously, and Doris didn't care for it. Phil, however, seemed flattered, and it was Phil who would eventually have to choose.

·4·

Betrayal

'Can I give you a lift?'

A buzz of curiosity ran down the bus queue. When gentlemen in shiny black Daimlers pulled in to the kerb on a rainy night it usually meant only one thing. But Christine Archer didn't hesitate.

'Yes, please,' she said, folding her umbrella. The man leaned across and opened the passenger door.

'I didn't know you were back, Squire,' she said, clambering damply in as Arthur Lawson-Hope moved some parcels to the back seat. 'You've certainly saved my shoes.'

The Squire laughed, released the handbrake and they moved off. The wipers clunked rhythmically in a futile attempt to clear the screen. Christine settled back against the leather seat with relief.

'I'm not sure I want to be back,' the Squire confessed. 'I gather this ironstone business has divided the village.'

'You're not going to let it happen, are you, Squire?' asked Christine passionately. 'It would be hateful.'

'It's not quite as straightforward as it seems.' The Squire slowed as he turned into the Market Square, deserted on this wet Wednesday evening. 'As far as Fairbrother's concerned, he's got the money, I've got the land. But the real point is that I don't own the mineral rights.'

'Who does, then?'

The Squire leaned forward and wiped the clouded windscreen with his gloved hand.

'I – well – I sold them when I was a bit ... embarrassed. To my cousin Percy. He's farming out in Kenya.'

Christine remembered talk in the village about the Squire's money troubles a few years back. He'd even had to sell a Georgian tea kettle that had been in his family since 1757.

'But surely your cousin's going to think the same way that you do, isn't he?'

The Squire heard the note of panic. He was fond of Christine. He was fond of all the Archer family. When he spoke there was a smile in his voice.

'Oh, Percy's a sound enough chap. I have no doubt at all that he'll put a very effective stop to Fairbrother's plans.'

• • •

'He can't have.'

Christine's fork clattered on to her plate.

'He has.'

Dan had interrupted his breakfast to take a telephone call. He shrugged on his old tweed jacket.

'Squire says he's heard from his cousin Percy in Kenya.' The shortness in his voice was his attempt at masking his feelings. It didn't work. 'Seems *he* hasn't got the mining rights to the Estate, either. Let 'em go during the war to some chap called Crawford.'

'But that means –' Christine began.

Dan opened the door to the yard and a rustle of oak leaves, which always collected by the boot scraper, scuttled in.

'Dan, you're not going out? You haven't finished your breakfast.'

'I've had enough. I'd better give Simon a hand with the calves.'

Dan plucked his hat from the peg behind the door. It clattered shut behind him.

Doris pursed her lips and poured herself another cup of tea. When Dan left half a rasher of bacon on his plate it was serious. When he left half a rasher and a heap of mushrooms, it was very serious indeed.

'Well, that's that.' Christine rolled her napkin and pushed it through its wooden ring. 'There's nothing and no-one now to stop Fairbrother going ahead with his beastly mine. We'll all be dug up and sent packing.'

Phil had said nothing. Abruptly he got up from the table. He had finished his mushrooms, Doris noticed, but left a whole piece of fried bread – usually his favourite.

'Makes me feel like throwing my job in,' was all he said.

Out in the yard, he avoided Simon and climbed up into the Jeep. Fairbrother often let him bring it home at night – one of the perks he would miss, he thought wryly, when he no longer had a job. His father came out of the workshop with an armful of fencing stakes and Phil raised his hand in greeting. Dan nodded a farewell. They'd talk tonight. They'd have to. Phil might be begging for a job back at Brookfield come the end of the year.

• • •

At Fairbrother's, Jane was dragging egg crates from an outbuilding. She had on a man's Aran sweater, which was unravelling at one wrist, and her cheeks were pink with exertion.

'You should have left those for me!' Phil called as he jumped down.

'And put myself out of a job? No thanks!' Jane replied.

'Whose is the car?' Phil indicated a prosperous-looking Humber parked near the house.

'Oh, great goings-on last night, according to Betty when she came to collect the eggs,' said Jane conspiratorially. 'Important guest from Felpersham, or London, or somewhere. Much fuss over dinner being just so. More fuss over the right wines. *Wines*, mark you. All stops pulled out to make a favourable impression because it's the first time they've met. A really special effort.'

'Fairbrother got a new ladyfriend, then?' asked Phil, bemused. 'Who is she? What's happened to Mrs Carey?'

'It's not a she,' corrected Jane. 'You might know that anyone Fairbrother was really anxious to impress would be a business crony.'

'Oh, new accountant, I expect,' remarked Phil dismissively. 'Jane, let me get that last crate. I can't just stand and watch you work.'

'It's never stopped you in the past!' But Jane stood back and let him drag the last crate from the furthest recesses of the outhouse.

She shook her hair loose from its ribbon, which had been failing to hold it in place, and retied it.

'I don't know who he is. His name's Crawford.'

Before Phil could reply – before he could think – two figures came round the side of the house. One was Fairbrother, the other was a smart, middle-aged man with slicked-back grey hair, who slid into the driver's seat of the Humber while Fairbrother put his travelling bag and attaché case on the back seat. After a final handshake, the car moved off, Fairbrother standing to watch it go.

So, there he was. The man who held the future of Ambridge in his hands, his shoes shiny from city pavements, well breakfasted on eggs from the flock Phil had reared, accelerating away from the chaos he was about to cause.

'Phil? I said, if you don't need me for anything else, I want to make a phone call about the egg-washing machine.' Phil blinked and saw Jane looking enquiringly at him.

'Yes, yes, fine. Let me know when you've finished, though. I need to use the phone, too.'

Phil knew he must let his father know how quickly things were moving. And then they must tell the Squire.

• • •

But the Squire, it seemed, was outmanoeuvred at every turn. Fairbrother told Phil bullishly and without a hint of shame that he had had a most productive meeting with Crawford who was, he confided, a man who 'talked his language'. Phil took this to mean balance sheets and profit margins, and kept his own counsel, but he received eloquent indication of how Fairbrother was thinking when he asked him a simple question about winter grazing for the cattle.

'Oh, you sort it out,' said Fairbrother airily. 'My mind's too occupied with the ironstone project to think about the farm.'

That said it all, thought Phil grimly.

The whole village was preoccupied with the ironstone project. Even the general election called by Mr Attlee could not hold their attention for long. Walter went to three political meetings and came back saying he didn't think much of any of the parties. He pledged his vote to the first one to offer him £10 a week for life and free beer, but since none seemed to consider this a priority for their manifestos, he lost interest, and so did most other folk in the village. Even the prospect of Mr Churchill returning at the age of seventy-seven to lead his first peacetime government caused barely a ripple of excitement in Ambridge. Instead, in The Bull, where Walter and Tom Forrest sat over their ale and dominoes in the evenings, at the WI, at the smithy – wherever people were gathered together, the talk was of ironstone and what it meant for Ambridge. And no-one had anything but a pessimistic view.

Only Fairbrother remained utterly confident, not only that the scheme would be good for the district, but that he could actually convince the villagers it would be so. He called a public meeting in the village hall. He plastered the village with posters and plans showing the proposed area of mining, the roads that would be widened, the number of jobs created. He shrugged off various unexplained incidents at his farm that could only be described as primitive sorts of sabotage – a gate lifted off and the Ayrshires roaming the road, the dairy flooded with engine oil. Fairbrother simply ordered padlocks on all the outbuildings and told PC Randall that he'd be having a word with the Chief Constable if things didn't improve.

Fairbrother even tried to play the squire, turning up in The Bull and offering drinks to the regulars. All were declined, not always politely, and Fairbrother was left nursing a half-pint by himself until he gave up the unequal struggle. Standing alone by a draughty window – Tom Forrest and Walter Gabriel had by ancient tradition the unequivocal right to the chimney corner – Fairbrother even managed to convince himself that he had tried to take the village's opinion into account. If no-one wished to hear his side of the story, he could not be blamed for their intransigence.

Draining his beer, which he had not wanted in the first place, but which he had thought looked more 'man of the people' than a whisky and soda, he resolved to drag Ambridge into the twentieth century – whether Ambridge liked it or not. When Dan and the Squire made representation to him on behalf of the village he told them politely but categorically that, whilst Crawford had not yet signed over the mineral rights to the Estate, it was only a matter of time before he did so.

'To tell you the truth,' he said, with a crass disregard for the other men's feelings, 'I feel lucky to have a chap like Crawford on board. He's a businessman and well connected in the City. If you ask me, he's not far off a knighthood,' he added. 'What I can tell you is that we do have a draft agreement on the mining rights and we've made our application to the Ministry of Town and Country Planning.'

'There'll be a public inquiry, you realize that,' said the Squire brusquely.

'I accept that, but I honestly don't think it will change anything.' Fairbrother's confidence was staggering. 'I'm certain that the inquiry will find in favour of the mine, we'll get our permission and, gentlemen, I can tell you, that being so, I shall mine that ironstone with or without the goodwill of Ambridge.'

• • •

All this time, Phil went about his work on the farm, much of it in Jane's company. Though her responsibility was purely the poultry, she took an interest in every aspect of the farm work, asking intelligent questions about seedbeds and calving ratios and twin lamb disease. Phil found her interest in the farming side alone gratifying and her interest in him, which he could no longer deny, even more so. Nor could he deny that he was beginning to feel for her something far stronger than respect and admiration as a fellow worker.

When he saw Grace, which was increasingly rare, he was polite but distant. Whatever had been between them in the early spring and summer, when the fullness of the trees and the thrum of the bees had seemed to replicate all the promise their relationship held, had withered with every leaf that had fallen. Now the skeletal shapes of the trees and the shortening days seemed to mark not just a change of season but a cessation of feeling. Grace was as coolly polite as he was and Phil could never tell whether, if she had been warmer, he might have thawed, or whether, if he had been less chilly, she would have responded. But there didn't seem to be any point in trying to find out when the question of the ironstone mine loomed between them.

• • •

Grace didn't know when she'd ever felt so desolate. The alienation she felt from the village she could stand: she had never sought company or social life there. The distance between herself and her father was harder to bear. He had changed. He had become obsessed with the ironstone. She almost thought he had gone beyond the stage of it being a sound financial proposition: it was now a point of principle to foist it on the village. But it was the void between herself and Phil that Grace found hardest of all. Seeing him working alongside Jane day in, day out, laughing together, giving her a lift home, once, even, giving Jane his hand as she climbed a gate, made her sense the distance between herself and Phil as a void inside herself. How else could she account for the emptiness she felt? She took herself up to London whenever she could. It was the season of balls and parties. She had plenty of invitations and plenty of escorts, but none of them engaged her like Phil.

One day in late October she returned from London to find two messages from her father scribbled on a piece of blotting paper and weighted down on her desk with the glass paperweight that had been presented to him as Industrialist of the Year by Borchester Chamber of Trade. One informed her that Crawford was coming to dinner, the other that her father's new fishing rods were ready for collection: could she possibly slip into Borchester for him?

Why not, thought Grace. It beats sitting around here wondering what Phil's doing and who he's doing it with. She changed out of her smart navy suit into a tweed skirt and twinset and drove into town. The fishing-tackle shop was tucked away in a side street and, as she stowed the rods in the boot, Grace realized that she was close to Borchester Dairies. It was ten to five. Why shouldn't she offer Christine a lift home? They had been friends – maybe still were.

Christine was delighted.

'This is very decent of you,' she said as she tied her bike to the rack behind the car. 'The battery in my back light conked out last night and I haven't had a chance to replace it.'

'Riding a bicycle without lights – I wonder how long you'd go down for that?' teased Grace. 'Same as for not returning your library books on time, perhaps?'

She put the car in gear and released the handbrake. Christine looked across at her. Her hair had the same lively gloss as ever, but in everything else Grace seemed somehow . . . diminished. Her face was pale and Chris could have sworn she was thinner.

'Have you lost weight?' she demanded.

'It's all these trips to London,' said Grace lightly. 'It's not the horn of plenty you have here up in town you know.'

'I thought you were at parties and balls having a high old time, scoffing your head off and drinking champagne out of your shoe.'

'I am at parties,' said Grace. 'But I'm not having a high old time.'

'Are you and Phil still off?' Chris asked quietly.

Grace dipped her head.

'Still, he's got Jane to console himself with,' she said brightly.

'I don't know that he has.'

'It's all right, Chris, I've seen them with my own eyes.' Grace changed down a gear to take a corner. 'You can't deny it. And it's all my own fault. For being a Fairbrother.'

Chris couldn't help feeling sorry for Grace. In the past she'd been irritated by her, by her assumption that everything would fall into her lap because of her background and Fairbrother's money, of the little tricks she pulled when it didn't. She had often wondered how Phil could stand it. But this wasn't Grace stamping her tiny foot because she wanted something and couldn't have it. Grace was genuinely suffering.

'You must come to supper,' she said. 'Come and see us. Stay tonight when you drop me off.'

A wry smile twitched Grace's mouth.

'I'm required at home tonight,' she explained. 'Mr Crawford is coming to dinner.'

'I see.' Christine looked out of the window. A billboard for the evening paper read: 'Mr Churchill hopes for "new beginning" if Tories win.' Of course! The election was tomorrow. It all seemed so irrelevant when Ambridge had its own troubles to contend with.

'Make sure you tell Phil and your father, will you?' Grace asked. 'And tell them I told you?'

Christine caught the note of appeal in her voice.

'Of course I will,' she said. 'And, look, I really wouldn't give up on you and Phil. I'll be perfectly honest, Grace,' she continued. 'I didn't think you were particularly well matched in the beginning. But as time's gone on, well, I think – I think you and he have something special.'

'Do you really?' Grace swivelled her head to look at her.

Christine turned down the corners of her mouth.

'I used to envy you two. Look at the hash I've made of my love life.'

'It's hardly your fault,' said Grace indignantly, turning her attention back to the road. 'It's just a pity that Basil Grove turned out to be such a – a chancer.'

'Serves me right for getting mixed up with a married man in the first place, doesn't it?' replied Christine ruefully. 'But he was so convincing, Grace. All that business about wanting to take me away. I really thought he cared for me.'

'I'm sure he did, in his way,' soothed Grace. 'But I suppose if he could lie to his wife he was just as likely to be lying to you.'

'Pity it took me so long to realize it.' Christine shook her head impatiently, as if trying to dislodge the memory. Basil had promised that they would go away together for Whitsun, as his wife was away. But when she came back unexpectedly he had panicked and Christine had been left sitting in a tea shop waiting for him to turn up. He hadn't even had the decency to try to get a message to her. Thankfully, Borchester Dairies had transferred him soon afterwards to their depot in Felpersham.

'It really knocked me, you know,' Chris added thoughtfully. 'Thinking I'd been so stupid.'

'You weren't stupid, Chris.' Grace slowed to take the turning to Ambridge. 'You were just being you. Loyal and trusting, and expecting everyone else to be the same.'

'It's not a mistake I'll be making again,' declared Christine firmly. 'From now on I'm keeping them all at arm's length. Platonic friendship, that's all I want.'

'Even with Dick Raymond?' Grace sounded surprised. Dick was a reporter on the *Borchester Echo* who, since he had met Christine, seemed to spend an inordinate amount of time seeking out stories in Ambridge. 'I heard you two had been seeing a lot of each other.'

'Especially with Dick Raymond. And the same goes for Keith Latimer. And Nelson Gabriel. *Especially* Nelson Gabriel!'

Grace laughed. Seeing Chris had cheered her up. She dropped her off at Brookfield, bike and all, and drove home with a lighter heart and less of a sense of emptiness than she had felt for a long time.

• • •

'Grass keep to rent!' said Phil scornfully. 'Pasture to rent!'

'What on earth – you've made me lose my place now.'

Jane was totting up columns of egg receipts.

'I'm sorry.' Phil threw himself down in the ancient captain's chair covered in cracked ox-blood leather, a cast-off from Fairbrother's study that had found its way into the farm office.

Jane laid down her pencil.

'This is the grass keep Walter Gabriel told you about? Wasn't it any good?'

'Good? It was perfect! But can we get it? Not a ghost of a chance.'

'Why not?'

'Same old story. I said I was interested. They said, fine, but who was it for – my father or for Fairbrother? And when I said Fairbrother, they didn't want to know. Since the ironstone business there's not one of 'em would lift a finger to help him.'

'Doesn't help us much, does it?' Jane inked in a pencilled figure. Phil watched the delicate bones at the back of her neck flex as she raised her head and looked at him. 'The farm can only work in the future on the basis of hiring keep to replace the land taken up by the mine.'

'And if we don't get it we're going to be hopelessly overstocked,' he confirmed, forcing himself to concentrate on the facts. 'QED. Look, do *you* want to have a go at telling this to Fairbrother? He doesn't seem to listen to me.'

'No thanks, you don't pay me well enough!' retorted Jane. She sat back and folded her arms. 'We'll have to think again. I'll stay late tonight.'

'You don't have to.'

'I'm not letting you have all the glory!' Her eyes were teasing him, willing him to laugh with her. 'After all the work we've done on the replanning, I want to see it through.'

With little argument, Phil gave in. It would be much more pleasant to have Jane stay late with him tonight than to toil on here alone. She finished her calculations and then offered to run across to the house to ask the cook to cut them some sandwiches for supper.

'I wouldn't mind seeing what's going on, anyway,' she confessed. 'See if Crawford and Fairbrother are on first-name terms yet and have a look at what creation Grace is wearing.'

When she came back she had much to report. She had even been asked to join them for a sherry.

'But I declined,' she said. 'Told them you were cracking the whip and wanted me back sharpish.' As she spoke she poured coffee from a flask. 'Fairbrother and Crawford are definitely at the back-slapping stage. Grace looked a bit left out.'

'And what *was* she wearing?' asked Phil casually. He could still see Grace in the dress she had worn to the hunt ball – a black velvet bodice and a huge skirt of white net, with a necklace of garnets winking at her throat.

'Uh, I hardly noticed. She was very quiet. Blueish, I think. Sort of fussy bodice.'

Phil knew the one. It was the colour of the delphiniums in his mother's flower border. The bodice was ruched and it had elbow-length sleeves which he always wanted to slide his fingers inside to feel the softness of her arms.

'Phil? Coffee.'

With an apologetic shake of his head, he took the cup Jane was holding out to him.

'Well, shall we make a start?'

Phil worked her hard. Thoroughly churned up by feelings that he did not want even to try to identify, sitting side by side with one woman whilst thinking of another, he forced himself to concentrate on crop rotation and stocking levels and made sure Jane did the same. From time to time he ate a sandwich absent-mindedly – bloater paste or Spam, talk about the crumbs from the rich man's table – and Jane kept his coffee cup topped up. He hadn't even noticed that the stove had gone out till Jane shivered beside him.

'Gosh, I'm sorry.' He pushed back his chair and shook some coke from the hod on to the fire.

Jane stood up and stretched. He saw a tiny patch of bare midriff where her jumper raised up and her shirt had come untucked from her trousers. She walked over to the fire and squatted down, holding out her hands to the smoky glow. Her mouth worked as she stifled a yawn.

'You're fagged out,' said Phil. 'I should have realized. I'll drive you back to your digs.'

'You're not finished.' Jane yawned as she spoke. 'I'll walk.'

'You'll do nothing of the sort.'

'I can't drag you away now. It's going too well. All along I've been hoping this replanning of ours was a waste of time, that the ironstone wouldn't go through. But now it looks as though it's not destined for the dustbin.'

Phil thought quickly. He hadn't got much more to do.

'Give me half an hour and I'll run you home. Yes?'

'Of course.'

Phil looked around. The room was perfectly adequate as a farm office but there was nowhere comfortable for Jane to rest while she waited. She guessed what he was thinking.

'Don't worry. I'll just put my head down on my desk like we used to do at school after lunch.'

Phil fought hard to chase away an image of Jane as a flaxen-pigtailed five-year-old dozing at her desk.

'No, look.'

He got up and went to a corner of the room where he had flung a couple of bundles of sacks that had been delivered earlier in the week. With his pocket knife he cut through the twine binding them and spread them out into a thick mattress.

'It's not the Ritz, but it'll have to do,' he said.

Jane smiled gratefully. She snuggled down on the sacks whilst Phil rolled up his jacket to make a pillow.

'Comfy?' he asked.

'Mmm.' Jane sounded half-asleep already. She was lying on her side with her legs drawn up under her. Gently he laid his overcoat on top of her.

'Sleep well,' he said softly.

• • •

Thanks to her conversation in the car with Chris, Grace had approached the evening in a very different frame of mind from the time she had last met Mr Crawford. Then, she had been demure and silent. But this time, encouraged by Chris's assessment of her relationship with Phil, wanting desperately to believe that something could still be revived between them, she had resolved to speak up. She might not articulate it very well, but she could at least try to convey to him that the rosy picture painted by her father of the villagers' acquiescence to the mine was framed entirely by his own blinkered vision.

Her opportunity came after dinner when, having thanked the cook for her superlative effort with the chicken and the baton carrots and the tiny sprouts tossed in precious butter, not to mention the bramble fool, Grace rejoined her father and Crawford in the sitting room. The port decanter was unstoppered and each was puffing on a foul-smelling cigar. Crawford was telling Fairbrother that before he'd come out, he'd had a phone call from the Squire asking him round for a chat.

'You'll find him a bit of an old woman,' warned Fairbrother, topping up Crawford's glass. 'Still a believer in the feudal system.'

'I don't know about that, Mr Crawford.' Grace gripped the mantelpiece with one hand to steady her nerves. 'He just happens to think the same way as his tenants. Doesn't see the fun in being ruined.'

Her father stared at her. Crawford cocked his head on one side.

'I'm listening.'

'Ruin? Nonsense!' Fairbrother cut in. 'We've allowed for compensation. No-one will be out of pocket.'

'I'm not talking about the money,' said Grace quietly.

'So there is opposition, is there?' Crawford's voice was calm.

'Not so as you'd notice,' said Grace lightly. 'Apart from the little matter of our cattle getting out, and the engine oil in the parlour – oh, and the drill bit being stolen, of course. Did Daddy mention that?'

'It's the Industrial Revolution all over again,' asserted Fairbrother with a quelling look at Grace. 'Just taken 150 years to arrive in Ambridge.' He put his glass down on a console table. 'I didn't know you felt so strongly, Grace,' he said silkily. 'Might I ask whose side you are on?'

Grace bit her lip. She decided she'd risked enough.

'There's an awful fug in here,' she said. She moved to the heavy velvet curtains and pulled them apart. 'I think I'd better open a window.'

Glad of the diversion, Fairbrother came over to her.

'Good Lord, there's still a light on in the farm office!' he exclaimed. Turning to Crawford, he added: 'My farm manager, bright young chap, keen as mustard. Very capable. Full of modern ideas.'

Taking Grace's arm and squeezing it unnecessarily hard, he pushed her towards the door.

'Go and ask him for a drink, Grace. He deserves one for working this late.'

Glad to escape, still trembling from her daring and fearful of the inevitable inquest with her father still to come, Grace slipped out of the room. She opened the side door of the house and leaned for a second against the frame, taking in searing breaths of night air, which made her gasp as it hit the back of her throat. The sky was peppered with stars and a frost was beginning to glitter on the cobbles. This was a God-given opportunity to make some sort of gesture towards Phil. Proud of the stand she had made in front of Crawford, she felt that for the first time in months she could look him in the eye and not feel ashamed of her actual or assumed connivance with her father's plans. She pulled the door to behind her and set out across the yard.

• • •

Figures were beginning to blur in front of Phil's eyes. Sheet after sheet of paper was covered with estimates of next year's prices, yield per acre, weekly consumption per animal, labour, wages and man-hours. Reluctantly, Phil knew that he had done all he could for tonight. Stretching out his legs and extending the aching small of his back, he looked at his watch. Eleven o'clock.

He turned to look at Jane. Her fair hair was massed around her shoulders and she had one cheek pillowed on her hand. He knew that if he woke her, her face would bear the pink imprint of her fingers and he had a sudden unreasonable urge to kiss away the mark. It was all so complicated. It wouldn't be fair to get involved with Jane when he knew, in truth, he hadn't sorted out what he felt for Grace. If it was over between them, why did he spend some part of each day wondering what she was doing? Why did he question Betty the maid oh-so-casually after Grace had come back from her trips to London to see if there was mention of a boyfriend? Why did he see her face last thing at night before he drifted off to sleep? And it was sleep he needed now. He wasn't going to get anywhere thinking about Grace this late in the evening, just as he wasn't going to get anywhere poring over forward projections.

He stood up and went over to Jane. Crouching down, he shook her gently by the shoulder.

'Hey, Goldilocks.'

She gave a sleepy sigh.

'Who's been sleeping on *my* sacks?'

Still asleep, she rolled over on to her back and flung one arm above her head. With the other she partly pushed the covering coat away and he saw the outline of her breast through her sweater. Fascinated, he watched it rise and fall with her steady breathing. It was all he could do to stop himself reaching out to touch it.

'Come on, sleepyhead.'

She murmured something in her sleep. It sounded like his name.

Tenderly, Phil bent down. He crooked an arm under her neck and gently pulled back his coat.

'Jane?'

Slowly she opened her eyes and looked straight into his. Her eyes were extraordinary. Still that fascinating tawny pale. She frowned slightly, confused about where she was. Then she realized and said his name again. Definitely his name this time. Phil did not move.

'Phil,' she said again. 'Oh, Phil.'

She was wide awake now. They both knew what they were doing. She reached up and slid her arms round his neck. Her face was inches from his. Slowly he bent his head and found her lips.

• • •

Grace took a deep breath before she reached out and turned the handle of the office door. She felt calm and at peace. Somehow she had found a new strength. She and Phil belonged together – Christine had said so, and Christine was no sentimentalist. The ironstone had been, and would be, difficult for them. But it was something they could overcome. Swiftly she turned the cold iron handle. The door swung open easily and she remembered how Phil was always complaining about the draught. To her surprise, he was not at his desk.

Later, it seemed to her that it had taken her ages to find him in the room. In fact, it took only a split second for her eye to pick up a slight movement in the corner and to take in, in one sickening rush, what she saw.

Jane Maxwell was lying on what appeared to be sacks. Phil was kneeling beside her, his head drawn down by her arms, his hand supporting her head as he brought her lips to his. Grace made a tiny noise, a sort of whimper, then she turned and ran, slithering on the cobbles, hearing Phil call after her as she reached the house.

She slammed the door against his cry and leaned against it, too shocked for tears.

'Grace? You've been an age. Have you got Philip with you?' Her father's voice called from the study.

Grace pinched her cheeks viciously and gripped her upper arms as if to stop herself from falling apart. Her voice when she spoke sounded dangerously high, but she knew her father wouldn't notice.

'No, he's not coming in. He's still busy,' she called. 'And I think I'll go straight to bed, Daddy, if you don't mind.'

·5·

Resolution

The village hall had been laid out like a courtroom. There were rows of chairs and, on the stage, a trestle table had been covered with a navy-blue blanket and laid with blotters, pencils and a couple of carafes of water. Grace idly wondered who had supplied them: when she had last been to the village hall it had been for a bring-and-buy in aid of the Organ Fund and they had given her a cup of tea in a thick white cup. She was sure the village-hall kitchen didn't run to carafes. Now she was here, she felt blank, as if nothing could touch her, but whilst getting ready, she had had to wipe her lipstick off twice and start again, and then had got powder on her blouse and had had to change. Driving down to the public inquiry with her father, she had felt as if the tumbrils were rolling, though he, of course, remained supremely confident.

His lawyer had stayed over the previous evening at The Bull, and the two men had dined there on sole and a rather good bottle of Chablis. As they had emerged through the public bar under the mutinous gaze of the locals, Fairbrother had felt his usual irritation replaced by contempt. Did they really want nothing better for their children than the lives they had led, tilling the soil, taking beasts to market, and in the evenings hunching over a smeared pub table with a pint of cider and fistful of dominoes? They might not be able to see what he was offering them now, but in time, he knew, they'd thank him.

'Seems pretty pleased with himself, don't 'e?' commented Walter as Fairbrother ushered his lawyer out. 'I hates to say it, but I reckon it might even go in his favour.'

Tom rubbed his nose and laid down a domino.

'That feller Crawford hasn't signed over the mineral rights yet, don't forget,' he said. 'From what Dan said, when the Squire met him, it sounded as though he might be more willing to see sense than Fairbrother.'

'At least Philip's seen sense,' grunted Walter. 'Seems he's dropped Grace Fairbrother once and for all for that lass who keeps the poultry.'

Tom nodded. Doris had told him that Phil had been seeing more and more of Jane over the last couple of weeks.

'If you ask me, he's well out of it.' Walter popped a pork scratching in his mouth and crunched on it alarmingly. ''Er always seemed a flighty madam.'

• • •

'This is very good of you, Mrs Archer.'

'What, the food, or the access to the phone?' Christine grinned as she watched her mother heap a second helping of cheese and potato pie on to Dick Raymond's plate.

'Both.' Dick picked up his knife and fork and tucked in. 'You've no idea what my landlady in Borchester feeds me. Two sild and the heel of a small brown loaf last night.'

Doris clucked disapprovingly.

'You can't be expected to do a good day's work next day if that's all you've had to eat. You're to come here every evening, Dick, while the public inquiry's on. You can phone through your report, then have your supper with us.'

'He won't need telling twice!' Christine leaned over and stole a forkful of swede from Dick's plate.

Dick had been a frequent visitor at Brookfield since the end of the summer. In his job as a junior reporter on the *Echo*, he had been allocated Ambridge as part of his patch. He had swiftly assessed it as a place where nothing ever happened and found that by contacting the vicar for births, deaths and marriages, and standing Walter an occasional mug of cider in The Bull for the gossip, he could easily fill the odd column with Ambridge goings-on, leaving him free to sniff out the bigger stories in Borchester with which he hoped to make his name.

The discovery of ironstone had, however, put Ambridge on the map. Dick was secretly thrilled that his editor had agreed to let him report the inquiry and he knew that if he could unravel for his readers the Byzantine complexities of the opposing barristers' arguments and summarize them in simple language, he would do his career no harm.

'How do you think it's going, Dick?' Dan, who found sitting in a stuffy hall all day gave him more of an appetite than working in the fresh air – perhaps because he had nothing else to think about – had been giving his attention to his supper.

'You're not going to like this, sir, but I honestly think it's going in Fairbrother's favour. According to the experts, the ironstone will yield about 5000 tons a week. That's forty years' work for sixty men. The Town and Country Planning people will like that.'

'Where are we going to put sixty men and their families?' protested Doris. 'It'll mean a housing estate in the village, for sure.'

'And how the heck will I ever find a farm worker?' demanded Dan. 'I shan't be able to match the earnings the iron blokes'll give them.'

'I'm packing it in right now.' Phil spoke for the first time. 'Sixty blokes, each pinching one chicken a month for the pot, that's 720 a year or a loss of a thousand quid –'

They all laughed.

'It's a point, though, isn't it?' said Phil.

Dick agreed.

'You're right. Our cartoonist might be able to make something of that, you know.' He pushed his plate away. 'That was spot-on, Mrs Archer. Another triumph. Would you mind if I made that call to my office now?'

'Go ahead, lad.' Dan was in the process of stuffing his pipe. 'You know where it is.'

Dick moved out into the flagged passage. He flipped open his reporter's notebook and checked that he could read back his short-hand before picking up the receiver. As soon as he did, he heard high-pitched, distorted voices. He'd got a crossed line. Impatiently, he was about to put the receiver down when one phrase jumped out at him. Something about sabotage. Someone was planning to sabotage the diesel engine on the drill rig at Fairbrother's that night.

• • •

Grace had left the inquiry early, when they had broken for tea. All day she had sat beside her father, listening to interminable evidence about the market prices of foreign ores and trying not to look too obviously at Phil. Grace didn't want to meet the eyes of any of the audience. Though Chris had given her a friendly smile when she had walked in, Grace felt a communal hostility to herself and her father which she did not want to have to acknowledge. Phil was seated at the back, with Jane Maxwell beside him, of course. Grace fixed her eyes on the cretonne curtains at the window nearest him. From time to time, when she thought it was safe, she would allow her eyes to slide across and rest on his features as he leaned forward to catch what was said, frowning. Though once she had the agony of seeing him whisper something to Jane and Jane's immediate smile, he never once, that she was aware of, looked in her direction.

At tea, with her head throbbing, she escaped into the murky November afternoon. Most of the village, except those who could not be spared from their work, were at the inquiry. A chatter of mothers was waiting at the school gates and Grace heard them fall silent as she approached. With her eyes on the road, she passed by and with no thought for her new tan kid shoes, took a footpath over the fields to be more quickly out of earshot. In the hedge bottom a squirrel scuttled between one cache of food and another and a robin tried and failed to attract her attention with his flaring breast and song. Grace plodded on miserably, stumbling on the damp grass, until she reached home, thoroughly chilled. She flung herself on her bed, aching for sleep.

By six, when she heard her father return, she had done nothing but doze fitfully and her headache was, if anything, worse. She ran a bath, splashed cold water on her eyes and changed for dinner. Downstairs she found her father more optimistic than ever.

'You should have stayed, Grace!' he admonished her. 'My chap didn't half sock it to 'em. It's going really well.'

'Is it?' With a small gesture she declined his offer of a sherry.

'Crawford's been held up in London till the end of the week,' he went on, 'but I'm having a transcript of the evidence so far sent up to him by teleprinter and – Grace?'

Grace sank down into an armchair and put her face in her hands. Tears spilled from between her fingers, marking the white satin of her evening gown.

Fairbrother moved quickly to her side.

'Grace! Tell me what's wrong.'

Her shoulders heaved helplessly. For a long moment she couldn't speak.

'You know what it is!' she said at last.

'Oh, Grace.' He perched on the arm of the chair and pulled her against him. 'You're not still fretting about what the village thinks of us.'

She tugged violently away from him.

'You don't understand. It's not just the village. It's individuals.'

'All right, who?'

Grace bit her lip. The pain in her head had been subsumed in the pain around her heart. Then, raising her head, 'Phil.'

'Philip? What about him?'

Grace moved her head impatiently. How could her father not have noticed her unhappiness?

'He doesn't care about me any more. He's got Jane now.'

'And it's because of the ironstone?'

'Oh, of course it is! We'd have been fine without it. But you know how . . . how principled he is!'

Fairbrother had a moment of guilt. All he had observed, on seeing Philip and Jane together, was how satisfying it was to see they'd made the right choice in employing her. But, ever the businessman, his brain began to process the new information he'd been given and to come up with solutions.

'What do you want me to do then?' he asked. 'Sack him? Or sack her?'

'It wouldn't do any good,' said Grace sadly. 'I've lost him.'

• • •

Phil was in the office at Fairbrother's, looking for a torch. Despite his mother's concern, when Dick had told him about the sabotage, Phil hadn't hesitated. He hated and deplored the idea of the ironstone, but Fairbrother was his employer. Fairbrother's land and everything on it – from cattle to ironstone drills – was his responsibility and he couldn't knowingly let a couple of hotheads cause expensive damage. Anyway, experience had shown that these acts of vandalism didn't make any difference to Fairbrother – if anything, they had increased his determination to push on with the mine.

Dick, thirsting for a story in which he could play an active part, had said he would meet him at the farm – he still had to phone through his copy. On the way, feeling that what they still lacked was muscle power, Phil had called in at Jim Benson's. Jim was one of Fairbrother's workers, six foot three of solid sinew and just the sort of bloke you wanted on your side in a fight.

'It may not come to that,' explained Phil. 'But if it does, Jim, I'll be counting on you.'

'Trust me, sir. I won't let you down.'

Phil had just located the torch – shoved, for some reason, at the back of a drawer of the filing cabinet – when he heard the office door open. Still mindful of another occasion when the opening of that door had caught him unawares, he looked up sharply. But it was only Dick.

'Look who I found on the way!'

Standing behind him, in wellingtons and a battered fawn mac, was Jane.

'Jane? What the devil are you doing here?'

'I rang Chris to see what you were doing tonight. She told me you were on a mercy mission. I've come to lend a hand.'

'Oh, no, you don't.'

Jane's tiger eyes held his and there was no warmth in them now.

'I don't mind it during the working day but don't tell me what I can and can't do out of hours, Phil, please.'

Phil was aware of Dick studying the ceiling and he knew Jane was not going to give way.

'All right, then,' he reluctantly agreed. 'But you'll have to be careful.'

Footsteps outside indicated Jim Benson's arrival and, after a quick explanation of their planned route, assuming that the saboteurs would come from the south, across the open fields, thus avoiding the trout stream, the four of them stepped into the yard.

Phil couldn't explain why – perhaps it was something that would not have stood up to analysis, anyway – but he suddenly felt that he needed to see Grace. All day in the inquiry he had been aware of her looking at him and he had had to force himself not to look back. He felt desperate about the coldness he was showing to her when he knew that she needed support, but he knew he couldn't carry in his head, still less in his heart, his conflicting feelings about the ironstone and about her.

Since she had disturbed him and Jane, her aloofness had taken on a new edge, distinguished not by coldness but by a pain that was almost tangible. He knew how much he had hurt her and he was fearful of hurting her more. Yet he wanted her to know that tonight, in taking steps to protect her father's property, he felt closer to her than he had for months.

Sending the others on ahead, telling them to keep the torch beam covered and to keep down low, he went to the front door of the house and rang the bell. He hoped they had not already started dinner, but when Betty showed him into the morning room she said not. Apparently Grace and her father had spent longer over drinks than usual. Cook, she added, wasn't very pleased.

Phil stood with his back to the fireplace, watching the door. He saw the low, oval brass handle turn and braced himself for Betty's return with a message that Grace didn't want to see him. He would hardly have been surprised. But it was Grace herself, Grace at her loveliest in white slipper satin, off the shoulder, her hair held back with two combs of jet. He braced himself for one of her sarcastic openers, but she said simply, 'You were the last person I expected.'

'I know.' Phil realized with horror he hadn't a clue what he was going to say. He knew what he needed to say, but he couldn't get it all out in the five minutes he had before he had to rejoin the others on the dark path through the winter wheat to the drill.

'I just wanted to let you know,' he mumbled inadequately, 'not to worry if you see a light on in the office. I – um – I've had to come back to finish something off.'

'I see.' Disappointment dulled her eyes. 'And you're warning me off, is that it? So I don't interrupt anything?'

'No! Grace, I wouldn't have had that happen for anything. And I've wanted to explain –'

'Oh, Phil. It doesn't need explaining, does it?' In the hall, the gong boomed for dinner. 'Well, does it?'

Phil didn't move. He couldn't take his eyes off her.

'Say something!' she pleaded.

The clock on the mantelpiece behind him began to whirr, then to chime. It was already eight, the time the saboteurs were due.

'I'm sorry, Grace, I have to go.'

Abruptly Phil pushed past her, feeling her hand clutch his arm. In a stumbling run he crossed the yard again, out into the oblivious darkness of the winter fields.

• • •

He found the others ankle deep in mud in a ditch behind the hedge.

'You haven't missed anything,' whispered Dick. 'Well, only me getting hooked up on some barbed wire.'

'Shh!' Jim's ears had picked up a footfall along the lane. Then the gate rattled and someone climbed over. Dark in the darkness, a couple of shapes were crossing the field towards the drill.

'Now?' asked Jane.

'Now!' ordered Phil.

At a run, they all broke cover and headed for the drill. They could hear a metallic clatter and the whine of rope then, somehow, the saboteurs seemed to sense their approach. All three scattered in different directions.

'This one's mine!' Dick, fly half for his grammar-school rugby team, swooped for the man's legs and they crashed to the ground together. The man squirmed out of Dick's hold and, as he moved, lashed out with his feet, catching Dick on the shoulder and then on the cheekbone. Dick cried out in pain, but, as the man broke free and made for a gap in the hedge, Jane was with him. When he paused to duck under the wire she lunged at his leg and held on to it, matching his curses with her own.

'It's a flamin' girl!'

The man kicked his leg violently to shake her off and, as Dick pounded up behind, Jane was thrown to one side.

'He's getting away!' she shrieked.

But Dick jumped neatly over her and lurched after the man through the gap in the hedge. Jane sat for a moment to catch her breath. She couldn't see Phil or Jim and hoped they had had better luck with their targets. Hoisting herself to her feet, she squelched over to the drill. Benson thudded up the lane and clambered over the gate.

'Lost 'em, both of 'em,' he announced, fed up. 'Chased 'em all the way to the Squire's woods an' all.'

'Would you know them again?' asked Jane.

'Couldn't see to tell.'

'Where's Phil?'

'He's coming back through the water meadows in case they double back.'

'What a fiasco.'

Dick panted up, limping.

'I would get the one who cut up rough,' he moaned. His clothes were daubed with mud and when Jane put her hand to his cheek it came away sticky with blood.

'Fine vigilantes we are,' lamented Jane. 'Didn't catch one.'

'Saw 'em off, though.' Jim had been examining the drill. 'Everything's still here.'

'Oh, well, that's terrific.' Jane dabbed Dick's cheek with her handkerchief. 'When the inquiry finds in his favour and the planning permission comes through, it's really cheering to know that Fairbrother can start drilling straight away. I don't know why we came really, since we're all against it.'

'It's just something you have to do, isn't it?' said Dick. 'It's called adventure.'

• • •

The public inquiry dragged on. Phil had had to tell Fairbrother about their failed attempt to catch the drill saboteurs and Fairbrother clearly wondered whether Phil had let them go on purpose. But Phil insisted that while he was Fairbrother's farm manager, he would always safeguard his property, whatever he might think of the ironstone scheme and, eventually, Grace's father conceded.

When Phil saw Grace they watched each other guardedly, like two wounded animals who had hurt each other in the past and were frightened of causing themselves more pain. Jane watched them both, aware without knowing why that something had shifted on the night that she, Phil and the others had gone after the saboteurs. But she decided to bide her time. If Phil and Grace had drawn closer together again, surely the outcome of the public inquiry, which everyone seemed sure would find in Fairbrother's favour, would push them apart once and for all?

In the village, feelings still ran high and the ironstone remained the only nightly topic under discussion in The Bull.

'Fairbrother'll get his way, his sort of toff always does,' Bill Slater asserted in the public bar on the night before the inquiry was due to deliver its verdict. Bill, who had been responsible – albeit inadvertently – for the ironstone discovery in the first place, might have been supposed to be one of its champions, but he was vehemently opposed to the scheme. Some reckoned it was because he hadn't been allowed any of the glory. They said he reckoned Fairbrother owed him something – after all, Fairbrother would be making thousands out of the mine – and Bill felt disgruntled he hadn't been offered even a token 'thank you'.

Bert Matthews, a farmworker from Penny Hassett, who was not one of Bill's favourite people, but was one of the few who would drink with him, took a pull at his pint. Keith Latimer, who, since Christine had been seeing so much of Dick had little else to do with his time but prop up the bar at The Bull, pocketed his change from the round he had just bought.

'There's no point talking about it, Bill, old man,' he said. 'The verdict's *sub judice*.'

Bill sniffed. 'Aren't you the swank, knowing Greek,' he sneered.

Bert laughed.

'It's Latin, you clot.'

'What did you call me, Matthews?' Bill's breath smelt sickly sweet of beer.

'Come on, Bill, no need to get nasty.' Keith put a hand on his arm but Bill swatted it off.

Bert turned his back. He wasn't looking for a fight but Bill spun him round to face him.

'Say that again. To my face,' he taunted.

Bert pushed him away angrily. Bill got on his nerves with his pasty face and his constant moans. Bill staggered backwards – he'd had several pints already – and collided with a pillar, making the horse-brasses on it jingle. Recovering his balance, he came at Bert head down – and that was the point at which Sam Saunders, the landlord, ejected them.

'Tek 'im and put his head under the pump,' he advised Keith. 'And when he comes round tell him he's not welcome in here no more.'

Keith was busy collecting everyone's coats and by the time he got outside a crowd had gathered. Bert was standing over Bill, his fists loosely clenched at his sides.

'I didn't even want a fight,' he was protesting. 'I never even tapped him. He was putting up his fists to hit me, then he just keeled over, hit his head on the horse trough.'

Keith bent down and lifted Bill's eyelids one by one.

'Can you hear me, Bill? Bill?' he called.

• • •

'I don't know where Bill can be,' grumbled Mrs Perkins to Jane. There had been a WI sale of work earlier that evening and though it would not normally have been Jane's chosen entertainment, her self-imposed ban on seeing Phil had meant she had been at a loose end. She had encountered Mrs Perkins bargaining for a thread-work tea cosy and, the purchase completed, Mrs Perkins had invited Jane back for a cup of cocoa. She felt rather sorry for her, living in those miserable digs on the Hollerton road, and, as she'd told the girl earlier, if she hadn't had her no-good nephew living with her, she'd have offered her a room herself. 'He didn't turn up for his tea and it don't look as if he's been home,' she went on, removing her hat and repiercing it fiercely with a hatpin in the shape of a parrot. 'If he had, I hoped he'd at least have built the fire up.'

The fire in the grate was a sorry collection of embers and the coal scuttle was empty.

'I'll fetch you in some coal, shall I?' offered Jane. All the way back to the cottage, Mrs Perkins had been telling her what a martyr she was to her lumbago.

'Would you, duck? You're a good girl.'

While Mrs Perkins made the cocoa, Jane let herself out of the back door, heeding Mrs Perkins's shouted warnings to mind the washing line and the uneven paving stones. She opened the coal house door and started to shovel.

'Caught you!'

Jane leapt up with a gasp.

'Dick! Will you stop fooling about?'

Dick's head appeared round the garden gate.

'Is Chris with you?'

Jane shook her head and continued shovelling.

'Drat. Someone said they saw Mrs P walking home with a blonde girl and I thought she might be here.'

'Sorry to disappoint you,' smiled Jane. 'I'm just doing my bit for the old and infirm.'

With the last shovelful of coal, she stood up, then stooped again as she saw something glinting in the coal dust at the bottom of the pile. She leant forward to get a better look.

'Dick! Come and look at this!'

Dick came and squatted down beside her. He let out a long, low whistle. They were looking at the stolen drill bit that had gone missing from Fairbrother's drilling equipment weeks ago when the sabotage had first started.

'Are you all right out there?' Mrs Perkins's voice carried across the dark garden. 'Jane? Who's that with you?'

'Come in with me, Dick,' urged Jane. 'We'll decide what to do with this later.'

Dick thought for a moment, then pocketed the drill bit and followed her back up the path.

· · ·

Bill Slater, whose condition in Borchester Infirmary was 'giving cause for concern', missed the end of the inquiry. He was not in Ambridge to hear that, in fact, he had been right in his assessment of the outcome of the business of the mine. Fairbrother did get his own way. Dick Raymond phoned the news through to Brookfield. Dan took the call.

'The Ministry of Town and Country Planning have reached their decision,' he announced when he came back wearily into the kitchen. 'Fairbrother can go ahead with his blessed ironstone scheme.'

The village had waited so long for the verdict that the outcome of the inquiry was almost an anticlimax. The fight and the fire seemed to have gone out of even the scheme's fiercest opponents. In The Bull, dominoes were shuffled and played with resignation. In the shop, talk was already turning to how the village might make the best of the influx of newcomers who would be coming to work the mine.

'Might be a couple of handy footballers amongst 'em, I suppose,' Jim Benson, in his spare time the Ambridge team's goalkeeper, mused out loud to Phil as they strawed down the cattle. Phil merely grunted. He didn't care if the miners turned out to be all-round athletes and demon batsmen to boot; the coming of the mine would still mean the destruction of all he had worked so hard to create at Fairbrother's. It would also mean, he felt sure, the destruction of all the hopes he had nurtured, not just about his career as Fairbrother's farm manager but maybe, one day, also as his son-in-law . . .

But then, quite unexpectedly, there came another piece of bad news for the village to deal with. Bill Slater slipped into a coma as the result of his head injury and, early one November morning, about the time when he would normally have been helping Dan with the milking, he died peacefully in Borchester Infirmary.

Dick, who had found out about Bill's death when he was doing his usual tour around the hospitals for the paper, came and found Jane. She was moving the poultry fold-units to another section of the field.

'Bill was definitely the saboteur, wasn't he?' she said when he'd told her. 'Or one of them.'

'No doubt about it.' Dick ran his hand through his hair. 'I never told you, but when I was struggling with that bloke the night we went after them, I tore a button off his jacket. And the night we found the drill bit, there was a jacket hanging on the back of Mrs Perkins's door that had exactly the same button and bit of cloth missing.'

Jane chewed her lip. Dick had presented her with the missing jigsaw-puzzle piece – the inevitable, elusive bit of sky. She should have felt triumphant but instead she felt sickened and strangely wary.

'What are we going to do about it?'

Dick, too, was no longer the fearless investigative journalist. He was a twenty-year-old cub reporter, seriously out of his depth.

'Tell Fairbrother, I suppose.'

'I've got a better idea.' Jane suddenly knew just who to tell. 'Let's tell Phil. He'll know what to do.'

. . .

At the back of Jane's mind, she had still not given up hope. The granting of planning permission for the mine, could still, she thought, conspire to pull Phil away from Grace and back towards her for once and for all.

But there were other factors that were beyond Jane's control. Crawford, Fairbrother's partner in the venture, had long been having second thoughts. Not wanting to prejudice his investment until the outcome of the public inquiry had been announced, he had allowed things to unfold. Once the inquiry had found in Fairbrother's favour, however, Crawford had begun to play for time. Before drilling could begin he insisted that they engage a proper mining contractor to come and survey the site. Fairbrother had disagreed.

'We've got Keith Latimer's site drawings and measurements,' he reasoned. 'Surely that's all we need.'

Crawford protested and when Crawford disagreed with someone he could be very disagreeable. Fairbrother had to relent and, within the week, a terse, impatient man called Lenton arrived to pace the site. He trudged this way and that over the muddy fields, looked at the geological surveys, and consulted Keith Latimer.

The whole of Ambridge was by now resigned to the worst and Lenton, with his interminable cigarettes and broad Yorkshire accent, seemed an unlikely saviour. But, as he told Fairbrother and Crawford over lunch, he had grave doubts. The problem in the end, he said, was the difficulty of transporting the stuff. With the nearest railway station being at Hollerton, and no chance of the line being extended to Ambridge, he judged it unworkable to load the ironstone into trucks and drive it to the station: yet it would be too costly to transport it to its final destination by road.

As word of Lenton's pronouncements spread round the village,

Ambridge held its breath. Everyone expected the resourceful Fair-brother to find a solution even to this.

'Helicopter? Hot air balloon? He'll get it out somehow,' declared Walter cynically in The Bull.

But Lenton's verdict made Crawford's waning enthusiasm wane still further and, standing alone, Fairbrother no longer seemed to have the stomach for the fight. For once his decision was not made on economic grounds. Fairbrother was not the sort of man who would ever admit that he had been touched by something personal, yet Bill Slater's death – the lad was only nineteen, after all – had disturbed him greatly. The inquest ruled that Bill's death was 'accidental' and that Bert Matthews, who had never wanted the fight, should bear no part of the blame.

Fairbrother knew that if the village blamed anyone for Bill's death, it was him. Emotional talk that got back to him about how he had 'blood on his hands' should not have affected him, but somehow it did. He thought about it long and hard as he walked his fields, unable, for once, to take any pleasure in the fine numbers of pheasant he saw, which would mean a good shooting season. Bill Slater had found the ironstone, after all: maybe it should be laid to rest with him.

So, on the day Bill's funeral was held in a sooty church in Hackney, George Fairbrother let it be known that, though he could go ahead – he didn't want people thinking he was completely soft – he had decided, on balance, not to take up the option to mine the ironstone. Ambridge was ecstatic. Phil was ecstatic. And Grace had her first good night's sleep for months.

· · ·

'What's this?'

'What does it look like? Read it.' Jane carried on with her book-work.

Phil ripped open the envelope that he had found lying on his pad. He had just got back from market, where the prices for pedigree Ayrshire calves had been very pleasing. He read the letter through once. Then he read it again. He strode over to Jane and banged it down in front of her.

'You're resigning? Don't you think we might have discussed it instead of just sending me a formal letter?'

'What did you expect?' She kept her voice deliberately light. 'Tear stains and tragedy?'

Phil picked up a copy of the *Borchester Echo* which was lying on her desk. Its headline read: 'NO MINE FOR AMBRIDGE' and the by-line was 'By Our Special Reporter, Richard Raymond'. He chucked it back on the desk and stuffed his hands in the pockets of his whipcord breeches.

'What are you going to do?'

Jane leaned over the wastepaper bin to sharpen her pencil. Her hair hid her face. The shavings fell in perfect curls.

'Oh, I shall go home to Bath. Mummy's desperate to have me home for a bit. She loves to mother me.'

'There'll be a lot to do here, Jane,' said Phil gently, 'now Fairbrother's abandoned the scheme.'

'Oh, I'm pretty sure you'll soon find someone to take my place,' said Jane, raising her topaz eyes to his one last time. And he knew that she didn't mean with the poultry.

·6·

Missing the Moment

'So here I am, reporting for duty.'

Grace beamed up at him, her eyes shining. Phil suppressed a smile and leaned on the broom with which he had been sweeping the yard.

'Dressed like that?'

Grace looked down. 'What's wrong?'

She was wearing tapered, sage green trousers in some sort of worsted cloth and a matching sweater in what could have been fine merino wool but, knowing Grace, was probably cashmere. A patterned silk scarf was tucked into the neck and pearl studs glimmered in her ears.

'Why – nothing,' he smiled. 'You look marvellous. The slacks are smashing and the sweater's just the job – but those clothes are far too good for working clothes.'

Grace laughed.

'Well, I wasn't proposing to start this morning. I merely wanted to be formally introduced to the poultry.' She looked at him from under her lashes and added wickedly, 'Then you can have me in dungarees and a leather jerkin if you like.'

Phil still harboured grave doubts about Grace taking over Jane's job with the poultry, but when she had returned from a holiday with her father and learnt that Jane had resigned, she had been adamant. Phil's reservations were not simply to do with the fact that Grace had never before shown any interest in the farm: they were as much to do with the distraction of having her around – even, or perhaps especially, in a leather jerkin. But Phil did not feel he had any choice in the matter. Fairbrother was all for it, and since Phil was relieved still to have a job after all the business with the ironstone, he did not intend to cross Fairbrother unnecessarily.

When Phil had seen Grace, her father and Mrs Carey, now Fairbrother's constant companion, off to the south of France for Christmas, his boss had not even committed himself to returning to the village. To have him and Grace back and continuing in farming was more than Phil had dared hope for. In the month before Christmas, Phil and Grace had tentatively taken steps towards re-establishing their relationship, and by the time she had come to leave they were fonder of each other than ever. He had written to her immediately at the hotel, and she had phoned him several times, careless of the expense, to tell him how much she was missing him.

'You wouldn't believe how dreary it is here!' she complained.

'Oh, I'm sure it must be terrible,' Phil sympathized. 'All that food and wine, and the casino and the cafés and the society crowd. I bet you're hating it!'

'I am, Phil,' she replied. 'I hate being anywhere that you're not. And I'm going to make sure it doesn't happen again. I'm going to make sure Daddy never leaves Ambridge!'

Eventually, they did return, Fairbrother lightly tanned and acting as if the ironstone idea had never happened. Phil sensed that while they had been away things had moved on somewhat between George Fairbrother and Helen Carey, too. Even today, Fairbrother was teaching her to cast at the trout stream, and it seemed as though Grace's matchmaking might finally pay off. If so, and Mrs Carey were to take on Grace's old role of running the house, Grace would need something to occupy her and Phil guessed this was not far from Fairbrother's mind. As usual, Phil felt caught in the middle and knew he would be pulled both ways trying to please everyone.

• • •

'Look! Is that or is that not a callous?'

Grace extended her pink palm to Christine. Chris stooped to release Daffodil from the milking machine – and to hide a smile. Her own hands were crisscrossed with lines and scratches, their skin hardened by work and weather, particularly so since she had left the milk depot and begun work at Brookfield. Grace was pointing to a miniscule raised patch of skin which, she claimed, she had acquired through lugging cornmeal about in a galvanized bucket.

'Do you really think you're cut out for farming, Grace?' grinned Chris.

Grace shook her head ruefully. 'What do you think? Or has Phil discussed it with you?'

'Not really. He's the soul of tact.'

This wasn't strictly true. Grace had only been doing the poultry job for a month, but Chris knew from Phil that she was nearly driving him demented with her non-existent timekeeping – what was she doing over here at Brookfield in the middle of the afternoon, for a start? – and her complete lack of feeling for the hens.

Chris slapped Daffodil's rump and the cow lurched off with a bellow into the yard. Grace stepped back in alarm as a tethered cow released a torrent of urine.

'Ugh! Honestly, Chris, how you can bear to do this twice a day I don't know.'

'There's nothing wrong with milking, except it's slightly tedious. For real hard work, you want to try getting the cows into the crush for their injections, or trimming the sheep's feet.'

Grace shuddered. 'No, thank you.' She looked at Chris closely. 'Are you really set on making a go of things here?'

Chris shrugged. Since Dick Raymond had gone off to work first in London and then as a junior correspondent in Malaya, Christine had had to give up any thoughts for now of being swept off her feet. She and Dick were writing to each other, of course, and his letters were more gratifyingly affectionate than she had expected. But after her previous experience of building up her hopes and being let down, Christine was trying to play it cool.

'I don't see myself as mistress of Brookfield in years to come if that's what you mean,' she laughed. 'Dad only took me on because Phil's too headstrong to take orders from him. But to be honest,

I think Dad's had quite a surprise. I don't think he was expecting *me* to question him quite so much.'

'So you're finding it a bit of a strain?'

Christine released another cow from the milking machine and wiped its teats.

'Grace,' she said patiently, 'you're talking like some sort of agricultural agony aunt. It's just not you. What are you getting at?'

'Oh no!'

Another cow was messily and enthusiastically relieving itself in front of Grace. She wrinkled her nose.

'I can't talk to you here, it's too . . . animal. Meet me at The Bull later, can you? There's something I want to ask you.'

• • •

By eight-thirty they were cosy in the lounge bar at The Bull, having ejected Simon Cooper and Christine's Uncle Tom from the fireside by claiming women's prerogative. The two men had retreated grumpily into the snug with the cribbage board, muttering about today's young women being brazen enough to drink on their own in public houses, something that would never have happened in their day.

'When was that? The Stone Age?' asked Christine. 'I wouldn't mind but I'm only having a bitter lemon.'

'Forget them,' urged Grace. 'I've been dying to tell you. I can't wait to see your face.'

'Well? Don't tell me my dear bro's proposed at last? Or has someone else beaten him to it?'

'Oh, if I wait for Phil I'll wait for ever,' said Grace dismissively. 'Mrs Perkins has more chance of walking up the aisle with Walter Gabriel than I do with Phil at present. No, this is something that concerns you and me.'

Christine sat forward.

'Well?'

'I'm thinking of setting up a riding school at Grey Gables,' said Grace in a low voice. Grey Gables was the local hotel and country club, owned by a rather raffish character called Reggie Trentham, who was passionate about horses. 'No-one else knows. And they're not to, yet. But I'd like you to come in with me. A partnership.'

'A partnership? But hang on, I haven't got any money.'

'No, but I have,' said Grace. 'What I don't have, apart from the sheer love of horses, is the expertise. That's what you'd bring to it.'

Christine let out a long breath. This was so unexpected, so astonishing, so perfect she couldn't take it in. And just when she had been feeling as if life was passing her by.

'Even Jack and Peggy have got away from Ambridge!' she had burst out to her mother only the other night. They had just finished listening to *Much Binding in the Marsh*.

Doris had sighed and poured milk into the pan for cocoa. She wasn't at all sure about the arrangement Jack had recently entered into in Cornwall with his wartime crony, Barney Lee. When Barney had come to Ambridge, Doris had not been impressed by his ferrety face and thin moustache. Even Dan had thought he looked like a spiv. But all Jack could see were the pound signs ringing up in front of his eyes. He went down to Cornwall to have a look and came back raving about the soil, the climate and the air. ('Much better for the kids, Mum!' 'Better than Ambridge? I doubt it!' Doris had said stoutly.) But there was no arguing with Jack when he got an idea in his head and he had packed up the family and persuaded Dan to take over the smallholding.

By comparison, Doris knew that Chris felt trapped. She had thought she might have the opportunity to travel to Ethiopia as a companion to a rather eccentric author, Lady Hylberow, who had taken a shine to her, but, rather to Doris's relief, the offer had been withdrawn at the last minute. Chris had had to resign herself to working for her father for the foreseeable future – or at least until Dick came to his senses and returned from South East Asia to marry her.

All this spun through Chris's head as she played with the stem of her glass and tried to assimilate everything that Grace had said.

In her wildest dreams she had never imagined that she might actually be able to have a career with horses. From the time her parents had bought her her first pony, a fat creature called Snowflake, straight out of a Thelwell cartoon, she had been captivated by them. She and Phil had held gymkhanas in the paddock near the orchard with old oil drums supporting the poles and a rudimentary water jump over a tiny tributary of the Am. Her mother had stitched Snowflake a horse blanket and Christine had painstakingly embroidered his name on it in pink chain stitch. With his old box Brownie her Dad had taken pictures of her proudly holding Snowflake's bridle and feeding him windfalls. When the poor animal had overeaten the spring grass and suffered the most terrible colic Chris had slept in the hayloft above his stable for a full three nights and had offered to pay for the vet out of her pocket money.

But Snowflake was long gone. Nowadays she rode Dasher, a roan mare that Dan had bought broken-mouthed at Borchester market and who was a sweetheart, though really past it for riding. Chris had often envied Grace her beautiful thoroughbred horse, and now she was being offered the chance to work with other lovely horses, schooling them, taking pupils, maybe in time doing livery work . . . Chris realized that her mind was running on ahead and she hadn't even given Grace an answer. She checked herself to find Grace studying her with amusement.

'You were miles away! Is that a good sign?'

'Oh, Grace, yes! It's a marvellous opportunity and – thanks for thinking of me!'

'My dear, I thought of you straight away. All I ask is that you don't breathe a word to anyone, not your mother and father, or Phil, until I've done a few more sums.'

'Where is the money going to come from, Grace?' Chris felt she had to ask.

'My mother left me pretty well off when she died,' Grace explained. 'Till now, I haven't known what to do with it. Then one day last week I was cleaning out the chickens and *hating* it. My back was nearly breaking and there was a biting wind whistling under the henhouse door. I suddenly thought: if I don't want to do this, and I can't go back to looking after Daddy once he marries Helen, which is only a matter of time, what would I most like to do? And there was only one answer.'

It sounded perfect – too perfect.

'I know we both love horses, Grace, but even with your money behind us, have we really got the knowledge to pull it off? I mean we'll need three or four good horses to begin with, plus ponies for the children: there'll be hay to buy in bulk and tack and –'

'I've thought of all that.' Grace laid a hand on her arm. 'I've already asked someone else to help us out.'

'Who?'

'Mike Daly.'

'Mike Daly?' said Chris, startled.

Mike was a somewhat colourful Irishman who was renting Blossom Hill Cottage. An experienced horseman, he was planning to breed pigs while working on a book. Chris hadn't had much to do with him but she knew he was utterly charming – and blessed with a very Irish gift of the gab.

'He knows ever such a lot about horses,' said Grace. 'And you know all these rumours that Reggie Trentham has started about him being some sort of spy?' she went on, smiling. 'Well, at least I thought he'd be able to keep our secret.'

• • •

Grace's insistence on secrecy led to not a little complication, especially when Reggie saw her car outside Blossom Hill Cottage at eleven o'clock at night and happened to let this slip in The Bull. But by the early summer, all the financial arrangements were in place to Grace's satisfaction and she and Chris were able to announce their proposal for the stables to their respective families. Grace was at last able to reassure her father – and Phil – that she was not having an affair with Mike Daly and Chris could reassure her father that she wouldn't leave him in the lurch at Brookfield, but would continue to work for him part-time.

Phil was relieved to know that Grace's late-night assignations did not mean anything more sinister and he knew that Fairbrother was relieved, too. Grace needed a project to occupy her. George Fairbrother and Helen Carey had, in a satisfying vindication of village gossip, been married at St Stephen's at Easter. After all her machinations, Grace had been as enthusiastic as anyone for the match but had found living under the same roof as Helen something of a trial. When Helen had found out – to Fairbrother's delighted surprise – that she was pregnant, the atmosphere had become even more strained.

'Grace doesn't like the competition, does she?' Chris commented wryly as she and Phil washed up for Doris. 'Helen will be the centre of attention for the next nine months, then there'll be the baby. And being shoved to the sidelines is not what Grace is best at.'

But for all her faults, Phil was becoming more and more convinced that he and Grace were meant to be together. A short holiday in Cornwall with Jack and Peggy had made him realize what an unhappy relationship was like. By comparison, his ups and downs with Grace were trivial. At least they had the fun of making up, and at least they usually managed to laugh about their disagreements. By contrast, the atmosphere at Jack and Peggy's was like a war of attrition: constant niggling and bickering over the tiniest things, most of them, to Phil's mind, utterly unimportant. What did it matter if Jack ate his supper in his working clothes once in a while? He was tired and hungry at the end of a long day – why should he be bothered to change? Was it really his job to entertain the girls when Peggy took Anthony William Daniel (fancy lumbering the child with three names, another affectation of Peggy's, thought Phil) for his bath? Phil realized he was bound to defend his brother, but he honestly couldn't blame Jack for taking himself off to the pub most evenings. After a few hours in Peggy's company, Phil was only too ready to join him, and he couldn't wait to get back to Ambridge. As summer eased itself into autumn, he wasn't surprised when a telegram arrived saying that Jack and Peggy were coming back themselves.

'Things haven't quite worked out as we hoped,' Peggy wrote

cryptically in a letter that arrived next day, putting both Doris and Mrs P – as Mrs Perkins was widely known – into a fever of speculation. When they met them at the station, everyone privately agreed that Peggy looked washed out, but it was not until a few weeks later that it emerged that they had had to leave Cornwall because Barney, Jack's partner, was getting rather too interested in her. But by then Jack was engrossed in another of his schemes: despite having no previous interest in public houses except as a customer, he was hatching a plan to take over The Bull when Sam Saunders retired at the end of the year.

· · ·

As the days grew shorter and the shadows lengthened on the grass, Phil found himself thinking more and more about himself and Grace. He had to admit he had finally been spurred into action by something Grace had said. It was to do with Mike Daly. The irony of Reggie's suspicions about Mike was that, to an extent, they were true. Mike had been a spy in the war – but he hadn't, as Reggie had thought, taken a dead hero's identity as his own. Instead, Mike had been involved in the most amazing cloak-and-dagger stuff behind enemy lines – all of which only came to light when Reggie, determined to prove his case against Mike, ran to earth another agent Mike had worked with and brought her to Ambridge.

Her name was Valerie Grayson and with her exotic good looks she certainly fitted the image of the beautiful spy. During the war, it appeared, she had posed as Mike's fiancée to provide cover for some of their assignations. And while Mike, she revealed, was still working for the intelligence services and might at any moment be dispatched on another job, she had given up her war work.

'It was fun while it lasted,' she said nonchalantly. 'But a girl has to settle down sometime.'

The idea of the flamboyant Valerie 'settling down' anywhere less cosmopolitan than Monte Carlo seemed unlikely to Phil, but to Reggie's delight – he was clearly rather smitten with her – she announced that she intended to stay in Ambridge and make it her home. Grace thought it was all frightfully romantic.

'Makes life in Ambridge a bit dull in comparison, doesn't it?' she'd remarked as Phil drove her back from an evening at Blossom Hill Cottage during which Mike had told them the full story.

'I don't know about that,' said Phil defensively.

Grace tossed her head.

'Oh, come off it,' she said. 'You don't get any thrilling spy dramas going on under your nose in Ambridge.'

'We just have had,' said Phil, puzzled.

'Don't take me so literally. You know what I mean,' snapped Grace. And she refused to be jollied out of her temper for the rest of the drive home.

'Well, anyway,' said Phil heartily, trying to win her round, as he pulled up beneath the swagged and sagging mulberry tree in front of Fairbrother's. 'I, for one, shall certainly look forward to reading Mike's book.'

'You'd expect them to marry, wouldn't you?' said Grace abruptly. 'Having undergone all that together.'

'I don't know,' replied Phil. 'I don't suppose living in that rat-infested cabin in Switzerland that Mike was going on about was highly romantic.'

'Oh, Phil, of course it was! Two people alone together against the odds! In any self-respecting book or film, Mike and Valerie would just have to marry at the end of it all!'

'I don't think Reggie would be very impressed if they did. Did you see him? He was hanging on Valerie's every word.'

'Oh, you're hopeless!' Grace scrabbled for the door handle.

'Jealous or something?' teased Phil somewhat heartlessly – as he would later come to realize.

Grace turned back icily to face him. 'No, I'm not jealous. I'm just trying to speed the happy ending.'

'Who for?' She did not reply and, thinking this was a comment on his poor grammar, he corrected himself. 'Sorry – for whom?'

'Mike and Valerie, of course,' she said. 'Who do you think?'

• • •

When he *did* think about it as he ringed the hens and drilled the winter barley he did eventually realize that she had been hinting about the two of them. He wasn't sure if he was being deliberately dense or merely cautious. He certainly wasn't being intentionally cruel but, as Christine lost no time in telling him, that was how it was beginning to seem.

'For goodness' sake, it would hardly be indecent haste if you were to propose to her tomorrow! How long have you known Grace now?'

'Um – well, over two years, I suppose.' Phil picked up a pudding basin from the wooden draining board. It was his turn to dry.

'You men, I give up!' Christine rinsed a saucepan aggressively and banged it down. 'You either get engaged on a whim or you hang about for ever!'

Phil knew Chris was still smarting from news of Dick Raymond's sudden engagement to a tea-planter's daughter out East which, to add insult to injury, she had learnt of from a caravanner who was visiting Ambridge on Dick's recommendation. Admittedly, the post from Malaya was somewhat unpredictable, and when Dick's letter containing the news eventually arrived, the postmark revealed that it had been posted two weeks previously. Although Dick had expressed his decision in terms of not holding Chris to a 'boy-girl romance', Chris still felt she'd been given the brush-off.

'I didn't know she was that keen on Dick,' Phil had said, surprised.

'I don't think *she* did,' Doris had replied. 'It's a case of absence making the heart grow fonder. Poor Chris. Nothing ever seems to work out for her in affairs of the heart.'

Even allowing for Chris's justifiable element of pique, however, Phil had to agree there was something in what she said about him and Grace. Grace had put on a brave face throughout her father's sudden engagement and speedy marriage to Helen Carey, while her own romance seemed to be going nowhere. Now her father and Helen were behaving in a completely soppy manner over this baby they were expecting. No wonder Grace felt disgruntled.

Sometimes Phil wished he had that streak of spontaneity that women seemed to appreciate. He wished he were the sort to turn up at the Fairbrothers' on a warm summer Sunday with a picnic hamper in the back of the car and whisk Grace off to Weston for the day, or to surprise her one drear November night when she had expected an evening at Borchester Little Theatre with a spray of orchids and tickets for a London show. But deep down he knew that he would never take off to Weston on a summer Sunday when there might be overtime to be worked on the harvest, and that a show in London would mean getting back to Ambridge at two in the morning – hardly compatible with a six o'clock start next day.

Sometimes he wondered what Grace saw in him at all – especially when there were more dashing chaps around, like Clive Lawson-Hope, the Squire's nephew, who had recently arrived to help his uncle run the Estate. Perhaps it was the thought of a possible rival that finally spurred Phil into action, but typically, not with Grace, but with her father.

He'd practised what he was going to say time after time in the mirror while shaving in the mornings, but on the day of his audience with Fairbrother, he still found himself almost completely tongue-tied. His boss stood with his back to the window, his hands clasped behind his back, as Phil stuttered out his thoughts.

'You see, sir,' he began. 'The position is a bit difficult on both sides. The quickest way to promotion – so they say – is to marry the boss's daughter – but I don't want promotion that way. And more to the point, I don't want people thinking that I want promotion that way.'

Fairbrother did his little trick of pulling at his moustache, as usual to hide a smile. He didn't want the lad to think he was laughing at him. He was so patently sincere with his clear, grey eyes and look of scrubbed eagerness.

'All this is very involved,' he said gently. 'Mind if I try and straighten it out?'

'Please do,' nodded Phil.

'Grace isn't exactly poverty stricken,' her father explained. 'If I cut her off without a penny, she'd still have a nice little nest-egg left to her by her mother. Financially, she's quite a good catch.'

'That sounds dreadful!' exclaimed Phil.

Fairbrother waved away his objection.

'Even if I disapprove, she can still bring enough money into the kitty to marry comfortably,' he continued. 'That what you wanted to know?'

'Thank you, sir.' Phil sounded dejected. 'But that's all right. Forget it.'

'Forget it?' Fairbrother was astounded.

'There's an awful lot of difference between sweeping a girl off her feet and setting out penniless to face the world and –'

'Hang on,' interrupted Fairbrother. 'Are you saying you'd prefer it if Grace weren't well off in her own right?'

'Of course I should, sir!' said Phil vehemently. 'I'd much prefer it!'

• • •

The realization that Grace was a wealthy woman knocked Phil for six. He had assumed that her investment in the stables with Chris had swallowed up all the money her mother had left her. All his instincts, all his upbringing had led him to expect that in a marriage he would be the provider. He knew Grace looked up to him and respected him. He felt he could give her advice that she might at first dispute but would eventually take. He felt he was the rock on which she could lean and on which they could build the foundations of a life together. But if Grace had her own money, everything was askew. He could not envisage a marriage where they did not come to joint financial decisions – where, dammit, they didn't have to struggle a bit. So when, finally, after his interview with her father, he spoke to Grace about the future, it was the financial side that exercised him as much as his feelings for her.

'Let me get this right,' she said, when he had laboriously explained what he proposed to do over Welsh rarebit in The Copper Kettle in Borchester. (He had planned to talk it through as they strolled by the bandstand, but they had had to seek shelter from the autumn rain lashing down outside.) 'You want me to wait around while you save £2000 so that you feel you're putting something into our partnership.'

'Into our marriage, Grace,' urged Phil.

'Yes, I know that's what you said.' The fingers of her conspicuously ringless left hand compressed and released the sunray pleats of her skirt. Phil watched, transfixed. 'But it sounds more like a partnership to me.'

'Isn't that what a marriage is?' asked Phil. He lifted her restless hand on to the table and covered it with his own. She seemed to be making heavy weather of this. He had been so pleased with the idea when he had come up with it.

'It's one aspect of it, yes,' agreed Grace, her fingers fragile beneath his. Her eyes were dark and troubled. 'But there are others. Love? Romance? Desire, even?'

Phil twined their fingers together.

'But – I feel all those things for you. That's why I'm here, for heaven's sake.'

Grace smiled and shook her head, more in a gesture of affectionate disbelief than anything else. He was so sweet and she could tell he had spent many a long evening figuring out exactly the right sum that would give him his stake in the marriage.

'How long will it take you to save that much money?' she asked.

'I've worked it all out,' he said eagerly. Next he'd be showing her his calculations. 'It won't be more than five years.'

'Five years?' The feathers on Grace's hat – dyed the same wine colour as her costume – bobbed as her head came up.

'But I hope I can do it sooner than that. I've an idea for pedigree pig breeding, you see –'

'Phil,' said Grace firmly, 'I care for you more than you know, but if you think I'm going to wait five years, you have got a lot more thinking to do.'

• • •

To her credit – and Grace was not known for her patience – she did wait: for a whole year. Much happened in Ambridge. In December, Christine was twenty-one, and, with Reggie Trentham's advice, Dan and Doris bought her a beautiful jet-black horse whom she called Midnight. Grace was a bridesmaid when Reggie, not Mike, married Valerie ('What did I say?' crowed Phil) and in the spring Chris left Brookfield to work full time at the stables.

In her place, Dan took on the rather dour Len Thomas who left his wife and baby behind in Welshpool, lived in and told Doris he liked his breakfast egg fried hard. It was Len who discovered an outbreak of swine fever at Brookfield and who, wife or no wife, soon seemed to be courting Mary Jones, a brilliant needlewoman whom Helen Fairbrother had discovered when she needed a layette made for baby Robin, who had arrived two weeks early in February.

Clive Lawson-Hope, as might have been predicted of a newly arrived man-about-Ambridge, paid Grace a lot of attention, which she was not slow to point out to Phil, but still Phil made no further move. Even when Clive proposed, Phil was phlegmatic. He carried on with his pig breeding, carefully depositing his profits in a savings account he had opened specially. 'You know my position,' he told Grace firmly. 'You must do as you see fit.'

Yet on Coronation Eve, Phil and Grace were inseparable as they roasted potatoes till four o'clock in the morning in the embers of the bonfire on Lakey Hill, one of a glowing chain that stretched from the Malverns across to the Hassett Hills. Next day they danced together at Walter's Coronation party, where half the village gathered to watch the young Queen Elizabeth take her solemn vows in Westminster Abbey on Mrs P's television set, for which Walter had wired his barn.

· · ·

Grace had seen out the winter months philosophically. Clive had provided her with a diversion. She liked him. He was attentive and attractive, but his main function was as an irritant to Phil – not that Phil had seemed very bothered. But on Coronation Day, with such an air of new beginnings, of promise, she ached more than ever for Phil to come to his senses and for the passionate declaration she longed to hear.

'Grace, this is crazy. I think about you every minute of every day. I don't care about the money, I just want us to be together.'

She waited for it, she imagined how, when he said it, she would fling her arms round his neck and press her face to his. But it never came.

'We've conquered Everest!' he cried instead – Sir Edmund Hillary and Sherpa Tensing had reached the summit the day before. 'Now all we need to do is win back the Ashes!'

No, thought Grace to herself, it needs something more drastic than that.

And so she arranged to go away for a year on a horse management course in Ireland.

'What on earth do you want to do that for?' Phil demanded when he cornered Grace in the stables, having heard the news from Chris.

'You're not the only one who has a career, you know,' Grace retorted, tightening Flash's girth. 'It'd be a different story if you wanted to go away to study pig breeding!'

'That's not the point!'

'Oh, I think it is,' said Grace. She led Flash out of her box and into the yard. 'It's called sauce for the goose, Phil.'

That Grace might leave Ambridge on her own initiative, leaving him, as Chris put it with her usual charm, to stew in his own juice, was something Phil had never even considered. In the six weeks before her departure he ran through every possible scenario. Should he beg her to stay? She wouldn't have taken any notice. Should he forget his plan to make £2000 and suggest that they marry straight away? Even when Mrs P generously offered to lend him some money to increase his pig numbers and maximize his profits, Phil couldn't bring himself to take it. It wouldn't be enough and he was still unable to reconcile himself to the fact that Grace would be bringing considerably more money to the marriage than he would.

In the end, he put aside the idea of declarations of any sort – Grace could always outdo him with words – in favour of a gesture that would tell her unequivocally what she meant to him and the certain plans he had for their future. It was a gesture he would make, he decided, at the last minute, on the platform at Borchester Station.

• • •

'That egg not to your liking, Len?'

Dan's farmhand was silent, hidden behind the morning paper.

'Expect the yolk's too runny for him,' grinned Dan. 'Bless me, Doris, you can't have had it in the pan more than ten minutes.'

But Doris motioned her husband to be quiet. It wasn't like Len not to touch his breakfast. Yet he'd seemed perfectly cheerful when he'd come downstairs a few moments ago, whistling and buttoning his cuffs.

'Len?' she queried gently. 'Are you all right?'

Slowly Len lowered the paper and Dan and Doris were shocked at the chalky colour of his face.

'Len, you can't be well.' Doris was already pushing her chair back. 'Open the back door, Dan, for some air. I'll telephone for the doctor.'

Len held up his hand. He shook his head.

'I'll be all right,' he muttered.

'Well, what is it, lad?' Dan always sounded gruff, even when he was trying to be gentle.

In reply, Len held out the paper to his employer. He indicated a small paragraph at the foot of the page.

'There.'

Dan took the paper, puzzled, and Doris got up from the table to come and stand behind her husband's chair. Together they peered at the printed word. It was the report of a road accident at Melin-y-ddol, near Welshpool, and the subsequent death from her injuries of a Mrs Marion Thomas.

'Oh, Len,' said Doris, realizing. 'I'm so sorry. It's someone you know, isn't it? A relative?'

'You don't understand.' Len was distraught. 'Marion was my wife.'

* * *

Dan was lucky to catch Phil up at Fairbrother's before he set off on his rounds of the fields.

'It's not a pretty tale,' Dan explained. 'This Marion had been seeing another feller. There was no marriage and no feelings left to speak of between Len and her, but there is the little lad – he's hardly more than a baby, I gather.'

Phil shook his head sadly. It sounded a mess. 'What's Len going to do?'

'All he can think of right now is getting home to find out what's going on. The little boy's with Marion's sister at the moment, apparently, but Len obviously wants to see how the land lies. I don't think he's too keen on having him brought up by her family.'

'He's not proposing to bring him to Brookfield, is he?' The postman opened the door of the farm office and threw a bundle of letters on to the table near the door, but they both ignored him.

'Phil, I've no idea, and I can hardly push him on it, now can I?' said Dan. 'Listen, all I came over for is this. I'm up to my neck this morning: I'm behind with the cultivations, the chain's off the harrow and the seedsman's due. Could you take Len to the station and see him safely off?'

'Me? But, Dad –'

'I know, I know, it's Grace's last morning. But all you have to do is put Len on the ten-twenty from Hollerton and you'll be in bags of time to get to Borchester to see Grace off at midday.'

Phil sighed. He had had other plans for the morning, such as sprucing himself up to say a proper – he hoped, a fiancé's – goodbye to Grace. But he knew how pressed his father was at present and how urgent it was to get the winter barley in.

'I can't very well say no, can I? Everything else seems pretty trivial at a time like this.'

'Thanks, Phil, lad. I knew I could count on you.'

Phil couldn't blame his father. Dan wasn't to know that Len was not, in the end, going to go quietly. When Phil arrived at Brookfield, thinking he was taking him to the train, Len announced that he had to go round to see his girlfriend, Mary, to let her know what was going on.

'I can't just head off without a word of explanation,' he insisted. 'She'll only hear all about it from someone else and she'll never forgive me.'

'And where will we find Mary?' enquired Phil.

'She'll be in Borchester, at the shop,' said Len blithely.

'But – your train's from Hollerton,' said Phil. Hollerton was miles in the other direction.

'That's right,' agreed Len. 'And I don't think I'll make the ten-twenty. But there's another an hour later.'

An hour! By the time he got back into Borchester, for the second time that day . . . Phil did a rapid calculation. He'd be lucky to get five minutes with Grace.

There was nothing he could do. He'd promised to help his father out of a jam. Len, though being intensely irritating, had to be his first priority.

'Come on, then,' he said, as graciously as he could. 'Let's get going.'

• • •

Phil took the stone stairs, sparkling with gypsum in the station gloom, two at a time. He had driven Len to Borchester, waited while he had his tryst with Mary, then sped him to the later train at Hollerton. Even then, he hardly felt he could abandon the poor chap on the platform, so had waited for the train to pull out – a full, agonizing five minutes late – with Len's face tragic at the window. Then he had driven like blazes back to Borchester in the hope of managing to catch Grace.

'Excuse me! Sorry!'

He dodged round a businessman with a briefcase lumbering down the steps and, reaching the top, swung round on the handrail, just in time to hear the guard blow his whistle and to see the train chug into life down the track. Phil let out a huge sigh of disappointment and frustration and held his aching sides.

'There you are!' Fairbrother approached down the platform, swinging his stick. 'You've just missed her!'

'So I see,' panted Phil, adding bitterly, 'She got off all right, then?' Fairbrother beamed.

'Oh, she's quite a seasoned traveller, is Grace. As long as it's not too choppy on the boat she'll be fine.'

'She didn't . . . leave any message for me?'

'Well, no, I'm afraid not,' Fairbrother replied. 'She bought herself an illustrated paper at the bookstall, I put her hatbox up on the rack, the guard took her trunk and – well, that was that.'

'Never mind. Thanks, anyway.'

'Sorry you've had a wasted journey, Phil. I – er – I take it the farm can spare you this morning, can it?' Grace's father asked with a mischievous glint in his eye.

'Don't worry about the farm, sir,' replied Phil glumly. 'It's going to be getting my full attention over the coming months.'

With Grace gone, there would be precious few distractions.

• • •

As Phil clambered wearily back into his car, he felt the sharp edge of something in his pocket dig into his leg. Slowly he reached in and brought out a small black leather box. He tapped it thoughtfully on the steering wheel before easing it open, not that there was any point now in looking at its contents, not without Grace. Inside, snug in a slit against cream velvet, was the sapphire and diamond engagement ring he had chosen for her and which he had intended to give her at the station.

·7·

To Have and to Hold

It was the longest year Phil had ever known. He felt as if he were living his life in parallel to, rather than with, those around him. Things that were cause for general jubilation, such as the announcement that all rationing would end next year, or plans for commercial television ('It'll never catch on!' swore Dan) didn't seem to touch him at all. Closer to home, in the village, he hardly noticed that Reggie's young cousin, Ann Trentham, had a crush on him, nor could he share Ambridge's interest in a newcomer called John Tregorran, who had turned up in a green caravan, having left academic life after a surprise win on the football pools.

It was the mildest December for twenty years, and before that for 200, but just when farmers were congratulating themselves on their good fortune, January brought with it a bitter winter followed by a cold spring. At the end of March, Chris turned down a proposal from Clive Lawson-Hope, who was about to leave for his Uncle Percy's farm in Kenya. She seemed rather more upset at the fact that four horses had died in the Grand National than at the prospect of losing another suitor, but Phil was outraged.

'The man's nothing but a predator!' he complained to Walter, for whom he was mending some fences as a favour. Walter didn't need any encouragement to dislike Clive, who had been hounding him since the start of the year about the state of his farm.

'My old granny would have had a word for him,' pronounced Walter, pushing his greasy cap to the back of his head as they took a breather. 'He's nobbut a blackguard!'

Even Clive's reforms – and he had improved the forestry management on the Estate, Phil had to grant him that – could not save the Squire from the ultimate indignity. He had already had to sell some of his land to Fairbrother, and one vivid May morning the Squire himself called at Brookfield to tell Dan that he had no option but to sell the entire Estate. He would do his best, he said, to set a fair price – if Dan were able to raise the money to buy. Fortunately, Dan had already sold the smallholding to an impressive young woman from Surrey called Carol Grey, but there were many tense meetings with the bank manager, the impassive Mr Helston, before Dan's offer price, plus £250, was accepted in July.

By then, the worry about buying the farm had almost been superseded by worry about Jack, whose odd outbursts and erratic behaviour had become more than Peggy could bear. Jack had succeeded in obtaining the licence of The Bull at the beginning of 1952, but within months the licence had had to be transferred to Peggy after the brewery got to hear about Jack serving drinks after time. What the brewery had tactfully called Jack's 'dilatoriness' had continued, though, and it was a relief to the whole family when he agreed to be admitted to the local hospital for nervous diseases for a four-week stay as a voluntary in-patient.

All this Phil told Grace in letters written late at night when he had given his weaners their iron injections and docked their tails, balanced his accounts and checked compulsively the mounting balance in his National Savings book. She wrote back with lyrical descriptions of the countryside where she was staying, the horses she was training, and the amazing old man in the village who had the knack of 'whispering' to horses and who could school the most impetuous colt. She was writing to Chris as well, and told Phil she was thrilled that Chris had the chance to ride at a two-day show at Belverston for a well-known local horseman, Paul Johnson.

She told Phil to give his Uncle Tom her love: myxomatosis was taking out vast numbers of the local rabbit population and Uncle Tom should have been pleased, but he hated to see any creature suffer and the 'myxy' dealt them a nasty, lingering death. She chided

Phil for not visiting her in Ireland and scolded him for not trying out the fishing rods she had sent him for his birthday in the trout streams of County Limerick. But Phil had no desire to see her in Ireland. He wanted to see her back in Ambridge and, increasingly, he wanted to see her back in Ambridge as his wife.

When, finally, she wrote to tell him the date of her return – 7 September – Phil knocked off work early and went over to Grey Gables to see Reggie Trentham. Phil knew that Fairbrother himself was quite capable of organizing a homecoming party for Grace, but Phil wanted it planned his way – and if you wanted a celebration organized, Reggie was the person to ask.

• • •

Phil had Christine making 'Welcome Home' banners and he himself spent the entire evening before the party blowing up balloons. Having missed seeing Grace off to Ireland a year previously, he was determined to meet her at the station on her return, but in the end Fairbrother met her in the Daimler. The first sight Phil had of her after all their time apart was when he arrived at the party (late, having been held up by a farrowing sow) to find her deep in conversation with Paul Johnson. Resisting the urge to rush over and wrap her in his arms, Phil helped himself to a saucer of champagne (when Reggie did something, he didn't do it by halves) and positioned himself so that he was half-hidden by a massive flower arrangement. Now he could watch unobserved.

She was as beautiful as ever. Her glossy dark hair, a deep, dark brown that was almost black, had been cut shorter, exposing the nape of her slender neck. When she looked up at Paul, she put her head on one side and listened attentively as he spoke. Phil knew that look. It made you feel as if you were the only man in the world. When Paul had finished, her mouth twitched at something he had said and her hand rested lightly on his arm. Phil knew that touch. He felt a sudden lurch of jealousy which was an actual, physical pain. He gripped the stem of his glass until he thought it would snap. He hadn't spent a year missing her for this.

For a year he had looked at no-one else, and hadn't wanted to. His waking hours had been spent working and building up his pig herd in his precious spare time. His evenings he had spent writing to her, thinking of funny little incidents that might amuse her and waiting for her letters in return. He had phoned once or twice – at Christmas and on his birthday, and she had urged him to visit her. But he hadn't gone. In his dogged, stubborn way, he felt that she was trying to prove something by going to Ireland. She was making him wait in the way he had made her wait – and he wanted to prove that he could.

A waitress passed with a bottle and Phil held out his glass for a refill. Then he walked over to Paul and Grace.

'Don't tell me,' he began, butting in, 'it seems as though you've never been away!'

Grace spun round to face him.

'Phil! Where've you been hiding?'

She flung her arms round his neck. Phil returned her embrace while trying not to spill his drink.

'We don't need to ask if she's missed you,' commented Paul with a sardonic smile. 'Shall I make myself scarce?'

Grace turned back.

'Oh, Paul, don't be silly,' she said. 'I've missed you all. Now go on, tell me more about Reggie at the Hollerton point-to-point.'

That was how it went on all night. Oh, she talked to Phil, but she talked to Reggie, and Jack, and Dan, and Paul of course – a lot to Paul – just as she would no doubt have talked to Clive Lawson-Hope if he'd been there – and to Alan Carey, too, come to that. By eleven o'clock, after Reggie had made a fulsome and slightly drunken speech, and when the older partygoers were starting to drift away, Phil was fuming. When Paul had finally left with Chris, Grace came and found Phil, seated on his own in a corner, making a pyramid out of Grey Gables matchbooks. She sat down next to him in a slither of aquamarine taffeta.

'I'm worn out! What a welcome back! How sweet of Reggie to host it.'

Phil noticed that she didn't assume he had had any part in it. 'Glad you enjoyed it,' he said stiffly. 'All part of the service.'

'You don't mean – oh, Phil, was it your idea? Well, you should have been making the speech, then.'

'Oh, I don't think that would have been appropriate, do you? After all, it's not as if we have a special relationship or anything.'

'Oh, Phil, don't be tiresome. Not on my first night home.'

Phil couldn't help himself. In his trouser pocket, his fingers closed around the smooth black leather box that had been lying in his sock drawer for over a year. In it was the engagement ring he had bought her a year ago. The opportunity hadn't arisen to give it to her then and it didn't look as if it was going to arise now.

'No, it wouldn't do to spoil things, would it? Not when you were having such fun flirting with all and sundry.'

'All and sundry? Charming.'

'All right, I'll be more specific. Paul Johnson.'

'Oh, for heaven's sake! We were talking about horses.'

'And I suppose that makes a pleasant change from pigs.'

'Well, you do have rather a one-track mind on the subject.'

Phil knew Grace was trying to tease him out of his ill-temper, but he couldn't rise above his intense disappointment with the way their long-anticipated reunion had gone.

'I think your father's trying to attract your attention,' he said curtly. 'Presumably he and Helen have got to get back for the nipper.'

Grace stood up.

'Shall I see you tomorrow?' she asked, more quietly now.

'I'll be at work as usual, if that's what you mean.'

Phil looked away from her as he spoke. A bunch of balloons had drifted down from the ceiling and was wafting about on the dance floor. Over the stage the home-made banner, written by Phil and coloured in by Christine, read: 'The Wanderer Returns!' But for how long? thought Phil. How long before she wanders off again, to somewhere or someone else?

• • •

'Oh, that is so typical!' Grace Fairbrother surveyed her car, parked in the garage at her father's farm where, under a tarpaulin, it had spent the past year of her absence. The front offside tyre was completely flat.

'Problems?' Her father approached from the house, dressed for the office in a pinstriped suit.

Grace indicated the tyre.

'I don't suppose . . . ? ' she asked hopefully.

Fairbrother shook his head. 'Sorry, old girl, I'm all spruced up for the office. Look, Phil's just out there in the yard. He's your man.'

Pecking her on the cheek, he climbed into his own car and started the engine.

'See you at dinner!' he called through the open window. And endearingly, though brusquely, 'Good to have you back!'

Grace wondered if Phil felt the same. He had behaved so oddly the other day at her welcome-home party, and since then he had seemed to be avoiding her. She badly didn't want to return to their old sparring ways, when they had seemed to vie with each other for the chance to occupy the moral high ground. Jim Benson passed, carting straw, and she was tempted to ask his help, but on the other hand, the flat tyre would be an excuse to talk to Phil – perhaps even to try to find out what was eating him. He wasn't exactly thrilled to be dragged away from his inventory of the chemical drums in the barn, but followed her across the yard anyway.

'You're a fine lot,' she said lightly as they reached the garage, 'letting a girl's car go to rack and ruin while she's away.'

'Look,' said Phil, taking off his jacket and hanging it on a nail, 'the car's been in here jacked up and properly greased the whole time.' He squatted down by the wheel and began impatiently loosening the nuts with a spanner. 'And I've started it up and left it ticking over at least twice a week for the whole twelve months.'

'Have you?' Grace was touched and surprised to realize he'd thought of it. But she couldn't think of anything else to say and Phil was silent as he concentrated, easing off the nuts, jacking up the car and putting on the spare for her. As he jacked the car down again and the replacement tyre met the ground, there was a hiss of air.

'The spare! It's going flat!'

'What?' Phil shoved her out of the way and crouched down again. 'It must be the valve.' It wasn't the valve. There was a puncture in the spare as well. Phil didn't even bother to suppress his curse.

Guilty at the irritation she was causing him and aware that the operation was occupying far too much of his time in the middle of the working day, Grace reacted as she usually did, by trying to shift the blame elsewhere.

'I wouldn't be a bit surprised if the tube's perished or something,' she complained. 'Really, you'd think somebody would have had the sense to take care of the car whilst I was away!'

Phil was bad-temperedly jacking the car up again. 'Pity you didn't think of giving someone the job instead of just hoping somebody'd do it. I suppose I'll have to mend the blessed thing now. You'll have to help me, though.'

'Me?'

'It's your car, as you keep reminding me. Won't do you any harm to wield a tyre lever for a change.'

'Well, thank you, Phil,' retorted Grace. 'You really are the perfect knight in shining armour.'

'Oh, I've got none of those sort of illusions,' said Phil bitterly, turning away. 'Let's be honest, I'm just the hired hand.' And before she could retaliate he added, 'Do get out of the way, Grace. And for heaven's sake, put that spare-tyre cover somewhere safe.'

It took another twenty sweaty minutes of struggling before the tyre was inflated and ready to put on again, but in the process something must have been knocked out of alignment and, try as he might, Phil could not get the wheel back on. As he struggled, Grace holding the tyre lever, his hand slipped and blood oozed from his torn knuckles.

'Blast!' Phil rocked backwards on his heels, straight on to the spare-tyre cover.

'Mind your feet, clumsy!' cried Grace before she could stop herself. 'Oh, Phil, look at the dent! It won't ever fit properly again!'

'That's right, blame me!' flared Phil. He sucked at his knuckles. 'You put the darn thing behind me when I wasn't looking. I said to put it out of the way – don't let go of the lever!'

With a tinny clatter, the tyre slipped off again.

'Now look what you've done!'

'I can't help it! You keep on criticizing!'

'It isn't my wheel! Did I ask for the job?'

'It's no good yelling at me!'

'Why don't you just do as I tell you?'

Suddenly they both stopped and the unexpected silence rang in their ears. Phil first, and then Grace, began to smile at their outbursts of temper.

'Oh, Miss Fairbrother,' chided Phil. 'Your temper.'

Grace took a handkerchief from her pocket and bound it tenderly round Phil's hand. 'We're a couple of fools, aren't we?' she agreed. 'Go on, hit me over the head with the mallet.'

'I very nearly did,' grinned Phil.

'Fancy us losing our tempers over a silly thing like that.' Grace finished off her makeshift bandage with a clumsy knot. Phil regarded his hand and tried unsuccessfully to flex his fingers.

'I'm not going to be able to put on the spare trussed up like this.'

'Oh, bother the spare,' said Grace. 'I'm so late for my manicure now it hardly matters.'

'You mean you had me toiling away, tearing my hands to ribbons, just so you could go to town for a manicure?' Phil shook his head in disbelief.

Grace nodded, her mouth twitching as she swallowed a smile.

'You do look funny when you're cross,' she observed. Gently she reached out and touched his hand. 'Poor old you.'

Phil looked at her. Her hair was all over the place and she had a smudge of dirt on her nose. She was impossible and exciting. She could be vicious – and vulnerable. He had never wanted her so much.

'Grace . . .' he said abruptly.

'Yes?' She looked up from under her lashes.

He took both her hands in his good hand and laid the bandaged one on top of them.

'Will you – will you marry me?'

It was as if he had thrown a switch. Grace's joy illuminated her whole being.

'Oh, yes, Phil. Yes, please!'

There was absolutely no point in a long engagement but, with Grace only just having got back, rushing things through before Christmas seemed equally unnecessary. Six months seemed a reasonable sort of time to wait and Fairbrother was delighted when Grace said that she'd always thought Easter, the time he had married Helen, was the perfect season of the year for a wedding. The following year, 1955, Easter Monday fell on 11 April. And despite Doris's dire warnings about the certainty of rain on a Bank Holiday, that was the date set.

• • •

'It's all your fault,' hissed Phil to Jack as they waited for the bride to arrive. She was now nearly ten minutes late. 'She's getting back at me for your stupid suggestion that we should bring forward the date to before the end of the financial year so that I'd save myself £90.'

'I still say you should have done.' Jack fidgeted his finger inside his tight, shiny collar.

'Yes, I could have,' snapped Phil, 'and found myself with a new date for the wedding and no bride.'

'You haven't exactly got a bride now, have you?' grinned Jack. He craned and looked back up the aisle. 'Still no sign.' His time in the hospital seemed to have done him the world of good: he was his old gregarious self again.

'How long have we been sitting here?' asked Phil in despair.

'Couple of minutes,' lied Jack easily. 'Not nervous, are you?'

'It feels like hours,' groaned Phil. 'Everybody's whispering. Even the vicar's looking at his watch.'

Jack swivelled round and beckoned to Dan in the pew behind.

'There's no hitch that you know of, is there, Dad?' he asked.

Dan leant forward and spoke in a whisper which to Phil's embarrassed ears sounded louder than his usual tone of voice.

'Mrs Fairbrother says Grace and the bridesmaids were ready and waiting when she left. Can't think what's happened.'

It was Phil's turn to swivel. 'Nip outside and see if anyone knows what's going on, Dad, please,' he implored. 'I can't stand this.'

Dan held up his hand to quiet him and stood up. He clapped Phil heartily on the shoulder as he squeezed past Doris, dignified in coffee silk.

'Stop fussing, lad. After the time it's taken you to get round to it, what's ten more minutes?'

After what seemed like another ten – to poor Phil, at least – there was an audible sigh of relief from the congregation as Dan sped back to his seat, followed soon after by the opening bars of the Bridal March. As Phil tested his shaking legs before moving to stand before the altar, Dan hissed an explanation – something about the starter motor on the bride's car getting jammed and the chauffeur having had to rock it free. Phil was hardly listening. It didn't seem to matter any more. She was here, she was coming, and she was soon going to be his – for life.

As she approached down the aisle, he couldn't resist turning round for a glimpse of her. She was a misty figure in tulle, slight and insubstantial, tiny as she clutched her father's arm. Under her veil her eyes were wide and, for the first time that he could ever recall, almost shy. Instinctively he put out a hand to squeeze hers as her dress sighed to a halt beside him. He knew he would never forget the scent of the lilies in her bouquet, the slipperiness of her satin-gloved hand or the tender look she gave him.

'Leaving me at the altar, eh?' he joked nervously. 'Am I glad to see you.'

'Explanations later,' she mouthed. And then, 'I love you.'

• • •

Once they were married, Phil often asked himself why on earth he had waited so long. Fairbrother had agreed to let them have the house at Coombe Farm for the nominal rent of £1 a week and, as they settled in to their newlywed routine, Phil felt that this was how his life had always been meant to be. He couldn't imagine now how he had lived at home with his parents and Chris; how he could possibly have wanted to spend his evenings any other way than by his own fireside, with Grace sitting opposite him; how he could have lain night after night in the narrow single bed he had slept in since he was twelve when he could have woken every morning to Grace's silky warmth.

For Grace, too, marriage was everything she had hoped it would be. Since her father had married Helen, she had not been involved with running the big house, but had concentrated on her work at the stables. Now that the business was established there, and Chris, with Paul Johnson's involvement, was only too willing to shoulder more of the burden, Grace found that she actively enjoyed the occasional morning playing the housewife, turning the mattress and dusting their wedding presents. She pored over recipe books, determined to make Phil something tasty for supper each night, and for someone who had never done more than instruct the cook, she proved to be a more than competent cook herself. She could sense Doris's surprise when her parents-in-law came round for tea and were offered drop scones and strawberry jam and lemon-iced sponge – all home-made. She noted Doris's well-concealed disappointment when a tour of the house revealed no crumpled pillowslip or smear on the kitchen sink and she had to swallow a smile when Phil sang her praises to his mother.

Phil was prospering at work both for himself and for her father, and the horse-riding school was doing well: all in all, Grace felt that those first few months of their marriage were blessed with a special charm – protected, almost, by a kind of magic. And when, in September, her father offered Phil a directorship and they went away for a few days to stay with a friend of Grace's at the seaside in celebration, it didn't seem as if things could get any better. Even the fact that, when they got there, poor Isabel had scalded her foot and they had to look after her baby, Ian, didn't dampen their spirits. Isabel was mortified and apologetic, but Grace found the little chap rather fun and, casting furtive looks at Phil as they pushed the pram, she could see that he too was enjoying every minute.

. . .

The night after they got back to Ambridge, she cooked partridge for supper and, with his approval, raided her father's cellar for a bottle of claret. She got out the best glasses, shone up the silver candlesticks that Reggie and Valerie had given them as a wedding present, and put slim pink candles in them. She changed, as she always did before Phil came home, but this evening dressed her hair with more care than usual and dabbed some perfume behind her ears and on the nape of her neck, where Phil loved to nuzzle as she stood at the stove.

When Phil came bounding in he was full of news of the autumn sale he was organizing for her father. Not surprisingly, he queried the candles and the silver but she parried his questions. She wanted to tell him in her own time. She placed the partridge on a serving dish and poured gravy, to which she had added a generous measure of wine, into a sauceboat. As she reached behind her to take off her apron, Phil's hands were there to untie the bow for her. He turned her round to face him and kissed her lingeringly.

'You're a clever girl,' he said. 'I don't deserve you.'

'Oh, yes you do,' she smiled. 'Now come on, the partridge will get cold.'

Phil took the hint and carried the birds to the table. Grace followed with the game chips and tiny – frozen – green peas, one aspect of her housekeeping to which Doris would never be reconciled. Phil began to carve.

'A beano like this is extending the holiday!' he exclaimed, placing slices of breast meat on her plate and passing it to her. 'Do you know,' he added as he served himself, 'I didn't mind pram-pushing one bit. Do you think anyone thought it was ours?'

The serving spoon chinked against the side of the dish as Grace replaced it. She said nothing. In the silence, Phil poured the wine.

'What's the matter?' he asked softly. 'I made a gag, no reaction.'

'I was just thinking,' said Grace. She shook out her napkin and placed it in her lap.

'What about?' Phil took a sip of wine.

'Well ...' Grace began, 'it's silly, but taking care of Isabel's baby over the weekend ... maybe you were right after all, Phil, and I was wrong.'

'What about?' But she knew that he must know. It had been the only time in the past six months that they had even come close to a disagreement. It had been when, lying close together one night, Phil had raised the question of children and Grace had said firmly that she thought they should wait. When he had asked how long, she had said the first thing which had come into her mind – five years. She had felt Phil tense, but he hadn't said anything. She knew he wouldn't push it. They'd hardly been married five minutes, which was, in fact, part of her logic. After all this time, she was so enjoying having Phil to herself that she didn't want any distractions. She didn't want to think about anyone else but the two of them and she could only imagine a baby getting in the way. But it hadn't been like that with Isabel's baby. He'd been so adorable, and it had tugged at her heart to see Phil rolling a little wooden elephant to him, and the baby trying to grab Phil's tie, and the soft downiness of the baby's head and the rough curls of Phil's bent over the cot at night ...

Grace put down her knife and fork and took a steadying sip of wine. Phil was looking at her intently.

'Well? What about?' he prompted.

'Waiting five years,' she said softly, 'for a family of our own. It was selfish on my part. I know it isn't really what you want and the week-end brought it home to me.'

Phil looked at her, his eyes bright. He said nothing.

'Well, I didn't do too badly with Isabel's baby, did I?' she prompted.

'Badly?' Phil had found his voice again. 'You're an absolute natural.'

Grace let out a sigh. After all her years of fierce independence, of challenging and sometimes almost wantonly defying Phil, she now found it the most satisfying thing in the world to say or do the things that would please him most.

'That's what I'm beginning to feel myself,' she said gently. 'You were right. Let's forget all this waiting five years nonsense.'

Phil covered her hand with his. Delight, astonishment and gratitude struggled for supremacy in his face.

'Let's forget the partridge,' he said. 'It'll keep. Hmm?'

Grace smiled. He pushed back his chair and came over to her. He held out his hands. 'What do you say, Mrs Archer?' he asked softly. 'Shall we make up for lost time?'

Grace placed her hands in his. 'The sooner the better,' she said.

. . .

Next morning, Phil was boyish with plans.

'If it's a boy,' he enthused, 'we could call him George Daniel . . . or Daniel George.'

Grace calmly took the breakfast plates to the sink.

'Looking ahead a bit, aren't we?' she smiled over her shoulder. 'I can tell you, if we had a girl I wouldn't dream of calling her Doris . . . or Helen.'

'No?'

'Not even to please the grandmas. Now,' she chided, 'we'd better put our skates on, Phil. Look at the time.'

Phil looked at his watch and pantomimed dismay. He gulped down the last of his coffee.

'I'll drive you over to Grey Gables,' he offered.

Grace was putting on her riding boots.

'There's no need, darling.'

'I insist.' Phil unhooked his working coat from behind the door. 'Anyway I want to see Reggie and Valerie. Book a table for tomorrow night. Celebration.'

'What are we celebrating?' asked Grace, as if she didn't know.

'Oh . . . just celebrating,' smiled Phil. He slipped his arms round her waist and pulled her against him. She slid her arms round his neck and leaned her head luxuriously against his shoulder.

'I'll ask John and Carol to join us,' he murmured, kissing the top of her head. 'Impress them with the urgent necessity of getting married. I really can't recommend it enough.'

• • •

Ever since Phil and Grace had finally made a go of it, Ambridge had been in dire need of a new pair of young lovers whose fortunes the villagers could follow, and it seemed as though Carol Grey and John Tregorran might finally fill the void. The potential romance between Christine and Paul Johnson had initially excited some interest, but after so many disappointments, Christine was playing her cards extremely close to her chest. Even the Ambridge rumour-mongers needed some slight evidence to go on, and Christine was not going to let them have the satisfaction. As long as she could maintain that she and Paul merely shared an abiding interest in horses, she would do so, though both of them knew that their closeness was beginning to be underpinned by feelings that had nothing to do with the riding school.

John, however, had made his feelings for Carol known rather more publicly – it was common knowledge that he had even proposed to her at one of Mike Daly's parties – but Carol was that new breed of woman who knew her own mind and who did not need a husband to give her an identity. Though there had been many doubters in the village that she would make a go of the market garden, she had battled on (with part-time help from Jack, who needed, it seemed, some involvement with the land), and had turned the run-down smallholding into an impressive business. The Ambridge matrons thought she had now proved her point and should sink gratefully into the manly arms of whichever suitor next presented himself – Dr Cavendish, who had established a health centre in the area, was the preferred candidate of some at the WI and Mothers Union, where these weighty matters were discussed – but Carol exhibited a wilful tendency to go her own way. She was perfectly happy to be paired off with John at dinner parties – like this one of Phil and Grace's, for example – but when it came to making the arrangement more permanent, she pulled back.

It seemed that there would be no escape for her from the subject of weddings, however, since the night of Phil's planned celebration fell on the day that Princess Ira von Furstenburg had been married in Venice. The wireless and television had reported it fulsomely – and it had been a sumptuous occasion.

'Guests in a fleet of gondolas with the gondoliers in white trousers, golden embroidered jackets and scarlet sashes,' marvelled Carol as a waitress placed a dry Martini in a chilled glass in front of her. Reggie Trentham had done wonders for the standards in the cocktail bar at Grey Gables.

'With high jinks like that going on, it surprises me that nobody fell in the drink!' Phil's face was flushed from his day in the sun. The autumn sale had been a great success: he had sold twenty-five in-calf heifers, eight barreners and two yearling bulls on Fairbrother's behalf, as well as fifteen culled-out cows.

'You never know,' grinned John. 'Somebody's probably awash.'

They all laughed and John was passing round a dish of olives when Grace suddenly exclaimed:

'Confound it! I've lost an earring.' She pulled off the remaining one, a twisted knot of black and white seed pearls. 'I think I remember . . . I've a feeling it came off as I was getting out of the car.'

Phil leapt up. It seemed he could not do enough for Grace at the moment. 'I'll go and look.'

But Grace was already on her feet, elegant in her panelled black dress. 'No, no,' she said. 'You stay here. I'm sure I'll find it on the floor of the car. Shan't be a moment,' she called back. 'Feel rather undressed without it!'

Phil watched her go, loving the delicate sway of her hips. He had trouble in dragging his attention back to John and Carol, who were chatting about the village concert, fête and field day John was organizing to raise money for the village hall roof repairs. Phil had just offered him the loan of one of Fairbrother's lorries and his services as a driver when Grace came tearing back into the cocktail lounge. Later Phil remembered how a stout man at a neighbouring table had slowly lowered the menu he had been studying and had stared as Grace dashed across the room. How the pianist had stopped in the middle of an arpeggio. How a paper cocktail napkin had fluttered to the floor in the draught from Grace's dress.

'Phil! Everybody! Help!' she shrieked. 'The stables are on fire!'

· · ·

Phil had never seen anything like it. It had been a warm day – it had been a warm week – and there was a light breeze that must have fanned the fire. By the time Phil and John had rushed outside, flames were leaping from the roof, zigzagging alarmingly against the dark sky and sending showers of sparks on to the gravel below. The heat was intense, the brightness almost blinding, but most chilling of all was the terrified whinnying of the tethered horses trapped inside.

Grace pulled on Phil's arm, dragging him towards the blazing building.

'We must get the horses out!'

'I know, Grace, but we must be careful. Anyone sent for the brigade?'

'On their way,' said Reggie as he ran up. 'Anything I can do?'

'Tap over there.' Phil indicated the stable yard. 'Get some water – a bucketful, anything. Sparks are dropping through from the loft on to the night beds.'

Reggie dashed off and Phil looked up to see Grace already emerging from the stables leading Cavalier, one of the hunters, as well as her own horse, Flash. He tore across to her.

'You mustn't go in by yourself, you silly girl! You should have waited for me!'

He took Cavalier from her and led him over to a tree well away from the fire, where he tethered him. Grace followed with Flash. Her face was streaked with dirt and tears and there was a deep scratch all down her forearm. She must have caught it on one of the wooden box-rails. He seized her by the shoulders.

'Are you all right?'

'Phil, please!' She pulled away from him impatiently, already half-running back towards the stables. 'Please. Let's just get the horses out.'

Together they went back inside, through the choking smoke and the frightening flickers of flame.

'Mind they don't lash out, Grace!' warned Phil as she untied Judy and Isabella, two of the ponies.

Phil heard John calling from the doorway, asking what he could do to help. He shouted back to him. 'You're not so used to them as we are! We'll get 'em out to you and Carol and you take 'em away!'

John shouted back his agreement and came a few tentative steps in through the smoke. Grace handed Phil Isabella's reins and he led the snorting pony, its head dipping and rearing, out to John, who struggled to lead her clear. Judy was even more difficult to deal with, jibbing at the flames that were snaking across the ceiling, licking their way down the wooden partitions that had been the horses' sleeping quarters. In the end, on Grace's shouted instruction, Phil had to fling his coat over the pony's head and lead her blindly to safety, passing her reins to Carol, who needed Reggie's help to restrain the flailing head and hooves. Phil fought his way back in to find Grace leading out Chris's horse, Midnight.

'That the last?' he shouted.

Grace nodded.

'Oh, Phil, they're so frightened.'

He came the other side of Midnight's head and took hold of her bridle.

'You've got them all out, that's the main thing. Now for God's sake, Grace, let's get clear.'

They emerged coughing into the air to find that Reggie had returned with some water.

'Seems so useless, just a bucketful,' he said as he handed it to Phil.

Just then there was a whoosh of flame and the triumphant

crackling of blazing straw. Part of the loft floor had fallen.

'My God, this is ghastly!' exclaimed Reggie. 'Come on, Grace, they're out now! Get well away!'

But Grace didn't move. With her arms wrapped around her body, rocking slightly, she stood staring at the blaze as if hypnotized.

'It's an inferno in there,' said John, awestruck. 'Place must be as dry as tinder.'

'Where the hell are the brigade?' demanded Phil. 'How long are they going to –'

'Midnight! Midnight!'

He broke off as Grace's cry sang through the air.

'Oh no!' Carol put both hands to her cheeks. 'Midnight's gone back in. And Grace is going after her!'

Silhouetted against the vivid flame, Phil saw the horse moving and then Grace in her black dress in the bright doorway.

He sprinted forward with a speed he didn't know he had, yelling with a power he didn't know he had. It had never mattered so much that she hear him.

'Grace! Grace! Come back! The roof's collapsing! For God's sake, Grace, come back!'

The smoke was thick, black and ugly, almost worse than the flames. Phil wished he'd thought to soak a cloth in water and wrap it round his face, but he hadn't been thinking of anything but Grace. As he had dashed for the doorway, he had heard the awed gasps of onlookers as the roof caved in in a perfect 'V'.

'Don't let him go!' he'd heard Carol shriek and he had heard John's footsteps on the gravel beside him.

'Phil! Phil!' John had implored but just then Midnight, eyes rolling, muzzle foaming, had come straight at them out of the stable. Phil knew that there were others who could cope with the horse. His one concern was Grace. He plunged for the stable doorway. John followed him in.

'Grace! Grace!' Phil was almost sobbing. 'Oh my God, where is she?'

'I can't see!' John was coughing in the smoke.

Phil charged this way and that, calling Grace's name. There was no order to the inside of the stables any more, with one blazing loosebox merging into another. Where the roof had fallen, vast cross-beams stuck up at odd angles like shipwrecked timbers.

'There! Look!' Phil cried. 'Under the beam!'

John was miraculously beside him.

'Get it off her! Go on! Help me! Heave!'

Grace was slumped on her side with the beam across her chest. The wood was hot and charred.

'I can't budge it!' cried John helplessly.

Phil's voice was as raw as his hands. 'Heave!' he howled. 'Pull your guts out! For God's sake, John, just do it!'

But it was too much for the two of them. It was only when Reggie stumbled in through the smoke and found them that the three of them, pulling together, managed to lift the huge beam. Then John and Reggie somehow supported its weight between them as Phil dropped to his knees on the straw and crawled underneath to Grace. Gently he put his arms under her and tugged her towards him. He couldn't imagine what injuries she might have and he was terrified of hurting her more. All the time he talked to her, the kind of soothing, crooning talk he remembered from when he was small and had banged a knee or grazed an elbow.

'There, there, my darling, I've got you, it's going to be all right. I've got you, there, there, you're all right now.'

His cheeks were wet with tears as he gently dabbed at a deep gash on her head with his sleeve.

'Grace! Can you hear me? Grace . . .'

He felt John's hand on his shoulder and he knew they had to get out. With Reggie and John to steady him he staggered to his feet with Grace in his arms. Reggie indicated that he'd help, but Phil shook his head fiercely and tightened his grip around her. He wanted her all to himself. He was the only person he trusted to make sure she wasn't hurt any more.

• • •

At Brookfield that night the lights burned late in the kitchen. Phil had gone to Borchester Infirmary in the ambulance with Grace. Doris had finally taken herself off to bed but Christine, who had been playing badminton in Borchester with Paul, couldn't believe that she had had no prescience of what had been going on at the stables.

'I'll never play badminton again!' she reproached herself. 'What a fool I was!'

'No-one knew the place would go up,' said Dan reasonably. 'They reckon it was a spark from someone's garden bonfire got carried on the wind, you know.'

'I just can't take it in. All the work we've put in – and now Grace could be laid up for weeks –'

'They reckon she was just knocked out,' soothed Dan. 'And you know Grace, it'll take something pretty serious to keep her away from her horses for long.'

Christine fiddled with the pompom on the knitted tea cosy.

'I should have been there,' was all she said.

Suddenly, the catch on the back door was lifted. Slowly the door opened and Phil appeared. His dinner suit was scorched with flame and streaked with dust and water, but he had obviously washed his face, which seemed unnaturally clean and pale.

'Didn't expect you back quite so soon,' said Dan, surprised. 'Chris and I were . . . Phil? Phil, lad.' Phil closed the door softly behind him. He looked dreadful. 'Phil? What's gone wrong?'

For a long moment Phil didn't speak. When he did his voice seemed not his own.

'In my arms. On the way to hospital. She . . . she's dead.'

·8·

Living and Loving

All Ambridge suffered under a pall of shock and pain. That Grace – so bright, so vivacious – could be taken from them so suddenly and so violently was something the village simply could not comprehend.

'Is Auntie Grace still dead?' eight-year-old Lilian asked Peggy a week after the funeral. And though Peggy took her gently on her knee and explained that Auntie Grace was dead for ever and would not be coming back, the child's innocent question framed the disbelief of everyone who had known her.

Phil just shut down. In the early days after Grace's death, Doris had tried to persuade him to come back to Brookfield, and when he had insisted on staying at Coombe Farm, she had gone to stay with him for a few days. It broke her heart to see him aimlessly wandering about in the evening, after he had dutifully eaten his untasted meal, picking up and putting down the ornaments that they had been given as wedding presents or flicking through one of Grace's equestrian magazines that were still lying around. Fairbrother, grieving himself, told him to take as much time off as he needed, but Phil refused. Numbed, he discussed with a visiting horticulturalist the prospects for blackcurrants on the Estate, which would require taking over eight acres of Walter Gabriel's land, and he even went to the annual sheep sales at Knighton. Somehow he felt that if he carried on, put one foot in front of the other, day after day, he might get through the blanketing weight of utter despair that wrapped him round, or at least carry the burden without collapsing.

For urban folk the year was ending, with shorter days and crisper mornings, but in Ambridge another farming year was starting. Phil had never felt less like walking the fields to check the seed beds for the winter crops or setting the men on to break down the earth on the heavier land near the river. He did it all, of course, but there had never seemed less point to anything and he honestly didn't care if he was still alive himself to see the first green shoots next spring. He closed himself off. He put himself beyond anyone's reach and would not allow them to help him.

'He's keeping it all bottled up,' his mother fretted as she cut back some faded chrysanthemums in the long border beneath Brookfield's red-brick garden wall. 'I'm sure it's not good for him.'

Dan paused in his forking of the flowerbed.

'Look, love,' he said gently. 'It's only natural. See how a sick animal behaves – a sheep, for instance. When it's got something wrong with it, it sort of – gets away from the rest of the flock. Gets itself apart from 'em for a bit. It's easy enough to understand.'

'I don't like to think of him alone at Coombe Farm.' Doris put out a hand to Dan and struggled up from her kneeling position. He kept her hand in his.

'I know you don't. His mind's made up, though. And you'd better face it, love, that's how it's going to be.'

• • •

And that was how it was. On every new day without her, Phil got up in the morning with a heavy heart made only heavier by the day's activities and the prospect of returning at night to an empty house, one which – and this was the worst thought of all – might soon have been home to a brand new baby. Walter, Phil's godfather – and a fellow widower – had given him a corgi, Septimus, for company, and Phil felt even worse about appropriating some of his land for the blackcurrants. In the event, Walter announced that it had given him the push he needed: he intended giving up his farm on Lady Day and setting himself up as the village carrier.

Brookfield was not without its problems, too. Early in the new year, two pigs went lame. Realizing it was serious, Dan called in Robertson, the local vet, but he was totally unprepared for Robertson's diagnosis of suspected foot-and-mouth. Dan was utterly perplexed as to how the disease could have got on the farm in the first place, especially as it was the indoor pigs that were affected, and not the cows or sheep that roamed the pastures. But the outbreak was confirmed and, by the end of February, Dan's entire stock – every cloven-footed beast – had been shot on the farm and the carcasses buried under six feet of earth.

'One thing,' said the Ministry vet, a Job's comforter if ever there was one, as he dipped his wellingtons in the footbath that had been placed at the gate, 'you'll be having your cheque through for the valuation you agreed. We'll disinfect the place and four weeks on, all being well, we can declare the farm clean and free from infection.'

Dan's eyes travelled over the empty fields, the silent cowsheds.

'Don't know as I'll restock with a dairy herd,' he said. 'Not for the time being.'

'And how should we live then, without the monthly milk cheque?' asked Doris, alarmed.

'I'll do me best to see that you don't go hungry, love,' replied Dan drily.

'It would be a pretty drastic decision.' The vet pushed his trilby to the back of his head.

'Been thinking about it,' said Dan noncommittally. 'Might give myself a rest from twice-a-day milking. See how we get on.'

Doris looked at her husband suspiciously. Dan Archer, looking for a rest? She'd been trying to get him to retire ever since Phil had left the Farm Institute five years before. This was the man who had back copies of *Farmers Weekly* piled up in the office because he 'never had time' to read them. The man who filled in time between milking and his breakfast egg being cooked by chopping a few logs and who spent his Sunday afternoons in the workshop extending the rick rod. She knew what was wrong with Dan. He was tired, tired out with the shame of bringing the disease to the district and weary with worry-ing round and round in his head how the blessed illness had got on the farm in the first place.

Phil tried to interest him in broiler chickens. Dan wondered about beef stores. Eventually Doris insisted they go away for a few days, and chose Aberystwyth as their destination. It was there that Dan recovered enough to tease her, pretending that he was thinking of selling up and moving to this beautiful but remote spot. And it was when they returned to Ambridge that Dan finally got the answer to his question, when his farmhand, Len Thomas, admitted that some uncooked – and obviously infected – liver had got into the pig swill. Never one for uncertainties, once Dan had an answer he was reassured, and from then on he began to take a proper interest in the farm again. By the summer he had replaced the sheep with eighty Radnor-type ewes and two Downland rams and was talking about restocking in the autumn with Friesians instead of Shorthorns.

Doris breathed a sigh of relief. It was not yet a year since Grace's death and the anxiety at Brookfield had, she felt, made her neglect Phil. Looking for an excuse to invite herself round to Coombe Farm, she did the only thing she could think of and the thing that came most naturally to her. She made him a batch of scones and took them over with a pot of cream and a jar of her strawberry preserve. It was a Saturday afternoon in July, that short gap between haymaking and harvest, so she was sure of finding him at home. As she walked across the fields with her cloth-covered basket, feeling like a latter-day Red Riding Hood, she could hear Septimus barking in the garden. As she rounded a belt of trees she could see her son, in khaki shorts and an open-necked shirt, throwing a ball for the dog.

'Fetch, Timus,' he shouted as he hurled the ball through the air with the powerful throw that made him the Ambridge cricket team's secret weapon. Yelping with excitement, Timus hurled himself after it, leaping up as it began its descent to catch it in his mouth.

'That's it, good boy, bring it back,' Phil encouraged him as the dog's stumpy legs covered the ground again.

Doris paused and smiled. She would have far preferred to see Phil romping in the sun with one of his children, but since that dream was obviously not to be fulfilled just yet, it was joyous to see him being himself again instead of the thin ghost he had become over the winter. Reassured, she carried on her way, the basket somehow feeling lighter now, and resolving to say a special prayer of thanks at evensong in the grateful hope that the worst of everything really was behind them.

As if she needed any more to feel happy about, Christine, at long last, finally announced that she and Paul Johnson were getting engaged – just when Walter had hoped she might make a match with his son Nelson! And, with typical perverseness, Chris and Paul announced that they were not going to hang around much before getting married.

'The sooner the better, as far as I'm concerned,' declared Christine with her mouth full of cold roast beef one Monday lunchtime. 'Pass the pickle, please, Mum.'

Doris did so, smiling to herself. It would take more than the excitement of an engagement to put Christine off her food. Doris had been staggered when Chris had first arrived home wearing the ring, a square-cut ruby shouldered by two flashing diamonds. Chris explained that it had been in Paul's family for years.

'You're marrying money, then, are you?' asked Jack, blunt as usual, as Peggy examined the winking stones on Chris's finger.

'I am, brother dear,' retorted Chris, 'and it won't change me at all. I shall still drop by The Bull for a pineapple juice, even if I do pay for it with a £5 note and tell you to keep the change!'

'I'm not proud,' her brother replied. 'I'll look forward to it.'

But for Doris, the Johnsons' social status was an uncomfortable reminder of the inadequacy she had felt when faced with Grace, daughter of the local landowner, as a daughter-in-law. Admittedly, Dan was now an owner-occupier at Brookfield, but, especially since the foot-and-mouth, it was still a struggle much of the time. Now they faced the prospect of having to pay for a wedding that would not lose them face with the Johnsons – Herbert and Hilda, as Chris had been invited to call them – and with only a few months to put anything by.

'We'll manage, love,' Dan reassured her one breakfast time. 'Even if we have to sell a few of our heirlooms.'

'Such as what?' Doris reached for another piece of toast. 'There's only the silver-gilt tea caddy and the barometer in the hall.'

Dan scooped a wobbling spoonful of Doris's bitter marmalade from the jar.

'I was thinking more of your chutneys, love, and maybe some of that blackcurrant jam. They'd fetch a fine price on the open market.'

'Oh, you!' Doris shook her head in exasperated affection. 'When will you ever take me seriously?'

'Never, I hope,' chuckled Dan. 'But admit it, you love me for it, don't you?'

• • •

Chris and Paul were too busy being in love to worry overmuch about arrangements.

'Don't fuss, Mum,' Christine chided when Doris tried to settle her down to make a list of what was needed. 'It'll all get done.'

'But there's the cars to book, and photographers and heaven only knows what we'll do about flowers at that time of year!'

Chris and Paul had finally settled on 15 December as the date for their marriage – two days before Dan and Doris would themselves be celebrating their 35th wedding anniversary.

'Keep it simple.' Chris was already putting on her coat to go and meet Paul. 'Christmas roses, lots of greenery and a few sprays of berries.' She stooped to kiss her mother's worried face. 'Just ask Carol Grey to sort it out!'

But though she was blissfully happy, beneath Chris's nonchalance lay a nagging worry that the Johnsons would make trouble over the wedding arrangements – and beyond. They had already tried to make the couple delay the date of the wedding, saying that Paul still had to make his way in business. Then Mrs Johnson had tried to interfere over where they lived, showing Christine brochures of a new 'estate' on the outskirts of Borchester, where the houses had half-tiled upstairs bathrooms and even a garage.

But Chris and Paul stood firm. They were going to make their home in a converted coach house at the stables at Walton Grange, where Chris now ran her riding school in partnership with Paul's sister, Sally, while Paul concentrated on horsebreeding and improving the bloodlines.

Even before the wedding, when the place was still empty, they spent happy evenings there emulsioning ceilings, planning where they would put the sofa and the standard lamp and admiring the spiral staircase that led out of the living room, a modern touch they were both very pleased with. One night, when they snuggled up together in the sagging armchair that Chris had rescued from the attic at Brookfield, the subject of Christmas arose. They both realized that they would be the subject of fierce competition between the two sets of parents for where they spent Christmas Day.

'So, what's it to be?' asked Paul, stroking the nape of her neck in the way that she loved. 'Christmas Day with my folks and Boxing Day with yours?'

Chris stared hard at the luminous bars of the electric fire.

Paul gently turned her head to face him. 'What's wrong?'

'Couldn't we have Christmas on our own?' asked Chris in a small voice. 'We shall only have been married about ten days. Just back from our honeymoon.'

'I know,' said Paul. 'But for the sake of peace and quiet . . . It's only a couple of days.'

Chris looked at him. He had such blue eyes – deep and deep-set. When he looked at her and she looked at him, her heart seemed to do a slow somersault that took her breath away.

'Paul,' she said, taking his hand, 'what would you like to do? Honestly.'

'It isn't about what I'd like to do,' he sighed.

'No,' she conceded. 'So what do you feel we ought to do?'

'All right,' Paul kissed her fingertips. 'Spend Christmas with the folks. After all . . . once the children start arriving we shan't want to spend Christmas away from home.'

Chris exploded with laughter.

'I love the airy way you talk about children,' she smiled. 'How many are you anticipating?'

'Not less than four,' Paul declared firmly.

She could see that he meant it.

'You won't forget that we've got a foxhunter competition to win, will you?' she chided him, sliding her arms round his neck and bending her head for his kiss.

'You leave that to me.' Paul's arm crept round her shoulders and pulled her towards him. 'In fact, leave everything to me.'

• • •

'Chris! Chris! Over here!' Balanced precariously on the churchyard wall, with John Tregorran holding his legs, Phil tried to attract the bride's attention.

Back in the autumn, after the first awful anniversary of Grace's death, Fairbrother had called Phil up to the house and in a transparent attempt to give him a new interest, had announced that he'd come up with the perfect Christmas present for him – a cine-camera.

'That's very good of you, sir,' said Phil, perplexed. 'But why mention it now?'

'Ah well, there's method in my madness.' George Fairbrother was slighter and greyer now – greyer in the face as well as round the hair-line. 'It's Christine's wedding, isn't it, before Christmas and it seems a shame not to be able to capture that on film.' He paused and stared out of the window. Jim Benson was driving by with a load of hay for the ewes. Both men watched the tractor pass and disappear up the track. Phil waited for Fairbrother to speak. When he didn't, he prompted him.

'Sir?'

'What? Oh, sorry.' This happened a lot these days. Since Grace's death, Fairbrother seemed to drift away in the middle of a conversation to a world of his own. Phil knew only too well who the only other inhabitant of that world was. 'Yes, now, what was I saying . . . ?'

'Paul and Chris's wedding.'

Fairbrother inclined his head.

'It's about time your family had something to celebrate, Philip,' he said. 'About time we all did. I don't want the day clouded for you by . . . memories. Of course it'll affect you. It'll affect all of us. But I thought if you had something to keep you busy, it might help.'

Phil was touched by the older man's thoughtfulness.

'Well, sir, I'm grateful,' he replied. 'And I'll do my best to make Chris and Paul a record of the day that they'll be proud of.'

• • •

The wedding scene was everything a budding cameraman-director would want. It was one of those startlingly clear December days, with piercing sunshine which, out of the wind, even felt warm. Chris, everyone agreed, looked a picture in her dress of white lace with its billowing paper taffeta petticoats. Paul, tall, dark and classically handsome ('Don't you hate him?' John Tregorran had whispered mischievously to Phil) was her perfect foil in his morning suit with a white rose in his buttonhole. The bridesmaids, Paul's sister Sally and a friend of Chris's from Borchester Dairies, looked stunning in turquoise velvet cut on the empire line. Doris was resplendent in a violet silk dress and jacket and even Mrs Johnson, whose presence had once been in doubt owing to a heavy cold, was there in an ivory-coloured hat and a full-length mink coat.

'Personally I'm surprised she's not wearing black,' Chris whispered to Peggy as they waited for the photographer to assemble all the guests outside St Stephen's. Mrs Johnson had made no secret of the fact that she thought her only son could have done better for himself than Christine. 'But I'm glad she's here.'

Phil darted busily around, dodging the gravestones as he tried to get cine shots from every angle. Sally had organized a surprise guard of honour of helpers and prize pupils from the stables mounted on ponies and Phil wanted a long shot of Chris and Paul making their way through it from the church porch. The horses were then to provide an escort for the bride's car as it made its way up to Grey Gables for the reception. Petrol rationing had been reintroduced earlier in the year and John Tregorran, as usher, had the job of fitting as many people into as few cars as possible for the journey. But since Carol Grey, who was in charge of the flowers, was a guest, it was no hardship for John: all the village knew he would do anything to be near her.

'Perhaps it'll give him a few ideas,' Reggie Trentham commented to his wife Valerie as the guests arrived at the country club for their lunch of minestrone soup and chicken Marengo.

'He's already got the idea, dear,' Valerie replied drily, straightening a place setting. 'Persuading Carol Grey that it's a good one is another matter. Now, do you think there are enough trays of sherry in circulation?'

Before they went through to lunch, Chris pulled Phil to one side.

'Did you get all your pictures?' she asked.

'I think I did,' mused Phil. 'Shan't know till the film's developed, though. The trouble is that you only get one chance at these things.'

'You don't, you know, Phil.' Chris suddenly put her hand on his arm, the unaccustomed wedding band bright and new. 'I know how hard it must have been for you today. But you will get another chance to be happy. You must,' she added fiercely, 'or there's no justice in life!'

Phil squeezed her hand.

'Look, you shouldn't be worrying about me,' he said. 'It's your day, yours and Paul's. I'm just very happy for you.'

'Oh, Phil.' Chris's eyes glimmered with tears. 'I don't know how you do it, I really don't. If I ever lost Paul –'

'Lose him? He'll be divorcing you for desertion if you don't get along and take your place at the top table with him. Now come on, Chris, no tears, please. Your guests are waiting!'

But he was touched by her concern for him on her own big day. And, yes, she was right. Today had been hellish. Phil knew that he must have come under consideration for the role of best man, but assumed that everyone had thought that having to stand at the altar, where less than two years ago he had himself stood as the bridegroom, would be too much for him. He was more and more admiring of Fairbrother's foresight in giving him the cine-camera, which at least had occupied his time before and after the church service.

He looked at his watch. Paul and Chris were leaving by the London train from Hollerton Junction at four. Less than three hours of jollity, then he could go home, change out of these confounded clothes, collect Timus and stroll down to the village. Timus, who had been shut up all day, would welcome the walk and the exciting, earthy, twilight smells and Phil knew just where they would walk to. He would go and lay his buttonhole on Grace's grave and remember how she had looked on their own wedding day and how – for him – she would always look.

• • •

Doris was glad to get away from the reception, too. Not wanting to look unsophisticated in front of the Johnsons, she had reluctantly accepted a glass of sherry from one of the circulating waitresses and at lunch had had half a glass of wine, as well as a few sips of champagne for the toasts. Now she had the makings of a throbbing headache, her feet had swollen in their black patent shoes and though she felt she couldn't eat or drink another thing, you could be sure Dan would be starving again by six and she'd have to stand at the stove frying him a couple of gammon rashers and an egg. But Dan could see that she was tired, and when they got home he steered her gently into the parlour, where he had laid and lit the fire before they left for church so that the room was comfortably warm. He brought her the footstool and they sat together in the half darkness, almost too tired to speak.

'Went well, I thought,' Dan said eventually. 'Didn't you? No hitches at all.'

'No, none,' agreed Doris. 'And she did look nice in her going-away suit, didn't she?'

Chris had chosen a fitted costume in raspberry-coloured tweed with a velvet collar.

Dan nodded.

'Aye.'

Doris knew without saying that he was thinking of Christine as a small girl in a similar coloured velvet dress she had had one

Christmas – a hand-me-down from someone. Doris couldn't remember who, but Chris had loved it. Doris sighed.

'I hope I don't feel this tired into next week,' she said. 'There's a lot to do. Jack's birthday, and the turkeys to pluck, and the whole house to get ready for Christmas.'

'Get Bess to come in and help,' said Dan, referring to Simon Cooper's wife. 'She'll be glad of a few bob extra this time of year.'

'Maybe I will,' said Doris.

Just then, there was a knock on the back door and it opened on its squeaky hinge.

'Where are you, then?' came a surprised voice.

'That you, Tom?' called Dan.

'We're in the other room for once,' called Doris. 'Come on through.'

Tom had done a sterling job, along with John Tregorran, in marshalling people into the waiting cars and in seeing that the pony escort got off on time.

'Thanks for all your help today, Tom,' said Dan as his brother-in-law settled himself on the other side of the fireplace. 'You'd be useful on point duty any time.'

''Twas no trouble. I thought it went off all right.'

'Wonderful,' agreed Doris.

It was a mystery to her why Tom, at forty-six years old ten years her junior, had never married. He always said his lifestyle as a game-keeper – late nights and early mornings – wasn't one that would suit a wife, but their own father had been a gamekeeper and their family life had been happy enough. Doris knew how much Tom valued being part of her and Dan's family at Brookfield and she knew that he must have felt a pang at today's ceremony.

'I'm too old for all that caper nowadays, anyhow,' he'd said brusquely when she'd last mentioned the subject of romance – the time when Agatha Turvey, a somewhat forthright widow, had invited Tom round to her cottage for the evening. But Doris, who would have liked to see Tom settled, wished he could meet the right woman – not Agatha Turvey, but someone homely who'd look after him, cook his dinners, mend his socks and give him a kiss before he set off to work. After all, he was such a good sort. Look at the help he'd been recently to Pru Harris, the barmaid at The Bull, helping her to sort out her mother's will. She sighed out loud.

'I've got a sort of flat feeling, though, now the wedding's all over.'

'Missing Chris already?' enquired Tom.

'S'pose I am really. Not that I haven't got plenty to be getting on with,' she added.

'Well, one thing's for sure,' grinned Tom. 'You might be thinking about her, but – and I don't mean this to be hurtful – I don't suppose she's thinking about you. Probably her mind's too full of her brand-new husband.'

'More than likely,' agreed Dan, relighting his pipe with a spill from the fire. He puffed on it thoughtfully. 'Still, if they have as good a time together as Doris and I have had all these years, they won't do too badly.'

Doris looked over at him lovingly. He was the best husband and father anyone could wish for. If Chris had one hundredth of the happiness with Paul that she and Dan had had together, she'd be doing pretty well. Oh, Jack and Peggy rubbed along together all right, and Jack was certainly pulling his weight at The Bull these days. Now that the children were older – Jennifer had already started at senior school, for goodness' sake – the tensions in the household seemed less. But it was still a scratchy marriage, and the living quarters at The Bull never seemed to have that safe feeling that only a loving atmosphere can create. Then there was Phil, still rattling around at Coombe Farm with only Timus for company, with his life – how had Carol Grey put it once? – with his life in cold storage. Surely, thought Doris, it didn't seem too much to ask for one of her children's marriages to turn out well? But before she could get too reflective, Dan stood up.

'I'd better look in on the cows,' he announced. 'And then, you know, Doris, an egg and a couple of rashers wouldn't go amiss. And I'll bet Tom could use a bite of supper, too, couldn't you, Tom?'

Doris smiled inwardly. She could read Dan like a book – and after all these years he was still her favourite reading material.

'That'd be smashing,' Tom concurred. 'Any chance of some fried bread?'

'Fried bread? Did you miss your breakfast or something?' demanded Doris, getting up. 'You haven't been looking after yourself properly.'

There was no doubt about it. Tom, like Phil, but for different reasons, definitely needed a wife.

·9·

A Shot in the Dark

Doris wasn't to know it – that's younger brothers for you, never tell you anything – but Tom was fonder of Pru Harris than he was letting on. Timid in the extreme, and rather plain with her scraped-back hair and funny old-fashioned clothes, Peggy had initially been surprised at Jack's choice to fill the bar job at the pub.

'She's hardly going to attract the customers, is she?' Peggy had said when Jack had announced he was keen on her for the position. 'She's no Rita Flynn in the looks department – or personality, come to that.'

'Ah, but the punters have you for that, my dear,' wheedled Jack, who was in an expansive mood. A rep had called with a selection of liqueurs that his firm was pushing for cocktails and Jack had sampled most of them, brilliant in their exotically shaped bottles. 'What we need is a hard worker who's not going to run off with a ploughboy and leave us in the lurch.'

'Hmm.' Peggy was unconvinced. 'Can she cook?'

'Pru Harris? Cook? She's been champion pickle- and chutney-maker at the village show for years. One year she pips Mum at the post, next year Mum snatches the trophy back –'

'I don't have time for making jams and chutneys, in case you haven't noticed, Jack. And I certainly don't have time to look at all the entries in the village show.'

'Well, there's your answer, anyway. She's more than capable of setting up a round of cheese and tomato sandwiches. And I dare say, if push came to shove, she'd make a mean steak and kidney pie to put on the menu.'

'Well, that's something. I certainly wouldn't mind spending less time in the pub kitchen.'

'That's settled then, I'll offer her the job. She's not on the telephone but I could send a message over with Uncle Tom. He seems to be sorting out her business affairs for her. Or at least,' he winked, 'that's his story!'

• • •

Jack and Peggy were, in a sense, right in their assessment. Pru Harris was no Marilyn Monroe. But she wasn't without suitors – some more welcome than others.

The trouble started early in the new year when Ned Larkin's brother, Bob, came to visit. Ned was a reliable sort of bloke. He'd proved himself a good worker at Brookfield since he had replaced Simon Cooper, who had retired to become the village's jobbing gardener. But Bob was a different story.

'If he reminds me of anyone, it's that no-good Bill Slater,' Dan told Doris one day when Bob had been hanging around waiting for Ned to finish work. 'Blow me if he wasn't eyeing up the slates on the barn. He'd have them off and sold before you could say steeplejack.'

'Dan, that's a terrible thing to say,' chided Doris.

'You mark my words. Bob Larkin is trouble, love. The sooner he goes back where he came from, the better.'

But Bob, it seemed, had no intention of leaving Ambridge alone. He took a shine to Pru, and every night you could find him in the public bar at The Bull drinking gin and peppermint and trying to persuade her to have a drink with him. Occasionally, for politeness' sake, she would accept a grapefruit juice, but in general tried to find excuses not to stand chatting, pleading customers to serve or glasses to wash. This was fine when the pub was busy, but one night in early January, the slush underfoot and the bitter wind contrived to keep everyone by their own firesides, and Pru found herself trapped in the bar parlour with a very insistent Bob.

'Come on,' he urged, 'one little kiss never hurt anybody.'

'No, Mr Larkin. Please, don't be like this.'

Pru prayed for someone to come out from the back, but it was Anthony William Daniel's bedtime and Mrs Peggy would be upstairs, while Mr Jack, she knew, was changing a barrel in the cellar. Just then the pub door opened and, along with a freezing blast of air, in walked Tom Forrest. Pru had never in her life been so grateful to see anyone.

'Are you all right, Pru, lass?' he asked brusquely, having seen the situation at a glance.

'Of course she's all right. Why shouldn't she be?' Bob took a defiant gulp of his drink.

'Just struck me she might be having trouble with one of the customers.' Tom's voice was cold.

'I'm the only customer here. Fill that up, will you, sweetheart?' Bob pushed his glass across the counter.

Pru reached out for it without saying a word. Tom settled himself on a bar stool.

'I reckon now as I'm here I might just have a half of shandy,' he said. 'If I'm not interrupting.'

Pru shot him a grateful look but Bob looked thunderous.

'Forget the drink,' he snapped at Pru. 'I'll come back another time when the atmosphere's less frosty.'

• • •

Next day, Tom confided in Doris. She had walked down to see him at the pheasant coverts, bringing him a seed cake.

'All I'm worried about is Pru,' he explained. 'I don't give a darn for Bob Larkin. And by all accounts he don't give a darn for anyone else either.'

'You're jealous,' said Doris astutely.

'That's enough of that talk!' Tom shut the gate on one of the release pens, where he had been checking on the birds. 'I've got a high respect for Pru Harris and I don't want to see her led up the garden path by Bob Larkin or anybody else.'

'Maybe you should have proposed to her then,' said Doris. 'Bob Larkin has – twice, by all accounts.'

Tom looked at his boots.

'Aye, maybe I should,' he admitted. 'But if he carries on bothering her like he's doing, or if he makes her a promise and then lets her down, he'll have me to answer to. And I'm telling you, Doris, I'd bash his face in soon as look at him.'

Doris had never heard her brother so vehement. Tom was the gentlest of men, but on top of all this business with Pru, it was the height of the shooting season and he was working all hours. There were poachers in the district and although Fairbrother, for whom Tom now worked, understood that his gamekeeper could not be everywhere at once, Tom blamed himself for every bird lost. He had been keeping vigil, sometimes throughout the night, and was clearly exhausted. And when people are exhausted, thought Doris, emotions always run high.

'Come to Brookfield for your tea tonight, Tom,' she suggested. 'Phil'll be there. He might have some ideas for beating these poachers.'

Apart from giving Tom a good feed, she didn't really expect the evening to achieve anything, but when Tom and Phil got to talking about the poaching, they actually did come up with an idea.

'What you need is to play the poachers at their own game,' urged Phil. 'You never know when they're going to be there. They never know when you're going to be there. But what if they knew for certain you weren't going to be there?'

'You've lost me, lad.' Tom scratched his head. 'If I'm not there, how can I catch the blighters?'

'Ah, but you will be.' Phil outlined his plan. 'How about you put a story around saying you'll be away. I don't know, gone to look at some new birds or something . . . '

'I could say I was going to Fordingbridge,' put in Tom, 'the game-rearing place. There's always summat to look at there.'

'Fordingbridge! Perfect.' Phil unwrapped another chocolate from the tin that Tom had brought with him and popped it into his mouth. 'Get the train from Hollerton, get off at the next station and I'll pick you up there. I'll even watch the night out with you if you like.'

Tom shook his head in admiration. 'Phil, that's brilliant. You're wasted working for Fairbrother.'

'Ah, to be sure, I learnt a thing or two about undercover work from Mike Daly,' grinned Phil, imitating Mike's Irish accent. 'So – are we on?'

• • •

But the plan, which had seemed so brilliantly simple in its description, was not as straightforward in its execution. Later Phil often reproached himself for getting his uncle into a situation which turned out so disastrously.

It really did seem as if it was going to work. Only Tom, Fairbrother and Phil knew that Tom was not at Fordingbridge, and once Phil had collected him from Merton Halt, the next station down the line, his uncle hid out the day in one of the poultry sheds, grabbing a bit of sleep on some sacking and waiting for nightfall. When dusk fell, at barely four o'clock, Tom went through the top half of the woods with the dogs, pushing the birds down to Long Cover, where he and Phil planned to lie in wait and where the poachers would have to come to find what they were looking for – and two people that they weren't.

It was the longest of nights. It was gone three before they heard the sound they had been waiting for: the sound of a four-ten being fired on the crest of the hill. From bitter experience, Tom knew that the culprit would work his way down on one side of the cover or the other.

'All we've got to do is separate and move round quietly. Keep about fifty yards apart,' whispered Tom. 'Don't rush it and take it steady. We'll hear him having another go or two. One or other of us is bound to stumble across him.'

Phil nodded his agreement.

'Don't forget.' Tom was already scrambling out of the shallow ditch they had scraped in the earth to conceal themselves. 'Whoever catches him, blow sharp on your whistle and the other'll come running.'

• • •

Phil was scrambling through some bracken when he heard it. Two sharp blasts on the whistle, way to his right.

'Uncle Tom?' Dodging the low branches, slithering on leaf mould underfoot, Phil followed the sound, straining his ears for any more noise. Soon he could hear the grunts of a struggle and knew that his uncle had got his man.

'Uncle Tom?' he called again.

'Over here!' Tom sounded desperate. There was the sound of greenery smashing as the two of them fell through some bushes, presumably struggling for control of the gun. The man was clearly a fighter. Then Phil heard Tom's voice, in a tone of utter surprise.

'Bob Larkin!'

'Gerroff! Leave hold of me!' It was the other man's voice.

'Go on! Give me the gun!'

'I'm coming, Uncle Tom! Hold on!'

But Phil couldn't get there quickly enough and he was still some twenty yards away when he heard the shot followed by an even more ear-splitting silence. Fearing what he would find, he broke through the undergrowth to find his uncle standing dishevelled over a dark shape on the floor.

'What – you're covered in blood!'

'I'm all right.' Tom's voice was low and trembling. 'Shine it on him down there. I know who it is.'

'Who?'

His uncle confirmed the name Phil had heard spoken during the struggle.

'Bob Larkin.'

Phil shone his torch down on the ground, then immediately wished he hadn't. The shot must have entered beneath the chin.

'Oh, my God.'

He turned away, sickened, and heard his uncle retch.

'Don't touch him,' Phil said, knowing he had to take charge of things. 'Don't touch anything ... Just stay here – or somewhere around.'

'I can't believe it.' The words were barely audible.

'Don't move him. Don't do anything. Here's the torch. Just stick around. I'll be as quick as I can.'

'Where are you going?'

'To fetch a doctor, of course. And I'll have to call the police. But Uncle Tom, listen to me. Don't move him. Don't go near him. And for God's sake, don't touch anything and don't move from here.'

• • •

'Murder? Our Tom?'

'Now you see why I made you sit down. Look, Mum, I'm sorry, but that's the charge.'

'They'll never make it stick, will they?' Dan poured boiling water into the teapot. Phil had warned his parents when he had arrived at the farm that a cup of strong, sweet, tea might be in order – and told his father that for once he didn't think his mother should be the one to make it.

Phil dug the apostle spoon into the sugar bowl, watching the heaped crystals slide over its surface.

'They've already taken my statement. I said it was an accident, which it was. Larkin was poaching. He had four or five birds on him. Uncle Tom caught him, they were struggling for possession of the gun and it went off. Those are the facts.'

'It's not just about the facts, though, is it?' Doris was crying quietly. She groped in her apron pocket for a handkerchief. 'They'll ask questions all round the village. Everyone knows there was no love lost between Tom and Bob Larkin.'

'Your Mum's right, Phil.' Dan carried the teapot over to the table. 'Do you reckon Tom knew who he was fighting with? Before he saw the body on the ground, I mean.'

Dan stirred the pot and covered it with the knitted blue-and-yellow-striped tea cosy. Phil had seen the big-bellied brown earthenware pot stirred thousands of times on this table but the simple action seemed new and incomprehensible. He had grown up with that tea cosy but today he felt as if he had never seen it before.

Shock, perhaps. And lack of sleep. He blinked and tried to concentrate on what his father was saying.

'I'm afraid so. I heard him say his name when they were struggling. He knew all right.'

Doris gave a little whimper and buried her face in her hands.

'Come on love. He'll be all right.' Dan put his arm round her.

'You don't understand!' Doris burst out. 'You don't know what he said to me! He said – he said he felt like bashing Bob Larkin's face in!'

'Did he? When?'

Doris explained about her conversation with her brother in the pheasant coverts. Phil looked thoughtful.

'You're not saying you think he meant it, are you, Mum?'

'Of course he meant it! But all he meant was he'd give him a good hiding if he made any more trouble. Not to . . . not to . . . not this!'

She buried her face in her hands again. Dan patted her awkwardly on the shoulder.

'All right, love, don't take on,' he soothed. 'It all depends whether he said anything similar to anybody else, I suppose,' he went on. 'I mean, we can keep it quiet, but –'

'It'd look bad for him if it came out, wouldn't it?' his mother said, raising her damp face again.

'Well, it certainly wouldn't help.' Phil said no more. He had enough to worry about. He was already wondering what the police would make of the Fordingbridge bluff when and if they found out about it – as they surely would. Would it be better to tell them before the ticket inspector from Merton Halt, where Uncle Tom had got off the train, read about the case in the papers and went to the police of his own volition? In fact, should he have mentioned it when he gave his statement?

There was a knock on the back door and it opened. George Fairbrother entered, stooping under the low doorway.

'Mr Fairbrother!' Phil jumped up to offer the older man a seat and Doris, embarrassed, dabbed her eyes and screwed her handkerchief into the palm of her hand.

'I haven't come to intrude,' said Fairbrother. 'You need to be a family at a time like this. I just want you to know that I'll do all in my powers to help Tom out of this. I've had the police round. There's no doubt in my mind that it was an accident and I want you to know that I've been on to Bannister, my solicitor, asking him to represent Tom's interests. For what it's worth, I shall also be putting a call in to the Chief Constable.'

Mention of the Chief Constable set Doris off weeping again and Dan ushered her out of the room, leaving Phil and his employer together.

'It's a mess,' Fairbrother said brusquely. 'But that doesn't mean we can't sort it out.'

'I hope so,' said Phil, though the more he thought about it, the blacker things looked for Uncle Tom.

'All the poor chap's worrying about is who'll exercise his dogs and check the tunnel traps. That's Tom for you. Utterly conscientious. An all-round good sort. Not the sort who goes to prison for murder.'

'No.' Phil looked at Fairbrother gratefully. 'Thank you for all you're doing, sir. And for your support.'

But even as he said it, Phil had never felt more despondent about Uncle Tom's chances.

• • •

Things got worse, as they always do. The charge was considered serious enough for Tom to be remanded in custody in Borchester jail between hearings. In the meantime, two people unfortunately let slip to the local policeman, Geoff Bryden, who had replaced Randall on his promotion to sergeant, that Tom had also said to them that he would bash Bob Larkin's face in. Though they went to great lengths to say that it had just been a figure of speech, the fact was still out in the open. The police also established that Tom had known from the start who he was fighting with and, as Phil had suspected, swiftly discovered the elaborate trick they had played over the supposed trip to Fordingbridge.

At the end of March, Borchester Petty Sessions Court decided that there was a case to answer, which meant another, longer, wait for a date at the Assizes. But at least bail of £100 – on a surety of £50 each from Tom and Mr Fairbrother – was agreed and Tom came home to Ambridge, thinner and paler, not so much from lack of food as from lack of fresh air and exercise. He stayed a night or two at Brookfield, but then insisted on going back to his cottage. Doris would have preferred to keep him under her own roof where she could keep an eye on him – and feed him up – but he was insistent. He even refused a lift back, saying he preferred to walk.

'Well, you can understand it, can't you?' said Dan thoughtfully. 'Maybe if you lived in a prefab and dived straight out of there on to a Tube in the mornings and then into a little smelly city office, then back on to the Tube again and back into your prefab at night, you might have got yourself adjusted to prison life a bit easier than Tom. Though I dunno, maybe not ... But for a chap who's been more or less a free agent all his life, with room to move around, it must be a pretty soul-destroying thing.' He paused for a swig of tea. 'That's why he wanted to walk, Doris. He wanted to get the feel of the turf under his boots again. To feel the wind in his face. To smell the land.'

Tom had been released just at the time when the land was coming alive again. He had always loved this time of year, the buds like little green buttons, the shivering catkins over the river, the busy blue tits building their nests. But this year spring had for him a luminous beauty. He could not look too long at the green grass before tears came to his eyes, and when he climbed Lakey Hill and surveyed the vastness of the Vale of Am stretching into the distance, it seemed almost incomprehensible compared with the tiny cell he had lived in and where, in his lowest moments, he imagined being incarcerated again for a much, much longer period.

One day in May he was busy cutting hazel boughs when PC Bryden came to tell him that the date for the Assizes had been set for 4 July. The hearing was expected to last at least two full days, but the charge would be manslaughter, not murder. Tom pretended to be consoled, since everyone seemed to think it was such good news, but always in his mind's eye he could see that cell, the tiny window letting in hardly any light, and certainly no air, and the grille in the door, which might be banged open at any hour of the night or day so they could make sure you hadn't done away with yourself. Tom knew that if they locked him up again, that's exactly what he would do. Somehow, he'd find a way.

. . .

The date of the trial meant that the first week of July would be a momentous one for Ambridge, for Saturday the sixth was the date of the annual village fête. The vicar, as always, was pondering how best to maximize the profits, which meant not just increasing the number of sideshows and attractions, but getting more people through the gate.

'And the best way to do that, it seems to me,' he declared at one of the interminable fête committee meetings at the village hall, 'is to get a celebrity figure to open it.'

A hum of interest went round the table.

'What sort of celebrity? You're thinking of someone local, I take it?' asked John Tregorran, who was always at the centre of village activities and was especially keen on getting young people involved.

'Not necessarily.' The vicar's eyes twinkled. 'But before you come under pressure from the youngsters at the youth club, John, I believe Rock Hudson's booked up until the year 2000 and Bill Haley and the Comets sadly have a prior engagement.'

Everyone laughed, but the vicar raised his hand for quiet. 'I'm serious. I think we should look a bit further afield than that chap from Waterley Cross who does the comic monologues on the wireless. What we want is – a star!'

The meeting broke up and everyone went away to think about it, instructed to come to the next meeting with suggestions.

'I think I'll concentrate on my lavender bags,' said Doris to Dan's sister-in-law Laura, who had arrived from New Zealand following the death of her husband, Frank, Dan's brother, and was staying at Brookfield. 'What do I know about stars of stage and screen?'

'You're overfilling those lavender bags, you know,' was all Laura said. She and Doris were not getting along. 'How much are you thinking of charging for them?'

• • •

One sunny summer Sunday, the vicar gave a particularly ebullient sermon about the three talents and buttonholed Phil and Christine after the service.

'I've fixed it!' he proclaimed. 'Somebody famous. And what a scoop for Ambridge!' Phil and Chris looked at each other, amused. The vicar was cock-a-hoop. 'Up to the minute, a modern celebrity. Go on, guess!'

'But – in what way is he famous? It is a he, I presume?' asked Phil. The vicar nodded.

'Yes, give us a clue. Politics? Art? Sport? Literature?' hazarded Christine.

Beyond suggesting 'art' the vicar didn't give them much help, and it was only when they had run through all the painters they could think of from Sir Gerald Kelly to Pietro Annigoni, who had recently painted the Queen's portrait, that he revealed that the celebrity's speciality was, in fact, music.

'If he's a skiffle expert or an Elvis Presley type, you're in trouble,' joked Phil. 'I don't think they're the speech-making sort. I can't understand what they sing,' he added, 'let alone when they speak.'

'I don't think you'll be able to say that about this particular musician,' said the vicar smugly. 'I can vouch for his being intelligible.'

'The Eton and Oxford type, what?' smiled Christine.

'The only chap I know who fills that bill is . . . no, you can't have!' exclaimed Phil.

'Go on,' urged the vicar.

'It isn't!' cried Christine. 'you don't honestly mean you've got Humph. The one and only Humphrey Lyttleton!'

But the vicar had done just that, apparently through a friend who was a curate in Humphrey Lyttleton's parish in London.

'Surprised, eh? I told you I'd find someone to pull 'em in!'

The news spread round the village like a forest fire and though some of the 'stick-in-the-muds', as John Tregorran called them, were initially suspicious, the reaction of everyone else vindicated the vicar in his choice.

'And if anyone does tell me outright they object, well . . . ' he said to John Tregorran as they drew up the plan of the stalls, 'I shall tell them not to be a bunch of squares!'

But as excitement mounted in Ambridge about the fête and its celebrity guest, the atmosphere at Brookfield was still overlaid with tension about the outcome of Tom's forthcoming trial. The only good thing to have come out of the whole business for Tom was a new closeness to Pru, who had come to see him in prison, immediately allaying any fears he might have had that she would want nothing to do with a 'jailbird'. When his day's work was over, he would regularly drop by The Bull for a half of shandy, and on her evenings off they would walk in the early summer sunshine on the banks of the Am. She loved the countryside as much as he did and understood his need to be quiet. Nothing more specific was said between them. They were not even officially 'walking out together'. It would have been ridiculous at their ages: he was forty-six, she was thirty-five. But there was an unspoken agreement that they should spend as much of this time together as possible and, though Tom hardly dared think beyond the date of the trial, maybe, in the future, even more.

· · ·

The fourth of July was warm and sultry. Thunder had rumbled over the Hassett Hills during the night, and as Tom clambered into his best suit and put on the fresh shirt and collar that Doris had laundered for him, he longed to be getting into his working clothes and setting off for the woods to feel the fretful sun on his back and the first inevitable spots of rain. He hoped the thunder would blow itself out before Saturday, the day of the fête, which depended on a sunny day for its success. And he hoped against hope he would be there to see it.

Dan, Phil, Walter, John Tregorran and, of course, George Fairbrother were in court to hear the case being tried. All day, with the ceiling fans whirring and the clerk to the court scribbling furiously, the same evidence was picked over time and again as different witnesses were questioned by Tom's counsel, Mr Cloudsley, and the barrister for the prosecution, Mr Grice. It was not long after the afternoon tea break and Phil was on the stand being cross-examined, when suddenly the foreman of the jury got to his feet. He was a short chap, wiry, with close-cropped grey hair and a suit that had seen better days but he had a quiet authority and it was easy to see why he had been elected foreman.

'My lord,' he said when he had got the judge's attention, 'having regard to the evidence we have already heard, my colleagues and I do not wish to hear any more.'

A murmur went round the court.

'Am I to understand,' asked the judge, 'that it is not necessary for you to hear any further evidence on behalf of the defence? And that you wish at this stage to return a verdict?'

'Yes, my lord.'

Tom gripped the rail in front of him. Dan sat forward, his hands between his knees.

'This is pretty unusual,' whispered John Tregorran to Walter.

'Ar. But is it good for Tom?' his neighbour replied.

But the clerk to the court was on his feet and addressing the foreman of the jury.

'Are you all agreed upon your verdict?'

'Yes, sir.'

'Do you find the prisoner guilty or not guilty upon the charge in the indictment?'

The pause before the foreman spoke seemed interminable.

'Not guilty, sir.'

• • •

Jack Archer replaced the telephone receiver and turned to Peggy, who had been standing at his elbow while he took the call. Phil had promised he would phone them as soon as the verdict was known.

'Well?' she asked eagerly.

'Discharged,' announced Jack triumphantly, 'without a stain on his character.' He grabbed her by the waist and whirled her round the hall. 'Here . . . give us a kiss to celebrate.'

'There's no time for all that.' Peggy disentangled herself. 'I've got to get the function room ready, or Walter'll never forgive me.'

Though the family, in their darkest moments, had had tremors of doubt, Walter had been convinced ever since Tom's arrest that he would get off.

'And that'll be the excuse for the best and biggest celebration Ambridge has seen since . . . since . . . well, since I last throwed a party,' he had declared in the public bar back in the spring, telling Peggy to reserve the function room for the night Tom's trial ended. 'And that's not all,' he'd added with a twinkle. 'I'll surprise him some other way too, you see if I don't.'

As Peggy bustled off to start cutting sandwiches, Jack called after her. 'Pru was there all day, apparently. Didn't miss a moment of the trial.'

'I should think not, after you'd given her the day off specially.'

Jack followed his wife through the swing door into the kitchen. 'Rumour says she and Uncle Tom are sweet on each other,' he remarked. 'And they say there's no smoke without fire.'

Peggy took a tray of eggs from the pantry and filled a huge pan with water to bring it to the boil.

'You should be the last person to talk like that, Jack Archer.'

'Me?' Jack watched her as she began to slice a large tin loaf. 'Why, what rumours are there about me?'

'Ooh, you'd be surprised. Good job you've got a nice, kind, under-standing wife who knows you.'

Jack came up behind her and slid his arms round her waist. Peggy pretended – not very convincingly – to try to shrug him off.

'Are you suggesting that I'm still a bit of a Romeo? Now that is flattering – and at my age, too! But you know something, Peg – there's only one lucky girl. You.'

'So you say,' smiled Peggy. 'Now, make yourself useful, Jack, and start buttering this bread.'

• • •

'Dan, lad, far be it from me to criticize, but don't you reckon young Phil here is tekkin' us a heck of a long way round?'

Phil was driving his father and his Uncle Tom back from Borchester and Walter had told him on pain of death he mustn't reach Ambridge before six. It would take him that long to get his 'surprise' organized.

'You've just been acquitted!' said Phil. 'You shouldn't be worrying about anything!'

'And what were you up to before we set off?' queried Tom. 'You were gone far too long to be obeying the call of nature, like you said.'

'Just had to make a couple of phone calls,' Phil replied. 'Spread the glad tidings about your release.'

'I thought Walter might have hung on to have a drink with us on the strength of it.' Tom sounded disappointed. 'Seemed he couldn't get away quick enough. And it's not as if he's got beasts to see to now.'

Dan shot Phil a look. Both of them knew perfectly well why Walter had rushed away so circumspectly.

'Probably had an urgent appointment to take tea with Mrs Perkins,' smiled Dan. 'And she's not the sort you keep waiting!'

But Tom's attention had been distracted.

'The bunting for the fête doesn't usually start this far out of the village, does it?' he said.

'Ah well, there's a visiting celebrity this time, don't forget,' said Dan facetiously.

'And look at the crowd of people round the bridge! Must've been an accident or sommat.'

Phil slowed the car.

'Looks like fellers in uniform,' Tom puzzled, straining from the back seat to see.

'Ah, well,' said Phil smugly, knowing exactly what was going on. 'We'll soon find out, won't we?'

At that moment, a cheer went up from the crowd and the men in uniform – alias the Hollerton Silver Band, specially convened for the occasion – burst into an exuberant rendition of 'For He's a Jolly Good Fellow'.

Tom gaped open-mouthed.

'Why . . . Dan . . . Phil . . . 'tis for me.'

'Reception in your honour, Uncle Tom,' Phil confirmed.

In great high spirits, Walter, as master of ceremonies, approached the car.

'Switch off your engine, Phil,' he commanded. 'We got a rope here and twelve more good men and true to tow you in proper. Right old reception committee we got for you, eh, Tom?'

'All this . . . for me?'

'Well, who did you think it was for?' cackled Walter. 'Humphrey Lyttleton? He's not due till tomorrow – and anyway, he's got a band all of his own!'

Then he was off again, making as if to conduct the band, but deciding in the end to lead the crowd in three cheers.

'I never expected nothing like this.' Tom was visibly moved.

'There's Doris waving, look,' smiled Dan, waving back enthusiastically.

'Where? I can't see so clear.' Tom's voice sounded muffled.

Phil shifted round in his seat. 'Sun in your eyes, Uncle Tom?' he asked gently.

'Over there, look,' offered Dan. 'With Chris.'

'Where? Ah, yes, I see her now.' Tom swallowed hard. 'Yes, that was the problem, Phil. Sun in my eyes.'

·10·

Moving On

'A *what* print?'

Phil followed Christine on to the escalator in Mitchells store in Borchester, leaving behind the heady perfumes of the cosmetics hall on the ground floor.

'A scarf print. It's as if you'd taken a scarf – well, several, really – and made a blouse out of them.'

Phil looked pained. 'And you want me to help you choose it?'

'You might just as well come with me as kick your heels waiting outside the main entrance.'

Phil was beginning to regret this shopping expedition. Paul Johnson was away for ten days looking at thoroughbreds near Kilkenny and Doris thought that Christine needed 'taking out of herself'. But quite how Phil had got roped into bringing his sister shopping in Borchester at the end of July when the barley was just days off ripening he could not fathom. He had accomplished his purchases – shaving cream and half a dozen initialled handkerchiefs – in a matter of minutes, and when he had met Christine after half an hour at the foot of the escalator he had expected to see her already sporting a stiff, navy-and-white Mitchells bag with the blouse inside it. To his astonishment she told him she had not even moved off the ground floor and had spent the entire time 'looking around'.

'A man always looks so out of place in a ladies' department,' he grumbled. 'And why do you suppose,' he mused, 'they always put ladies' lingerie on the same floor as bedding?'

'Don't ask daft questions,' scolded Chris, stepping off the escalator at the first floor. 'Come on, it's another floor up.'

'Hey, wait a minute.' Phil's attention had been caught by a display of kitchenware. In the distance, a girl with a blonde urchin-cut in a dress with broad, jade-green stripes was giving some sort of demonstration. Over a high-pitched whine, which reminded Phil of a lightweight power drill, he heard her say to the assembled crowd, 'And now I'll show you the fifteenth use to which this very versatile little household gadget can be put.'

Phil sidled closer.

'What on earth are you edging up there for?' Christine followed him.

'I'm interested,' hissed Phil, as the girl continued:

'Drill, screwdriver, saw, floor and shoe polisher, egg-whisk, vegetable chopper – and now, the heating element.'

With a flourish, she plugged in another attachment and switched on the motor.

'And so, ladies and gentlemen, you have a hairdryer. Would you care to feel that, madam? Nice blast of hot air, isn't it?'

'I don't believe it.' Chris whispered.

'Clever, eh?' said Phil admiringly.

'Not that. The girl. She's the one you took with your cine-camera at the fête. The one nobody knew. The one you've been asking about.'

'I know,' said Phil.

. . .

Fairbrother's gift of the cine-camera had been an absolute blessing to Phil. As well as filming Christine and Paul's wedding, he had been able to take before and after pictures of the improvements being made to the Estate buildings and, with John Tregorran's encouragement, had even set up a cine club in the village. Its first production, though hardly 'feature-length', promised to be a creditable effort. Phil had entitled it *Stranger in Ambridge*, and in it the village and its inhabitants would be seen through the eyes of a new arrival. There had been some embarrassment over the casting of the lead role after Phil had managed to promise the part both to Joan Hood, whose father Percy farmed Court Farm, and Elizabeth Lawson, who had come to Ambridge to nurse her aunt, Lettie Lawson-Hope. Phil, who, he had to admit, had been rather struck on Elizabeth, had been relieved when she graciously gave way and the filming continued with Joan as the central character.

As the church fête was a crucial date in the Ambridge calendar, Phil had naturally taken his cine-camera with him on fête day. After filming a snatch of Humphrey Lyttleton's speech, Phil had made his way round all the stalls, embarrassing his mother by making her hold up a couple of lavender bags for a close-up, before repairing to the tea tent where, in the queue, he had first caught sight of the girl. Her blonde hair gleamed and in her yellow dress she was like a pillar of sunlight against the damp gloom of the canvas. Phil watched out of the corner of his eye as she carried a tray of tea and two slices of cake – coffee and walnut, if he guessed correctly – to a table at the far side of the tent, where she joined an older lady.

When they got up to go, Phil followed them, and by cutting off a corner near Mrs Perkins's fortune-telling tent, found that he had a good view of them as they tried their luck on roll-a-penny. For the rest of the afternoon, there wasn't a general view of the fête that did not have the blonde girl and her companion in it. Phil wondered if the title of his film would be compromised by the fact that it now showed yet another *Stranger in Ambridge*, but he didn't care. He knew for certain that he was only interested in the identity of one of them – and she *wasn't* Joan Hood.

When he had the film developed and showed it to his family, he had to put up with a lot of teasing from Jack and Christine about the 'mystery woman'. But no-one – and he asked around as discreetly as he could – seemed to know who she was. And now here she was again, in Mitchells of Borchester, demonstrating a – what was it? – a House Drudge.

'You'd like one, wouldn't you, Chris?' Phil urged.

'What on earth for?' Christine was fingering a seersucker table-cloth.

'Well – um – perhaps you could polish your tack with it?'

Christine looked sceptical.

'I think you've gone doolally,' was all she said.

Phil was undeterred. With a tentative gesture he tried to attract the demonstrator's attention.

'Yes, sir?'

And – oh, joy – the girl came nearer. She had calf-brown eyes and the softest-looking skin he had ever seen.

'Um – could you tell us a little more about this thing?' he asked.

'What would you like to know?'

'What your name is,' he blurted out. 'I mean – Chris, you want one of these, don't you?'

The demonstrator put her head on one side quizzically.

'I'm not really interested, thanks,' said Christine. 'He's the one who's interested,' she added pointedly.

'Oh, yes,' agreed Phil. 'I'm convinced. The House Drudge is an absolute must. As far as I'm concerned, it should have been invented before the wheelbarrow. We'll take a dozen!'

The girl looked at Phil in a way that he couldn't quite read and that he hoped wasn't what it looked like – indulgent pity. He knew he was gabbling, but he couldn't help himself. He couldn't believe that he'd actually been given the opportunity to see her again and to talk to her – and all thanks to Chris's search for a blouse!

'I'm going up to fashions,' his sister said now, reminding him of the original purpose of their trip. 'Are you coming?'

Phil shook his head. 'I'm too interested in the House Drudge. Meet me here – then you won't lose me.'

With a despairing look, Christine headed for the escalators again. As if speaking to a very small and rather tired child, the demonstrator said kindly to Phil, 'Now, what do you want to know?'

'About the House Drudge? Nothing,' said Phil, emboldened now that his sister had gone. 'You were at Ambridge church fête.'

'Ambridge?' The girl's eyes clouded. 'I did go to a village fête somewhere about three weeks ago.'

'Everyone was wondering who you were,' confided Phil. 'Well, I was, anyway.'

'And now you know,' the girl said briskly. 'So, the House Drudge. Are you sure you want to buy one? Your wife didn't seem very keen.'

'Chris?' The idea was laughable. 'That wasn't my wife.'

'Your fiancée, then.' The girl turned away and moved back to her stand. She began to collect up heaps of chopped cabbage and slivered cucumber from the previous demonstration.

'That was my sister,' said Phil urgently.

'She was wearing a wedding ring,' said the girl, sweeping the piles of mutilated vegetables into a bin.

'That's because she's married,' explained Phil.

'Are you married?' The girl stopped what she was doing and looked at him directly. Phil's heart felt as though it was in a cable car.

'No,' he said simply, and added, 'my wife died.'

There was a long pause while the girl looked at him. A woman with a shopping basket on wheels tried vainly to attract her attention but in the end turned away, defeated.

'I'm sorry,' she said quietly, at last.

'That's all right,' said Phil. 'You couldn't have known.'

She took out a cloth and wiped the counter.

'I like you,' he said earnestly.

She gave something that was between a laugh and a gasp, and he could understand her surprise. He wondered how he was finding it in him to be so bold.

'You don't even know me,' she said, adding to a dawdling shopper, 'There'll be another demonstration in about fifteen minutes, madam.'

'I like the look of you and I know you better than you think,' said Phil. 'I've got movie pictures of you at the fête. In colour.'

She stopped what she was doing, the cloth lying limply in her hand.

'What on earth for?'

'I suppose I liked you then,' said Phil weakly. 'Couldn't we have dinner?'

But Jill – her name was Jill Patterson, he established after he had told her his – said she couldn't have dinner with him that night.

Tomorrow would be her last day in Borchester before she had to make her paperwork and order book up to date, tidy up her demonstration stand, pack her bag and pay her hotel bill before moving on to Scunthorpe. Phil had to be satisfied with a half-promise of dinner on the night of the Borchester Show, a whole ten days away, because House Drudge would be having a stand there. Even then she was reluctant to commit herself.

'It all depends on the trade,' she explained, separating eggs for her next demonstration. 'Do you like meringues?'

'No,' replied Phil.

'Neither do I,' she said. 'But one of the things the House Drudge does beautifully is to beat up egg whites. I have to do it a dozen times a day.'

'I bet you do it beautifully, too,' said Phil, meaning every word.

Jill looked at him from underneath her lashes.

'I think you should know,' she said, 'that I've done a lot of travelling around on this demonstration game both here and abroad. I can say "no" in five languages and mean it.'

'I'm sure you can,' said Phil. 'But I never want to hear you say it in English. Dinner after the Borchester Show. I'll find you.'

She shrugged.

'You're certainly persistent.'

'That's us Archers for you. And Jill – you'd better get used to it.'

• • •

He found her all right, squeezed between a stall called Nose To Tail (Equestrian Supplies, est. 1930) and one selling cow licks. But while she kept her promise – though it was more a quick snack than a dinner because she said she couldn't stay long – they had hardly sat down and looked at the menu when she dropped another bombshell.

'Yes, I must be ready to leave again by nine-thirty tomorrow morning,' she said matter-of-factly, putting down her menu and straightening the candle shade on the barley-sugar twist wooden lamp on the café table. 'I'll have sardines on toast and a pot of tea, please.'

'I'll have the same.' Phil put down his menu without looking at it. 'Where to tomorrow, then?'

'Venice,' she said brightly. She clasped her hands under her chin.

'Venice! Don't tell me there's a colossal export trade of House Drudges to the Venetians.'

Her unvarnished nails were pink and pearly with perfect half-moons. Phil couldn't take his eyes off them.

'If there is, I couldn't care less. This happens to be my annual holiday.'

Blithely she told him she was going for two weeks with friends – girlfriends, or so she said. They were taking the car over and driving down.

'Venice,' said Phil, depressed. 'Gondolas . . . serenades . . .'

'Mmm,' replied Jill. 'And all that ice cream. I can't wait!'

After they had eaten, she let him walk her back to her hotel – well, more of a B & B, really.

'Shall I see you again?' he asked.

'That's the sixty-four-million-dollar question, isn't it?' She looked at him in the light of the streetlamp. 'Oh, don't look so miserable!'

'Sorry,' said Phil.

'I'll do you a House Drudge at a special price if it'll cheer you up,' she offered. 'I get a good discount.'

'You know it's not a House Drudge I'm interested in,' he said vehemently. 'It's you.'

Impulsively, she took a piece of paper from her bag.

'Have you got a pen?' she asked.

Phil gave her his fountain pen – the one Grace had given him for his birthday the year they were married. Jill scribbled something down.

'This is where I'm staying in Venice,' she said, shoving the pen and paper back at him. 'If you want to write to me, I can't stop you.'

'I'd like to see you try! There'll be a letter waiting when you get there!'

'You've got great faith in the Italian postal system, I must say!'

'I've got great faith in the way I feel about you.'

She looked at him gravely, then smiled. 'I have to go,' she said. 'Thanks for my sardines.'

. . .

Phil wrote to her as soon as he got back home. It wasn't a long letter. He didn't write a hundredth of what he wanted to say because he was afraid of frightening her off with the strength of his feelings. But he did remember to ask her the one burning question that he had forgotten to mention before they parted. When exactly was she coming back and would it be to Borchester? Every day he watched the post and finally, after days of waiting, Timus, whom he had trained to pick up the letters, brought him, along with his bank statement, a postcard of the Grand Canal. On it, she had written: 'Arriving Borchester 3.30 p.m. August 20th. See you there?'

'You bet!' thought Phil. Timus whined. He had done just as he did every day and had not even received a pat on the head when normally there was a doggy chocolate drop in it for him.

'Sorry, boy,' said Phil, realizing. 'Am I forgetting about you?'

In truth, he would have been prepared to forget about everything and everybody. Desperate to meet her train, he cooked up some excuse for Fairbrother about having to meet an important sales executive – well, it was sort of true – in order to get the time off in the middle of the afternoon, and in the middle of harvest, too.

When he saw her step off the train he noticed her feet first, slim and tanned in cream strappy sandals, then looked wonderingly at the rest of her as she came towards him down the platform, the porter carrying her suitcase.

'Welcome back,' he said when she drew close, adding, 'You look wonderful.'

'Thank you,' she smiled. 'I had a wonderful time.'

'Good, good,' he said, distracted. 'I was going to ask you . . .'

'I'm sure you were,' she said kindly. 'Do you mind if I put this down?' She lowered a brown-paper parcel to the floor. 'It's a hand-blown vase. Murano glass. It weighs a ton.'

'I'll take the young lady's case from here.' Phil tipped the porter. 'No, what I was going to ask you was . . .' Phil said when the man had gone, 'Look, I'm sorry if this seems repetitive, but will you have dinner with me tonight?'

This time she agreed with less reluctance, he thought, but that was probably because she was still on holiday and didn't have to go haring off anywhere the next day. She was booked to do a fortnight of demonstrations split between Underwoods in Borchester and Allens in Felpersham but then, she had already warned him, she was due to go to Scotland for two whole months. Phil had refused to think about it, concentrating as he was on seeing her safely back from Venice. But now she was here and the prospect loomed, he began to wonder about asking Fairbrother for some holiday. It wouldn't be an unreasonable request. He hadn't had any time off since the spring, and a salmon-fishing holiday in Scotland would be a perfectly fitting way for a young widower to spend his time, even if the delights of Princes Street did feature heavily too . . . He wondered about broaching the prospect with Jill over dinner.

• • •

At least the setting was more salubrious than their last meal together. After much deliberation, and in the fervent hope that she would say yes to dinner, he had booked a table at The Feathers in Borchester, which had a new French chef who was supposed to be a wizard in the kitchen. The menu even offered dishes flambéed at your table – something which, as far as he knew, was even beyond the capabilities of the House Drudge, unless it had a flame-throwing attachment he had not yet seen.

Jill certainly seemed to enjoy the evening. She was less harassed than on both the previous occasions he had seen her – in the store and on the day of the Borchester Show. She told him all about her holiday. About their ride in a gondola, and how Jacqui, one of her friends, had almost tipped them in. About how they'd swum at the Lido and drunk frothy coffee on the piazzas between visits to churches and galleries. He told her how the harvest was going, about the fuss in the village over the madeira cake recipe for the Flower and Produce Show and how (though he rather regretted this – after all, it was hardly romantic) one of Dan's best heifers had gone down with bloat.

'Enjoyed yourself tonight?' he asked as she nibbled an after-dinner mint with her coffee (black, no sugar, he noted).

'Oh, yes. You've made a tremendous fuss of me,' she smiled.

He loved her smile.

'It was a pleasure,' he said, understating the case somewhat.

Jill smoothed out the golden foil the chocolate had come in.

'And all this on the strength of three meetings.'

'And a postcard from Italy,' he put in quickly.

'Exactly.' Jill licked her fingers. Phil's stomach clenched itself into a knot. 'I ask myself . . . why?'

'Why?' Phil shrugged. 'Because I like you. That's why. No harm in that, is there?'

'I don't know yet. Haven't had this high-pressure attack before.'

'Not even in Italy with Jacqui?'

Jill giggled – not a high-pitched, silly, girlish giggle, but a low, warm burbling, deep in her throat.

'Not even in Italy. So why? Why did you meet me today?'

'Why did you let me know what train you were coming on?' retaliated Phil.

'Because you wrote and asked me,' she parried.

'But you needn't have written back and told me. You must have wanted to see me again.'

Jill's mouth twitched in a would-be smile. 'You save your fishing for Scotland, if you ever get there,' she said. (Phil had decided, emboldened by the claret he had chosen to go with their steak, to mention his proposed trip.) 'Look.' She laid her napkin on the table. 'It's been a lovely evening. But it's also been a long day. I was up at five. I must get back and get some beauty sleep.'

'That's something you can do without very comfortably.'

Phil's eloquence seemed to know no bounds. Sometimes he heard himself say things to her and he had no idea where they'd come from. Jill raised her eyebrows – perfectly shaped, like the rest of her.

'You're full of pretty speeches tonight.'

'You inspire them.'

'Thank you,' she said, inclining her head. 'But . . .'

'Go on,' he said.

'At the same time, I still ask myself . . . where is all this leading? Where do we go from here, Philip Archer? Because I don't see any future in it. Do you?'

No future? What was she talking about? If he had not realized it before, Phil knew at that moment with utter certainty that he wanted to spend the rest of his life with this beautiful, strong-willed, rather spiky girl, and that if he couldn't, it would simply not be worth living.

'What sort of future had you in mind?' He was playing for time.

'Be reasonable,' she said. 'I have a job. It takes me all over the British Isles. Quite by chance I happen to have paid three visits to this area and I've somehow seen you each time.'

'Thanks to my pressure tactics.'

'Agreed. Entirely thanks to your pressure tactics. But it's pretty obvious that our beautiful friendship is going to fold up pretty soon. It has to.'

'No, it doesn't.' Phil could hardly keep a quaver of panic – or was it desire? – out of his voice.

Jill spread her hands – those lovely hands.

'I'm scheduled to travel all over the country. I shan't be in this neighbourhood again for a long time.'

'In that case,' said Phil, thinking on his feet, 'I must somehow wangle it so that I can come up to wherever you are and visit you. We must see more and more of each other and get to know each other better and better and . . .'

'And?'

'Well – what would you suggest?'

She smiled, showing her perfect teeth. Actually, one was slightly crooked, but they were perfect to Phil.

'Oh, you're impossible. But listen, Philip. Just to put things square right from the 'beginning – and to avoid any disappointments or misunderstandings. I'm not the kind of girl who could ever become a farmer's wife.'

Phil gulped. That was straight from the shoulder. And it seemed to have hit him in the solar plexus.

'I've got no roots in the soil,' she shrugged.

'Everyone in these islands has some roots in the soil,' he bluffed. 'Everybody.'

Jill looked at the ceiling and sighed. 'Not me. I'm a townie. Born and bred. I know nothing about farming, country life – village life. I'm used to the cities and the bright lights. And I love them. I could never settle in the country. I wouldn't know how to go about it.'

'Country folk are like everyone else, Jill, make no mistake about it. They like nice people. And you're a nice person. I'm sure they'd like you.'

He knew what was bothering her. She'd already told him that she was an orphan. Both her parents had died when she was quite young and she had gone to live with her aunt, Daphne, who had been her companion at the fête and who lived in Crudley, a small industrial town in the north of the county. Phil had no time for amateur psychology, but after three meetings he felt such a close bond with Jill that he felt he could guess what she was thinking – and he could understand it. Because of her background, she was not used to, and could not imagine, the closeness, the connectedness, of family life – and, by extension, village life. She dreaded feeling a permanent outsider and it was easier for her to lose herself in towns and cities – indeed, in a job that kept her always on the move, and thus unable to make connections – than to risk being rejected. She didn't think she'd fit into village life and she wasn't prepared to take the risk of finding out.

'No, I'm serious.' She leaned towards him and he just wanted to take her face in his hands and cover it with kisses. 'I couldn't and wouldn't marry a country farmer because I'd only make a flop of being his wife. I'd let him down. I wouldn't be able to help him run the farm and socially . . . well, it just wouldn't work.'

'I see.'

'I'm only saying this to save any embarrassment, Phil.' Her eyes never left his face. 'No misapprehensions on either side.'

'None at all,' said Phil bitterly. 'I think you've put the whole thing perfectly. You don't want me to ask you to marry me, and if I did, you'd say no. Well, I think that covers most eventualities. I'm really glad we got that straight. Shall I get the bill?'

·11·

Rescue

He did ask her to marry him, of course. He couldn't help himself.

The day after they had been out to dinner Jill had phoned him at the farm office. 'I'm sorry,' she said in a small voice. 'It's just me. I honestly meant well. But I know I hurt your feelings last night.'

'Yes, you did.' Phil was too surprised to hear from her – and too grateful – to come up with any clever remarks. 'And –'

'Yes?' He could hear her catch her breath.

'Just this once I'm prepared to overlook it.'

'Oh, Phil, thank you. I'm so glad you said that.' He could imagine her cradling the receiver in a public telephone box and smiling her incredible smile. She gave a short, embarrassed laugh. 'Good intentions. The road to hell is paved with them, or so they say.'

'Mm.'

But Phil had been on the road to hell once before in his life, and he knew that this wasn't it. He knew that wherever he went with Jill, it would seem like paradise.

'You must think I'm completely devoid of imagination, but I have to ask you,' he said. 'Will you have dinner with me tonight?'

And so the rift was healed, and for the fortnight she was in Borsetshire Phil saw her as much as he could. But the fortnight went too fast, as fortnights have a habit of doing when you are falling in love, and with indecent speed it was early September and time for her to set off for Scotland. In the end, Phil had done nothing about asking Fairbrother if he could take a holiday. September was such a busy time with the cultivations, and Len Thomas, who had left Brookfield to work as shepherd at the Estate, was anxious to go round the sheep sales with him and buy in some breeding stock.

'I suppose we can write,' said Phil as he stood on the platform with Jill – at New Street Station in Birmingham this time.

'And phone,' she said.

Phil nodded bravely. 'It's better than nothing.'

'Yes.'

He knew she was feeling the parting as much as he was. All the spark had gone out of her voice and her eyes were dark.

'It's grim, this, isn't it?' he said.

She nodded. 'Not much fun.'

As if to spare them any more anguish, the guard came along the platform, shutting all the doors.

'I should get on now, miss, if you're going,' he said.

Jill looked at Phil, then impulsively leant forward and kissed his cheek.

'Bye,' she said quickly.

Phil took her by the shoulders and pulled her towards him, kissing her on the mouth.

'You're not getting away with just a peck,' he said. 'Not when I'm going to miss you as much as I am.'

'I know.'

The guard raised his flag.

'I have to go.'

She climbed in and Phil slammed the door behind her. Jill lowered the window and leaned out.

'Don't forget to write,' she said.

The guard blew his whistle and the train began to move off. Phil began to walk, then jog, alongside it. 'I won't,' he said. 'And don't forget you're going to marry me.'

'Am I?' There was a glimmer of Jill's usual self. 'I thought I'd vetoed all that.'

'Oh, I didn't believe a word of it.' Phil was running alongside the train now. 'I still don't and I never will.'

She said something in reply but he couldn't catch it and eventually he had to stop running as the train picked up speed. It scythed out of the station and away down the track, but he could still see her head, a blonde blur at the window, and even when the shining rails were completely empty, he waved and waved.

• • •

He saw her again, sooner than he'd expected, after just a month. In late September, when he and Len had been away on the Welsh Borders looking at sheep, he returned to Ambridge late one evening and called in at The Bull just before closing time. Two surprises were in store. One was a crayfish supper – Walter Gabriel had had a record catch and had offered them to Jack at a knockdown price. The other was to find Jill there waiting for him. There was much nudging and winking among the regulars as Peggy prepared Phil a plate of crayfish and ushered him and Jill into a private room.

'I'll make sure you're not disturbed,' she said, closing the door behind her.

'Do you feel as conspicuous as I do?' asked Jill.

'Don't worry about it. It's just their way,' said Phil. 'Oh, come here. It's wonderful to see you.'

He hugged her close but he could sense her tension. 'What is it?'

Jill broke away from him. She held the back of one of the moquette-covered dining chairs that were grouped round the small table.

'I wanted to see you because – well, something rather important's happened. It could affect the future.'

'Tell me.' Phil couldn't stop himself from moving towards her. 'Have you definitely made your mind up – about me, I mean?'

'I've been offered a promotion,' said Jill abruptly. 'My boss has given me the chance of being in charge of all the demonstrators in our firm. He's a shrewd man, Phil,' she added. 'He's realized that you – that somebody – had shaken my calm a little.'

'You mean . . .' Phil tried to work out the logic behind the offer. 'He thinks he might lose you so he's trying to produce a counter-attraction.' He let out a breath. 'Well, what did you say?'

'If I were to accept . . .' Jill's finger traced the raised pattern in the upholstery fabric. 'I think there would be an unspoken agreement between him and me that I didn't intend to marry – at least not for some years.'

Phil felt a surge of relief. At least she hadn't accepted the job offer straight away.

'You're building up my hopes, Jill,' he smiled. 'Are you crazy enough to marry me?'

'That's what I want to find out,' she said evenly.

She told him that she had a rare day off the next day. What she wanted to do was spend it in Ambridge, meeting people, looking round the place, getting a feel for it. Phil knew at once what a concession this was, given all her reservations about village life. If he could just break them down and convince her that Ambridge would welcome her, both in her own right and as his future wife, then surely any remaining doubts on her part would be removed.

'Friday . . .' he mused out loud. 'Payday for the chaps. Heck of a lot to do. Fairbrother's going away next week . . .'

'It doesn't matter if it's a problem,' Jill said sadly.

'Wait . . . wait . . .' said Phil, thinking quickly. How many times in his life, and in his love affairs particularly, had he cursed himself for not being more spontaneous, for not giving in to the feeling of the moment? Jill was offering to meet him on his home territory, more than halfway, as it were, and he was thinking about mundane things like wage packets! They'd just have to manage without him for once.

'I'll take the whole darn day off!' he declared. 'I'll work like stink Saturday and Sunday to make up for it.'

• • •

He showed her everything. He took her round all his boyhood haunts – the best spot on the Am for catching tiddlers, the secret place on Lakey Hill where he had gone when he ran away from home at the age of eight after some row with Chris, the reason for which he could not even remember. After coffee in the kitchen, with Jill and Doris exchanging biscuit recipes, he walked her round Brookfield, introducing her to the cows by name and explaining all the field names – Round Robin, Pikey Piece. He took her to meet Walter, who mischievously promised to carve her a love spoon and, on the village green, on their way to The Bull for lunch, they even bumped into the vicar.

'Lovely girl,' the vicar whispered while Jill was in conversation with Mrs Perkins, who happened to be 'just passing'. 'When do you want me to put the banns up?'

At The Bull, Jack and Peggy insisted they had lunch and drinks on the house, then Phil drove Jill round the Estate, calling in on Uncle Tom for a cup of tea before returning to Brookfield for supper with his parents.

'I am exhausted,' said Jill, when he drove her back to her lodgings in Borchester. 'I felt like the Queen must on one of her foreign tours.'

'It is tiring, being on show.' Phil took her hand and squeezed it. 'You were wonderful. They all loved you.'

'Really?'

'Almost as much as I do.'

• • •

Phil didn't feel he could do any more. He knew that he had fallen in love with Jill at first sight, at the fête, but he could see that she had to weigh things up before committing herself. She was not a schoolgirl: she was nearly twenty-seven, an independent woman with a career which, as she realized, she would have to sacrifice to marry him. He hoped that he had at least convinced her that, if she did change her mind about being a country farmer's wife, Ambridge would be a friendly place in which to do it. And he took comfort from the fact that she was still stalling her boss on the question of the promotion.

Then something happened that rocked Phil back on his heels. He had taken Jill back to Coombe Farm after a night out. It was only the third time she had been there – in fact, she had just said something in jest about it being 'third time lucky' for her, when there was a knock at the door. Opening it, Phil found himself face to face with someone he had never expected to see again – Elizabeth Lawson.

He had first met Elizabeth at the beginning of the year, when Chris had set him up on a blind date with her at a Pony Club dance. She was a relative of the Lawson-Hopes, a nursing sister, and she had come to Ambridge to care temporarily for her Aunt Lettie, who had become very frail. Elizabeth was good fun. Phil had got her involved in the cine club and they had been out several times, though she had made it plain from the start that she was engaged to a junior doctor at a hospital in London. That hadn't stopped Phil from becoming quite fond of her, as was his tendency, and though he had still been keen on her when she had left Ambridge in the spring to return to London, her last words to him came back to haunt him when he saw her standing on his doorstep.

'I shouldn't be surprised,' she had said, 'if, in four or five months' time, I phone up asking to speak to Philip Archer and the phone is answered by a female voice saying, "This is Mrs Philip Archer. Can I give him a message?"'

And now, just when her flippancy might have turned out to be prophetic, she was back again, telling him that her engagement was broken off, and, presumably, thinking or hoping he might still be carrying a torch for her.

What could he do? He took her inside and introduced her to Jill.

'Er – Jill's a demonstrator of a household gadget, Elizabeth,' Phil faltered, aware that the introduction was both clumsy and inadequate. Even more clumsily, he blundered on, 'We – um – I know her very well.'

'Really?' Elizabeth sat down proprietorially in a fireside chair, fastidiously spreading out the skirt of her fashionable windowpane-checked suit. 'I don't ever remember you speaking about her.'

'Phil and I met quite recently,' put in Jill smoothly. 'If you're an old friend –'

'I suppose you could call me that,' said Elizabeth coquettishly, looking up at Phil from under her lashes. 'Comparatively old, anyhow. Old enough to think you'd be interested, Phil, to hear about my romance that went wrong.'

'Oh, yes, I would,' said Phil cloddishly, not knowing what else he could say. 'Yes.'

Elizabeth smiled with, it seemed, some satisfaction. 'Obviously this isn't the time to tell you about it. No need to bore the company. When shall we meet? Tomorrow?'

Phil did at least have the presence of mind to stall her on that one and Elizabeth had the decency – or sense of self-preservation – to leave reasonably quickly, apologizing for disturbing their evening. Jill appeared to have coped with the situation perfectly easily, but when Elizabeth had gone, Phil knew from what she didn't say that she was both curious and jealous. As someone who hadn't got a deceptive bone in his body, Phil was in a torment to think what it might have looked like, or that Jill might think he was still in any way fond of Elizabeth. She was a complete irrelevance now, and if he had ever been struck on her, any feelings he might have had were totally eclipsed by what he felt for Jill. He was desperate to tell Jill all this, but understandably, she asked him if he'd drive her home, saying she needed an early night.

'It's chilly,' he said. 'I'll get the car rug.'

'Good,' Jill replied. 'I like attentive people.'

'How much?' Phil came closer, wondering if he dared put his arms round her.

'Reasonably well,' said Jill. She leaned towards him. 'This Elizabeth Lawson . . .'

'Yes?' Phil held his breath.

'Just remember that I've come into your life now,' said Jill seriously. 'The same rules don't apply that applied before I knew you.'

'No,' agreed Phil. 'They don't at all.'

He wrapped his arms around her and pulled her close. Then he held her tight, swaying gently with her, sighing, until all the awkwardness of the evening had ebbed away.

• • •

But the return of Elizabeth Lawson to Ambridge unsettled Phil. He felt as if he were playing a game where the rules were being torn up and rewritten every five minutes. He had never thought of Elizabeth as a schemer, so he could not understand why, when she could see clearly that his affections were engaged elsewhere, she kept contriving to seek him out. So desperate did she seem for his company that she even managed to persuade him to take her to a potato-harvesting demonstration. Phil got through the day somehow, hating it, not knowing how to introduce her to fellow farmers they met, just wanting to be with Jill. After he had dropped Elizabeth off he drove straight to see Jill. She had managed to fix things so that she was doing all her demonstrations in the Midlands, so she had taken some lodgings with a well-meaning but rather talkative widow in Borchester.

'I wasn't sure whether I'd find you in.' Phil had gone through agonies waiting to see if anyone answered the front door.

'I haven't been back more than half an hour.' She was in her work clothes, a navy suit and tie-necked blouse, but had obviously kicked off her shoes the moment she came through the door because they lay abandoned in the hall.

'My landlady's decided to go to the pictures,' she announced, leading the way into the front room. 'If we put a match to the fire it'll soon warm up.'

Phil drew the curtains as she did so. The flames began to lick at the coke and kindling in the grate and, as she straightened, Phil took her hand and led her to sit on the sofa beside him.

'How was your demonstration?' she asked conversationally. But she took her hand away.

'Quite interesting, really,' Phil admitted. 'But I wished I'd taken Craddock – you know, the farm foreman – with me to see it. Yes,' he said, from the heart, 'I really do wish I'd taken Craddock. That would have simplified a lot of things.'

The fire crackled and a flame leapt up the chimney.

'I want to talk to you,' he said.

'Go on, then.'

Phil took a deep breath. 'It's Elizabeth Lawson, Jill.'

He felt her tense beside him. 'No, it's not what you think. Everything I've told you about her is the truth. But there were things she said today – at the demonstration – she's talking about picking up the threads again. I don't know if she means it or not.' He turned to her and took her hands. 'Jill – won't you say you'll marry me before she tosses a spanner into the works?'

There was a long silence. They both watched a spark from the fire leap on to the rag rug and snuff itself out. Then Jill spoke.

'You really are one of the most extraordinary people I've ever met.'

'Will you *marry* me?'

'I begin to wonder,' said Jill, 'whether you want me to marry *you*.'

'Heavens above!' Phil burst out. 'Haven't I begged and pleaded?'

'So what difference does Elizabeth Lawson make?'

Phil let go of her hands and ran his own through his hair. 'I've said the wrong thing again,' he despaired. 'Jill, look at me. I'm quite sure of myself. Quite sure. She couldn't make any difference to the way I feel about you. And I don't want you to let her put you off me, either.'

There was another silence, then a bubble of laughter rose up in Jill's throat.

'You are funny,' she smiled. 'Getting into a tizzy.'

'Of course I do,' Phil defended himself. 'I'm in such a state waiting for you to say yes or no that I build things up. I may not show it to other people, but I'm walking a tightrope.'

Jill took his hands back in hers. 'If I said yes,' she began gently, 'would you come down off it?'

'No,' replied Phil. 'I'd probably leap up clean through the heavens.'

Jill laughed.

'I'll risk it. Phil – I want to marry you.'

'Oh, Jill! Say it again.'

'I want to marry you, Phil. I love you.'

• • •

Phil would have married her the next day, with a special licence, forgetting an engagement and everything. In the end some vestiges of sanity prevailed and they agreed on a short – very short – engagement. They set a wedding date of 16 November, at Jill's parish church, St Luke's, in Crudley. Jill had already told her uncle and aunt that 'an awfully nice man' (which made Phil squirm) had asked her to marry him. They very reasonably, in Phil's opinion, said that they thought it was high time she got married and that they trusted her judgement to pick a man who would make her happy. Phil wished that his own parents – his mother particularly – could see things in such a generous light. Doris was very doubtful about the marriage from the start, so much so that Jill even called round to see her about it.

'I've nothing against you at all, Jill,' Doris explained as she poured the coffee. Jill had protested, but no-one was allowed over the threshold at Brookfield without something passing their lips. 'But as Phil's mother I'm all against rushed marriages.'

'It's Phil who's doing all the rushing,' smiled Jill, adding quickly, 'Mind you, I want to marry him.'

Doris pushed the milk jug and sugar bowl across to her but Jill shook her head. 'Philip isn't the one who'll be the target of malicious gossip.' Doris reclaimed the sugar bowl and sugared her own cup. 'Hurried marriages always lead to malicious gossip.'

Jill took a sip. 'Heavens,' she said. 'I'm not bothered. Let them gossip.'

Doris pursed her lips. Jill still had a lot to learn about living in a small community, even when she was marrying someone as well regarded as Phil. And there were other implications which she wondered if Jill had even considered.

'You're taking on a lot,' she said boldly. Someone had to say it. 'You're stepping into someone else's shoes.'

Jill looked down at her coffee cup, then raised her eyes to Doris's. 'Grace's,' she said.

Doris nodded. 'And as you know, Phil's way of life is as different from yours as chalk from cheese. You've a lot to learn.'

'With help I *will* learn, though.'

Despite herself, Doris couldn't help admiring her determination.

She hadn't been at all happy when Phil had announced that he was getting married again – for heaven's sake, she and Dan had only met Jill a couple of times – but Jill impressed her with her quiet confidence. It wouldn't be easy, settling into Ambridge after the life she had been used to, but Doris knew that she could do it. And although – because of the speed at which things had happened, which had predisposed her against Phil's choice – she would almost have liked to take against Jill, she could not. Deep down, though it felt almost disloyal, she suspected that Jill would make Phil a better long-term partner than Grace would ever have done.

• • •

One of the things Jill would have to learn very quickly was that she would not be able to do anything in Ambridge without it getting back to Phil, and sure enough, he heard from three different sources that she had visited his mother at Brookfield.

'I see it all,' he challenged Jill, as they snatched a quick bite to eat before going to a film. 'Behind my back you're having a mad affair with Ned Larkin.'

Jill laughed her deep, velvety laugh.

'But seriously,' Phil went on. 'How come you were at Brookfield so early?'

'I wanted to talk to your mother with you off the scene.'

'You got the impression she didn't approve of you? That it?' asked Phil.

'Well . . . yes. But it appears it's the rush she doesn't like. She says it's not fair to me.'

Doris had emphasized the fun Jill might get from planning a wedding, building up her bottom drawer and choosing her trousseau. And simply from being engaged.

Phil straightened his knife and fork. 'Maybe I have rather rushed you,' he confessed. 'I didn't want to take any chances on losing you.'

She reached out and touched his hand. 'I felt the same. About you.'

Phil didn't want to say it – it was the last thing he wanted – but he felt he had to. 'Maybe you'd better think it over more carefully, Jill. I don't mind waiting.'

What was he going to do if she did ask for time? All he wanted to do was to be married to her. He should have known her better.

'Well, I do,' she said defiantly.

'You mean . . . we go ahead as planned?'

'Yes.'

He leant over the table and kissed her on the lips, then sat back, beaming.

'There's one thing, though,' he said, 'where I do agree with Mum.' He reached into his jacket pocket and brought out a small leather box. He had managed to find out her ring size by buying her a dress ring for her birthday, which meant that he had been able to choose the three-stone diamond with utter confidence. 'Put your finger out,' he said. 'Third finger, left hand.'

She did so and he eased the ring over her knuckle.

With a tender smile she withdrew her hand from his and turned it this way and that, watching the ring sparkle under the light. Then she reached forward and took his face in her hands and he felt the unaccustomed coldness of the gold band against his right cheek. She kissed him lovingly.

'Phil,' she said, 'it's beautiful. You're a darling. You really are.' Phil grinned, pleased by her pleasure. 'Now try and get out of marrying me, if you dare,' he retorted. 'I'll sue you for breach of promise, heartbreak, alienation of affections, habeas corpus – the lot.' Then he added, seeing her staring dreamily at the ring, 'Here's the waitress, so take the stars out of your eyes and concentrate on the food.'

• • •

The wedding went off without a hitch. Those had all happened beforehand, like the mix-up over Phil's suit, which had resulted in his being given one three sizes too small. Luckily, he had tried it on at home and was able to change it before the wedding, combining the errand with a visit to John Tregorran's newly opened antique shop to choose the wedding present John wanted to give them. On the wedding morning, from the hotel in Crudley where he and his parents were staying, he telephoned Jill at her aunt's.

'I know it'd be bad luck to see you before the wedding,' he said. 'But that doesn't mean I don't want to. So I thought I'd phone.'

'It's lovely to hear your voice,' she said. 'It's chaos here. I look a wreck but the hairdresser's coming in a bit.'

'I bet you don't look a wreck,' he said. 'Just come to church as you are.'

'You want to marry a woman with a head like a disused mop?'

'I don't care what you look like. I never will. I want to marry you, full stop.'

'Well, I feel the same.'

Her voice came down the line, warm and promising.

'I love you, Jill.'

'I love you. See you later.'

'See you *soon*.'

• • •

St Luke's was a much smaller, simpler church than St Stephen's in Ambridge. It had plain, whitewashed walls hung with brocaded banners to the gospel saints. There were no side chapels or altars, no statues in niches or rood screens. Just a straight, simple aisle leading between the stained wooden pews and at the end an altar with a silver crucifix. Phil knew that Jill had particularly wanted the service at St Luke's because it only held about sixty people and she was already aware of how bare 'her' side of the church might look. But though her aunt, uncle and cousins, her boss and her fellow colleagues only filled about three rows, Ambridge took care of the rest. Walter Gabriel, Uncle Tom and Pru, now officially 'courting', Mrs Perkins, John Tregorran and Carol Grey, the Trenthams, the Fairbrothers, the men from the estate, the men from Brookfield – they had all made it plain to Phil that, though they realized the reception was for family only, they would not miss the service for anything. And they had meant it.

Jill did not keep him waiting as Grace had done. A minute before two-thirty, Phil, seated once again with Jack beside him as best man, was told that she had arrived. Phil and Jack took their places. But it still seemed an age whilst the photographer took pictures of her outside before the organist played the Bridal March and she came down the aisle towards him – he couldn't resist turning round to peep – gripping her uncle's arm tightly. And as they gave their holy vows, the vows he had taken once before, Phil sent up a silent prayer that, this time, God really would grant them the rest of their natural lives together 'till death us do part'.

· · ·

Jack, as best man, behaved just as Phil had expected him to do – with total impropriety. He made every embarrassing joke possible during his speech and, with Christine's husband, Paul, planned a full-scale sabotage of the suitcases involving sewn-up pyjama legs and film-star pin-ups of the appropriate sex in both Phil's and Jill's cases. Knowing that he was likely to put kippers in the car engine and scatter the interior with confetti, Phil had wisely booked a taxi to take him and Jill away from the reception.

'Time we made a move, isn't it?' he said to her when all the speeches had been given, the cake cut, the champagne drunk and the guests mingled with. 'They won't think us rude, will they?'

Truly, he couldn't wait to be on his own with her.

'Well,' she smiled at him. The camellias anchoring her veil had slipped slightly and he straightened them. 'My folks won't.'

'Come on then, Mrs Archer.'

Phil took her hand and led her across the room.

'Mum, Dad, we're thinking about going,' he explained.

His father clapped him on the shoulder. 'Quite right too,' he said. He pushed Jill's veil back slightly and stooped to kiss her cheek. 'Welcome to the family, love.'

'You *are* a family, too, aren't you?' Jill said. Then, the smile that had been in place all day left her face for a moment as she remembered her own family. 'Still –' she gave a little shake of her head, not wanting unhappy memories on a day like this. 'I hope you've enjoyed yourself.'

'I have,' said Dan. 'I think we all have. Most of all I think I've enjoyed seeing our Phil looking like he used to. He's been far too serious-minded these past couple of years, you know. And it's you that's brought about the change.'

'Well, he's changed my life pretty effectively, too,' Jill smiled at Phil. 'And I know it's going to be for the better.'

In the taxi, however, on the way to The Hare and Hounds Hotel, where Phil had stowed the car in a lock-up garage, Jill turned to him with a worried look on her face.

'Phil,' she said. 'You've got to tell me. What's the difference between a sack and a bag?'

Phil realized with a start of amusement what she was talking about. He had come in on the end of a conversation between her and his father about milking and mastitis, of all suitable topics for a wedding reception, and he could be sure his father would have used the term 'bag' for a cow's udder. Delighted, he laughed out loud.

'There,' she protested. 'You're laughing at me!'

'Oh, darling, darling.' Phil reached his arm round her and snuggled her against him. 'You don't have to worry about things like that. You'll learn. There's plenty of time.'

'But there is a difference?' she insisted.

'Yes, but you don't have to worry about that on your honeymoon!'

Jill kissed his neck, then nuzzled his earlobe.

'All right, darling,' she agreed. 'Let's leave the sacks and bags until after the honeymoon. And the gilts and stores and silage and heifers and compost and whatever it is they all are. You'll have to teach me, though. I'm terribly ignorant.'

'Ignorant in some things, maybe,' Phil concurred, feeling more comfortable and right in himself than he had done for years, and quite possibly, than he had ever done. 'But not in the things that matter.'

Then he cupped her face in his hands and kissed her full on the lips.

'Thank you, Jill,' he said.

'What for?' Her eyes shone in the darkness.

'I think you've probably saved my life. In fact, I know you have.'

·12·

A Tale of Two Marriages

Phil was a married man once more. He could not believe the change it made in his life. He had thought he had coped pretty well on his own: people had congratulated him on it. He knew that after Grace's death, his mother would have moved in on him and taken over, or even moved him back to Brookfield, but Phil had stood firm. He had taken a pride in learning how to cook for himself, recipe book in one hand and wooden spoon in the other. He was never going to master the pies and casseroles he had been brought up on, but he had worked his way determinedly through omelettes (harder than you'd think) and chops (tough, grill too high for too long) to macaroni cheese (note: next time make half the quantity). He had done all his own washing. He had even ironed after a fashion – at least, the bits of a shirt that might show if he had a meeting with Fairbrother.

And his life was not just lived at Coombe Farm. If, at the end of a working day, he didn't feel like his own company, he had only to walk into the bar of The Bull to find half a dozen regulars he could chat to. He was invited out a lot. Everyone, it seemed, wanted to feed him. His family had been wonderful. The door was always open at Brookfield and he called in or phoned to speak to his mother every night. Doris left pies and cakes on his kitchen table, in tins to protect them from Timus. The Fairbrothers asked him to rather awkward suppers, which he only got through by talking shop with his boss while Helen looked on sadly, fiddling with the lid of the coffee pot.

Jack and Peggy invited him round for meals: scratch family affairs in the back kitchen at the pub, when Anthony William Daniel showed off his latest 'invention' (typically a suet carton, a few lolly sticks and an elastic band) and Jennifer and Lilian squabbled over whose turn it was to clear the table. Phil felt out of place with Jack and Peggy, but then he always had. Their family life was loud and boisterous, unlike what he remembered of life at Brookfield when he had been growing up, regulated by his mother's placid presence.

He went beyond the village, too. Chris and Paul, in an attempt to 'take him out of himself', frequently took him to the theatre, but he was not comfortable with them, either. He felt as if he was intruding on their togetherness and once, aware and unable to bear the fact that when the lights went down, Paul and Chris had twined their fingers together in her lap, he had pleaded a headache and had left after the first act. The play had been – he would never forget it – *Separate Tables*. That was how Phil felt. As if he would be at a separate table, looking in on other people's happiness, for the rest of his life.

Now he had rejoined the party and it amazed him that he could have tolerated being on his own for as long as he had. A good evening then had consisted of whiling away an hour in The Bull, not burning the potatoes, *Take Your Pick* on the television and congratulating himself for remembering to turn on the immersion for a bath before bed. Now he saw what a half-life he had been living, the bitter tedium and the sheer loneliness of every long day. Now he could not wait to get home to see Jill turn from the stove, pushing a wisp of hair off her forehead and lifting her face for a kiss. Instead of coming in to darkness and Timus's cold nose, the house was warm and lit and alive. Jill would have laid the fire in the sitting room and plumped up the cushions on the settee. A pan of stew and dumplings would be simmering on the stove. But the thing that mattered most was Jill's smile as his arms closed around her.

'Home,' he would murmur, 'I'm home.'

• • •

Jill was loving married life and country life more than she had dared hope. Nervous about giving up her job and her independence entirely, she had arranged unpaid leave of absence for three months while, she told her boss, she saw how her new life suited her. Although he wasn't keen – the three months would be over Christmas, House Drudge's busiest sales period – Jill told him firmly that her only other option was to resign, and since he didn't want to lose her, he had no choice but to agree. Even so, when they returned from their honeymoon, Jill was still wondering if she had done the right thing. But she kissed Phil a dutiful, wifely goodbye as he went off to work on that first Monday morning and went back into the kitchen to wash up the breakfast things.

It felt very strange. Even Grace had worked, she knew, and Jill had always earned her own living. And it wasn't just the money. It was about having friends of your own, a life of your own, a life that she was not sure Ambridge could supply. She wondered what on earth she would do with her time. The washing up – two plates, two cups and the cutlery – took precisely four minutes. Phil would be back for lunch, but it was hardly going to take long to open and heat up a can of mock turtle soup and lay out sliced tongue and ham on a dish. If she wasn't careful she'd turn into the sort of woman who hovered around in the kitchenware departments where she had once done her demonstrating, buying devices to make radish roses and cut zigzag shapes in tomatoes.

But just as she was wiping her hands, the phone rang. It was Doris, asking her if she'd like to go to Brookfield for coffee and then proposing that they walk down to the shop together. And did Jill or her aunt have any left-over wool? The W I were sending blankets to Eastern Europe and thousands of squares were needed. Incidentally, had Jill ever done much knitting? Jill smiled to herself. She couldn't wait to tell her former colleagues that her life now revolved around cups of coffee, a trip to the village shop and knitting squares out of scraps. But sceptical though she was, she found as the winter weeks went by that these activities not just passed the time, but passed it very pleasantly. As someone who had always taken life at a run, Jill had to learn to slow down – and the village helped there, too. She soon found out that it was impossible to try to hurry Walter Gabriel in one of his anecdotes or to refuse tea and rock buns with Mrs Perkins should they bump into each other on the village green.

'You're blooming, my love!' Walter told her when he called in one morning to deliver the promised love spoon he had carved. 'You'm looking rare bonny.' Jill smiled. At first she had blamed her tightened waistbands on the endless biscuits (when Doris said coffee she never meant just coffee) and the rock buns. But early in the new year, when there were other signs that she could not ignore, she went to the doctor. He confirmed what she suspected. She was pregnant.

She told Phil one drab January Sunday when they had prised themselves away from the fire to take Timus for a walk. The rooks were making their usual racket in the high-rise housing estate they had constructed on Ten Elms Rise. Timus, outraged, took their calls as a personal slight and charged at the trees, barking.

'He's quite mad, isn't he?' said Phil fondly, squeezing Jill's fingers, which she had slid inside his jacket pocket.

'He still thinks he's a puppy.'

They walked on for a while in silence, twigs cracking damply under their feet. Mist was gathering in the valley. The rooks clattered busily in the trees.

'I wonder ...' Jill began. Phil looked at her enquiringly. 'I wonder how he'd get on with children.'

'Timus? He'd love them. Constant playmates. As long as they weren't too noisy, of course.'

'Hm.' Jill looked at him. The damp cold had made his hair even curlier. One springy lock of it was bouncing over his eyes. She loved him so much.

'I don't think there's any guarantee of not getting a noisy one,' she said.

Phil stopped. There was something in her tone, a hint of smugness, a touch of teasing, which made this conversation different from any they had had on the subject before.

'Jill? Are you trying to tell me something?'

Jill smiled mischievously.

'I think you've already guessed,' she said. 'Daddy.'

Phil didn't say a word. He turned to her and hugged her fiercely to him. Through his several layers of clothing she could feel him shuddering and she knew it was nothing to do with the cold.

Phil wanted to go and tell his parents straight away, but Jill found, rather to her surprise, that it was something she wanted to do herself. Doris had found it hard to accept her in the beginning, Jill knew, but in the couple of months since the wedding, she had come to feel like Jill's own mother. Fleetingly, Jill wondered what sort of mother she herself would turn out to be. She knew that she could do a lot worse than follow Doris's example. Perhaps, though, she might adapt a few things for the modern world. She couldn't imagine that a child who would come of age in the 1970s would think much of being told to wear a flannel vest all winter or being dosed with syrup of figs.

'Well, I'm blessed!' Dan exclaimed when Jill had left after telling them the news. 'They haven't wasted much time!'

'Dan, really!' Doris drained the water off the sprouts and added a dab of butter.

'Sorry. Steak and kidney, is it?' he added hopefully.

'Is that all you can think about?' Doris banged a dish of peas and carrots down on the table. 'What I want to know is, has anyone said anything to our Chris about it? This should make those two sit up and take notice!'

· · ·

Chris did sit up and take notice. When Phil and Jill invited her and Paul out for a drink at the country club, she sat up bright and tall when they told her Jill was expecting.

'Oh, congratulations!' she cried, seizing Jill's hands. 'Oh, Phil! I'm so pleased!'

That way she did not have to meet Paul's eyes, and, anyway, he rushed off to order champagne, leaving Chris to ask what she knew to be all the right questions. Was Jill feeling well? Perfectly. She certainly looked it. When was the baby due? The beginning of August, apparently. Chris did a quick calculation. It must have been conceived on honeymoon. And she and Paul had been married for over a year.

She couldn't help but let it get her down. The feeling dragged on right through the summer, the time of year Chris normally loved most, when the horses could be turned out, when she could ride out all the lazy afternoon, listening to the hedges alive with birds, charting the progress of her Dad's corn from stiff shoots to droop-eared ripeness.

'Something's wrong, Chris. You're not – what you used to be, somehow. Are you sure you feel well?'

'I'm all right,' Chris replied shortly. Paul's sister, Sally, who was her partner in the riding stables, was very good at her job and very popular with the customers, but she was not someone Chris would have ever chosen to be friendly with. She much preferred to keep their relationship on a business footing.

'Then what is it?' Sally persisted.

'I don't know,' said Chris bad temperedly. 'I just don't know. Maybe it's growing up . . . getting old . . . getting disillusioned.'

But everyone was growing older. Jill was a year older than Chris and she was anything but disillusioned. Only the day before, Chris had seen her at Brookfield for Sunday tea, looking gorgeous – if enormous – in a pink cotton sundress.

'Disillusioned with what?' Sally probed, rubbing at a stubborn mark on a piece of tack.

The worst of it was that Chris knew every detail of the conversation would get back to Mrs Johnson, Paul's mother. And wouldn't she just love to think there was something wrong with the marriage.

'It's nothing really,' Chris said quickly. 'Nothing specific.' She laughed. 'Can't pin it down to the Sputnik or this credit squeeze that Paul's been going on about . . .' She sighed. 'I suppose I'm just plain silly.'

'You haven't had a tiff with Paul?'

'No. We haven't.'

'That's what Paul says, too.'

So she'd checked. Marvellous. Chris threw down her bit of rag so fiercely she sent the lid of the saddle soap spinning to the floor.

'It's true,' she said fiercely. 'We haven't.'

Sally just looked at her, biting her lip. Chris suddenly felt she'd been unfair on her. In fact, Sally didn't get on with her mother any more than Chris did, so it was unlikely she'd go telling tales about anything that was said. And she did seem concerned. Chris put out a hand and squeezed the other girl's arm.

'I'm sorry, Sally. But I've just got a vague feeling that something's . . . well . . . missing. I don't know what – but something's missing.'

Of course she knew what. It was what Jill was about to have. A baby.

Or two, as it turned out to be.

'Well, no-one can accuse us of half-doing a job, can they?' grinned Phil when Jill told him one day over breakfast. Jill hadn't been feeling well – lethargic and breathless – and he had been desperately worried that something had gone wrong. But now the doctor had told her that she was carrying not one healthy baby, but two.

'I still can't get over it, you know.'

'Finish your breakfast,' said Jill fondly.

'Give us a kiss first!' he demanded.

'Why?'

'I dunno,' he shrugged. 'The occasion seems to call for one.'

He moved the teapot so that he could lean across the table. She tasted of bacon. She tasted delicious.

'Go on,' she said, laughing. 'You're all eggy.'

Phil laughed and sat down again.

'I've been thinking about it, you know,' she mused. 'I don't see that it will be much more trouble bathing two than bathing one.'

'I haven't quite got down to the practicalities.' Phil mopped his plate with the last piece of toast. 'I suppose it'll mean more of every-thing. Nappies, for a start.'

'Twin pram. Another cot.'

'Whatever.' He pushed his plate away and wiped his mouth. 'But mind you do just what the doctor ordered.'

Jill folded her hands over her tummy.

'Ooh, they're kicking, the little horrors,' she said. She reached for his hand over the table. 'Don't worry,' she added. 'I will.'

. . .

Mrs Perkins passed Doris a cup of brick-coloured tea and pushed a plate of cakes towards her. 'Have a fancy, Mrs Archer.'

'Ooh, thank you.' Doris reached for the nearest, which had a large piece of crystallized lemon lodged in the icing. 'I know I shouldn't.'

'Won't do you no harm.' Mrs Perkins settled herself and took her Siamese cat, Whisky, a present from Walter Gabriel, on her lap. 'What's the news from the hospital this morning?'

Jill had been admitted with pains the night before: the babies were certain to make an appearance today. Doris swallowed before replying.

'We didn't phone,' she explained. 'Phil said he'd let us know as soon as there was anything to report. Didn't want to make a nuisance of ourselves.'

'Quite right too.' Mrs Perkins poured a drop of milk into her saucer and offered it to the cat. 'Twins, eh? You wait till the glamour has worn off and she's washing two lots of everything.'

'Oh, I don't think she'll mind. I expect Jill will get as much help as she wants. And I can't imagine Phil not being a help to her.' She smiled ruefully. 'Things were a bit different in our day, weren't they?'

Mrs P pursed her lips. 'When I had our Peg, I wouldn't have given a thank you to have anyone else bathe her or dress her,' she snorted. 'Not like these modern women. They'd rather be at a cocktail party' – she made the very idea sound like a typical day in Sodom and Gomorrah – 'or,' she paused for effect, 'having a career!'

'Ah, but you're old-fashioned, Mrs Perkins.'

'A woman's place is in the home,' asserted Mrs P. 'Bringing up her family and keeping house for her husband . . .'

Doris could tell that Mrs P was bringing out another of her mental soapboxes. She was about to reach for another cake to sustain her through the diatribe when there was a furious knock at the front door.

'Who on earth is this? Middle of the morning!' clucked Mrs Perkins. She eased the cat off her lap. 'Sorry, Whisky.'

'Milkman calling for his money, I expect,' suggested Doris.

'He's early, usually calls around dinner time, when he knows the kettle'll be on,' observed Mrs P tartly.

She stumped off down the passage, muttering to herself about 'cheeky young blighters'. The door took some more punishment from the knocker.

'All right! I'm coming as fast as my legs can carry me!'

Doris smiled to herself and wished the plate of cakes didn't look quite so tempting. She was having a real battle with her weight these days. Whisky jumped up on her lap and she occupied herself in stroking him, whilst keeping an ear cocked for what was going on at the front door. It wasn't the milkman. It was Christine.

'What's going on?' asked Doris as Chris, dishevelled and in her working clothes, was shepherded into the room by Mrs P.

'Been trying to find you,' Chris explained. 'Have you heard the news?'

A glance at the two older women gave her her answer.

'Jill's had her babies,' she explained. 'A boy and a girl. All three doing remarkably well – and the father still conscious!'

Doris put a hand to her chest. 'Oh, thank goodness. That's a weight off everyone's mind!'

'I said all along everything would be all right,' chimed in Mrs P, who had been nothing but a harbinger of doom about piles, varicose veins and backache. 'All along I said it.'

'Phil rang Brookfield, but everyone was out, so he got hold of me and I said I'd spread the news,' said Chris brightly. 'So I'm an auntie five times over now.'

'I suppose you are, dear,' said Mrs Perkins. 'But do you know, we were just chatting about young women like you.'

'Oh, yes?' Chris sounded guarded.

Doris shot her daughter a look. She knew that brittle tone in

Chris's voice and the smile that turned up the corners of her mouth when her heart was down in her boots.

Mrs P blithely collected up the cups and put them on the tray.

'I'll make us another pot, shall I?' she offered. 'Yes, Christine, I just happen to think that when a woman marries, she should settle down and devote her time to looking after her husband and family. In fact, I think it's high time you swapped horses for babies. And nothing will alter my views. So there.'

Chris could feel her mother's eyes on her.

'Well, I happen to think differently,' she sallied bravely. 'But you're entitled to your opinion and I'm entitled to mine.'

'Now you're just being tactful,' Mrs P snorted, peeved at being done out of the chance of an argument. As Walter Gabriel was always finding out to his cost, there was nothing she liked better than a good old ding-dong.

'It's no good, I'm not going to argue,' smiled Chris. 'I'm full of goodwill towards everyone. And I'm dying to see the babies. Mum, when d'you think it would be decent to go along? You coming with me?'

'Just you try and stop me!'

But the person Doris most wanted to see in bed in the maternity ward of the Cottage Hospital was Chris herself, with her very own baby. She knew for certain from everything that hadn't been said that it was what Chris wanted, too. So Mrs P might be proved right yet.

• • •

'On behalf of my wife and me I'd just like to thank all of you for your gifts and everything you've done for us . . . and Jack and Peggy for this fine reception. And look here, Peg. You and Mrs P's supposed to be guests, so stop forever popping out to see how things are going in the kitchen.' Uncle Tom paused, glass in hand, to let the laughter in The Bull's function room subside. 'You've all made it a very happy day for us. So now let's drink up and get on with the party!'

His last few words were almost drowned out in a torrent of

applause and cries of 'Hear, hear!' One of the unlikeliest matches the village had ever seen had resulted in one of the simplest but happiest weddings. Uncle Tom was nearly fifty; Pru Harris – now Pru Forrest – was thirty-seven, yet to see them together was like looking at a couple of teenagers. There was no question that it was a real love match.

'Just please don't let them have any children!' Chris thought to herself, watching her uncle and her new aunt mingle with the guests, their arms wrapped round each others' waists. Then she put her elbows on the table and propped her head in her hands. What was she turning into? Could she really not bear anyone else's happiness?

'Penny for them?' Paul flopped down beside her. Always the life and soul of the party, he had been scheming with Walter Gabriel to play some sort of joke on the couple when they got back to Tom's cottage that night. Chris felt suddenly weary.

'Just tired,' she said. He took her hand and kissed the palm, then brought it away from his face and looked at it.

'Hm. Future's looking good,' he said.

She smiled and stroked his cheek with her fingertips.

'Paul? Do you love me?'

'What sort of a question's that?'

Chris lifted her shoulders in a minute gesture.

'Oh, so you want proof?'

Paul leaned abruptly forward and kissed her hard on the mouth. Her hands flew up to his shoulders and she eased away from him, embarrassed. Her parents were only at the next table, talking to Squire Lawson-Hope.

'Paul! Not here!'

Paul curled a lock of her hair round his finger.

'Listen to Miss Prim and Proper!' he teased. 'All right, let's go home, then. Get an early night?'

She looked into his deep-set eyes and saw herself reflected there.

'Oh, yes, please,' she whispered. She gave him her hand and he pulled her up from her chair.

'Of course I love you,' he said. 'Don't ever doubt it.'

'I know. It's just me. I'm being silly.'

'You certainly are.You're the silliest, most lovable little goose ever.'

But however much he loved her and however much she loved him, they still didn't seem able to make a baby.

• • •

By December, with her own twenty-seventh birthday and their second wedding anniversary looming, Chris couldn't stand it any longer. One impossibly bright day she rode over to Coombe Farm to ask Jill a favour. She had to steel herself to visit the place now, finding the nappies drying in front of the fire and the rattles and rag books on the settee just too poignant for her. Thankfully, though, Jill was outside, wearing gumboots and one of Phil's overcoats. Shula and Kenton, as they'd named the twins, were asleep in their pram in the yard.

'I'm giving Phil a surprise,' Jill panted as she tipped pig nuts from a massive sack into the trough in the pigsty. 'He had to dash off urgently for something after breakfast and he was cursing because he'd have to come back specially to feed his pigs. I'm going to ring him and tell him I've done it.'

'Golly, you're brave,' said Christine. 'He'll be over in a jiffy to make sure you've not given them the wrong stuff.'

'Oh, I've watched him so many times I couldn't go wrong.' Jill dumped the sack on the floor of the sty and dragged it back into the yard. 'Still, you didn't come here to talk about pigs, I bet. Come in and I'll put the kettle on.'

Midnight skittered on the concrete surface of the yard and Chris reined her in.

'No, I shan't stay a minute. I shan't even dismount,' she said. 'Jill . . . I want you to do me a big favour.'

'Just name it.' Jill was scratching a sow's back with a long stick. Chris marvelled at how she had taken to the life of a farmer's wife. Chris wouldn't have dared feed Phil's precious pedigree pigs.

'I want you to come and see a doctor with me in Felpersham,' she said baldly.

'Me? See a doctor? But there's nothing wrong with . . .' Jill tailed off and blushed fiercely. 'Oh . . . sorry . . . what a clottish thing to say. Yes. Of course I will.'

'Thanks.' Chris could have hugged her. 'I hoped you'd say yes. I just want someone to come with me, that's all.'

Jill nodded understandingly, though she looked puzzled.

'Does Paul know?'

'No. Definitely not.' Midnight picked up Chris's vehemence and danced a few steps towards the sty. Jill backed off. Chris knew that horses still rather frightened her and she yanked at Midnight's bridle. 'Nor must Phil,' added Chris urgently. 'Or anybody else.'

'Don't you think your Mum should . . . ' Jill began tentatively.

'No. *No.* I want you to come with me.' Chris could feel herself beginning to get upset. She saw Jill register this and decide to indulge her.

'All right.' Jill extended a cautious hand to pat Midnight's neck. 'Just give me twenty-four hours' notice to fix up the twins and I'll be right along.'

'And it's just a shopping expedition for Christmas, Jill, see?' added Chris anxiously.

'Of course. If that's really all you want me to know at this stage.'

Chris leaned down towards her. 'There's nothing else *to* know at this stage, believe me. Anyway, thanks, Jill . . . for not asking too many questions.'

Jill was utterly dependable, Chris knew. She wouldn't tell a soul. Their trip to Felpersham could be kept a secret and, whatever the gynaecologist, Mr Goodman, told her, Chris would have time and privacy to come to terms with it.

The appointment duly came through for 19 December, two days before her birthday. Jill said she would fix for Mrs Rogers, a village woman who helped her with the twins, to take care of them for the day so that she and Chris wouldn't be under any pressure of time. 'We might even do that bit of Christmas shopping,' she told Chris on the phone. 'Then at least our alibi looks convincing.'

The one thing they hadn't reckoned with was the fact that Felpersham would be full of people, Ambridge villagers among them, on genuine Christmas shopping expeditions and, when she emerged from Mr Goodman's rooms, Chris was horrified to find that, of all people, Jill had been accosted by Mrs Perkins. Talk about trying to keep it quiet! Chris might as well have put up posters in the window of the village shop.

'Hello, Chris,' Jill greeted her warmly, seeing her approach. 'Look what the wind's blown along.'

'Hello, Mrs P,' Chris was amazed to hear her own voice sounding so composed. 'How nice to see you. Just in time for us to have a cup of tea together.' Her mind went back instantly to that day in the summer when she had burst in on her mother and Mrs P having tea, bringing them the news of the twins' arrival. It all linked together horribly neatly. 'Been doing your Christmas shopping?' she persisted, taking the older woman's arm and guiding her down the street. Jill followed at a trot behind.

'Just having a final look round,' Mrs P panted, her feet tapping on the pavement as she tried to keep up with Chris's long strides. 'I like Felpersham better than Borchester, but why were you . . . ?'

'Oh, so do I.' Chris endorsed Felpersham's charms. 'It's a much prettier town.'

'Mind you, Phil was livid because we chose to do our shopping here instead of Borchester.' Jill had now caught them up and they were walking three abreast with Mrs P in the middle like a recalcitrant child. 'He was trying to invite himself along. He'd got visions of entertaining two charming young women to lunch.'

'Instead of which, we're having the pleasure of Mrs P's company at tea.' Chris could hear an almost threatening note in her voice. If news of her visit to the doctor got back to Paul through Ambridge gossip, she knew he would never forgive her.

'Christmas shopping? Fiddlesticks!' chuckled Mrs P. 'You've been paying a call on a doctor's and don't want to discuss it very much. It's all right, love, I can put two and two together.'

'And make five?' enquired Jill.

'But you needn't take any notice of me,' Mrs Perkins went on.

'I can promise that I haven't seen either of you if you don't want me to have seen you.'

'You can say you've seen us, but not outside the doctor's,' Jill pleaded.

'All right.' Mrs Perkins sniffed. 'But I'm very curious and I don't mind admitting it.'

'Well, you needn't be,' Chris said firmly. She'd had quite enough of the subject. 'Now let's stop nattering about nothing and have this cup of tea, then I'll drive you back to Ambridge. Come on, Jill, my tongue's hanging out for a cuppa. And I know a really nice tea shop. It's down here somewhere . . .'

• • •

'I thought we were never going to get rid of her!' Jill groaned as she got back into Chris's car after delivering Mrs P and her several parcels safely to her front door. 'And when she got out those combinations she's bought for Walter in the middle of the tea shop I thought I was going to die!'

'Me too!' Chris started the engine and turned the car in the direction of Coombe Farm. 'I'd better get you home. Your husband will think you've abandoned him, not to mention your babes in arms.'

'Oh, they can do without me for a few hours,' Jill said airily. 'I'm more interested in you. I've been bursting to ask you. Oh, but don't tell me unless you want to,' she added quickly, before giving herself away again with: 'What did he say?'

'Mr Goodman?' Chris waved to Uncle Tom, who was crossing the village green towards The Bull with a brace of pheasant in his hand.

'Well, of course. But really, only if you want to.'

'You're a poppet, Jill – and most considerate.' Chris indicated right at the crossroads. 'But I'll put you out of your misery from one point of view. I'm perfectly fit and healthy – in fact, a very normal female – and there's nothing wrong.'

'Oh, good.' Jill sounded about as relieved as Christine herself felt. 'So – how do you feel about it?' she asked excitedly.

'Hm? Oh – all right, perfectly all right.' And then, realizing, 'Oh, Jill – did you think I was pregnant?'

Jill looked crestfallen. 'You mean you're not?'

Chris laughed out loud. 'No. I'm not pregnant – yet. All I wanted was to know if there was any reason why I shouldn't be. And there isn't. So – Paul and I will just have to keep trying!'

'Well, that's no hardship, is it?' Jill's mouth curved in a smile.

'Not at all. In fact, I'm looking forward to it.' Chris turned into the drive at Coombe Farm and the headlights picked out the old millstone lying in the centre of the yard and the porch leaning lazily against the house.

'Home again,' she said, pulling up. 'And Jill – thanks again for coming with me.'

'Don't mention it,' Jill squeezed her gloved hand as it lay on the steering wheel. 'And I really hope I'll be saying congratulations to you and Paul some time soon.'

'I hope you will be, too. Perhaps I'd better brush up on my knitting over Christmas. I gather the little darlings get through an awful lot of clothes.'

'Well, if I've got one piece of advice for you, it's to start with just the one,' grinned Jill. 'I think that probably helps.'

'Yes,' agreed Christine. 'One would be plenty for me.'

·13·

Family Life

'You're not! How marvellous! Congratulations!'

Chris felt Jill's arms go round her and she closed her eyes against the coming tears. Jill, pregnant again, and the twins not six months old . . .

Jill pulled away and looked at her.

'I've been dreading telling you, Chris. I know how hard it must be for you. But it will happen soon for you and Paul, I'm sure of it.'

Chris nodded, not wanting to speak in case her voice came out all wobbly. Her head was throbbing with the effort of not howling out loud.

'Has Jill told you the glad tidings, then, Chris?' The back door was flung open and Phil came in from the yard in a blast of freezing January air.

'Boots!' called Jill automatically.

'All right, all right.' Phil hopped on one foot, easing his wellingtons off. 'We're after the family allowance, to tell you the truth. All those extra bobs in the kitty.'

'I suppose I'm just surprised because it's so soon after the twins.' Chris heard her voice, though she had no idea if what she was saying made any sense.

'We thought we'd have them close together and grow up with them,' put in Jill. It sounded as though she was making excuses.

'Grow old, more like,' grumbled Phil, padding across to the table in his socks. 'I could sleep for a week.'

'Shula's started teething,' Jill explained. 'She had us up three times in the night.'

'And Kenton had us up twice. Funny how they don't wake each other up, but they never fail to get to us.'

Chris smiled politely. It didn't matter how much Phil and Jill tried to point out the bad side of having babies, she would never be convinced. She would have given up sleep for the rest of her life if it had been her and Paul pacing the floor at three in the morning with a damp, inconsolable little bundle.

'It's about time we had some good news, anyway.' Phil fetched himself a cup from the dresser and sat down. Jill poured him some coffee.

'Are you still worrying about this chap Grenville?' Chris held up her hand to stop Jill pouring her another cup.

'Worrying? That's the real reason he hasn't been sleeping, isn't it, love?'

· · ·

It had all started back in the autumn. George Fairbrother had simply not been the same man since Grace's death. Little by little, he had lost interest in the Estate, until Phil was running things more or less on his own. Phil didn't mind: far from it. He had loved the responsibility, making decisions, ordering equipment, taking on staff. Although he had always kept Fairbrother informed, Grace's father had made him feel as though the Estate was his concern, and Phil had not seen why the situation shouldn't continue. However, back in October, Phil had been summoned to see his boss up at the house. Expecting to go through the herd pedigrees or the lambing averages, Phil had gone armed with a sheaf of files. But when he got there, he was not shown into the study, where they always had their business meetings, but into the sitting room. Helen had changed the house a lot over the years. Gone were the dim velvet curtains and the plump Victorian upholstery. The sitting room was painted in eau de nil with flowered chintz curtains and low, linen-covered chairs. Helen was sitting in one of them, close to the window, doing her tapestry. Phil expected her to leave when he was shown in, but she simply smiled a greeting and carried on with her work.

After a brief preamble, Fairbrother stood with his back to the fire and told Phil why he had asked him over.

'There's no point in dressing it up, Phil,' he said. 'I'm selling up. I've had enough of Ambridge. If everything goes well and a buyer comes forward at the right price, the Estate should change hands next Lady Day. And don't be surprised if you don't see much of me in the meantime. I'm winding up my business interests in London and Birmingham, too, and that'll take up a lot of my time. Anything to do with the Estate, you can refer to Helen here.'

For the next couple of months, that was exactly what Phil had had to do, and he had not found Helen easy to work with. Fairbrother had not been a countryman, but he had understood business. With all due respect, Helen had not done anything much more taxing in her life than organize a Christmas bazaar, but instead of letting Phil get on with things, she queried every decision, which was not just irritating, but incredibly time-consuming.

'And in the end,' he fumed to Jill, 'she has to admit I'm right – and of course I'm right; these are things I've been doing all my life!'

'It won't be for ever, will it?' soothed Jill. 'There'll be a new owner soon, won't there?'

'And that'll improve things, I suppose! What if they're some jumped-up city type who knows nothing about farming and expects me to teach them? My life's going to be a picnic!'

And both of them knew that that was just one scenario. The new owner might even be a hands-on farmer, or he might be coming from another estate and bring his own farm manager with him. Phil might be out of a job . . . and with a wife and babies to support.

He had at least expected things to go quiet concerning the Estate sale over Christmas. As they had done every year since Grace's death, the Fairbrothers took themselves off to London. Phil breathed a sigh of relief.

'A week or, if I'm lucky, maybe even ten days without Helen's interference!' he exulted to Carol Grey, whose market garden had been absorbed into Fairbrother Enterprises, making her a director along with Phil.

'You'll be able to come to our little celebration, then?' she smiled. She employed about fifteen women at the packaging plant at this time of year and when they finally broke up for Christmas, they always had a rare old party.

'Wild horses wouldn't keep me away! I'll bring the bottle of sherry the feed merchants sent over. And don't think your girls are going to get me and Jim Benson playing postman's knock, like last year!'

But life wasn't all sherry and silliness: there were other claims on Phil's time. Dan was planning a big reorganization at Brookfield, investing something in the order of £2500, and wanted Phil's advice. After the festivities, he and Phil spent much of Christmas evening going over the figures.

'Shooting tomorrow, that'll blow the cobwebs away,' his father said, stretching, after they had been poring over paperwork in the Brookfield farm office.

'I can't wait,' said Phil. 'It may not seem very fair to take it out on the rabbit population of Ambridge, but if I don't let off some steam somehow . . .'

'You'll enjoy it, lad,' smiled Dan. 'You always do.'

But the next day Phil did not turn up at the hide on Heydon Berrow as expected. Tom, Walter, Dan and Jack had bagged half-a-dozen rabbits, six pigeons and two hares by the time Phil drove up in the Estate shooting-brake.

'Sorry, you blokes, really,' he began. 'I've been chasing round like a bluebottle.'

'Nothing wrong, I hope?' asked Dan, who knew the answer already. He could see that Phil was preoccupied.

'I don't know,' replied Phil. 'Remains to be seen. I had a wire to contact Mrs Fairbrother urgently.'

Four pairs of eyes looked at him expectantly. Finally he relented.

'Well, if it's a secret now, it won't be for long. It's all over, chaps. In other words, we shall remember this Christmas for a long time.'

Everyone looked even more worried, especially Uncle Tom, who worked for the Estate and would depend on the new owner for his livelihood. Jack, too, worked for Carol Grey as manager on the soft fruit side of her business. But they weren't the only ones. There was no-one in the village who would not be affected by the Estate sale. Dan was no longer a tenant of the Estate and Walter had given up farming, but the character and style of the new owner would affect them and everyone else who lived in Ambridge. The owner of the Estate was the nearest thing the village had these days to a squire. His personality imprinted itself on the entire neighbourhood and could mean the difference between a prosperous and pleasant place to live and a village with all the life squeezed out.

Walter produced an old medicine bottle from his jacket pocket and uncorked it.

'Sloe gin,' he explained. 'I reckons we all needs a swig.'

They took turns to pass the bottle round. The liquid went straight to the solar plexus, from where it radiated heat to the furthest extremities.

'Blimey, Walter, this is strong!' exclaimed Uncle Tom.

'If you ask me, the sloes themselves were about thirty per cent proof!' Jack wiped his mouth with the back of his hand. 'Here, give us another swig!'

When everyone had drunk what they wanted and Walter had recorked the bottle, Phil told them what had happened.

'The Fairbrothers,' Phil explained, 'have had a firm offer for the Estate and they want to accept. Carol Grey and I have to go to London tomorrow for a directors' meeting. Not that we shall be able to do very much about it, I'm afraid. It looks to me as though it'll all be sewn up within a matter of days. Then the new broom will sweep in, and it's anybody's guess who will be swept out. So this is it, blokes, this is it.'

• • •

As Phil had predicted, the sale had gone through. The only glimmer of hope, from Phil's point of view, was that the new owner, Charles Grenville, was something of a protégé of old Squire Lawson-Hope. The Grenvilles themselves, it appeared, had been landowners for three or four hundred years but the family had practically died out since the First World War. In 1939, their whole estate had been taken over for military use and Grenville had shipped out to a colonial post somewhere in Africa, where instead of drinking pink gins and playing polo in his spare time, he had built up several thousand acres of ranching on the side. Now he had sold his ranch, spent a year touring the world looking at agriculture and, presumably, intended to put his experience to good use in Ambridge. In some ways he sounded like a squire of the old school. At least he intended to keep on the Manor House for his own use.

'Just try to keep an open mind,' Jill begged Phil as he prepared to meet Grenville in Ambridge for the first time one day in late January. 'Give him time, see how the land lies.'

'I'll give it time all right,' protested Phil. 'I just hope he feels the same.'

Maybe it was Phil's own fault. Maybe he had so convinced himself that he was not going to like Charles Grenville that it could only happen that way. But from their very first meeting there was friction between them.

'I don't think he's such a bad sort, but I'd say there's a ruthless streak in him,' concluded Carol when they had finally escaped from their audience with the great man and had beaten a retreat to Phil's office.

Phil, who was still smarting from the way Grenville had batted back all the questions he had asked about delegation of responsibility, blew out a breath in an attempt to release some of the tension from his shoulders. He poured a finger of whisky into two smeared glasses and concealed the bottle behind a box file.

'That's all right,' he asserted stubbornly, passing Carol her drink. 'There's a ruthless streak in me, too, but people don't see it very often. And there's one in you,' he added.

'In me?' Carol turned her great dark eyes to him.

'Yes. Otherwise you'd have married John Tregorran long ago.'

Carol laughed exasperatedly. The entire village was still trying to pair them off.

'Oh, get along with you,' she said. 'Concentrate on the subject in hand.'

Phil leaned back in his chair and rolled a sip of whisky round on his tongue.

'I shall do the same as you. Do what he suggested and give him six months' trial. If at the end of that time I'm crawling up the walls with frustration, I shall pack in my job. Start up on my own somewhere.'

'Well, I like working with you,' said Carol warmly. 'I intend sticking it out if it's humanly possible. I don't want to throw away several years of patient work any more than you do.' She looked at him for confirmation and he gave a brief nod. That was the truth of it. All the hours he had put into building up the pedigree herd, the cold nights in the lambing sheds, the field trials with different strains of wheat . . .

'I just don't think I made a very good first impression, somehow,' Phil confided. 'Still, we'll have to see how it goes.'

It didn't go well for many, many months. Phil always felt that Grenville was trying to trip him up, to get him to admit that he'd made mistakes, that the ram he and Fairbrother had chosen hadn't performed well or that the poorly drained patch of land by the river would have been better left as pasture than ploughed up for potatoes. The new owner wanted more detailed egg and milk production records kept, and he wanted copies on his desk every Friday, or posted to him if he was away. He wanted the progeny-testing people to take a look at the dairy herd and he was convinced it was worth experimenting with other breeds of sheep to see which were best suited to the Estate land. Most of all, he was not a bit interested in what he called 'pretty-pretty' animals aimed at the show ring, which would surely mean the sale of the pedigree Hereford herd that Phil had painstakingly built up over the years for Fairbrother, who had been interested in rosettes. Even on pigs, Phil's real area of expertise, Grenville had his own ideas.

'I'm not convinced that your double-A-plus-grade bacon pig is necessarily the best – the most economical to produce, that is,' he opined during one of their first, frosty meetings during that cold spring when he took control.

'We always produce to get best prices,' objected Phil, colouring, as he did when he felt under attack.

'And I think you waste a lot of pig-meat doing just that.'

Grenville stared him out, his grey-green eyes hard on Phil. Phil looked back stonily, wondering if he would last six weeks, let alone six months.

Grenville didn't seem to be as tough on Carol, Phil noticed, though, as she said, she had the advantage over their new boss because, for all his farming experience, horticulture was new to him and he had to trust her judgement. Even so, he made her draw up a plan of the refrigeration and packaging plant's total capacity over the next twelve months, as he was determined to increase it.

'You can't argue with it, Phil,' Carol said mildly when Phil complained. 'He wants to get the best return on his investment. And you must admit, he knows his stuff in a way Fairbrother never did.'

But Fairbrother's way had suited Phil and he chafed under the new regime. There were many nights when he got home to Jill and cursed the Fairbrothers for ever leaving. And when Helen Fairbrother returned to Ambridge in the late spring, it was with another piece of news that would not be comfortable for Phil.

'I'll come straight to the point,' Helen explained, having asked Phil if he would join her for tea at the country club, where she was staying. 'I've got something in my handbag here I'd like you to see.'

Phil couldn't imagine for a moment what it was. A map of the ironstone development that Fairbrother had been so keen on, for old times' sake? Or surely not . . . something to do with Grace?

'George and I have felt for some time – from the moment we knew we were leaving, in fact – that something should be done about Grace.'

So it was to do with her.

'Ambridge is her last resting place.'

'I don't need reminding,' said Phil quietly.

'I'm sure you don't.' Helen passed him a heavy scroll of paper.

Phil unfurled it, bemused.

'It's a stained-glass window,' she explained. 'All the formalities have been gone through and it's going to be installed in place of one of the plain windows at St Stephen's. That's the final approved design.'

Phil rubbed his forehead, the gesture to which he always resorted in times of distress. He stared at the design, which was of the lion lying down with the lamb, until the brilliant colours blurred in front of his eyes.

'I do feel I might have been consulted about this before now,' he said at last. 'After all, I was her husband.'

Helen's hands fluttered over the tea things.

'It's exactly for that reason that George and I thought you'd be the last person to object.'

'I'm not objecting. I think it's a very nice gesture of you both.'

'Then why that expression? Surely you approve?'

Helen reached for the roll of paper.

'Oh, I approve,' said Phil, passing it back to her. 'It wasn't me I was worrying about.'

'Who, then?'

How could she be so dense?

'Jill,' stated Phil. 'I was wondering what her reaction's likely to be. She may not care to be reminded. It's rather a different position for her.'

· · ·

'And so there it was, Jill, love,' he told her when they had bathed and settled the twins, had supper, washed up, put the nappies to soak, folded the ones that had dried, fed Timus and laid the table for breakfast next day. 'A *fait accompli*. They'd said nothing to me about it at all.'

Jill sat down heavily on a kitchen chair. She was five months pregnant now and, unable to get the rest during the day that she had had when expecting the twins, was feeling every second of it.

'Well?' she asked.

'Well, dash it,' said Phil, retying the ribbon round the neck of a pink knitted teddy bear for something to do, 'when we came here to Coombe Farm you said you wanted to erase those features of the place that expressed Grace's personality, didn't you?'

'I said so, yes, and what's more, I did it,' said Jill quietly. He had admired the tactful way in which she had redispersed the wedding presents, changed a pair of curtains here, a set of cushions there, and, one weekend when he'd been away at a conference, had completely redecorated their bedroom. 'It was a bit uncomfortable trying to settle down with Grace, but we've done it, haven't we?'

'*I* thought we had, yes, until this blessed business of the stained-glass window cropped up.' He propped the teddy bear up against a bottle of gripe water. 'Jill –'

She interrupted him. 'I know you loved Grace. But you love me, too. If Grace hadn't died, you wouldn't have loved me, though. You wouldn't have looked at me.'

There was a long silence. Timus sighed contentedly in his basket. In his dreams, at least, rooks dropped from the trees into his waiting jaws.

'I think that's true,' said Phil at last.

'You know it is,' said Jill.

'So – do you mind? The window, I mean?'

Jill picked up the teddy bear and walked it across the table and back.

'I really don't know.' She shook her head. 'I'd be clottish if I did, I suppose, but . . . I don't know, Phil. I suppose it'll be there when – when the five of us go to church.'

'Years hence.'

'Yes, years hence.' She stroked the teddy's ears. 'It's sweet, isn't it? Mrs Perkins knitted it. There's a blue one, too, but Kenton threw it out of the pram into the midden and I haven't washed it yet.'

'Jill, really? Do you mind? Because if you do, I'll fight them on it –'

'Oh, Phil, honestly.' Her voice was warm and rich with love. 'How can I mind? A stained-glass window against those two upstairs? Against the heartbeat that I've got inside me? Against what I know about you as my husband?'

Phil got up and came round the table to her. He stood behind her chair and leaned forwards, wrapping his arms around her.

'You're too good to be true, you are,' he murmured into her hair.

She tipped her head back so that she could look into his eyes.

'I know you loved her,' she said seriously. 'But it is possible to love more than one person in your life. You love me too, don't you?'

'Oh, darling, you know I do.'

He kissed her softly on the mouth and when he drew his lips away she pulled him back to her for more.

'Then I don't mind,' she said when she let him go, 'about the window, I mean. It'll always be there. We'll tell the children about it when they grow up and are old enough to understand.' Phil nodded, his heart too full to speak. 'Oh, dear,' Jill sighed. 'Those Fairbrothers. They've caused some heart-searchings in their time, haven't they?'

• • •

With Phil's blessing, and, more importantly, Jill's, the window was installed at St Stephen's, and perhaps its most surprising consequence was to provide Mrs Perkins with a husband. Arthur Perkins was the stonemason contracted to do the job and like most visitors to Ambridge, he put up at The Bull. Mrs P had met him there, and before long he had been invited round to her cottage for several suppers, to Walter Gabriel's great disgust. A proposal, wedding and Mediterranean cruise followed, and Mrs P and her 'second Perkins' left Ambridge to live in Arthur's London home.

'Ambridge won't be the same without you,' Jill had told her when Mrs Perkins had called round to Coombe Farm to say her goodbyes. Jill was even more heavily pregnant now. Shula, always the more forward of the twins, was dragging herself up on the furniture, trying to stand, and Jill knew that the relative peace she had gained by being able to put the two of them in the playpen and get on with a few chores would not last much longer. Not that there would be much peace at all when the new baby arrived in the middle of September.

'Well, I daresay I won't be the same without Ambridge,' reflected Mrs P. 'But Arthur's a good man. He's not a drinker, for a start, and that's worth a lot.'

'Oh, yes,' Jill agreed with a secret smile.

'Jack's a bit too fond of the bottle, if you ask me. Worst job out for him, keeping a pub. But there you are, Peg wouldn't thank me for saying it, so I don't.' She shook her head. 'Children, you never stop worrying about them, you know, Jill.'

'Thanks, Mrs P. That's really cheered me up.'

Mrs Perkins drained her glass of lemon barley.

'You've got nothing to worry about. You've got a sensible head on your shoulders, and you've got a feller in a million in Phil.'

'I know I have,' said Jill fondly. 'I hope you and Arthur are as happy.'

• • •

'What are they doing up there?' demanded Phil.

'Settling Jill and making her comfy, I expect. For heaven's sake, sit down, Phil.' Doris glanced at the clock. 'I think I'll go and make a cup of tea. I expect the doctor and nurse could do with one, anyway. They'll tell you when they're ready.'

It had been a long night. Jill's labour pains had started in the early evening and Phil had finally woken his parents just after midnight. Since the twins' birth had been so straightforward, Jill had opted to have this second delivery at home, but no-one had reckoned with a thunderstorm which had put the phones out of action, meaning that Phil had had to leave Jill in the care of a neighbour and go for the district nurse himself. To make things worse, Jill had had a delayed second stage of labour, and the doctor had been called out to give her something for the pain. It was now nearly four a.m. and the baby's first cries had only just been heard.

'I'll never have another at home, straight I won't.' Phil was hovering near the doorway anxiously. 'It's too wearing. Dash it, I'll never have another.'

'It'll be a miracle when *you* have your first,' said Doris tartly.

'Mmm? Whassa time?' Dan, who had been snoozing in an armchair, opened one eye.

'Oh, go back to sleep, Dan Archer. You're no help!'

'Oh, hello Phil.' Dan had still not registered that he was in Phil's sitting room at Coombe Farm and not in his own chair by the fire at Brookfield. 'What did it turn out to be? Am I going to get me calf subsidy?'

'Men!' declared Doris in contempt. 'All he can talk about is that heifer that's due to calve.'

'It's her first time, see, and she's a darned good milker,' muttered Dan sleepily.

'May I come in?' The district nurse opened the door from the hall and Phil leapt back as if electrocuted.

'How is she? Can I go up?'

'Is it a boy or a girl, nurse?' Doris asked eagerly.

'It's a boy,' the nurse smiled. Her name was Janet Sheldon and she was new to the area. She looked to Doris too young even to know where babies came from, let alone to be delivering them. 'You must have heard him bawling. He's healthy enough!'

'Thank goodness!' Phil sank down weakly. 'And Jill's really all right?'

'Fine. Just a little tired.'

'Another boy.' Doris dabbed at her eyes with the hankie she always kept up her sleeve. 'Well, well.'

'That's saved you the price of a wedding reception later on, anyway, Phil.' Dan was fully awake now. 'That's the first thing I said to myself when our Chris was born: "Dash it, I'll have to pay for her wedding!"'

'Of all the fibs!'

Doris reddened in case the district nurse might take Dan seriously, but she was smiling broadly.

'You can go up in a minute or two, Mr Archer,' she said. 'If you think you can manage the stairs!'

. . .

'Darling . . . Poor you . . .'

Phil held Jill's hand tightly. He never wanted to let it go. She seemed paler, her skin almost translucent apart from two bright red cheeks. There was a plaster on the back of her hand where the doctor had given her an injection for the pain. He'd explained that that was why she seemed so sleepy.

'Have you seen him?'

The nurse had taken the baby next door to give them a few moments together.

'He looks wonderful. But are *you* all right?'

'Just a bit tired.'

Her voice was very low, not his usual ebullient Jill at all. Her lips looked cracked and dry. Phil lifted a glass of water from the bedside table to her mouth.

'It seemed ages.'

She sipped and looked at him tenderly.

'I must have been obstinate . . . Or he was.' She gave a satisfied sigh. 'Another son.'

'An heir and a spare,' agreed Phil, pleased to see her smile. 'Is there anything I can do? Anything at all?'

With a wince which it hurt him to see, she moved slightly in the bed. She closed her eyes.

'Just stay a little while until the nurse comes back. After that,' she yawned, 'I think I'll go to sleep for a while.' She opened her eyes again and, typical Jill, thinking of him, added, 'You look tired too, Phil. You ought to get some rest.'

'Gosh, you . . . ' he said, moved. 'You're wonderful. Absolutely wonderful.'

Next door, their new son, David, began that tiny newborn mewing.

'Shall I go to him?' asked Phil, half up from his chair.

'No, the nurse is in there. She'll bring him in in a minute. See if he's ready for a feed yet.'

Phil relaxed again. 'Fathers are pretty useless at times like this, aren't they? Everything depends on Mum.'

'You know, I think I shall complain to Mr Grenville over this latest effort.' Jill smiled a glimmer of her usual wicked smile. 'You couldn't have fed me the right concentrates.'

Phil laughed and brought her hand up to his lips. 'You're wonderful, Jill. I love you. And I'm so proud of you.'

'I love you, too,' she whispered as Janet Sheldon poked her head round the door. She had David in her arms, his little limbs fighting the shawl that was tightly wrapped round him and his mouth a dark 'O' in a furious pink face.

'Young Master Archer's making himself known already, as you can hear.'

'He can cut that out.' Phil sounded almost stern. 'We don't train them to howl at night in this establishment.'

Janet brought the baby in to the room. She handed him to his mother and Phil watched lovingly as Jill expertly settled him in the crook of her arm. Jill put her little finger in his mouth for him to suck on and the grating cries subsided to whimpers.

Janet looked meaningfully at Phil. 'Let's see if we can get him settled, then you can get some sleep too.'

'Time for me to go, eh?'

Janet nodded. 'I think Mrs Archer's pretty exhausted. She had quite a time of it.'

Phil stood up reluctantly. He really didn't want to leave her. 'Night, Jill love.' He bent down to kiss her. 'Get a good sleep in if you can.'

'Night, night, Phil. See you in the morning – well, later on, anyway.'

'You bet your darn life you will. I'll be hanging around you and making a fuss of you all day.' Jill arched her eyebrows.

'Grenville will love that, won't he?'

'Grenville can go hang,' declared Phil. 'If he can't spare me on a day like this, it's a pity. I bet when he has a son it'll be a different story.'

Phil was, in fact, getting on better with Grenville these days. The six-month trial period was almost up and Phil was sure of staying on. There had been difficulties on either side, but gradually the two men, after circling around each other suspiciously, had sniffed the air and found that, in the end, they had the same thing – the Estate's best interests – at heart.

'And who have you got lined up as *Mrs* Grenville?' Janet's fair hair shone under her cap as she placed a pillow under Jill's arm to help support the baby.

'Carol Grey would be the obvious choice. After all, they have to work pretty closely, don't they, Phil?'

'Oh, come on.' Phil defended himself. 'The entire village has had her paired off with John Tregorran for years.'

'John Tregorran?' Janet looked at Phil.

'Antique dealer in Borchester,' Phil supplied. 'I don't suppose you'd have come across him. Unless you collect eighteenth-century rattles and feeding bottles and stuff.'

'On my pay? I should be so lucky.'

'I wonder . . .' Jill stroked the baby's cheek. He was still sucking her finger contentedly. 'I wonder if John and Carol will ever marry.'

'It's funny, isn't it?' observed Phil. 'Two seconds ago Jill was half asleep and I was being sent out of the room, but the minute we start speculating about the romantic affairs of the few single people we know, everyone's wide awake.'

Jill smiled. 'Well, when you're a boring old married couple like us, you have to take an interest in these things, don't you agree, Janet?'

Janet finished taking Jill's pulse. She laid her wrist down on the sheet before replying.

'It's not just old married couples. Us single people take quite an interest, too, you know.'

Jill looked at Phil. Like Janet, she had once been new to the area, and she had gone on to meet and marry here. Now she could not imagine any other life. She couldn't think how she had resisted Phil's proposals for so long. Everything was so perfect and felt so right. A happy tear slid down her cheek and dropped on to the baby's shawl.

'Jill? You're not hurting too much?' Phil grasped her hand.

'I'm just so happy.' She bit her lip. 'I'm so happy, Phil.'

'Me too,' he confirmed. Out of the corner of his eye he saw Janet tactfully leave the room. 'It's not been the easiest of years, has it, with the Estate sale and everything? I don't know how you've put up with me sometimes.'

'I love you, you clot,' smiled Jill. She leaned forward to kiss him, and the baby, jolted from his doze, began to cry.

'Here we go,' said Phil. 'Another rival for your attention.'

'You don't mind, do you?'

'Of course not. Three healthy children and the most darling wife in the world? Jill – I'm the luckiest man alive.'

·14·

The Other Woman

'I don't believe it! Every time you go away there's some romantic entanglement!'

Jill's voice came down the phone line, as warm and rounded as the cherry brandy Phil was drinking in his Amsterdam hotel room. It was only midday. Phil would never normally drink at lunch time, but he had had a cold morning tramping round glasshouses with Carol Grey and Grenville and he felt he deserved it.

'It's never mine, though, admit it,' he replied defensively.

'True. And make sure you keep it that way,' she told him. She was smiling, he could tell. 'But Carol Grey and Charles Grenville, engaged . . . wait till I tell your mother.'

'You can tell who you like,' said Phil. 'There's going to be an announcement in the *Echo* tomorrow.'

'I hope Carol's rung John Tregorran.' Jill sounded concerned. 'The poor chap'll be devastated if the first he knows of it is a bald announcement in the "Personal" column.'

'I really don't know,' said Phil, who had been so amazed by the news himself that he hadn't considered how John, Carol's faithful suitor for years, would feel. 'I can't very well ask. It's bad enough playing gooseberry as it is. Look, I've got to go, Grenville's behaving like a dog with two tails. We're supposed to be driving to Rotterdam this afternoon, taking a trip round the harbour by luxury motor launch and then having dinner on top of the Euromast.'

'It's a hard life, isn't it?'

'Don't worry,' Phil assured her, though he knew from her tone she was only joking. 'I'm planning to fit in a little shopping. Bring you back something extra special for being such a lovely, understanding wife.'

'What is it you get from Amsterdam? Tulips? Edam cheese?'

'Something a little more intimate than that. And lots of chocolate for the kids.'

When Phil had rung off, Jill replaced the receiver thoughtfully. Was she a lovely, understanding wife? She'd never even thought about it. She was just herself with Phil, always had been – but because they got on so well in every area of their marriage, it was perhaps easy for her to be. Chris didn't seem to find it so easy to be open and trusting with her husband. Phil's last trip abroad had been a 'boys only' holiday with Paul in the summer, and Christine had kicked up no end of a fuss.

Jill had been baffled by Chris's attitude to the proposed trip and she had told Phil as much when they were sitting outside at Coombe Farm with glasses of ginger beer. It had been a hot and airless July and the late-afternoon sunshine was still powerful enough to make them seek the shade. Ten-month-old David was crawling about on the picnic rug, constantly having to be lifted back to the centre and protesting every time. Kenton and Shula were playing – for the moment anyway, before the next fight broke out.

'I don't know what's brought about Chris's change of heart.' Jill built up a tower of bricks for David, who gleefully demolished them with a sweep of his chubby arm. 'Last week she was saying you and Paul deserved a break. Now she's totally against the idea.'

'Seems Chris thought we'd stay in England and do one or two agricultural shows and a couple of experimental farms,' Phil explained.

'You can do that any day of the week!' Jill leaned over and plucked David from the edge of the rug. 'No, sweetheart, the sheep and cows eat the grass, not you. What's happened to make her change her mind?'

'Well, it's our deciding to go to Paris, isn't it.'

Phil and Paul had opted for a five-day break in a city not best known for its contribution to agriculture.

'What's she afraid of? Losing Paul to some French piece?'

Phil shrugged. 'Could be.'

'Oh, for heaven's sake! I suppose she thinks you're going to bump into Brigitte Bardot on the Champs Elysées.'

'Well, that's always a possibility . . .'

'Oh, yes,' agreed Jill facetiously. 'And she'll say – in her lovely, fractured English, of course – that she's been waiting for two country bumpkins from Borsetshire to turn up and show her what she's been missing in life.'

Phil drained his glass.

'*Bien sûr.*'

Jill looked at him wryly. Before they were married her demonstrating work had taken her not just all over Britain, but abroad as well. Phil always said that one of the first things he could remember her saying to him – on that first day they had met in Mitchells, when he had been behaving like a complete idiot and she had been trying to get rid of him – was that she could say 'no' in five languages, and mean it. She knew for certain that Phil would do the same on this trip.

She held David out towards him. 'Before you start brushing up on your conversational French, love, perhaps you'd like to change your younger son. He's absolutely soaking.'

• • •

Deep down, Jill knew why Chris felt so unsure of Paul. Jill had three perfectly good reasons for not worrying about Phil, but, with no sign of a baby yet, Chris could not feel either the security or the fulfilment in her marriage that Jill found in hers.

Chris and Paul had had a tricky year in lots of ways. The agricultural machinery business which Paul had set up had got into deep financial trouble and he'd had to sell out to a concern which, it turned out, was run by Grenville. Paul now had a five-year contract, doing the same job he had been doing before, but as a salaried employee and, being Paul, he wasn't liking it much. There seemed to be no area of certainty in Chris's life. She was trying to build up the breeding side of the riding stables, but she had had to sell some of her horses to try to bale Paul out. The seeming solution to Paul's money troubles was not suiting him temperamentally. Worst of all, for Chris, was the fact that she wasn't able to provide him with one, let alone the four children they had blithely discussed having before they got married. And now he had announced a trip to Paris without her.

'I'm just not happy about it,' she said slowly, when Jill had tackled her on the subject. 'Right from the first moment it was suggested I wasn't happy.'

'But why . . . why?'

There was a long pause and Chris shook her head.

'I don't honestly know, Jill. I can't explain. But I've just got a feeling about it. And I don't like it.'

Jill was not a great believer in 'having a feeling' about things: with three children under the age of two there wasn't time to indulge in anything that wasn't washing nappies, mashing carrots, brushing hair and wiping noses. She personally thought that by behaving in the way she was, Chris was asking for Paul to go off the rails, and she told her so. But the dreadful thing was that Chris's feeling turned out to be right. As Phil had told Jill down a crackly cross-Channel phone line, they'd been sitting in a café when Paul had seen a young woman whom he had known when she was a girl and who had obviously had – perhaps still had – an enormous crush on him.

'Who on earth is she?' Jill had demanded on Phil's return home, dabbing on a little of the 'Je Reviens' he had wittily brought her as a gift.

'She's called Marianne Peters. Her father's with the embassy out in Paris. Supposedly the families have known each other for years. The last time Paul saw her she was thirteen and he'd just left school. They obviously got on well, but the age difference at the time meant that it never went any further. But now she's – what? – twenty-three and he's coming up to thirty; well, it could be a different story, couldn't it?'

'But he's not going to see her again, surely?'

Phil yawned. It was gone eleven at night and what with the late night at the Folies-Bergère – which he'd told Jill about, naturally, as he had nothing to hide – and sitting up late with Paul listening to all the 'this thing is bigger than both of us' nonsense, he could do without Jill starting to play the midnight marriage counsellor.

'I wouldn't bet on it,' he replied wearily. 'I had the devil of a job even getting him to come back with me. On our last night there he began giving me all this guff about spending a few days with her, just to go over old times . . .'

'I bet!'

'Exactly. What were they going to do, play Scrabble and go scrumping for apples? And you know Paul. He's always had – well, a bit of a – a wild streak.'

'Not like you, you boring old thing.'

'Luckily for you, no,' said Phil. 'Now can we please go to bed? I'm absolutely whacked.'

Phil didn't really see how Paul could arrange to meet Marianne again. The one good thing about the whole situation was that the girl was in Paris, and even Paul, who had to do some travelling in his job, couldn't wangle trips abroad that often. But when he next saw Chris he was worried. There were huge dark rings under her eyes and she seemed very subdued.

'Have you and Paul kissed and made up over our little French trip?' he asked her. She was teaching Jennifer to ride and they both watched as the fifteen-year-old cantered round the paddock, her blonde hair fluttering out from beneath her hat.

'I don't know, Phil.' Chris shook her head impatiently. 'I did a lot of hard thinking while Paul was away. Made up my mind that there'd be an end to all the silly bickering that we get up to.'

'And has there been?'

'Yes, I suppose so,' she sighed, 'but only because we don't really talk about things that'd lead to arguing. We don't discuss money, or children – or anything that really matters. It's just, "Saw Mr Braddock today. He says Jolly's shaped up into a really fine hunter," or, "Nice piece of steak, Chris. Can you pass the mustard?" It's killing me, Phil.'

Phil put his arm round her and hugged her.

'I am sorry. Anything I can do? Want me to have a word with him?'

'No! Don't do that!' Chris turned to him appealingly. 'He'd just think you were interfering, or I'd put you up to it . . .'

'I can't stand by and see you being made so unhappy, Chris. And I've got to tell you, Mum and Dad are worried too.'

'I know. But it's not just me being made unhappy, Phil, it's Paul as well. I sometimes wonder if we're just incompatible. Different temperaments, interests – everything.'

'Oh come on, you've got lots in common,' protested Phil.

'Like what – horses? That's about the top and bottom of it.'

'Be fair, Chris. You laugh at the same jokes, don't you? Enjoy doing the same things – going out, the theatre, music . . .'

Chris tugged impatiently at a bit of baler twine that had got caught on the gatepost. 'I could do all those things with you, or with a friend. We're supposed to be talking about the man I love.' She sighed. 'Once I'd got used to the idea, I hoped those few days away in Paris would – I don't know – bring Paul back to me somehow. But since he came back, he's seemed further away than ever.'

The conversation hardly did much to reassure Phil. But no amount of worrying by any of the family could alter the fact that things were not right between Paul and Chris. Suddenly, to everyone's horror, Paul began to talk about moving away from Borsetshire. He talked about Buckinghamshire, Sussex, Kent, even. Then he seemed to go off that idea and approached Grenville about a travelling job in sales, which would have taken him away from home on a regular basis. Phil liked the sound of that even less.

'What about *you*?' he asked Chris. He found he was making a point of dropping in at the stables most days on almost any pretext to see how she was.

'I stay at home and keep the home fires burning and he comes home at weekends,' she shrugged, leading a pony out into the yard.

'And what d'you say to that?' Phil watched as she expertly tightened a girth before handing the pony over to one of the girl grooms to be led away for a lesson.

'What can I say? I'd rather he was at home all the time, but if he'd be happier in a job like that . . . plenty of men do that sort of work and their wives just have to put up with it.'

'As long as you don't get cynical.'

'Cynical? Why d'you say that?'

'Well . . .' Phil didn't quite know himself why the word had come to mind. 'It was just your attitude. Sort of "couldn't care less – take things as they come". You know – casual.'

'Oh, Phil.' Chris leant against the warm wall of the stable in the fitful late summer sun. 'I've tried the possessive wife, the sulky wife, the martyred wife . . . the meek and mild wife . . .'

Phil rubbed his forehead. Chris and Paul's marriage seemed very complicated.

'Do you have to try all these different sorts?' he asked, bemused. 'Can't you just be yourself?'

'I'm as natural with Paul as I can possibly be,' said Chris fiercely. 'And I love him, I really do. But I sometimes get the feeling I don't register with him, Phil. So I get all worried and frustrated. Then I start trying to be somebody different, to get his attention back. I try to be – oh, forget it.'

'I can't forget it,' said Phil. 'It worries me.'

'Well, don't let it,' said Chris, straightening as another of her girl grooms came back into the yard leading a small child on a pony. '"You're all right, Jack." You look after your own little family and leave me to worry about Paul. Tell you what, I'll try and bring him over to tea at the weekend. I could do with a natter with Jill anyway.'

• • •

In truth, Chris was as bemused as Phil by the situation. She didn't know what had happened with her and Paul. She didn't think that on their wedding day they had looked less happy, or had *been* less happy, than Phil and Jill on theirs. She even got the wedding photographs out to check, and Paul came in one night to find her sitting in the darkness watching the cine film that Phil had shot. She couldn't tell him why she was watching it, of course, and that hurt her even more, and seemed to underline the problem. She didn't talk to him any more about the things that were really important to her, and she wondered if she ever had. He was like a lot of men – he would rather pretend that something wasn't happening than talk about it, and she felt as if she had become in some way infected by the same disease. Whenever, in the past, she had tried to talk about anything emotional, Paul listened patiently, but he had never had anything to contribute and he was, she could tell, always itching to close the subject off. Now it didn't seem worth bothering any more.

She became obsessed with the state of other people's marriages. Even at home, with her parents, she watched the affectionate familiarity with which Dan teased Doris about her weight and the way Doris grumbled back and wondered if she and Paul could ever feel anything similar. She knew that the real reason she wanted to go over to Phil and Jill's was not to chat to Jill or to see the children but – although it sounded ridiculous, even to her – to see if by gesture and by nuance she could pick up any tips, almost, about what a marriage was supposed to be like. All she knew was that it should be something different from hers.

Every time she thought about it she came back to the subject of children. Even Uncle Tom and Pru had fostered a couple of lads, Johnny and Peter. Her parents had three, Jack and Peggy had three, Phil and Jill had three. She felt as if she was destined to be a perpetual auntie.

She and Paul had given up talking about children, as well. After she had finally plucked up the courage to tell him about her visit to the specialist, Paul had amazed her by volunteering to go and be checked out himself. She had been so touched by this that she had got up, rushed round the table, and hugged him right in the middle of the country club, where they were having dinner. The waiter, who was just wheeling over the dessert trolley, had had to make a deft diversion, and a couple dining at the next table had broken out in spontaneous applause. Chris had sat down, blushing, but she had kept hold of Paul's hand all through her *crème brûlée* and when they got out into the car park she had held him tight and kissed him hard.

'Thank you,' she'd whispered. 'Thank you for not minding.'

Paul's visit to the doctor, though, had been no more conclusive than her own. He, too, had been declared A1 fit, and they had been sent away and told not to worry about anything. It would all, they were told, happen in the fullness of time. But then Paul's business had hit its bad patch and he had been frantic with worry. After the buyout, Chris had hoped that the removal of total responsibility would calm him down, but the opposite had happened. He had become restless and dissatisfied. And then there had been Paris.

• • •

She wondered afterwards, for months she wondered, how she could have been so dense. Yet in all the difficulties she was having with Paul, during all the strained silences in the artificial conversations, she had never really considered that his remoteness might be due to the fact that he had met someone else. How naive and stupid could she have been? How easy to deceive . . . Even when there were obvious signs, still she accepted his explanations.

One morning, just after Paul had left for work, and just as Chris herself was about to go out, the phone rang.

'I have a call for a Mr Paul Johnson from High Wycombe,' announced the operator.

Assuming that it was business, Chris asked her to put the call through. She could always take a number and get a message to Paul.

'Hello?' she said into the receiver after the call had been transferred. 'Hello? This is Mrs Johnson speaking.'

There was no response at the other end, and after a moment the receiver was replaced with a tiny click. Puzzled, Chris dialled the operator and explained what had happened.

'Are you able to give me the caller's number?' she asked.

'I'm afraid I can't do that, madam.'

'Can you tell me if it was from a business or a private number?'

'A private number, madam. It was a personal call. Perhaps the caller will try again later.'

'Perhaps.'

She couldn't waste any more time thinking about it: she had a pupil at nine. But all day, as she shouted instructions about keeping a straight back and not pulling the horse up too sharply, the phone call was lodged in her mind, as irritating as a snagged nail. Surely it couldn't mean anything? It could have been a legitimate customer who just happened to be calling from their home number. It might even have been a wrong number – but no, they'd asked for Mr Johnson. All day the thought nagged at Christine. All day she picked at it. That night, she mentioned it to Paul. He was in one of his romantic, flights of fancy moods. He was talking now about travelling the world, just taking off with no agenda, no itinerary, and seeing what transpired.

'We've got enough money to go, you know,' he insisted. 'For months if we like.'

Chris drained the potatoes. They still had to eat.

'And come back to *what*? Put the cruet out, will you?'

'What's it *matter*?' demanded Paul impatiently, doing as he was asked. 'We can start again.' He flung down the napkins as well. 'What's the alternative? We go on stodgily sweating away at the same jobs we've been doing for years, saving our money in the bank. What's the point?'

'Go on, keep at it,' smiled Chris, her heart filled with fear. 'You'll soon have me convinced. Then I'll call your bluff and say, "Right – when do we start?"'

'It isn't a question of calling my bluff at all. I mean it.'

She knew he did. How could she possibly keep him in Ambridge? How could she keep him at all? She concentrated on mashing the potatoes.

'Talking of calls reminds me,' she said lightly, her back turned to Paul. She couldn't look at him, just in case. 'There was a personal call for you just after you left this morning.'

There was the minutest of pauses.

'Personal? Who from?'

Chris mashed some more. These would be the smoothest potatoes ever.

'As you weren't here they didn't say and whoever it was didn't speak.'

'What part of the country did it come from? Local?'

'No,' said Chris. In an indifferent sort of way she checked the chops under the grill. 'High Wycombe. Where's that?'

'Um . . . Buckinghamshire, I think.'

'Aha.' Chris turned to face him at last. 'The place you wanted us to go and live. And you get a personal mystery call from there.' She managed to make it sound joking.

Paul shrugged. 'To be fair, when I mentioned Buckinghamshire I mentioned plenty of other places as well. All I was interested in was being near to London.'

'So who'd be ringing, d'you think?' Determinedly casual, Chris put the mint sauce on the table. The jug was too full and a drop spilt on the cloth, spreading luridly green.

'Search me. A customer maybe. Or,' Paul smiled his irresistible smile, 'some glamorous stranger out of my murky past.'

'Well, if she rings again,' said Chris bravely, though the conversation had done nothing to reassure her, 'I shall send her off with a flea in her ear. Anyway, supper's ready.'

'About time too,' said Paul. 'I'm starving. I thought you'd never finish with those potatoes.'

· · ·

Another month went by. It was a dull and rainy October, not the weather for being out of doors, but Chris had no choice. These days she never mentioned her long-cherished dream of an indoor riding school, something that she and Paul had talked about non-stop when they were engaged. The so-called savings they had in the bank were only a few hundred pounds – enough for air tickets perhaps, but not for anything major. Most of the money laid aside for the stables had gone on trying to save Paul's business, and Chris hadn't resented a penny of it. But as she stood with the rain dripping down her neck, watching talentless eight-year-olds on soaking ponies, she wished with all her heart that her life could have been different. Then one evening, a stormy evening after another rainy day, when Paul was at a Chamber of Commerce dinner in Borchester and Chris was planning tomatoes on toast in front of the television, there was a knock at the door. Cursing, Chris went to open it. Standing on the step was a young woman – a girl, really. She had on a short mac in a sort of peacock blue and her long hair trailed sodden over her shoulders.

'Mrs Johnson?' she said. 'Is Paul in? I'm Marianne Peters.'

• • •

'More coffee?' asked Christine.

'May I?' The girl held out her cup. The sleeve of the pullover Chris had lent her drooped over her hand. 'It just seems to hit the spot.'

Chris poured the coffee. She had insisted that Marianne had a hot bath and, while she was doing so, had hung her clothes up to dry in front of the fire. The real casualty were her shoes, which had started out as low-heeled tan court shoes and were now mahogany-coloured canoes that looked as though they might never recover.

'And you say you and your family have known Paul since you were young?' Chris sat back in her chair and tried to sound as if she were just making polite conversation. All the while she felt as though she were fighting for her marriage.

'It must be at least ten years.' Marianne's hair was drying in the warmth of the fire and Chris could see how it shone, in different shades of natural blonde.

'Funny he's never mentioned you before.' Chris took a sip of her own coffee. She didn't want it and felt it coat her teeth unpleasantly.

'I suppose we just sort of ... drifted out of contact,' offered Marianne.

'And how did you drift back into contact, then?' Chris smiled, still working hard at keeping the edge out of her voice.

'Oh, didn't he tell you? We just knocked into each other. Quite a casual meeting. In Paris.'

• • •

'Just *listen*, Chris. Listen to what I've got to tell you.'

Christine folded her arms in front of her. After Marianne Peters had finally gone off in a taxi (still in Christine's clothes, swearing to return them, although Chris couldn't imagine that she would ever want to wear them again), Chris had tidied away the coffee things, raked the fire, left the porch light on for Paul and gone to bed. There she had lain, rigid and tense, going over everything Marianne had told her – innocent as it sounded – in her mind. According to Marianne, all Paul had done for her, as a favour to an old friend, was to fix her up in a job with a public relations firm in Borchester that was run by someone he knew. The reason for Marianne's visit tonight had been to thank him in person. It all sounded plausible enough. Just because she was a young woman – an attractive young woman, at that – was that any reason to doubt either her motives or Paul's? No, of course not, *if* Chris had known any of this beforehand. But the fact remained that it was over two months since Paul and Marianne had renewed their touching youthful friendship in Paris – and not a word had been said to Chris about it. And that was what had kept her lying awake all night, feigning sleep when Paul came in, but all night wide-eyed in the darkness, wondering. Worrying.

'I still don't understand,' she said next morning, 'why you didn't tell me when you got back.'

Paul sighed. He looked as wrecked as she felt. He had had a fair bit to drink at his dinner. She knew he had been planning a gentle morning working at home, sustained by lots of aspirin and black coffee. Instead she had had some satisfaction in waking him at seven, and telling him over breakfast that she had had a visitor whilst he had been out.

'Come and sit down, Chris, please. Don't look at me like that.'

'How am I supposed to look at you?'

'I don't know. But don't look so – stern. At least, not until you've heard what I've got to say.'

Chris chewed her lip. Then, abruptly, she sat down at the table opposite him. Outside, in the leafless garden, a blackbird practised its winter cadences, a fluting football rattle of song.

'Go on, then.'

'It was a very . . . strange situation, Chris. By now I'd hoped the whole thing would be forgotten. Past history.'

'Yes? What "whole thing"?'

'You know that Marianne is an old friend of the family. The last time I saw her she'd be about thirteen, but I first knew her when she was about seven.' He lit a cigarette. Chris watched him, how he placed it between his lips, still talking, then paused, twisted his mouth to hold it and brought up the flame of his lighter. The lighter she had given him for their second anniversary, one of those new gas ones, with his initials on. He drew on the cigarette and exhaled. 'She was always very fond of me. She said she'd marry me when she grew up. If I'd wait for her.'

Chris frowned. 'That's a bit fanciful, isn't it?'

'She was only thirteen, remember.' Paul drew on his cigarette again. 'Naturally, I kidded her along and said I'd wait. Who wouldn't have done?'

'And don't tell me she did wait?'

'Precisely that. Never even had a boyfriend, so she says.'

'It's unbelievable,' said Chris softly.

'Exactly. I couldn't make up a story like that, could I,' appealed Paul, 'and expect to be believed? But I wasn't worried,' he added. 'She was in France and I was in England. Until she suddenly moved over to High Wycombe. Her father's retired there. And she wrote asking for a job at my place.'

'And you got her a job,' put in Chris, 'albeit somewhere else. Wasn't that asking for trouble?'

Paul met her eyes for the first time. She should have felt angry with him, she knew, but instead she felt sorry for him, even though he had caused her so much pain. If she had been naive, then so, perhaps, had he.

'In a way, I suppose it was. I suppose I didn't really think it through. But now she's arrived on our doorstep – to see you . . .'

'She came to see you.'

'I know.'

Paul tapped his cigarette against the ashtray – the painted pottery ashtray that her parents had brought them back from their holiday in Torquay this year. Chris thought of all the little things that they had accumulated during their life together. Did they represent anything? Or were they insignificant, was she insignificant, against Marianne?

'Is this why you've been so edgy and irritable? Because all this was going on?'

'Yes.' They both watched a curl of smoke from his cigarette. 'I was flattered, I suppose. We'd been going through a rough patch. Meeting her again seemed like . . .'

'If you say fate,' snapped Chris, 'I'll scream.'

'Well, all right. I was going to, but I won't. But think about it, Chris.' He leaned forward, impassioned. 'Borchester's too small a place to conduct an affair, even if I wanted to. Far easier from that point of view if I'd left her down in High Wycombe and gone to see her every now and again.'

'But you did think of that, didn't you? All that talk of a sales job?'

'Maybe. And I also talked of us moving to Buckinghamshire – or away, anywhere – but the two of us, Chris, you and me. I was just in such a muddle. I didn't know what I wanted.'

'And now? Do you know what you want now?'

'I'm going to tell her. Tell her straight. We couldn't ever be anything to each other.' He reached suddenly for Chris's hand and gripped it. 'I'm married to the best wife in the world. And the sooner Marianne finds herself a nice boyfriend of her own, the better it'll be all round.'

Chris didn't pull her hand away, but she didn't respond to the pressure of his either.

'And what'll she say to that, do you think?'

'I don't care what she says. It's all I've got to say on the matter. The whole thing was impossible. A storm in a teacup. And now the storm's blown over.'

Indeed it had. Last night's rain had washed the sky clean. Streaks of cloud chased each other in and out of the bare trees.

'I see.' Chris was still trying to take it all in, to think through all the implications. 'Well. Thanks for telling me.' She wanted to, but didn't, add 'at last'. He was still holding her hand. He stroked it gently.

'I'm so sorry if I've hurt you, Chris. It's been a nightmare. You see, Phil saw this reunion in Paris and got the whole thing wrong . . .'

So that was why Phil had been so solicitous towards her.

'But never mind all that,' Paul went on. He ran his hand through his hair. Chris noticed for the first time that he was beginning to get one or two grey hairs at the temples. 'I'm fed up with the whole thing, to be honest. It's been putting me off my work . . .'

'And off your wife?' Maybe it was the grey hairs that did it. He seemed so vulnerable. So lost. And if she didn't look after him, he'd find someone else who would. She curled her fingers round his. Paul smiled. It wasn't his usual confident smile, more an apologetic grin.

'There's one sure way of proving that one way or the other. Come here.'

She didn't move, but waited and watched him. He got up from his chair, their hands still linked, and moved round the table towards her. He pulled her up to face him and she let herself be pulled. She looked into the face she loved so much and felt her heart turn over. If she had lost him, her world would have ended.

'Oh, no.' She shook her head in mock despair. 'That's your answer to every problem.' Paul took no notice. He pulled her against him and started kissing her all over her mouth, starting at the corners, with tiny, fluttery kisses. She smiled against his lips.

'No, look, Paul, it's quarter past ten and I've got work to do. Paul! Mmmm . . . Paul . . . Mmmm . . . Oh, Paul, what am I going to do with you?'

. . .

'So, what are you going to do about it?' Jill bit off the end of the thread and rolled it into a knot. She was mending a tear in Kenton's dungarees. Outside, the twins could be heard shrieking as they 'helped' Phil to sweep up leaves for a bonfire. Little David was asleep in the pram in the hall.

'Jill, what *can* I do?' Chris looked round the kitchen at Coombe Farm, Timus snoozing in his basket, the miniature jumpers and vests drying in front of the stove, the blobs of Plasticine on the floor. She loved it here. 'Look, I know Paul's got his faults. He's impetuous, vain, and he's always looking for something new. But he's my husband and I love him. That hasn't changed.'

'Well, good for you.' Jill pinned a corduroy patch on the material. 'Some women would find it rather harder to forgive and forget.'

'Oh, I'm not finding it easy. Don't think I don't jump when the phone goes or when there's a knock at the door. Don't think I don't think about him every minute of every day, when I'm at the stables and he's – Lord knows where. But I am trying to put it behind me, Jill. If I don't, it'll eat away at me. It'll devour us both.'

'You have to learn to trust him again, I suppose.'

'Yes,' said Chris simply. 'And I don't quite, yet. But I will. I have to, Jill, for us to go forward. And it's made me realize . . .' Her voice tailed off.

'What?' Jill looked up from her sewing.

'It's Paul that matters to me. It's him I want. All this stuff about having a baby . . . well, if it happens, it happens. If it doesn't, it doesn't.'

'Really? That's quite a change of heart for you.'

'I know. But I'm going to stop bashing on about having children, Jill. You won't hear any more from me on the subject. I've got the man I want and that's good enough for me. As long as I've got him, I'll be all right.'

·15·

Changing Times

'I can't believe it, Mr Sinclair. I'm sorry, I just can't.'

Doris dabbed at her eyes with a ball of damp hankie. Andrew Sinclair, the manager at the Estate, who had taken over the job last year when Phil had finally decided to join his father in a cooperative venture, Ambridge Farmers Limited, with another farmer, Fred Barratt, shook his head.

'I doubt if there's any of us can, Mrs Archer,' he said in his broad Argyllshire accent. 'I just thought I'd maybe better come along and clear up what I can – since you were all such good friends.'

Doris let out a pained cry, then bit her lip against the tears. 'I wish you didn't have to say "were" like that . . .' she whispered.

'Now, don't upset yourself, love.'

Dan laid his big, work-toughened hand on her shoulder. But he, too, was shocked beyond belief. The news that Andrew Sinclair had brought them was that Charles Grenville had been badly injured in a car crash – and that in the same crash, John Tregorran's new young wife, the former district nurse Janet Sheldon, had been killed outright. John had been courting her since the beginning of the year and they had only been married a few months. Dan knew just what Doris meant. It was simply too much to take in.

Andrew Sinclair had been there the previous afternoon it happened, when he had been invited back by Grenville for a cup of tea at the Manor House after a long meeting to discuss crop rotation on the Estate. The way Andrew told it, it had begun as the most innocuous of tea parties. He and Grenville had walked into the sitting room to find Carol and Janet gossiping by a welcoming fire. Grenville,

253

Andrew had told them, had been in a particularly ebullient mood.

'Well, well, there you are!' he'd apparently exclaimed. 'Two genial witches over their brew!'

Janet and Carol had smiled. It was Hallowe'en.

'I haven't seen you for a long time, Mr Sinclair,' Janet had said.

'Keeps himself hard at the grindstone, this Calvinist of ours,' Grenville had joked. 'Snatched him away from it for five minutes for a quick cup, Carol, if there is one?'

Carol Grenville had felt the pot and decided that it would do. She began pouring. There were two spare cups on the tray.

'Haven't time for one myself,' Grenville had told her, explaining that he had to race over to Felpersham before the end of the working day to do a deal on a new grain contract. Janet looked at her watch and registered the time with dismay.

'I really ought to get back,' she exclaimed, looking around for her things. 'I've stayed much longer than I meant to.'

'Give you a lift if you like,' declared Grenville. 'Andrew,' he ordered, 'you stay and talk to my wife about her witcheries. Now, if you're ready, Janet . . .'

Janet stood up, clutching her handbag and gloves.

'Thanks very much indeed for the tea, Carol.'

'Not at all,' Carol Grenville had smiled. 'Come again as soon as you can.'

Then, in a confusion of goodbyes, the two of them were gone, Grenville assuring Carol he'd be back by seven, Janet promising that she and John would be at the fireworks party that the Grenvilles were holding the next week, and saying how much they were looking forward to it . . .

'Poor wee lassie,' Andrew said now. 'She wasn't to know.'

• • •

Everyone had been surpised, but delighted, when John and Janet had made a match of it. She was younger than he was by about twelve years but, as Tom had been the first to say to Doris, that hadn't been a bar to his and Pru's happiness.

'It's not so much that, it's what they'd have in common, though,' mused Doris. 'John Tregorran's such a – well, such an arty chap. And Janet's very down to earth. She has to be, in her job.'

'They say it was pottery as brought them together.' Thanks to his lengthy sojourns in the public bar of The Bull, Tom could always be relied on to know those delicious details that add such piquancy to gossip.

'Pottery?'

'Seems Janet was doing an evening class, throwing pots. She bumped into John on her way home one night and showed him something she'd made. He was so impressed he even took a couple of her pieces to sell as curios in his antique shop.'

'Well, I never. What sort of pots was she making?'

'Oh, give a chap a chance, Doris!' protested Tom. 'You'll be wanting to know what perfume she was wearing and the colour of John's socks next!'

The laughter and excitement of John and Janet's courtship and marriage seemed a long way off now on this most miserable start to the winter.

From what Andrew Sinclair had told Dan and Doris, it had been the most avoidable of accidents, and, as with all accidents, hedged around with 'buts' and 'if onlys'. It seemed that a couple who didn't know the area, on their way to a Hallowe'en party at Hollerton, had stopped to check their map. Not being country people, they'd assumed that they would be the only traffic on the narrow road and had scarcely bothered to pull off on to the verge. Grenville, coming round a bend in the lane, had had to swerve to avoid their car, careering into a field gateway where he had skidded on mud dropped by a tractor after the cultivations. Then the car had slewed all the way across the road again before hitting a telegraph pole on the passenger side.

'Janet must have been killed outright, Mrs Archer,' Andrew Sinclair said gravely. His red hair gleamed like Doris's copper warming pan under the kitchen light, which was still on, even though it was mid-morning. All Souls' Day, 1 November, had brought its own personal ghosts. 'She wouldn't have known anything, for a mercy.'

'And Mr Grenville's pretty bad, is he?' Dan asked after another pause to comfort Doris.

'Aye, I'm afraid he is.' Andrew Sinclair sighed. 'It's his legs and his chest mainly, where the steering wheel crushed him. And there's some head injury, too, from the windscreen.'

Doris shook her head and started to weep again. Dan patted her shoulder roughly.

'There, now, Doris, there, love.'

'I don't think he's regained consciousness,' Andrew added. 'Mrs Grenville's with him at the hospital. They've got him under blood transfusion.'

Doris wiped her eyes. She clutched the edge of the table, striving for control, her bulbous knuckles pitiful against the worn oilskin cloth. She swallowed hard before speaking.

'It . . . it just doesn't seem right, Dan. I saw Janet only yesterday. I was thinking how pretty and happy she looked. Poor, poor John.'

Dan nodded. There was nothing to say.

'And as for Carol . . . it's so terrible, it's all so terrible.'

Tears rolled down her pouched cheeks again. Andrew Sinclair shifted awkwardly in his chair.

'Wheesht, Mrs Archer, don't upset yourself.'

Dan knew her better. 'No, best have it out, Doris, best have it out.' He sat down beside her. 'Come on, old girl.' He gently eased the sodden handkerchief from her fingers. 'Look at that, that's no use, is it, eh? Here you are, use *my* hankie . . .'

• • •

All day, Doris couldn't get the news out of her head. She was supposed to have been meeting Carol, who was President of the Ambridge WI, for a meeting about the annual Christmas Fayre. Ever since Doris had organized a superbly successful Fayre a couple of years ago, where the gimmick had been a mystery Santa Claus –

ironically, played by John Tregorran – Carol had insisted that she be on the committee. There would be no meeting now. A couple of the other committee members telephoned Doris anyway, though they, too, had heard the news and their voices were flat with shock. With the day stretching empty in front of her, Doris knew she had to fill the time somehow.

When Dan had something on his mind, he would take himself off for a walk round the farm. 'The best manure,' he often said, 'is the farmer's boot.' Doris would sometimes go with him. He would rarely speak. As he paced the fields of wheat and barley, depending on their stage of ripeness, he would examine a growing plant for mildew or pull off an ear of corn and chew a grain or two. In the springtime, he would examine the buds on the apple trees in the orchard, noting which holes in the bark the woodpeckers were favouring for their nesting places this year. In the autumn, with the berries ripe and the birds busy in the hedgerows, he would fill a basket with sloes or blackberries for cooking or bottling.

He always seemed to gain strength and peace of mind from the simple natural activity, from being in touch with the land. He would be walking the farm today, Doris knew, thinking through the implications of Grenville's injuries for Brookfield, for Phil, for Paul, for Jack and for the whole village. She so wished she could go with him, but her legs were playing her up and it was so dull and misty she could scarcely see to the end of the garden. She knew that if she went out of doors her nose would start to drip and the damp air would lie heavy on her shoulders, where she already had a touch of rheumatism. So Doris turned to what had always been her greatest comfort in times of trouble. She would do some cooking.

She got out the huge crock of flour and two pats of butter, which she herself churned from the milk from the herd. She took from the larder glass jars of caster sugar and currants, packets of mixed peel and a jar of stem ginger. Out came the desiccated coconut and the glacé cherries, the golden syrup and the black treacle. When Ned Larkin came in to get his flask of tea refilled, she asked him to bring her over some apples from the store and to fetch the eggs from the henhouse, which she had not had time to collect. Happy for the first time on that drab day, surveying the store she had laid out on the table, she began greasing tins. This would make her feel better.

Yet as she creamed butter and sugar, whisked eggs and sifted flour, all she could see, like snippets of film shot by Phil on his cine-camera, were pictures of John and Janet Tregorran and Carol and Charles Grenville. As if it were yesterday, though it was over two years ago – 18 September 1961 – she could picture Carol and Grenville's wedding day. Doris couldn't remember such a big village event since the Queen's Coronation. Ambridge had been in a delirium of excitement for weeks. It had been decided that the reception would take place at Arkwright Hall, which served as a village community centre, as there would be more seating under cover if the weather should be chilly.

'You'd think the circus was coming! I wish it *was* the circus!' ten-year-old Anthony William Daniel had lamented to his grandmother after seeing the marquees go up. 'All this fuss for a blooming wedding!'

'You watch your language, my lad.' Doris had rapped him on the knuckles with a fork. She had been baking that day as well, but only because there was to be a special send-off for Carol at the WI that evening and she had offered to make the sausage rolls. She was glad she didn't have the job of making the wedding cake. It had fallen to Doughy Hood, the baker, to create the most elaborate five-tier confection, the details of which were a secret guarded with his baker's shovel, for Doughy took his responsibilities very seriously. Then there were the two coaches ordered from Wainwright's garage to collect the outlying Estate workers for the party, and the staff at the market garden had been working night and day to make sure that the choicest blooms would be fresh and ready for the big day: gardenias for Carol's headdress; roses, stephanotis and lilies for her bouquet. With Jill, Doris had been invited by Carol to see the dress beforehand, and she had gasped when she had seen the simple beauty of the heavy oyster grosgrain, with its high neckline and sweep of train.

'It's exactly what I'd expect of you, Carol, dear,' she'd said. 'Perfectly simple and uncluttered.'

'It reminds me of something.' Jill was frowning, searching for the comparison. 'I know, those pictures of medieval court ladies. Yes, Carol, I can quite see you and Charles as Arthur and Guinevere!'

'This is supposed to be my wedding, not a fancy-dress party!' Carol had laughed. But she knew, as they did, that she had chosen just the right thing for her severe, classical looks.

The Archers were to be involved on the day, as well. Harvey Grenville, Charles's cousin, was to be best man, but Carol, who had no close family, needed someone to give her away, and had sought out Phil on the farm to ask if he would do her that honour.

'It's me who'll be honoured!' he'd said, busy heaving fertilizer bags on to a trailer. 'Are you sure about it, though?' He indicated his worn work shirt and overalls. 'I'm hardly high-society material, you know.'

Carol held out her hands. 'I've still got dirt under my fingernails, look. Just because I'm marrying Charles, it doesn't mean I'll forget who my old friends are.'

The wedding day had been perfect: soft September sunshine with the first leaves swimming lazily down on gentle currents of air. When the simple ceremony was over and everyone had enjoyed the reception, Walter Gabriel and Ned Larkin had organized games for the children and a special peal of bells had been rung by the Ambridge team to mark the occasion. Then Carol and Charles – as no-one in the Archer family would ever feel able to call him, though he told them he wanted them to – had set off for their honeymoon in Venice.

'Good do, weren't it?' Walter, reeking of his special shaving soap, 'Ashes of Roses' ('Dog roses, more like,' Dan had muttered), swayed up to Doris. Wine, beer and cider had been flowing freely all afternoon – much of it down Walter's throat.

'I'm surprised to see you here, Walter,' Doris had said. Walter had been a perfect nightmare as a tenant, but he was still resentful of the treatment he'd received all those years ago, first from Clive Lawson-Hope and then from George Fairbrother, which had led to him giving up his farm. As a result, Walter had sworn that he wanted no more to do with landowners.

'I've come for Carol's sake,' he said defiantly. 'Her's a good 'un. No side to her. I never would have forgiven myself if I hadn't have seen that ring go on her "Amen" finger.'

'I see John Tregorran left early,' Doris observed.

Walter shook his head sadly. He and John were close friends.

'He's a broken man,' he said, never one to underdramatize. 'I don't suppose we'll see him smile again this side of paradise.'

'Oh, Walter, you do exaggerate.' Doris straightened the rose in his buttonhole, which had developed a drunken list. 'But it can't have been an easy day for him.'

It took John Tregorran a long time to come to terms with the fact that Carol was married. The village was desperate to pair him off with anyone who came along, which hardly helped. He had something of a flirtation with Dawn Kingsley, who helped him in his antique shop, but it seemed as if he felt that he and Carol were meant to be together. He had missed his chance – several chances – and if he couldn't have her, he didn't seem to want anyone else. He still saw Carol and they remained friends, but he was a sad and isolated figure. But if John was made miserable by her marriage, in those early months Carol had never looked happier.

Doris smiled to herself. It was funny. She never would have believed she could feel so close to the woman who was, after all, 'lady of the Manor'. But she and Dan had known Carol for years. They were the reason she had come to Ambridge – to buy what had originally been Jack's smallholding and turn it into the successful market garden it was today. Although she had always been smart and well spoken and, it had to be said, rather a modern woman for Doris's taste, Doris knew Carol as a hard worker. She wasn't the type to give herself airs and graces just because she was going to live at the Manor House. Even before they were married, she had nearly called off the engagement because she had feared that Grenville wanted a rather more staid, hat-wearing, bazaar-opening, good works sort of wife. Carol had fought hard for her independence and it didn't come easily to her to give it up. But when, within six months of marriage, she had found out that she was pregnant, she had had no alternative. Someone else had to be brought in on the management side of the market garden and Carol, always so slender, always so elegant, had blossomed into a rather less slender, but still effortlessly elegant, excited, expectant mother.

It was Doris who had been with her when the baby started. Grenville was in London at a meeting and, having got Carol safely to the nursing home and delivered of her baby, it was Doris who rang him – in the middle of a business dinner, apparently, not that he minded – to tell him he had the son he had always wanted.

'The loveliest little boy you ever saw, Dan,' Doris burbled excitedly when she bore the good news back to Brookfield.

'Yes, my love, so you said – forty-five times since you've got home,' replied Dan wearily, not even glancing up from an article on foot rot in his farming paper.

'I reckon Mum called somewhere before she came home, you know,' grinned Phil, who had popped in at teatime and had stayed on to keep his Dad company.

'I called in at The Bull and had a glass of sherry,' Doris said, trying to sound dignified, though even to herself her words sounded a little slurred. 'Told them all the news and then Jack gave me that bottle of champagne to bring home. And all you two can do is look down your silly noses at me as if I was a naughty child,' she concluded, indignant.

'I know, love, but anybody'd think you'd had the baby yourself,' pointed out Dan.

'Well, I'm tickled pink.' Doris sniffed. The trouble with champagne bubbles was that they came down your nose when you least expected it. 'I was able to give Carol a bit of company – and reassurance . . . You know, after I saw her, she was like a different person, somehow.'

'Sure you weren't seeing two of her, Mum?' Phil helped himself to another glass.

'I hadn't had a drop. She was – oh, I don't know, softer . . .

gentler, somehow. You know Carol, always so efficient. But now she looks . . . relaxed . . . '

'In other words,' said Dan, admitting defeat and laying down his paper, 'she looks like every other mother who's just had her first baby.'

'Yes,' said Doris, as if realizing it for the first time. 'That's just how she does look.'

'If you ask me, Dad, our very respectable Mum has got herself a bit tiddly,' grinned Phil. 'I think I'd better put the kettle on. Tea all round?'

'Ooh, Phil, I'd love one.' Doris pushed away her glass. 'This stuff's all very well, but it doesn't quench your thirst.'

It must have been the arrival of the baby – to be called Richard Charles, and entered even before his birth for Grenville's old school, so confident was his father that it would be a boy – that convinced John Tregorran that Carol's marriage was a reality. After a growing friendship with Janet Sheldon, he took her away on a touring holiday of the West Country and, at St Just-in-Roseland, proposed. If Carol now had a taste of what life had been like for John during the past couple of years, witnessing her engagement and marriage, she quickly stifled the feelings, and by the time John and Janet were married at the end of June 1963, the couples had become so close that Janet was married from the Manor House.

Doris rerolled the pastry trimmings to cut out leaf shapes for the top of her apple pie. The kitchen was already filled with the spicy smell of gingerbread and cut-and-come-again cake. A batch of scones and a malt loaf to make and then she'd have to start thinking about getting Dan's tea. She heaved a deep sigh. Just four months married, and now John was a widower and Carol, a mother with a tiny baby not yet one, was sitting by the bedside of her husband, willing him to live.

Doris had been a churchgoer all her life, and her faith in God was unshakeable, but just at this moment she wondered how such things could possibly happen, and to such good people. No doubt the vicar would have something to say about it on Sunday, when they would all, as a village, pray for Janet's soul and for Charles Grenville's recovery, and send their thoughts and prayers to Carol and to John . . .

· · ·

'Hello, Jennifer! I shall be able to hear you coming now, shan't I?'

Doris's hens had scattered to the furthest corners of the yard. Some had skittered into the barn. A couple of the silly things had even tried to fly over the chain-link fence into the orchard.

'Hello, Granny. Does it make a terrible noise, then?' Jennifer switched off the engine of her moped and removed her helmet, which made Doris think of the pictures of spacemen that had been all over the newspapers recently. Jennifer shook out her long blonde hair.

'No, not really.' Doris watched as she propped the bike up on a little metal prong and came over to kiss her. It was the middle of February, Jennifer's half-term from teacher-training college, and there had been a hard frost in the night. The lower halves of Jennifer's legs were protected by her knee-high boots, but there was still, to Doris, a frightening amount of exposed flesh before her heather-coloured tweed skirt started.

Managing somehow to stop herself from saying, 'You'll catch your death, my girl,' she went on, 'If you don't mind me saying so, I don't know what young ladies are coming to. In my day, it was thought very daring to ride on the pillion seat. And here you are, in control of the machine itself.'

Jennifer smiled. It would have been fairer if Lilian had had the looks and Jennifer the brains, thought Doris, but Jennifer seemed to be blessed with both.

'Well, I think it's marvellous of Dad to buy it for me. It means I'll be able to come and see you more often.'

Jennifer's college was in Walsall, on the outskirts of Birmingham. She loved it there, sharing a flat with three other girls, and why wouldn't she, as Jack observed wryly, sitting up all night drinking cheap white wine and putting the world to rights.

'Well, let's go on in and get the kettle on.' Doris shivered. 'It's a lazy wind, this –'

'Can't be bothered to go round you, goes right through you!' sang Jennifer, completing her sentence. 'Oh Granny, I do miss you and your funny old sayings!'

'Hey, less of that, madam!' Doris put her arm round her and Jennifer snuggled in close as they walked towards the kitchen door.

'What, the funny, or the old?' Jennifer grinned mischievously. 'That's stumped you, hasn't it?'

As Doris got out the cups and Jennifer put the cake on a plate – not too grown up to stick her finger in the icing and hope I haven't noticed, thought Doris – Jennifer demanded to be brought up to date on all the village gossip.

'What's the latest with the Estate?' she asked.

Doris poured water into the teapot and brought it to the table. She sat down heavily. It was over three months since the accident and Charles Grenville was still in hospital.

'It's not good news,' she said. 'They're going to have to amputate his leg after all.'

Jennifer sucked in her breath. 'Yeurgh.'

'I know.'

Doris could still remember seeing amputees from after the war – both wars – begging on street corners. You didn't see them much nowadays. She wondered what had happened to them all.

'Will he get an artificial one?' Jennifer sounded gruesomely fascinated.

'That's the idea. But in the meantime, while he's waiting for the wound to heal, he's got to go around in a wheelchair with his trouser leg pinned back . . . it's not a very appealing prospect for a man like Grenville, is it, really?'

'So who's running the farms?' Jennifer had got over her distaste and spoke through a mouthful of cake.

'Andrew Sinclair. With your Uncle Paul as sort of second-in-command. Carol's very involved – they discuss everything with her. And Mr Grenville chips in as best he can from the hospital.'

'That doesn't sound very efficient.'

'Maybe not, but your Grandad's just pleased they didn't drag your Uncle Phil back to see things through.'

Phil, Dan and Fred Barratt were just starting to get things going the way they wanted with the cooperative. Dan must have been feeling confident, which was unusual in one so cautious: he had even bought an extra hundred acres from a local farmer, Hiram Parsons. And it wasn't just on the farm that things were starting to settle down. Phil had given up Coombe Farm when he had left Grenville's and he, Jill and the children were just starting to feel as if Hollowtree farmhouse, where they now lived, was home.

'It's all change. Dad says Admiral Bellamy's estate might be coming up for sale.' Jennifer sipped her tea to which, Doris noted, she had added three spoons of sugar. Yet she was as thin as a rail. Still, at her age Doris had had an eighteen-inch waist, and look at her now . . .

'I don't think your Grandad'll be interested. He's got more than enough on his plate.' The truth of it was that Doris hoped Dan wouldn't be interested. He would be sixty-nine in October and still no thought of retiring. Luckily, Admiral Bellamy's land was not especially convenient for Brookfield, and Dan had never seen the point of having parcels of land all over the county. He liked to be able to walk or drive round his holding on farm roads. He resented the time the men would spend travelling between one field and another and he worried that at busy times, like harvest, he would not be able to keep a watchful eye on everything.

The truth of it, though, was that no-one knew what Admiral Bellamy's son, Ralph, who had an estate of his own in Cambridgeshire, would do. The land might be parcelled up into convenient lots and sold off. Parts of it might come up for rent. Or the whole estate could be sold, kit and caboodle, to the highest bidder. There didn't seem to be any shortage of people with pots of money these days. The pop singers you heard so much about, for a start. Heaven forbid one of them came to live in Ambridge!

'Well, I'd like Ralph Bellamy to come and live here,' said Jennifer dreamily. 'It's a good name, isn't it? If ever I write a romantic novel, I think my hero might be called Ralph.'

'A novel? Get on with you!' Doris poured them both another cup of tea and cut two more thin – well, thinnish – pieces of cake.

'Why shouldn't I? Teachers have jolly long holidays, you know.'

'And I should think they need them, the way some children behave nowadays.'

'Oh, that doesn't bother me,' shrugged Jennifer. 'I've got a younger brother and sister, don't forget. No, I want Ralph Bellamy to come and live here and be Master of Foxhounds and fall in love with me and live happily ever after.'

'You've got your life all worked out, haven't you?' smiled Doris incredulously. 'I didn't think girls of your generation believed in marriage any more.'

'Oh, it would have to be on my terms,' declared Jennifer. 'Otherwise, what's the point? You have to know where you're going in life, Gran.' She dabbed her finger round her plate, picking up crumbs. 'And I'm going on a diet tomorrow!'

• • •

Doris was thrilled to see Jennifer so happy in what she was doing. Lord knew, Peggy and Jack had had worries enough with her. When Jennifer was barely fifteen, Jack was already fretting about the way she was developing.

'It isn't her fault if she's blossomed out, is it?' Doris had said mildly. 'You can't stop 'em growing up.'

This had been no comfort, as Jack told her it was exactly what Peggy said, thus was not what he wanted to hear.

'Well, she's right,' confirmed Doris. 'The time for you to start worrying about Jennifer is when Peggy starts worrying.'

'Peg's got a different attitude of mind, don't forget,' warned Jack.

'Well, you'd do well to change yours,' retorted Doris.

She knew what the trouble was. Jack had always had big ideas. First they had been for himself. He was going to turn the smallhold-ing, when he had had it, into the most productive plot of land in

England. But that had been too much like hard work, so he had uprooted the family and taken them off to Cornwall for a year to try to do the same down there. By the time he came back to Ambridge, he had had enough of hard graft. He seemed to think running a pub would be a better bet, but after the licence had had to be transferred to Peggy, thanks in part to his drinking, Jack had found himself with time on his hands again. Odd-jobbing for Carol Grey, as she then was, had led to a job as her market-garden foreman, but Doris knew that Jack always felt he had not lived up to what he saw as his early promise.

No wonder, then, that he had once had ambitions for Jennifer to go to university, not just to college, and even now was talking about Lilian becoming a vet, when she would be lucky to get a handful of GCEs when she took her exams this summer. Yet if Jack expected the girls to work hard, he didn't want them to play hard. It was no wonder that a girl as lovely as Jennifer had no trouble in attracting boys, and Jack found fault with every one of them. Even when she had met a really nice lad, Max, on a skiing trip a couple of years back, Jack had played the heavy father and tried to make her give him up. It had lasted quite a while, nevertheless – nearly two years, which was a long time at Jennifer's age. Jennifer had confided in her Gran that Max had asked her to marry him, but she had refused.

'I'm far too young to get married!' she'd said. 'And anyway, he's the first boy I've been out with properly. Unless you count Gary Kenton, of course,' she added, 'but he was more interested in his broiler chickens than me.'

'You've got the right idea, Jennifer. You girls have far more opportunities than we had in my day,' Doris had advised her. 'You take your time.'

Jack had heard the marriage rumours. He had huffed and puffed and anticipated the worst. That was Jack's trouble. He thought Jennifer was so intelligent, but he never gave her credit for having any sense at all.

Doris had no worries about Jennifer, or Lilian, provided Jack didn't push her too hard, nor about Anthony William Daniel, who had progressed from electric trains through chemistry sets to his latest craze, a soil-testing kit, which he was busy trying out at Brookfield and charging Dan the handsome rate of a shilling a field. No, if Doris had had to worry about anyone down at The Bull, it would have been Jack himself. And when, in the spring, Jack came round, beaming fit to burst, and told them he had some good news, her heart filled with dread. What harebrained scheme had he come up with now?

'So – what are you going to do with it, Jack?' Dan had asked after what felt like a full minute's silence, during which time Dan and Doris had begun to digest the fact that Aunt Laura, who had always favoured Jack and Peggy, was to give – not lend, mark you, but give – them £25,000.

'I don't know.' Jack was practically bouncing round the kitchen. The usual, dull, defeated look had gone from his eyes. 'It's like – I just don't know – it's like winning the pools or something. I don't know if I'm on my head or my heels.'

'Well, you stay on your heels, feet on the ground,' said Doris firmly.

As well as Jack's over-exuberance, which was worrying in itself, she couldn't help but be suspicious of Laura. There had never been any love lost between her and Doris, and Laura's special treatment of Jack and Peggy in the past had always caused resentment in the family.

'She said something about – apart from the fact that me and Peg have been kind to her – something about death duties. Avoiding them. Says she might as well give it to Peg and me.'

'You've got to be careful, Jack,' warned Dan. 'It's five years before a gift's free from death tax.'

'Don't you worry,' grinned Jack. 'Aunt Laura's good for another ten years at least.'

'If she dies before the five years are up,' emphasized Dan, seeing the way Jack was going, 'you've got to pay back all the tax yourself, even if you've spent the money in the meantime.'

'If I were you,' chimed in Doris, 'I'd get her to have a check-up at the doctor's – before you go on a spending spree.'

• • •

'Do you think we'll ever stop worrying about them?' Doris asked Dan as he climbed into bed that night.

Dan was more worried about whether, if he turned out the cattle tomorrow, they would poach the grass. Even if they did, would it be a better option than keeping them indoors on the fag end of the winter rations, when they were scraping the sides of the clamp for silage and there was no goodness left in the hay?

'Eh? What's that, love?' he said, his usual tactic when playing for time.

Doris knew exactly what he was doing. His mind had been else-where – out on the farm somewhere. But she helped him out, as she always did.

'I'm talking about our Jack. Will we ever stop worrying about him?'

'I don't suppose you will, no,' smiled Dan, snuggling down. 'Here, that electric blanket Phil and Jill gave us for Christmas is a god-send, isn't it?' He turned his portion of the sheet neatly over the eiderdown. 'The fact that he's a grown man hasn't stopped you in the past.'

'He acts like a child, though, Dan. You saw him today. He'll be like a kiddie in a sweetshop with that money. Ooh, it's vexing of Laura, it really is.'

'And this is the same person,' protested Dan, 'who told Jack off for worrying about Jennifer.'

'Oh, Dan Archer, go to sleep, why don't you, you're no help.' Doris yanked the cord pull and put out the centre light.

'Come on, come and have a cuddle,' coaxed Dan. He moved his arm so that she could lie against him. She eased herself down in the dark.

'Seriously, Dan. I'm worried about him.'

'And he's worried about Jennifer and Lilian and I'm worried

about the cows. When will any of us learn that we can't worry it better, hey?'

He kissed the top of her head.

'Hey?'

'I don't know,' Doris replied sleepily.

'You get a good night's sleep,' yawned Dan. 'It'll all look better in the morning.'

'I hope so.'

Doris kissed his cheek and slid out of his encircling arm.

'Now you turn on your side or you'll be snoring.'

Grumbling, Dan did so. Doris stroked his back with the back of her hand.

'Night, night, love,' she said.

'Night, Doris.'

'And Dan?'

'What now?'

'For what it's worth, I think you should turn the cows out tomorrow. They look fed up of being indoors to me.'

Dan turned back over, with much rustling and slithering of eiderdown. He raised himself up on his elbow, then lowered his face to hers and gave her a kiss.

'Do you know something, Doris,' he said. 'For a wife, you're the best cowman I'll ever have.'

·16·

The Young Generation

'Well, Mum, what do you think?'

'Oh, Peggy, it's beautiful.'

Doris ran her hand over the pink, grained surface – Formica, Peggy had explained, wipe-clean and very practical – into which the hand basins in the new ladies' toilets at The Bull had been counter-sunk. The toilets themselves, with the new 'low-flush' cisterns, were pink also, and Peggy had chosen a deep, crushed-strawberry carpet (Carpet! In a pub toilet! How times had changed!) and paler pink emulsion for the walls. There was a white china cat with painted-on eyelashes crouched on the window ledge and some sweet williams from the garden in a cut-glass vase. Doris marvelled. She could still remember when the 'conveniences' at The Bull were a plank over a hole in a shed at the bottom of the pub garden, an area now covered in tarmac and signposted as the special parking area for coaches.

Over a year had passed since Aunt Laura had made her surprising and generous gift to Jack and Peggy, and the extensions and improvements at The Bull, which was how Jack, unbelievably sensibly, had decided to spend the money, had finally been completed. For months, Peggy had told Doris, the builders had seemed like part of the family: she had heard about their wives' difficulties in childbirth and their luck (or not) at the bingo. She knew which football teams they supported and how they would be voting in the election, which had been held in October 1964 and which had finally – but only just – brought a Labour government to power. She had even bought tiny Christmas presents for their children.

271

Now they were gone, leaving behind them the smell of fresh plaster, curious, unnoticed breakages and the odd cracked window pane where a ladder had slipped. But Peggy was so pleased to see the back of them she didn't care.

There had been some grumbling among the regulars when Jack had announced plans to scrap the old 'bar parlour' and knock it together with a storeroom to make a bigger drinking area.

'It'll be all smarted up, you'll see,' Walter Gabriel had prophesied to Ned Larkin over one of their regular games of dominoes. 'They won't want the likes of you and me suppin' our ale in here no more.'

'Where shall we go?' worried Ned. 'The Cat and Fiddle down the Hollerton road's full of rowdies on motorbikes and scooters. They won't want us there, neither.'

'If the worst comes to the worst,' decreed Walter, laying down a domino thoughtfully, 'we shall stay at home and drink our way through my home-made wine. That'll put a dent in Jack Archer's profits. Your go, Ned.'

But in the end, the locals had been pleased with their new parlour, the 'snug'. The old chairs and tables, with a few additions, were retained, and the fireside corner was reclaimed by Walter, Tom and Ned. The horse brasses gleamed against the newly painted walls, but everyone knew it would not be long before the cosy fug of tobacco smoke from roll-ups and pipes smeared the brass and stained the paintwork the same ochre colour it had been before. The collecting box for the Royal National Lifeboat Institution, which enabled you to roll your contributory penny down a slipway, was reinstated on the bar by popular demand, along with the pickled eggs. Ear-splitting and tooth-cracking pork scratchings were still available and honour was satisfied.

For the more sophisticated drinker, the crowd Jack was really trying to attract, there was a newly decorated 'lounge' bar with a scrolled maroon carpet, a cocktail menu and salted mixed nuts in little cellophane packets. Jack's ideal customer would live on one of the new 'executive' estates on the outskirts of Borchester, and would drive out along the bypass in his Cortina on a Saturday evening or a

Sunday lunch time. He would be a young man in a professional job, a bank clerk perhaps, or climbing the junior management ladder at the canning factory. His wife might work as a shop assistant (preferably in a department store like Underwoods or Mitchells, rather than in Woolworths), as a nurse or a teacher. He would drink beer, but only in halves, whilst she would ask for a gin and bitter lemon.

But more importantly, they would eat. They would go through into the new dining room and order rump steak and chips for him and half a roast chicken for her, followed by Peggy's mandarin orange gâteau and sherry trifle and an Irish coffee apiece. And when they drove away, relaxed and replete, they would tell their friends and come back again. It was for customers like these that the ladies' toilets had been carpeted. Times were changing, as Doris had observed, customers were more discriminating, and The Bull couldn't afford to stand still.

Peggy explained all this to Doris as she made them a pot of tea when the grand tour, including a peek into the flat that had been built for Aunt Laura over the dining room, was completed. It was a warm day and Peggy carried the tray out into the garden which, at four in the afternoon, was empty of customers. Doris followed, flapping her hand in front of her face to try to get a breath of air.

'And they say summers aren't what they used to be,' she wheezed, lowering herself into the deckchair that Peggy had set up. The wooden benches were fine for the customers, but not the place to get comfortable and have a really good gossip. 'Well, Peggy, I congratulate you. It all looks lovely. And Jack's pleased, is he?'

This was code for: 'How is Jack?' which Doris never liked to ask directly.

'Oh, Mum, I think we may have turned a corner.' Peggy passed her a plate. 'Shortbread?'

Doris helped herself, balancing the biscuit on her saucer, as Peggy went on, 'He seems much more settled. He's really thrown himself into these improvements. He seems determined to build up trade. Wants coach parties and Christmas menus and everything.'

'Not before time.' Doris sipped gratefully. Peggy always made a lovely cup of tea. 'After all the worries you've had with him. The worries we've all had.'

Peggy smiled sadly.

'I know. The only thing is . . .'

'What?'

'Well, it's all come a bit too late. For the family, I mean. Look at Tony, for instance. We never see him. He's up at your place tinkering with tractors the whole time. He doesn't seem to think of much else but farming these days.'

Anthony William Daniel was moving with the times, too. On his fourteenth birthday he had announced that from now on he wished to be known simply as 'Tony'. It had taken Doris some time to get used to it, but it suited him.

'Dan's delighted,' Doris said, brushing shortbread crumbs from her lap on to the grass, where the tireless blackbirds, now raising their second or third brood, would get them later. 'He was saying the other day how nice it would be to have another farmer growing up in the family.'

'It's in the blood, isn't it?' said Peggy. 'He's given it all up now, but Jack still misses the land.'

Jack seemed finally to have accepted that his future lay with the pub. Though Doris had always thought it at best tactless and at worst asking for trouble, Phil had been keen for Jack to invest his £25,000 at Brookfield, where he, Dan and Fred Barratt were expanding the herd and building a modern herringbone milking parlour. It was Jill who had squashed that idea.

'I think Jack and Peggy have done jolly well together and worked jolly hard,' she'd declared. 'I'm glad they've suddenly touched lucky and I don't begrudge them a penny of it. So far as Aunt Laura's concerned, it's a certain fact that nobody else deserves anything.'

'You don't mince your words, do you?' Doris had looked at her admiringly.

'It's true, though, isn't it?' Jill had continued. 'Jack and Peggy have been good to her while we've all seen her as a bit of a nuisance and a busybody. A troublemaker if ever there was one.'

'Yes,' agreed Doris grimly. 'And make no mistake. This could be the biggest piece of trouble she's ever caused in the Archer family.'

'Well,' said Jill sensibly, 'it'll only do that if the rest of us start getting jealous and all try to steal a piece of Jack and Peggy's cake. I can promise you Phil and I won't, whatever Phil may say.'

So Ambridge Farmers Limited, apart from a small investment which had been at Jack's insistence, had had to find a more conventional way of raising the money for their expansion. That, too, was done now. The first batch of cows would be arriving this week, to be introduced into the expanded parlour and to meet the new cowman, a young Irishman with flaming red hair called Paddy Redmond, who would be looking after them.

'And then there's Jennifer who's practically left home.' Peggy continued her lament. 'And when she is back home on holiday, she's out the whole time.'

Jennifer was now in her second year at teacher-training college. She was learning fast about life. There had been trouble last Christmas when she had lent her flat to friends. They had repaid her generosity by holding a rowdy party and, on her return, the landlord had bluntly told her to quit. Jennifer had been incensed by the injustice ('I wasn't even there and it was mostly my things that got broken! My Rolling Stones LP and my Mary Quant mirror!') and infuriated by Jack's somewhat pious attitude to the incident. Doris knew that Jack worried about Jennifer's wild streak, never seeing that it was the same wild streak that had given his mother so much cause to worry about him over the years. His latest concern was over how she looked.

'Who do you think is going to give you a job as a teacher, looking like that?' he had demanded when she had come home for the weekend dressed from head to foot in black, with a sort of woven waistcoat and strings of beads round her neck. 'They want someone the kids can respect, not a beatnik!'

Jennifer had raged at her father for his concern with her appearance, saying it was the person she was that mattered. Was he saying he didn't like that either?

'I don't know any more!' Jack had raged. 'I don't recognize you!'

When Jennifer had reported this, indignantly, to her grandmother, Doris had had to hide a wry smile. She could remember Dan having exactly the same conversation with Jack, except Dan had accused Jack of looking like a 'spiv', owing to the way he slicked back his hair and the money he'd spent on silk handkerchiefs.

'And what kind of influence is Jennifer having on Lilian,' Doris asked astutely, holding out her cup for a refill, 'with this new "with-it" mood or whatever it's called?'

'That's one consolation.' Peggy poured russet-coloured tea into Doris's cup and added milk. 'It doesn't seem to make any difference to Lilian at all. She's been working up at Valerie Trentham's stables for a year now and she's still loving every minute. She even condescends to wear a skirt now and then as a change from her jeans and jodhpurs. In fact, she's wearing one today. Val's away at a show in Shropshire and Lilian had to show some prospective pupils round.'

'Will they be back this afternoon?' Doris swatted away a wasp which was buzzing round the rim of her cup, attracted by a few damp sugar crystals. 'I don't seem to have seen them for ages.'

'Jennifer's walked up to collect Lilian from work,' explained Peggy. 'If I know them they've stopped off on the bridge to watch the world go by. Not, as Jennifer keeps telling me, that anything worth seeing ever happens in Ambridge.'

• • •

Jennifer sat on the parapet of the bridge, the bridge over which a Roundhead army, on its way to confront the forces of Charles I at Edge Hill, had marched out of Ambridge, leaving behind them a wounded drummer boy who supposedly made ghostly tappings at The Bull. Careless of its history, Jennifer swung her blue-denimed legs in a totally modern fashion and regarded her sister.

'Lilian, it's raining in Paris.'

'How on earth do you know?' Lilian looked incredulous. She was leaning over the low stone wall and gazing into the water. The Am was low. 'Do you remember how we used to play Pooh sticks here?'

'Never mind that. Charlie's dead.'

'Charlie? Who's Charlie? What on earth are you nattering about?'

'Don't be a drip, Lilian! It's snowing in Australia. In other words – down under!'

'Oh, I get it!' Lilian straightened up. 'My petticoat's showing.'

'Haven't you heard any of those expressions before?' Jennifer lit up a cigarette ostentatiously.

'Only the Australia one. What are they teaching you at that college?' Lilian hitched up her underskirt. 'Better not make a display of myself.'

Jennifer blew out a perfect smoke ring. That was something else she'd learnt at college. And it wasn't always tobacco that she practised with. 'Not that there's anybody much to make a display to in this village,' she complained. 'Strictly Dragsville.'

Lilian was busy checking that her bra strap wasn't showing, either. 'There,' she said, 'perfect.' She turned and surveyed the road to and from the village. 'Wow,' she said in a low voice. 'And only just in time, too.'

'What do you mean?' Jennifer's curtain of hair obscured her vision and she turned her head to look in the same direction as her sister.

Lilian hoisted herself on to the wall and clapped both hands to her chest.

'I'll have to sit down. Throb-throb-throb . . . that's my heart,' she declared dramatically. 'Look, coming along the road. Use your eyes, girl. And wow is the word!'

Jennifer was loathe to admit that there was anything or anyone in Ambridge that could possibly command her attention. Trying to look as if she didn't give a fig, she looped her hair behind her ear and glanced up the road. Coming towards them and towards the village was a tall young man, with dark, straight hair worn long over his collar. He was wearing sunglasses that hid his eyes, but if Jennifer knew anything, they would be a luscious dark chocolate brown. He was wearing jeans, pretty tight ones, too, and a mauve, short-sleeved shirt. He was gorgeous.

Jennifer could sense Lilian nearly bursting with excitement beside her. She took another slow puff on her cigarette and exhaled.

'Mm. He's OK,' she said casually. 'But I don't see why you should burst into sudden ecstasy.'

'But don't you think he's good-looking?' Lilian insisted. 'Simply fab!'

'Are you going off young Malcolm or something?' asked Jennifer shrewdly.

Lilian had been going out all year with Malcolm Taylor, whose father had bought Doughy Hood's bakery.

'No,' Lilian sounded defensive. 'But a change of scenery never did anyone any harm.'

Jennifer scrunched out her cigarette with the toe of her sandal.

'Who is he, anyway?' She wished she had a mirror in her bag to check how she looked.

'That's what I'd like to know myself. All I've gathered so far is that he's got some kind of tie-up with Sue Bent – or at least, he did have.'

Sue Bent was the new barmaid at The Bull. She had an impressive peroxide beehive and was rather over-liberal with her applications of 'Californian Poppy', which Walter said turned the beer.

'Better keep our voices down a bit,' Lilian added as the young man drew nearer. She hummed a snatch of 'She Loves You' to herself, before calling out, 'Hello there!'

'Hello.' He was still a good distance away.

'Remember me?' continued Lilian boldly, if not very subtly.

He was almost with them now.

'No, I – oh, yes, I think I do.'

No, you don't! thought Jennifer. You're just very charming.

'We met in that funny little café in Borchester,' Lilian went on brightly. 'You came over and asked me about Sue. Somebody had told you my name and that my father kept the nearest equivalent to a low joint round here.'

The young man smiled. He had the most even teeth Jennifer had ever seen.

'Far from that. Highly respectable, it seemed to me.'

He took off his sunglasses. No wonder he wore them: Jennifer had been right. Those chocolate eyes might melt in the sun – and he had a deep, dark chocolate voice to match. She thought it was about time she said something. No point in letting Lilian have it all her own way.

'Too respectable. The haunt of every old village square for miles around,' she said in the careless drawl she had perfected over the months at college.

'This is my older sister, Jennifer, by the way.'

The young man looked Jennifer straight in the eye. She felt as if she were starting to melt, too. Perhaps they had all been too long in the sun.

'How do you do?' he said.

'Hi.' It came out high, as well. So much for the casual drawl. Jennifer gave a little cough.

'And you're Roger Patillo,' continued Lilian excitedly. 'Sue told me. It sounds a bit improbable, doesn't it?'

'Sorry?'

'Your name. Sounds . . . I dunno – a bit made-up, sort of.'

'I don't see why,' he said slightly stiffly.

Jennifer cringed. 'Don't pay any attention to her. She's always like this, Pat.'

'The name's Roger, remember?' he grinned. 'You've got a short memory.'

Jennifer looked up at him from under her lashes. 'I'd still prefer to call you Pat for short.'

'Pat Patillo?' he queried with a smile.

'Mm. That's very good. Almost sounds like a pop star.'

'You play the guitar, don't you, Roger?' asked Lilian eagerly.

'Occasionally,' he admitted. 'How do you know?'

'Sue told me,' said Lilian archly. 'Or at least she hinted as much. Among a lot of other things.'

Roger looked slightly embarrassed. 'I was on my way to see her, actually.'

Jennifer looked at her watch. 'The Bull's just opening this minute, I should think.'

'Well, I'll be seeing you then. Both Miss Archers.'

'Bye,' Lilian smiled.

'See you around – Pat!' Jennifer called after him.

Roger turned round. 'Is that a promise?'

Jennifer had that melting feeling again. 'Could be,' she called. 'Anyway, bye for now.'

He raised his hand and walked on towards the village.

'So.' Lilian sounded triumphant. 'What do you think of that, then?'

'Not bad,' conceded Jennifer. It was his conversation and his sense of humour, as well as his looks, which had appealed. 'Not bad at all.'

'He's certainly a smasher to look at,' sighed Lilian.

Too old for you, Lilian, Jennifer thought, and miles too sophisticated. About time! There had never been anyone her own age in the village with whom she had felt she might have a decent conversation. There was John Tregorran, of course, and Walter's son, Nelson, when he was back from his travels, but they were both years older than she was.

'Sue says he really is quite good with the guitar and folk songs, you know,' Lilian continued. 'We ought to tell John Tregorran. He could put on a concert or something at Arkwright Hall.'

Jennifer nodded, thinking her own thoughts. What on earth was Roger Patillo doing in Ambridge? He surely couldn't really be here to see Sue, with her impossibly blonde hair and her cheap scent?

'What makes you think he's staying around?' Jennifer asked. She jumped down off the wall. 'Come on, we'd better get back.'

'He's met us now, he's bound to,' said Lilian. 'You must admit, it's about time Ambridge had a bit of young local talent – in every sense of the word, don't you agree?'

Jennifer thought about what Lilian had said as she poured sherry and pulled pints alongside Sue Bent in The Bull that evening. She usually helped her parents out in the pub during her holidays. It was true that there was simply no-one else, nor ever had been, as attractive as Roger Patillo in Ambridge. When, at about eight thirty, they had a lull in custom, Jennifer poured both herself and Sue a tomato juice and, trying to sound casual, said, 'I met your friend Roger Patillo today. You know him of old, do you?'

Sue looked at her cynically. 'He's a nice-looking bloke, isn't he?' she said.

'Well, yes, and I'm sure he's a very nice person as well,' replied Jennifer, feeling rather exposed.

'Dishy,' stated Sue. She took a swig of her drink, then dabbed the corners of her mouth with a shocking-pink polished fingernail. 'I knew him in Cambridgeshire. He used to drink in the hotel I worked in. Always very charming. When I told him I was moving over this way, he said he'd drop in if he was in the neighbourhood. And he has.'

'So he's just passing through, is he?' said Jennifer, feeling, to her chagrin, that she could not probe any further into the nature of the relationship between Sue and Roger.

'Well, funnily enough, when he popped in earlier, he said he rather liked it round here. And if he could find something interesting to do, he might consider staying.'

'Oh?' Jennifer hoped she didn't sound too keen. What sort of thing would a man like Roger Patillo consider interesting, she wondered. Aunt Laura was talking about getting someone to help her out – a sort of chauffeur-handyman. Or would that be a bit beneath him, with his exotic-sounding name and educated voice?

'I hope he won't cramp my style,' Sue continued, adjusting the pendant that lay on her psychedelic-patterned blouse so that it nestled between her generous breasts. 'There's one of the Estate workers – Steve someone or other – that I've got my eye on. So,' she concluded, 'if you are after Roger Patillo, feel free!'

• • •

'Well, are you happy with your new cows, then?' Doris asked, leaning on the gate beside her husband and son. Dan gave a satisfied sigh and all three of them gazed at the herd of black-and-white cows, calmly mooching and munching their way round the field. A red admiral butterfly fanned its wings on the gatepost. Overhead, in a cloudless sky, swallows looped and tumbled.

'Very nice indeed, that first batch,' proclaimed Phil.

'Aye, I'll confess I'm delighted with them myself,' concurred Dan. 'And just a few quid cheaper than I'd reckoned. Young Paddy's as pleased as punch,' he added. 'Feels he's really beginning to get somewhere.'

'He's turned out to be a good chap. Doesn't mind hard work, either,' agreed Phil, who, when Paddy had started, had had reservations, though more about Paddy's personality than about his work ethic. 'He's too charming,' Phil had said, anticipating Paddy winding himself and his father round his little finger. 'There'll be trouble, you mark my words.' But there hadn't been any trouble at all with Paddy. He kept his cottage and its tiny garden tidy, took a drink or two down at The Bull, but not to excess, and was passionately involved with his cows – sometimes, it seemed, to the exclusion of all other distractions.

'And he's a nice lad in himself,' added Doris. 'What he needs is a girl. He doesn't seem to have much real interest in them, does he, for all his charm?'

Dan slapped his hand on the warm wood of the gate.

'You and your matchmaking!' he laughed. 'You should set up one of these agency affairs. The Ambridge Matrimonial Bureau, Principal, Mrs D. Archer. Fully Experienced in Arranging Suitable Introductions!'

'Well,' asserted Doris, 'there never is any harm in a nice bit of young romance about the place – and we haven't much doing along those lines in the village these days. There aren't the young people around that there used to be.'

'Dear me, Mum, it's hardly any wonder,' grinned Phil. 'If they let themselves into your clutches, they'd find themselves married off and saving for a three-piece suite on HP before you could say "young generation". Youngsters today want to live a bit before they get married, you know.'

'Hah! Listen to the old married man talking,' scoffed his father.

'I seem to remember you having a few affairs of the heart before you settled down.'

'Yes, but it wasn't like today. Goodness, when I went to the Farm Institute we thought we were being daring if we sat up till half-ten with a mug of cocoa talking about store cattle. Now there's Jennifer away at college, wearing those funny peaked caps and waistcoats and what have you and never seen in a skirt any more, and Jack tells me the parties go on all night long, shaking themselves about to the music, talking about world peace and love-ins . . .'

'Not jealous, are you, Phil?'

'Who, me? I wouldn't swap my life with Jill and the children for anything, thank you very much,' declared Phil. 'To be honest, I wouldn't want to go through all that courting stuff again. You're looking at someone who was only too happy to swap the – what is it? – the hurly-burly of the chaise longue for the comfort of the double-bed.'

'I saw Jennifer and Lilian the other day after I left Peggy,' said Doris thoughtfully. 'They were on the bridge. Talking to a very nice looking young man.'

'What's this? A young man in the neighbourhood, possibly single, possibly eligible, that you don't know about? Doris, you're slipping!' chuckled Dan. 'That's him *and* Paddy to be paired off, then. How about one for Lilian, one for Jennifer?'

'Oh, Dan Archer, you never take me seriously,' scolded Doris. 'You know perfectly well that Lilian's walking out with young Malcolm Taylor. And as for the others, one's a complete stranger and Paddy – well, he's a lovely lad but I think Jennifer, with all her education, can do a bit better for herself than a cowman, don't you?'

'Frankly, my love, I think that's for Jennifer to decide,' said Dan gently. He put his arm round her shoulders and they strolled back to the house together. 'By the way, Phil, we must get the grain store swept out soon. Harvest'll be here before we know it.'

'That's right, get the conversation back to farming!' said Doris indignantly. 'That and your stomach, Dan Archer, they're your two favourite subjects!'

'Which reminds me,' Dan began mischievously. 'Did you promise me corned beef hash and jam roly-poly for my tea?'

'It's cold cuts and pickle and well you know it –' Doris broke off as Phil and Dan burst out laughing.

'Good old Mum!' smiled Phil. 'She's still the easiest person in the world to tease.'

Doris shook her head in exasperation and gave that little clucking sound which meant she knew she'd been had. Then, linking one arm with Phil and one with Dan, the three of them set off down the track beside the nodding elderflowers, secure in the knowledge that, whatever happened to the next generation of Archers, Brookfield would always be home.

·17·

The Way Forward

'Shula! Come on, darling, I think that's enough now!'

It was early July. Doris had invited Jill to bring the children over to tea after school, and had rashly mentioned the possibility of strawberries from the garden. While the boys had flung their satchels down in the kitchen, torn off their ties and raced off to see what farm machinery might be lying idle for them to clamber over, Shula had tidily placed her schoolbag on a chair and had asked Doris for a colander.

'I'll pick the strawberries, Granny,' she had said. 'It'll save your poor old legs.'

Jill and Doris had exchanged glances, Jill's a slightly worried one in case Doris was offended. But Doris had smiled broadly and reached down the cream enamel colander from its hook on the wall.

'Off you go, my precious,' she'd said. 'And mind that you put more in here than in your tummy – or you won't want any at teatime.'

Shula had scampered off, leaving her mother and grandmother to do the inevitable and make a pot of tea before turning their attention to cutting a vast pile of sandwiches.

'She's a lovely little thing,' Doris remarked, as she washed the lettuce under the tap, watching the not-quite-seven-year-old Shula crouched down industriously amongst the strawberry runners, her striped school dress thoughtfully tucked into her knickers.

'I know.' Jill popped a shred of ham into her mouth. 'The boys are lovely but – well, they're boys. It's not the same.'

'You were lucky to get a girl straight off,' said Doris, reaching for a clean tea towel. 'I had to wait nearly ten years for Christine.'

'And you haven't stopped worrying about her since,' smiled Jill. 'Well, have you?'

'I worry about all of them – except Phil,' admitted Doris. 'But then, he's got you.'

'Mum, you're a sweetheart. Thank you.' Jill came across to the sink and gave her a hug.

'It's true. You and Phil are so happy. You've given me three of the loveliest grandchildren – and at a time when I can enjoy them more than I could Jack and Peggy's. Things were such a struggle then, after the war.'

'You're still desperate for Chris to make you a grandma, though, aren't you?' Jill said gently. Doris went to deny it, as if the thought might have hurt Jill, but Jill went on, 'Don't worry, I can understand it. I can imagine it with my three. It's just the way it is. The fact is that David and Kenton's children will never mean as much to me as Shula's.'

Doris put the shiny lettuce leaves on the tea towel and rolled it up, patting them as she went.

'Oh, Jill, I've almost given up hope,' she sighed. 'I think Jennifer or Lilian'll be presenting Peggy with a grandchild before Chris, bless her, can do that for me.'

• • •

There was little discussion in the family these days about Chris and Paul's failure to have a child. No-one knew exactly what was going on in Chris's mind, still less in Paul's, but there was a general assumption that the longing for a baby had not diminished – at least, not on Chris's part – but that they had given up hope.

They had had plenty of other things to think about. If Chris had hoped that things might return to normal after all the business with Marianne Peters was finally sorted out, she was to be disappointed. The same restlessness that had prevailed since Paul had sold his business to Grenville and that had persuaded him to take the holiday in Paris in the first place had still not dissipated. One day, without any more preamble than a generalized dissatisfaction at the way work was going, he announced that he was quitting his job with Grenville's company and intended training as a helicopter pilot.

'A *pilot*?' Chris had said, astonished, having visions of naval helicopters winching shipwreck victims from the sea. Surely Paul, though only in his thirties, was too old for all that *Boy's Own* stuff? She passed him his after-dinner coffee all the same. 'Is it that easy?'

'Yes,' said Paul calmly, pouring cream over the back of his spoon so that it floated. 'It's not a complete change of direction.'

'Isn't it? I'd have said it was a complete change of *element*. At least your feet have been more or less on the ground before.'

Chris decided to take her coffee black. Now she knew why Paul had opened a bottle of hock to have with supper: he had been softening her up.

'Ah, no, darling, that's where you're wrong.' Chris watched as he pursed his lips to light a cigarette. There was the familiar clatter as the lighter went down on the table, the drawn-in breath, the pause, the smoke blown out. She had watched him do it thousands of times during their marriage and it never ceased to fascinate and charm her, even when, as now, he was in the process of turning her life upside down. She dragged her attention back to what he was saying.

'I'm going to get into crop-spraying,' he explained. 'Pesticides and insecticides sprayed from the air. Much less crop damage than taking a tractor into the field, no tramlines and crop loss where the wheels have been. It's the latest thing.'

So. It was another of Paul's schemes. Unlike Jack's, which were get-rich-quick schemes – though they never turned out that way – Paul's enthusiasms were not to do with money. They were more to do with whatever caught his somewhat febrile imagination. He always wanted to be at the forefront of any new development. He felt he had a sense for the market and the way things were moving: a sense of what people wanted. Crop-spraying. It sounded absurd to Christine. Wouldn't there be a lot of wastage? Surely the wind would carry most of it away? But she knew better than to challenge Paul. He had decided that he wanted a change, and for the sake of peace, for the sake of her marriage, Christine would simply have to go along with it. What she had not been prepared for was that Paul was also still hankering after a change of scenery. She knew he was not as wedded to Borsetshire, let alone Ambridge, as she was, but when he announced, after his pilot training was completed, that he was sending off an application for a job in East Anglia, she was flabbergasted.

'But it's perfect for us, darling,' he'd reasoned, and she knew he really believed it. 'Prairie farming, practically all arable, for me and the best horseflesh in the country for you!'

It was all so simple for Paul. But when Christine thought of those big empty East Anglian skies and the low fields stretching right to the horizon instead of Borsetshire's rounded curves and the sinking sun gilding Lakey Hill, she could have cried. And she did cry, in private, when he got the job. But there was nothing she could do. Her mother was worried about her, she knew, and Doris was even more worried when, within months of moving to a hateful modern house on the outskirts of Newmarket, Chris had a bad fall from a horse. Doris had come over to look after her and Chris had been hard pushed, feeling as weak as she was, not to collapse in tears and beg her mother to take her home. But throughout her marriage she had felt that her bed was made with Paul, and she must lie in it, despite the lumps and bumps. So she defended his decision to move, pretended she was liking it and scoffed at the thought that she was missing Ambridge.

'I'm missing Midnight,' she admitted. 'I wouldn't be in this state if I'd been riding her, I'm sure. She'd never have taken fright at a partridge flying out of a hedge bottom.'

'Well, Midnight's missing you,' Doris had assured her, fussing with her pillows. 'Lilian's been exercising her, but it's not the same.'

But fortunately for Chris, things were, for once, conspiring in her favour. Paul could not get on with his new boss, whom he blamed for the fact that the crop-spraying business was neither as exciting nor as lucrative as he had imagined, and within a year they were back in Ambridge, living in a rented house on the Estate, and Paul was working for Grenville again.

'And I can go back to my horses!' Chris had exulted to Jill when she and Paul went round to Hollowtree. 'At last! A bit of stability!'

But even the apparent security of Paul's job with Grenville hadn't lasted for long. Although he had recovered from the injuries he'd sustained in the car crash, or appeared to have done so, coping heroically with an artificial leg, the accident had altered Grenville. He had become restless in Ambridge, and everyone suspected it was something of a relief to Carol, who had had to cope with his moods, when he took himself off on a fact-finding trip to America.

It never occurred to anyone that this was anything but another flight of fancy which would probably come to nothing, but everyone was about to be surprised. Expecting a phone call to let her know when he was coming home, Carol was astonished to receive one in which an ebullient Grenville announced that America was where the future lay – for the whole family. He wanted them to emigrate. Distressed and isolated, poor Carol planned to fly out and try to dissuade him, but before she could join him, Grenville died suddenly, alone, of a brain haemorrhage. The doctors suspected it had been caused by a germ that he had picked up on his travels before he came to Ambridge and that it had lain dormant all these years.

That, at least, had been the official story, but village opinion held differently.

'Makes you wonder, doesn't it?' Doris had pondered. 'He did have a head injury at the time of the crash, but everyone made light of it. Maybe it was more serious than they realized.'

'I dunno. I think it goes deeper even than that, Doris.' Uncle Tom, who had come round to bring Doris a hare he had shot and had stayed for a cup of tea, replaced his cup on its saucer. Doris had got out the Royal Albert, which was normally for best, feeling obscurely that discussion of the Estate owner's recent death required some mark of respect. 'You see,' her brother continued, 'Grenville was a clever bloke. He'd seen a lot of the world, yet he came and tucked himself away here in Ambridge. I know he always had big plans for the Estate, and he was a great modernizer, but I wonder meself if he didn't try and cram himself into too small a channel. Too confined for him. And then he had the accident, and he went to America, and saw all the possibilities there and – whoosh! – it was like taking the cork out of a bottle.'

Doris shook her head doubtfully. It was a mystery to her quite what had happened to Charles Grenville, and it wasn't going to help his widow if the village formed the opinion that he had gone a bit funny in the head.

'Perhaps you should keep that idea to yourself, Tom,' she counselled. 'Poor, poor Carol. What a time she's had of it in the last couple of years. I should think sometimes it's only the thought of that little boy of hers that gets her out of bed in the mornings.'

• • •

'You really shouldn't have, you know, Paul.' For all the sadness in her life, Carol Grenville had remained as beautiful as ever and if it had also made her even more remote, there were some who found her aloofness compelling.

'You don't really mind, do you?' Paul Johnson sounded suddenly anxious. He took a sip of the pale sherry that Carol had placed on a table at his elbow. 'We did get though our business pretty quickly.'

Carol sat down on the brocade sofa and crossed her elegant legs in a swish of silk stocking.

'I know. You simply galloped through those notes from the solicitor. And I suspect,' she looked at him sideways, 'for one reason only. You couldn't wait to get upstairs with Richard and play trains. You really shouldn't have spent all that money on a three-year-old.'

'It wasn't a lot.' Paul stretched his legs out in front of him in the leather armchair, which had once been Charles Grenville's, beside the fireplace at the Manor House with the old Lawson-Hope coat of arms carved above it.

Carol gave him a sardonic look and popped a salted almond into her mouth.

'Don't tell me an electric train set's all that cheap.'

'Well . . . I've had a lot of fun out of it, too,' Paul confessed.

'You're telling me. You've been up in the nursery for the past hour.

Richard's usually had his bath and is in his pyjamas by now.'

'I'm sorry.' Paul was contrite. 'We were having a simply marvellous time. He takes the control box and sends the carriages whizzing round the track ... I'm the repair gang that comes along with a crane – alias my right hand – and puts them back on the rails again.'

'You are good to him.' Carol passed him the small silver dish of nuts. Paul helped himself to a few. 'And I do so want him to have some masculine influence in his life.'

'I'm telling you, the pleasure's all mine.'

Far off, in the hall, the doorbell rang.

'That'll be John Tregorran,' said Carol, smiling. 'He's come to read Richard a bedtime story.'

Paul stood up and drained his glass. 'Richard certainly won't be short of masculine influence tonight, then,' he smiled. 'Now I must go. If I'm too late, Christine gives me some very sour looks, I can tell you.'

As the maid showed John into the sitting room and Carol moved to pour another glass of sherry, she couldn't help wondering to herself. Only the other day Jill had been telling her how John Tregorran was always calling round at Hollowtree to see the children, and never went home without leaving them a 'little something' tucked under the clock.

'If their mouths are full of lollipops, they'll not be giving you any trouble,' he'd said to Jill.

'Of course, John should have had children of his own,' Jill had said, rather pointedly Carol had felt. She and John had both married other people. Both marriages had been tragically short. Would the village never tire of trying to pair them off, even after all that had happened? Now here was Paul Johnson, Jill's brother-in-law and, since Charles's death, Carol's business partner in the machinery and milling part of the Grenville Estate, spending rather more than lollipop money on her son.

Was it really because he and Christine hadn't any children of their own for him to play trains with? And how would Christine feel about it if she knew? Carol felt it placed her in a very awkward position and

Paul's reference to sour looks did nothing to reassure her. She knew that the Johnsons' marriage wasn't the happiest in the world and that Christine wasn't keen on the way that working alongside one another threw her and Paul together. How would Christine feel if she knew that it was Richard who was the real attraction? Would it make things better or worse?

• • •

'I'm home!' Paul flung his attaché case down in the hall and called up the stairs. 'Chris?'

There was no reply. He walked through the house. The French windows in the lounge were standing open and, guided by the sound of snipping, he found Chris in the garden cutting back a peony that had flowered in its wanton way and dropped its petals everywhere.

'Sorry I'm a bit late,' he said. 'Had some notes from the solicitor to go through with Carol.'

Chris carried on with her clipping, dropping the dead heads into a bucket. Paul watched her for a moment. He watched her gloved fingers as they moved among the leaves. The sleeves of her blue gingham shirt were rolled back and there was a bright pink weal down her forearm where she had scratched herself on a thorn. Beyond her, under the apple tree, midges bounced gently in a shaft of sunlight.

'Fancy a drink?' he queried.

'No thanks.' She spoke for the first time.

'Quite sure?'

'I said "no", didn't I?' She moved along the border and attacked a rose bush before savagely pulling up a clump of withered forget-me-nots. 'I hate these things,' she said. 'I don't know why everyone makes such a fuss about them, straggling everywhere.'

'There's something wrong, isn't there?' said Paul, trying to keep the resignation and weariness out of his voice. He did so wish that Chris would just come out with what was bothering her, instead of leaving him playing twenty questions.

'Are you sure you want to know?' She jabbed at a dandelion with her trowel. It resisted.

'Of course I want to know. Well?'

Christine sighed heavily, humping her shoulders. She abandoned the dandelion, pulled off her gardening gloves, straightened and turned to face him. 'I happened to go into Borchester today, Paul,' she began.

'Yes?'

'I was looking for a blanket for a pram.'

'Looking for what?' Paul was startled.

'Not our pram,' she said viciously. 'We'll never have a pram. It was a present for Joan Burton's baby.' Joan Hood had recently married Nigel Burton, Dan's former dairyman.

Paul grimaced. He knew what was coming and he dreaded it. 'It doesn't matter to other people that we haven't any children of our own, of course. When their babies arrive we have to do what's right and proper. We have to buy presents.'

He put out a hand towards her but she shrugged it away, not looking at him, talking to a point somewhere over his right shoulder. 'I find people with children have very little sensitivity towards us. I expect most of them think we haven't any children out of choice. That we're thoroughly selfish.'

'I do understand how hard it is for you, Chris,' he said gently. 'I'm sorry.'

'Anyway,' she said briskly, looking at him directly, looking for a response. 'I went into Brooks's. Do you know Brooks's?'

'Yes,' said Paul cautiously. 'It's in the High Street.'

'They sell prams . . . and blankets . . . and toys, don't they? Nice. So, I chose a blanket . . . pink, with a bunny rabbit in the corner. All very sweet and pretty. She's had a girl, by the way. They're calling her Juliet.'

She was still looking him straight in the eye. He held her gaze. A gunshot sounded far away in the woods, then another, and a dog barked into the dropping dusk. With a growing sense of doom, without daring to look away, Paul said, 'Well?'

'There's a very motherly assistant they have there,' Chris continued. 'When she gave me the change she said, "I often see you in

Borchester with your husband. You look such a nice couple. Tell me, how is your little boy getting on with his train set?"'

The gunshots sounded again. Uncle Tom, probably, protecting his pheasant poults from an impertinent predator who couldn't wait for dark.

'Train set?' Paul knew how stupid he must sound, but he didn't know what else to say. He had never for a moment imagined that Christine would ever find out.

'Yes, Paul, a train set.' Chris's voice was harder now. 'She told me how excited you were in selecting it ... "Fathers usually are," she said. Well, Paul? Would you like to tell me about it?'

Paul nudged the bucket of garden waste with his foot. Fat bees buzzed around the lavender in the border.

'It's a present I bought for Richard. Richard Grenville.'

'I suspected as much.' Chris gave a short laugh. 'I didn't really think you were raising another family somewhere else. But why didn't you mention it to me?'

Paul shrugged. 'I didn't think it was important.'

'Not important? A present of that size? What are we, then, millionaires?'

Lost for an explanation because he hadn't given one to himself, Paul looked up at the sky. High, high up, a group of swifts were zigzagging randomly this way and that, like iron filings drawn by an invisible magnet.

'If you want to know the truth, darling,' he improvised quickly, 'I'm trying to do a lot of business with Carol at the moment and as a ... a sort of persuasive lever, I bought the present for the child. You see, I'm a very low, public relations type, really. But there you are.'

'It's one explanation, I suppose.' Chris sounded doubtful.

'One explanation: it's *the* explanation.' All his public relations skills were going to be called for here, he could see. Something else suddenly occurred to him, and he added quickly, 'There's nothing sinister in it, darling. I'm not using Richard as an excuse to have an affair with Carol, if that's what you think.'

Was that what she thought?

'Paul – did I suggest that?'

She sounded shocked, so he needn't have worried.

'OK, just putting my spoke in first, in case you were going to.' The near-affair with Marianne would, he knew, always be between them, and between them and any other woman he knew. 'So what's really biting you, Chris?'

'Don't let's kid each other.' She picked up the bucket and carried it over to the compost heap. Paul followed her. 'It isn't just buying a present for the boy – or playing with him – it's keeping it from me.' She tipped out the contents of the bucket, then bent to remove the rose stalks, which wouldn't compost down. Paul knew of old that the more emotional she felt about things, the more necessary it was for her to busy herself with something. 'Because you didn't want to hurt my feelings. Make me feel inadequate or something.'

'Oh, Chris.' He pulled her up towards him, took the bucket from her hands and put it down. 'Can't you stop worrying your silly head about things and just enjoy life?'

She shook her head. 'No,' she said simply. 'And don't joke about it, Paul.'

Paul hated these discussions. Thankfully they happened less often these days, but they always involved going back over the same painful, pitted ground, coming up against the same obstacles and stumbling in exactly the same places. Once he had let her talk it all out again, and again, and again. She seemed to need to. But it got them nowhere and his instinct nowadays was to try to jolly her out of it.

'Listen,' he said patiently. 'I'm off to London for a few days for work, as you know. Come with me. I'll work during the day, you look round the shops – then we'll see a bit of night life when I've finished.'

She considered for a moment, then said slowly, 'No. No, I don't think so.'

'Why ever not?' he implored. 'There's nothing to stop you coming with me. Nothing at all.'

'I know,' she replied. 'And I think it's about time there was.'

'What does that mean?'

'It's high time we stopped evading the issue, Paul, and faced up to facts. The future. You go away to London and I'll stay here. And you do a bit of thinking and I'll do a bit of thinking. About adoption.'

• • •

'Keep your sisterly fingers crossed but I've an idea that we just might have seen the end of the swine fever. Pass us that oil can, will you?'

Chris reached under the bonnet of the tractor and handed it to Phil. It was the beginning of August. Harvest had started and Brookfield was a marathon of running repairs.

'Here.'

'Thanks.' Phil took the can and applied some of the contents to a bit of the engine that looked to Chris's untrained eye to be pretty oily already. 'Course, it's early days yet.'

Swine fever had started a month or so back on the Estate and had spread rapidly round the district. Brookfield had not escaped.

'I'm very glad, Phil, truly I am,' said Christine. She knew how worried her father had been.

'We'll see.' Ever cautious, Phil edged out from under the bonnet and regarded her properly for the first time. 'Come to that, you're looking pretty bright and cheerful yourself.'

'I am, as a matter of fact,' Chris confirmed. 'I just thought I'd take a good old-fashioned open-air stroll over here to see Mum.'

'Come to the end of your troubles as well?' asked Phil guardedly. Enquiring into the state of Christine's marriage could be dangerous and he knew things hadn't been at their best recently.

'Could be. Course, it's still very early days in this, too, but you never know, it could make quite a difference to Paul and me.'

Phil looked at her quizzically. He hoped it wasn't another change of direction for Paul about which Chris had to wear a brave face. Yet her cheerfulness sounded genuine enough.

'We've decided to adopt a baby.'

'Well, well.' Phil was flabbergasted. 'Three cheers for you.'

'We've been thinking about it for some time. Well, I have. And now we've discussed it and registered and been interviewed and everything. There are all kinds of things to be looked into, of course, the legal side and all the other problems . . . But – well . . . Do you think it's a good idea, Phil?'

Phil was touched that his opinion counted for so much.

'Best yet,' he said warmly. 'It'll be the very thing for the pair of you.' He wiped his hands on a bit of rag, considering. 'In fact,' he added, 'the more I think about it, the more it cheers me up. You should have done it ages ago.'

Chris made a little bobbing movement of her head.

'Well. We did keep hoping . . . you know. I mean – one of our own, maybe. But still . . .' Her voice dropped away but then she smiled and brightened again. 'I'm on my way to tell Mum.'

'Let me give you a hug,' said Phil. 'I'm not too oily, promise.'

She smiled and he opened his arms.

'I'm so pleased for you,' he said, holding her close. 'I'm sure everything'll work out. It'll be the making of you and Paul. And Mum's going to be so thrilled.'

· · ·

'Oh, Chris, he's beautiful.'

'Even when he's bawling his head off? Come on, Mum! Even I'm not that biased!'

'But he is!'

Christine placed the protesting baby in his pram. Baby Peter, as the adoption society had called him, was almost two months old now and had been with Christine and Paul for only two days.

'Peter is a compact baby with a long body and limbs which are nicely covered,' the printed information had told them. 'He has fair hair, dark-blue eyes and a very fair pink skin. He has a good-shaped head with a high crown, medium-sized ears, one of which protrudes sightly, and an oval face.'

Christine had thought she had visualized the baby perfectly from the description, but when she and Paul had gone to the society's baby home to look at him, she had felt breathless with the beauty of him and sheer exultation at the thought that he might be theirs. In the middle of October they had received confirmation that the adoption could proceed, though Peter would come to them initially for a sort of probation period. And now, with the last scraps of summer hanging crisply from the trees and the first frosts icing the grass, here he was, home with them at last.

'There now,' Chris soothed as she drew the soft cellular blanket over him. 'You mustn't disgrace yourself in front of your grandma, must you? You settle down in your lovely new pram and go off to bye-byes. There's a good boy.'

She took the handle and rocked the big carriage pram gently on its springs. Little by little, the baby's wails were converted into self-pitying whimpers and then into the occasional deep sigh and snuffle. Christine continued rocking him, though, until there was absolute silence. When she turned back to Doris, she found her mother wiping away a tear.

'Mum . . . what is it?' Christine came and perched on the arm of her mother's chair. Gently she took the navy-and-white sailor top that Doris was knitting for Peter out of her hands. 'Well?'

Doris blew her nose and smiled.

'It's just hearing you talk to him, Chris, and calling me his grandma. It's just so lovely.'

'Oh, Mum,' said Christine, moved. 'Don't. You'll set me off and then we'll all be crying.'

They both laughed self-consciously, Christine dabbing at her eyes with the back of her hand, and Doris bringing out her handkerchief again. Then the front door banged loudly and the baby, still only dozing, woke with a cry. Christine sighed.

'That'll be Paul back from work,' she said. 'He's got a lot to learn about the hours babies keep.' She went over to the pram and leant over it. 'Hello, young Peter. Did that naughty Daddy wake you up? We're going to have to train him a bit better, aren't we?' She reached into the pram and picked Peter up. 'I don't suppose I need to ask if you want to hold him,' she said, offering him to Doris.

Doris extended her arms. 'Just give him here,' she said happily.

'The district nurse said that if we keep picking him up he'll never get used to sleeping on his own.'

'Stuff and nonsense!' Doris settled the baby against her shoulder and rocked him back and forth, rubbing his back. 'I think he might have a bit of wind. Anyway, there's no baby ever suffered through too much cuddling, did they, my pet?'

'Mum, you're hopeless,' laughed Chris. 'I can see he's going to be spoilt rotten.'

'Chris,' began Doris firmly. 'I waited ten years for you and I've waited ten years for this. If I can't spoil him . . .'

'All right, all right!' smiled Christine. 'You win. I like holding him myself. I just put him in the pram because I thought you'd want to have a chat.'

'Chat?' exclaimed Doris in astonishment. 'We can do that any-time. But this little scrap, he deserves all our attention, don't you darling?'

The baby responded with a massive belch.

'Oh, dear! There, there, better out than in, eh?' clucked Doris.

'Billing and cooing again, I see!' Paul came into the room, foll-owed by Jack and Peggy. 'Look who I found on the step.'

'We're not disturbing you, are we?' Peggy said. 'Only Jill told me what a gorgeous baby you've got and we came to join the queue of admirers.' She came over and kissed Christine warmly on the cheek. 'Congratulations, Chris. I'm so happy for you.'

Doris held Peter away from her shoulder so that Peggy could see for herself.

'Oh, and he is gorgeous . . . what a poppet! Look, Jack.'

'Eh? Oh, yes, very nice.'

Jack was eyeing up the drinks tray on the sideboard, practically salivating. His drinking had escalated worryingly in the last few months, after a period of steadiness. Peggy watched him all the time.

'Do you remember when Tony was a baby, Jack?' she asked brightly, trying to get his attention. 'How he used to love you to tickle his tummy?'

'Did he?' Jack stuffed his hands in his pockets to stop himself from reaching for the whisky bottle. 'It's all so long ago. How's work, Paul?' Jack turned his attention to the only other adult male in the room in mute appeal. But even Paul was crouched down in front of the baby, tweaking his toes.

'We're not stopping, Jack,' put in Peggy quickly. 'I'm sure Chris and Paul have got things to do.'

'There's no hurry,' said Paul, standing up. 'Sit down, Peggy. How about a sherry?'

'Don't mind if I do,' said Jack. 'Or a whisky, if you've got it,' he added casually. 'No water.'

'A small Amontillado for me, please, Paul,' requested Peggy, shooting Jack a withering look as he followed Paul to pour the drinks. She sat down primly on the settee.

'How's Jennifer?' asked Chris, aware of the atmosphere. 'She'll have to think about applying for jobs soon, I suppose, now it's her last year at college.'

'Oh, I'm the last person to ask,' said Peggy tightly. 'She doesn't tell me anything any more. Make the most of Peter, Chris, when he's tiny. They soon grow up.'

'Jennifer'll do all right,' said Doris firmly. 'She's got spirit. I like that.'

The baby's head was drooping heavily against her bosom.

'He's dropping off again,' she mouthed to Chris. 'Perhaps you could pop him in the pram now. He's quite a weight!'

Doris handed the baby to her daughter. Peggy looked on indulgently.

'I must confess, though,' declared Doris, 'only in the summer I thought Jennifer or even Lilian'd be making you a grandma, Peggy, before I saw Chris with a baby.'

'Jennifer?' Peggy laughed. 'I doubt it, Mum. Like the rest of her generation, she's too busy changing the world to bother about changing nappies.'

·18·

A New Life

'God rest ye merry, gentlemen, let nothing you dismay –'

It was over a year later, ten days before Christmas, and Lilian sang cheerfully to herself as she tramped along the ridiculously slanting corridor that led to Jennifer's room. Jennifer had moved to this out-of-the-way corner of the pub's living accommodation when she was fifteen and had got her first Dansette record-player for her birthday. She was thrilled with it, but within days, tired of Elvis Presley's pitiful entreaties to 'Love Me Tender', their father had threatened to confiscate the thing. After a mammoth sulk (Lilian could remember spending hours in the stables with her pony, Pensioner – anything to get away from the atmosphere), Jennifer and Jack had reached a compromise: the record-player could stay if Jennifer moved rooms. And so Jack had cleared the rickety pub tables and cobwebbed garden umbrellas from what was once a lumber room and Jennifer – plus Dansette – had installed themselves there.

Jennifer's Dansette days were over now, though Tony, at fifteen convinced that the one thing The Beatles needed to broaden their appeal was a Borsetshire schoolboy on a trumpet, had claimed it for himself. Their father was either going deaf or had given up the unequal struggle with his children, but he did not seem to mind so much the never-ending choruses of 'A Hard Day's Night'. Or perhaps he just found its sentiments more in tune with his experience of life.

'For Jesus Christ our saviour is born upon this day –' Lilian trilled as she tapped on Jennifer's door and pushed it open. 'Can I come in?'

Her sister was sitting at her dressing table, staring into the mirror.

'Looks as if you have come in,' she replied listlessly.

'Sorry. Didn't want to disturb the great author.'

A year before, Jennifer had had a short story published in a magazine and she was working on a novel.

'You weren't.'

'Oh? Whatever happened to 'The Life and Loves of Jennifer Archer'?'

Jennifer looked away, towards the indigo square of sky at the window.

'I don't think I'll ever write another word of that novel,' she said.

'What? You've had an offer from a publisher!'

'I don't care.'

'But Jennifer . . .' Lilian didn't understand. Then she looked more closely at her sister. 'What's wrong? You look as if you've been crying.'

'It doesn't matter.' Jennifer picked up a hairbrush and drew it through her blonde hair.

'It does,' said Lilian vehemently. 'We've all noticed it, me and Mum and Dad. Something's been upsetting you lately.'

'Please don't, Lilian. Please just leave me.'

Jennifer seemed to be concentrating awfully hard on the simple act of brushing her hair. Lilian strode across the room and snatched the brush out of her sister's hand.

'No, I won't. What is it? Come on. Tell me.'

Strands of Jennifer's hair, made static by the brush, floated at her shoulders, a nimbus as fine as the angel hair their mother had just bought to drape on the Christmas tree. Lilian watched the halo of hair, fascinated, in the long silence that followed.

'I . . . I daren't,' said Jennifer at last. 'I daren't.'

Jennifer was older than Lilian by two and a half years, but suddenly the age gap seemed irrelevant. Lilian felt as if she were the older one. She felt as protective towards her sister as if she'd been a child of five who'd just broken a favourite toy. She gestured to

Jennifer to move up on the old cretonne-covered stool and sat down beside her. She put her arm round her shoulders.

'Come on, now,' she soothed. 'Come on.'

'Oh, Lilian!' Jennifer turned to her, no longer bothering to contain her tears. 'I've made such a terrible mistake! Such a terrible mistake!'

Puzzled, Lilian stared back at her and thought how lovely she looked, even with her eyes pink and puffed from crying. Then she realized what her sister was trying to tell her.

'You don't mean . . . You're not . . .'

'Yes.' Jennifer half swallowed the word. 'Don't tell anyone, please. Not yet.'

Then she burst into great shuddering sobs that shook her whole body. Lilian looked at her, so slender in her turquoise suede miniskirt and matching skinny-rib jumper. She simply could not believe that even now, inside her sister's body, a baby was beginning to form. Jennifer was nearly twenty-two, but she seemed to Lilian more like a little girl.

'Oh, Jennifer,' she said gently, still disbelieving, holding her and rocking her.

'Oh, Lilian,' Jennifer's voice was furred with tears. 'What am I going to do?'

• • •

Jennifer hadn't at first been able to believe it herself. The first month it happened she told herself there could be any number of reasons. She had just started teaching at Hollerton Primary: perhaps her body was merely reflecting the excitement of a new job. Or perhaps she was overtiring herself, trying to work on her novel when she came home in the evenings, as well as keeping up with her marking and planning classwork. She pushed the unthinkable thought down, deep down, but when, a month later, the same thing happened again, she knew with a heavy dread that she had to be pregnant. Some instinct she couldn't place made her get out all her old Elvis records, which she hadn't played for years. The plangent guitar and the lyrics of longing spoke to her of all the fear that she felt and the difficulties she faced. 'Are you lonesome tonight, do you miss me tonight, are you sorry we drifted apart?' murmured Elvis, and Jennifer clasped her arms across her chest as she listened. 'Does your memory stray to a bright summer day, when I kissed you and called you sweetheart?' Yes, yes, of course it did.

But all she could think about now was what her family would say. If something like this had happened to a girl who lived in London, or even Borchester, it wouldn't have been so bad. There would have been gossip, of course, but surely not the sense of shame her parents would feel as she eased her swelling belly behind the bar to serve customers when she helped out on Sunday lunchtimes, or when Elsie Catcher, the Ambridge schoolteacher, retired next year and Jennifer was unable to apply for the job she had always dreamed of because she was too busy with bottles and nappies.

For the past month all these thoughts had been whirling round in her head. Already her waistbands were getting tighter and she knew she wouldn't be able to hide her changing shape from her mother for much longer. If only it weren't Christmas! Gran and Grandad Archer would be over, with Gran asking coy questions about whether she had a 'young man' in tow – if only – and clucking over Auntie Jill, who was expecting another baby in April, and little Peter, Chris and Paul's adopted son, who at two would be toddling around looking suitably cherubic. Jennifer knew she was being cowardly and that she was buying time. She knew her parents would have to be told, but she knew she could not deal with it all before Christmas. She tried the idea out on Lilian, swearing her to secrecy, before making the phone call to Max Bailey, whom she had gone out with for two years and who, even after they had broken up, had remained one of her best friends. Max lived in Wolverhampton, where he had a top-floor flat in a modern block with an eye-level grill and a waste-disposal unit in the kitchen. You would expect Max's home to have all mod cons, as they called them in the estate agents' prospectuses. He worked as a surveyor for a property development company.

'Max,' she said down the phone, after he had accused her of forgetting about him because she hadn't been in touch since the summer, 'What are you doing for Christmas? I don't suppose I could invite myself over, could I?'

Her father was displeased and her mother was perplexed – understandably so – when she announced she was bypassing the delights of a family Christmas for a few days with Max, but Jennifer was adamant.

'I haven't seen him since the summer,' she defended herself. 'Now that I'm working it's not easy to get away. And his office is closed for a full week over Christmas.'

Finally, conceding ungraciously that she was an adult and could make up her own mind, her father drove her to the train.

'But your mother's worried about you,' he called as a parting shot as she went through the ticket barrier. 'And she's never wrong!'

• • •

Her stay in Wolverhampton was another mistake. Max was as charming and attentive as ever and his widowed father welcomed her with open arms. Unfortunately, it only underlined to Jennifer how different things might have been if she had made a go of it with Max. They might have been married by now and buying one of the new detached houses with ducted-air central heating, which he had pointed out to her on the way from the station. As Max's wife, she would have wanted for nothing, she knew. She could have had all the latest clothes – fun-fur coats and glossy patent boots, a car of her own (she had always wanted a Mini) and she needn't have worked, but could have concentrated on her writing. Max had adored her – still did – and in the end Jennifer had found it suffocating. So she had told him that though she didn't see a future for them, she really wanted to stay friends and, because he adored her, he had agreed. Now the comfort and security he could have offered seemed more desirable than ever before. But it was too late.

One other thing emerged from her few days away. Jennifer returned to Ambridge convinced that she could not have her baby there. She felt instinctively that she needed to get away – to hide in the anonymity of a big city. She wasn't going to run away: she would tell everybody who needed to know about the baby and she would have to work out a term's notice at school. But in the spring she determined to leave Ambridge for good.

First, though, she knew she had to tell her parents – and she just couldn't bring herself to do it. She thought round the problem every way she could. Should she sit them down and tell them together? Should she tell her mother first, gauge her reaction and then tell her father? Perhaps Peggy would offer to tell him. If she did, should Jennifer accept? And then, though she hardly dared think about it, came the question of telling the grandparents. Gran Archer would be bad enough, but as for Granny P . . .

All through the forced jollity of New Year at the pub, Jennifer turned the question over and over in her mind. As the regulars got more and more merry on New Year's Eve, Jennifer felt more and more removed from the celebrations and more and more alien. As her father nursed his hangover the next day, and her mother, tight-lipped, brought him liver salts and opened up the bar by herself, Jennifer took herself off for a long walk on Lakey Hill, despairing of ever finding the right moment – or the courage – to tell them.

It was on that walk that she thought of a way round it. She had never been a particularly 'churchy' person, but she had always got on well with Matthew Wreford, the vicar, who had tried to do so much for the young people in Ambridge. It was thanks to him that the Youth Club had been set up, and he encouraged anyone with musical talent to use it. He had helped Jimmy Grange, her Grandad's apprentice, with his skiffle group and now he was keen on the Sugar Beats, a group that Roger Patillo was setting up with Lilian and a few others. When she got home, Jennifer rang the vicarage to make an appointment to see Matthew. He told her he could see her on the following Thursday.

• • •

Sitting in his study, with the tortoiseshell cat coiled like rope in front of the fire and the grandmother clock ticking in the hall, Jennifer once again felt incongruous and out of place. She began to wonder why on earth she had thought this would be such a good idea. She felt as if she would almost be defiling the air by telling him what she had to tell him, but having got this far, she had to see it through. She also couldn't think of any other way forward.

'I've come to ask you a favour, Vicar,' she began when he had settled them both with cups of tea and slices of Christmas cake that she, at least, did not want. 'I'm in a terrible mess,' she went on, 'and it's all my own fault. I don't blame anyone and I'm going to face up to it – but my parents have got to be told and that's something I can't bring myself to do. Mr Wreford . . .' She looked at him with her most appealing wide-eyed stare, knowing that she was doing it and hating herself for it. 'Would you tell them?'

Outside, a branch tapped on the window. The clock ticked.

'And what would you like me to tell them?' he asked gently.

She knew he had already guessed, but he was going to make her say it. Jennifer looked down at the plate of cake in her lap. The plumply glistening raisins made her feel suddenly sick.

'I . . . I . . . I'm going to have a baby.'

She was expecting him to launch at the very least into a sermon about morals and the modern world, if only to show his disappointment in her after all he had done for her and the others. She expected a lecture on all the advantages she had had in life and how she had thrown them away. She anticipated the word 'sin' being used a lot. Instead he just looked at her and nodded. When he said nothing, she went on, in self-defence, 'I've been trying to feel ashamed, you know, Vicar. And I can't. I don't think I'm brazen – or pleased about it. I'd give almost anything for it not to be true – I'd love to be able to put the clock back. I've been a complete fool and I hate myself for it. And I regret it . . . But . . . I know everybody in the village will expect me to feel ashamed. And I can't, Vicar, I honestly can't.'

Now she had told him and explained her feelings, Jennifer felt nothing but relief. Matthew's reaction was far better than she had hoped for. He didn't judge her, and he was emphatic that she shouldn't make more problems for herself by imagining other people's reactions, especially when they were ungenerous ones. 'After all,' he smiled, 'if we're humble enough to admit it, most of us could often say, "There but for the Grace of God go I." '

However, although Matthew did reassure her, the one thing he refused to do was to tell her parents for her.

'Tell them,' he urged her, 'as soon as you can. They'll be shocked, horrified, hurt –'

'I daresay I deserve it.'

'Jennifer.' He leaned forward. 'No-one is going to be able to condemn you more than you condemn yourself. But this I promise you. Once you have made a clean breast of things, I'll be there to back you up.'

• • •

Jennifer did make a couple of attempts, she really did. She had decided that the way to do it was to tell Peggy first. She knew that her mother was worried about her. Jennifer even thought that she might suspect the truth, but whenever Jennifer came near to confiding in her, someone came into the pub, or once her father blundered in, chortling about some quiz show he had seen on television, and the moment was lost. Unable to find the right time or to form the words to tell her parents, Jennifer wondered if it might help if she talked to other people about it first. So she went to see Auntie Jill at Hollowtree and told her the news. Unlike Matthew, Jill asked some probing questions, such as who the father was. Jennifer refused to say.

'There's no chance of him marrying you, I suppose?'

'No,' she said. 'I'm quite sure he doesn't love me. Or even like me very much.'

Jill looked pained for her.

'Jennifer, dear!'

'Look,' said Jennifer. 'I haven't come for sympathy.'

Jill reached out and touched her hand.

'It seems hard on you, though. Bearing the whole burden yourself.'

'I brought it on myself,' replied Jennifer ruefully. 'I thought I was smart. I knew all the answers. Oh, other girls might get caught, but not me. Not in this day and age. Little did I know. You play with fire, you get burnt.'

Jill – she told Jennifer not to call her Auntie Jill any more, saying it was ridiculous when by the summer they would both be pushing prams together – was marvellous. Jennifer had always admired her, taking on Uncle Phil after his first wife died, running the house and raising the children, all apparently effortlessly. But that night she confessed to Jennifer how worried she had been when she first came to Ambridge, convinced that people would take against her as an outsider, a pretender in Grace's place.

'If I've got one piece of advice for you,' she said, 'it's to give people time. And don't prejudge them. Sometimes people's reactions can be better than you expect.'

• • •

Jennifer only wished that had been the case with her Gran. Jennifer had phoned and asked if she could call on her one January afternoon before the school term started. She arrived at Brookfield to find her grandmother lifting a tray of scones from the oven.

'Just in time!' Doris laughed. 'You must have smelt them cooking!'

Jennifer turned down tea and scones – the vicar's tea and cake had been bad enough. That alone was enough to get Doris worried: she could not bear a visitor in the house without a cup and plate in their hands. Reluctantly she led a resolute Jennifer through to the parlour, where the fire was glowing happily.

'Off you go, dear!' Her Gran propped her feet up on a sagging pouffe. 'Say your piece and then we'll have a nice cup of tea. I'm just dying for one.'

'Oh, Gran, it's difficult. And it's my own fault.'

Doris's mild moon face puckered.

'Jennifer? Whatever is it?'

Jennifer took a deep breath.

'Get ready for a shock, Gran. I'm going to have a baby.'

Her grandmother gave a little shake of her head, as if trying to dislodge what she had just been told and did not want to hear. For a long time she stared into space, then, with another shake of her head, seemed to pull herself together.

'Well, I . . .' she said at last. 'I just don't know what to say.' And then, her voice rising, 'You must have taken leave of your senses. Whatever could you have been thinking of?'

'That's just the trouble,' said Jennifer in a small voice. 'I didn't think. At least, not hard enough. Anyway, I've told you now. Perhaps I'd better go.'

But she didn't move. She sat transfixed. She felt as if she could almost see the thoughts crossing her grandmother's mind.

'There's never been anything like this in the family.' When she spoke at last, Doris sounded stunned. She was talking more to herself than to her granddaughter. 'The Moores had it once, I remember. And the Evans's had it in their family. But we've never known such a thing. Not in the Archers.'

'Well, there it is, Gran.'

'Out of wedlock . . . think of the child . . . I just don't know what to say.'

'I think you've said quite enough, Gran.' Jennifer's voice was stiff with the effort of holding in her tears. She hadn't exactly expected her grandmother to approve but she had never expected such a hard edge of disgust. They had always got on so well. She knew how many times her Gran had stood up for her when her Dad had been having a go. Perhaps she had been hoping for too much from someone who was, after all, from a very different generation. 'Enough to show me how you feel. I must be a big disappointment to you. But I'm only human, after all.'

Jennifer left then, walking quickly down the farm drive, leaving behind her in the kitchen the tray of cooling scones, the home-made jam and the pot standing ready for the tea that had never been made.

. . .

Now that she had told her Gran Archer and Jill, who would have told Phil, Jennifer knew she had to tell her parents. It was not fair to them. Though she had sworn her grandmother and her aunt to secrecy, family was family and it was perfectly possible that someone might let something slip. It was now more dangerous not to tell Peggy and Jack than to tell them.

It was Friday the 13th. Lilian had gone to see a Cliff Richard film with Roger, who'd become a good friend. Tony was at the Youth Club. After a supper of liver and onions – Jennifer would never forget it, nor ever know how she managed to keep it down – she cleared the table and put the kettle on for coffee. One of the regular barmaids was opening up the pub, so Jennifer knew that she could have a decent length of time with her parents both to tell them and to allow them the chance to recover before they had to go and be 'mine hosts' to the usual collection of regulars.

'Let's go and sit in the other room,' she suggested.

The living accommodation at the pub was pretty cramped. There was a kitchen-cum-living room and a small lounge that was hardly ever used but that felt the right place for something like this. 'I've put the fire on,' she added.

'Is it a special occasion?' grumbled Jack, as Peggy, realizing the scene was being set for an announcement, shepherded him through.

Jennifer busied herself spooning instant coffee into cups.

'Not specially,' she said. 'I've just got something to tell you, that's all. You go on through. I won't be long.'

'Please, God, give me the strength to do this,' she whispered as she poured on the boiling water and watched the brown powder froth angrily. 'If I never ask you for anything again, please will you give me that now?'

As soon as she'd told them, Jennifer knew that she had been right to dread it so much. Her mother wasn't as shocked as she'd expected – but then, as Jennifer had suspected, Peggy had guessed all along. She was upset, though, very upset, when Jennifer said that she had every intention of keeping the baby and yet no intention of marrying the father. Again she flatly refused to tell her parents any details about him. Her father, on the other hand, was incandescent with rage.

'You know what people will say if you don't name the father,' he shouted, leaping to his feet to loom over Jennifer. 'They'll say you don't know who the father is! Well, do you? Do you?'

'Yes, of course I do.' Jennifer's reply was almost inaudible.

'Do you? Do you? I wonder!' said her father bitterly.

'Jack –' Peggy put in tentatively.

'He ought to be made to marry you. Or –' He had a sudden thought. 'Perhaps he can't. He's not married already, is he?' he asked contemptuously.

Jennifer shook her head.

'Jack, please –' Peggy put in again.

But Jack was not in a mood to be reasoned with.

'You know what I ought to do, don't you?' he railed at Jennifer. 'Throw you out! Because that's all you deserve.'

Jennifer would have packed her bags and gone, willingly. Her father's reaction was what she had expected, and was, indeed, what she felt she deserved. It was her mother and Lilian who persuaded her to stay.

'Just until he calms down,' her mother urged her. 'He overreacts, you know he does. It's been a shock to him, that's all.'

Jennifer agreed, against her better judgement, and had to put up with a weekend of frosty silence from her father and her brother. Tony had declared he was 'too ashamed' to speak to her and retreated to his room where he nearly wore the Dansette out with his new 'Revolver' LP. Jennifer decided she'd give it till the end of the month, and if things were no better at home, she would definitely move out. She had already asked a teacher colleague who rented a cottage at Penny Hassett if she'd consider having a lodger for a while and the girl, who was, ironically, saving to get married, had agreed enthusiastically. Yet, to Jennifer's surprise, things did improve. By the middle of the following week, her father was actually trying to dissuade her from moving away.

'Where would you go?' demanded Jack over breakfast one day when she reiterated her intention to leave. 'Who do you know, away from these parts, who'd take you in and look after you before the baby's born?'

'Believe me, Dad,' replied Jennifer, 'I'm not so worried about trying to find somewhere and someone before the baby's born. It's after I'm worried about.'

Jack stirred his tea, more for something to do than because it needed it. Peggy had already done that for him. 'Look, Jennifer,' he said awkwardly, aware of what he had so recently said on the subject, 'there's always a home here for you. Before, during and after the baby. If that's how you want it.'

Jennifer, who knew what it must have cost him to change his mind, was moved. She didn't know that her grandfather had had stern words with his elder son about his attitude and in particular his worry for his own reputation over and above Jennifer's predicament. 'Surely she deserves our support, not our condemnation?' Dan had demanded, when Jack had gone round to Brookfield playing the heavy father and talking about throwing Jennifer out. Jack had argued the toss with his Dad because each was as stubborn as the other – that was probably where Jennifer got it from – but in the end, he had left Brookfield feeling sheepish and knowing that he had to make amends at home.

Jennifer went along with Jack's change of heart. Deep down, she doubted if she could stay in Ambridge after the baby was born, though the school had been very understanding. The timing of the birth was near perfect: the baby would be due at the end of June, so she could leave at Easter, or even May half-term if she was feeling well, and could be back teaching in September. So, gradually, life returned to normal, or near normal.

Even so, the pub regulars had to learn that the one topic of conversation that most fascinated them would, if they were overheard, probably get them barred. They had to find other things to talk about, like the fact that Nelson Gabriel, who had taken his father off on a sudden cruise last autumn, had still not returned from abroad. Or that the match the village had been waiting for for over ten years was finally going to happen: John Tregorran had proposed to Carol Grenville and had been accepted! Sadly, though, the gossips were cheated of a big wedding. Instead, it took place at St Stephen's so quietly as to be almost invisible. Afterwards, all Ambridge wished the Tregorrans well, though there were some in the Mother's Union who never quite forgave Carol for denying them their chance to pronounce on the dress, the flowers and the couple's prospects of happiness.

• • •

Jennifer missed the elusive Nelson. She longed to talk to him about the mess she'd got herself into. She knew that he'd say something sardonic about the small-mindedness of the village and make her laugh. As someone who himself had never conformed to Ambridge expectations, Nelson, Jennifer was sure, could have made her feel better about things. A couple of times she had been round to Uncle Walter's workshop, where he was turning out rocking chairs for John Tregorran's antique shop, to ask if he'd had any news. The answer was always no.

Jennifer didn't think what her visits might be doing to the old man, who began to worry that Nelson, though fifteen years Jennifer's senior, might be the father of her baby. If he had voiced these fears to Jennifer, she would have laughed till she cried. She had been out with Nelson a couple of times before he and Walter went off on their cruise, just as she had been out with Henry King, a student who worked in the bookshop that Roger Patillo managed, and with Roger himself. But they were friendships, nothing more. She enjoyed Nelson's barbed sophistication, a world away from the narrowness of Ambridge life. Henry had rather a crush on her and Roger had a passion for books and literature that she shared and that made his conversation more stimulating than any she had known since her college days. But as she had told her father, there was only one man who could be the father of her baby.

• • •

She had seen a lot of him over the summer. He was charming – very charming – and attentive and possessive and demanding. He had told her that he loved her and that he always would. He'd used phrases like 'for ever' and 'never-ending' as he kissed and caressed her in his cottage that sultry September evening, with the thunder tumbling over Lakey Hill and the sky outside purplish, like a bruise. She had always resisted before, but this time, when he led her towards the narrow stairway that opened off the living room, she made no protest. He had laid her down on his own bed with his working clothes crumpled in a corner of the room and a picture of his parents outside their cottage back home in Ireland on the bedside table. There he had made love to her and she had stroked his hair and marvelled at the compact muscularity of his body. She knew she couldn't stay overnight. Her mother, even now, lay awake until she got in and, anyway, she didn't relish the thought of sneaking out of his cottage in the morning and coming face to face with her Uncle Phil, for whom he worked as a cowman.

'Paddy,' she said as they lay together afterwards. 'Do you love me? Really?'

'Jenny,' he said tenderly. He was the only person who made her shiver when he said her name. 'I'm your man.'

A few days later, he announced he was taking a week's holiday which was owed to him and was going to visit his people in Ireland. Jennifer accepted it without question. It was a quiet time on the farm, after all. But when Paddy Redmond came back to the village, he announced that he'd got engaged to his long-time girlfriend, Nora, and that, in the fullness of time, she'd be moving to Ambridge to join him.

'I hope you understand,' he told Jennifer. They'd gone to The Griffin's Head in Penny Hassett, where he'd ensconced them in the darkest corner. Their meetings had always been in secret. 'It's just the way things are.'

'Oh, I understand all right,' said Jennifer. 'You got what you wanted. I was a challenge. Someone a bit different. But once you had it, I wasn't interesting any more.'

'Now, there's no need to be bitter.'

'I'm not bitter,' replied Jennifer. 'I'm just cursing myself for being so naive.'

How naive she had yet to find out.

• • •

'Come on Jennifer! Push! One last time!'

The nice Scottish midwife who'd been with Jennifer from the start allowed her to grip her hand.

'I can't,' said Jennifer weakly. Never in her wildest nightmares had she thought it would hurt this much or feel this lonely.

'Of course you can! I can see the baby's head! What lovely red hair!'

Just like Paddy's, thought Jennifer as she strained every nerve of her body to push the baby out.

'There, that's the head out! Now one last push!' the midwife encouraged her.

'You said that last time!' Jennifer was almost in tears.

'Never mind that. You push with the next contraction for me. Push the baby out.'

Groaning and panting, Jennifer did as she was told.

'Well done!' exclaimed the midwife in the same tone Jennifer had used to her six-year-old pupils when they got a sum right. 'You've got a lovely little boy.'

They whisked the baby away, saying they were going to clean him up. A student nurse came and washed Jennifer's face and helped her change her nightdress, then they brought the baby back to her and placed him in her arms. All Jennifer could think was that his hair was red – very red. There would be no point trying to hide the identity of the father, thought Jennifer. Everyone would know at a glance.

But if anyone guessed, nobody said anything, at least not to Jennifer. When she brought the baby home, she was touched to find that her parents had bought her a pram, which she had been too superstitious to order before. There was a pile of cards and presents for her in her room and Gran and Grandad Archer said they would buy her a cot for him. Still flooded with the emotion of it all, Jennifer broke down in tears.

'I don't deserve all this!' she sobbed on to her mother's shoulder. 'I've been nothing but trouble to you!'

'Oh, Jennifer, love.' Her mother held her tight. 'Don't think that. Don't think it at all.'

• • •

A couple of weeks later, it was Gran Archer's birthday – her sixty-seventh and, as Dan pointed out, her first as a great-grandmother. The whole family were invited to Sunday tea at Brookfield. Gran had laid a long table under the apple tree. They were all there – Jack and Peggy, Lilian and Tony, and Phil, Jill and the children. Jill was feeding eleven-week-old baby Elizabeth who had given them all a scare back in April when she was born a 'blue' baby with a defective heart valve. The poor little scrap had already had one operation and would need another when she was five, but for now the family were just glad that she seemed to be putting on weight and was starting to take an interest in the world around her. Auntie Chris, Paul and little Peter, proudly seated on his new tricycle, were there, too – and Jennifer, of course, with three-week-old Adam.

After Gran had blown out the token candles on her cake and it had been cut and passed around, everyone was ready for another cup of tea. Jennifer offered to put the kettle on again. In the cool of the Brookfield kitchen, she held her tiny son and hummed while the kettle started to sing on the Aga behind her. Suddenly she was aware of someone else in the room and turned to find her grandmother there. She had seen Doris several times since the baby had been born, but they had never been on their own together.

'Do you think I could have a little hold of him?' Doris asked almost shyly.

'Of course!' Jennifer handed Adam over carefully. The baby, half asleep, hardly stirred. Doris settled him in the crook of her arm. 'I think I'm lucky,' Jennifer added. 'He seems very placid.'

'It's no more than you deserve,' her grandmother replied, one hand supporting the baby's weight, the other cradling his head. 'After the time you had of it carrying him.'

Jennifer shrugged. 'He's here now. That's all that matters.'

'Yes, it is,' agreed Doris. 'But I've got to say it, Jennifer, I'm ashamed of the way I spoke to you when you told me you were expecting. I was too hard on you and I'm sorry.'

'Oh, Gran!' Jennifer moved and hugged her as best she could without disturbing the baby. 'Don't, please. It's all right now.'

Together they stood and looked out of the open window at the family group – four generations of Archers gathered in the same place.

'You won't be leaving Ambridge now, will you?' Her grandmother's voice was almost pleading.

'I'm not sure, Gran. You've all been lovely to me, and the village has been lovely. But – I'll have to see.'

'I'd hate to think we'd driven you out. You and this lovely baby.'

'He is lovely, isn't he?'

Jennifer stroked Adam's cheek softly, still amazed herself that something so precious could come out of such a muddle.

'He is,' her grandmother agreed. 'He's another Archer – another generation. But more than that,' she went on, 'he's a little person in his own right, just as you are. He'll have his triumphs and failures the same as we all do. But for now – well, a baby's a baby, Jennifer, and that's all that matters.'

Behind them, the kettle worked itself up into a frenzy of whistling and Jennifer moved to take it off the heat.

'What's this? Mother's meeting?' Her grandfather came into the kitchen. 'Where's that tea you promised us, Doris? Or have you two been too busy with baby talk?'

Jennifer and her grandmother exchanged glances.

'Something like that,' said Jennifer, smiling.

She knew then that even if she did leave Ambridge, she would never, ever be able to leave her family behind. None of them would: Gran and Grandad would make sure of it. The bonds were too strong for that.